TIDES OF LOVE

What Reviewers Say About
Kimberly Cooper Griffin's Work

No Experience Required

"*No Experience Required* is full of realistic, multidimensional characters. …I liked the honest and straightforward way that bipolar disorder was discussed, and I feel like I understand how those with the disorder feel a little bit more than I had before. I think that so much of this book is relatable to readers in different ways, and can help us all stop and think about others and the bigger picture a bit more. Even if readers do not know anyone with bipolar disorder, or are not in a same sex relationship, the matters at the heart of the story are universal. …*No Experience Required* is a well written and engaging book. I thought the issues of dating advice and mental health were very well handled, and I honestly would love to see more from all the characters in the book. I will be reading more from the author."—*Sharon the Librarian*

"The author does a thorough job of explaining Izzy's condition, her internal workings, hopes and fears. …This book straddles a space between a being a romcom and something more serious (given that the protagonists are dealing with a mental disorder and paternal homophobic physical violence). One of the best things about the book is that at the end we feel that this couple will really be happy together because they seem to have got their shot together and have learnt how to be a couple that communicates and cares for each other."—*Best Lesfic Reviews*

Can't Leave Love

"Sometimes you just need a romance that will melt your heart, bring a tear to your eyes at least once or twice, and leave you with a warm, happy feeling at the end. Add a couple of the cutest dogs, and you have a wonderful story. That is exactly what I found in *Can't Leave Love* by Kimberly Cooper Griffin. Besides being a beautiful love story, this book deals with some serious issues which is where the occasional teary eyes may happen. ...This is a well-written romance with well-developed characters (both human and canine), set in a lovely small town, with just the right amount of angst to make the story interesting. It is exactly the type of romantic tale that I love to read. In fact, I think I've found a new author to add to my list of favorite romance writers. I will definitely be looking for more from this author."—*Rainbow Reflections*

In the Cards

"Both main characters are very well developed and easy to connect with. The secondary characters are also well-written, especially Marnie, Daria's younger sister who is autistic. As the mother of an autistic son, I can tell you that Marnie is realistically written. The romance is fairly lighthearted and uplifting though the two mains do have several hurdles to overcome. They get a bit of a paranormal/magical push to help them find and fall in love with each other. ...I truly enjoyed this book."—*Rainbow Reflections*

Visit us at www.boldstrokesbooks.com

By the Author

No Experience Required

In the Cards

Can't Leave Love

Sol Cycle

Tides of Love

TIDES OF LOVE

by

Kimberly Cooper Griffin

2023

TIDES OF LOVE

ISBN 13: 978-1-63679-319-1

THIS TRADE PAPERBACK ORIGINAL IS PUBLISHED BY
BOLD STROKES BOOKS, INC.
P.O. BOX 249
VALLEY FALLS, NY 12185

FIRST EDITION: FEBRUARY 2023

CREDITS
EDITOR: BARBARA ANN WRIGHT
PRODUCTION DESIGN: SUSAN RAMUNDO
COVER DESIGN BY JEANINE HENNING

Acknowledgments

Thank you to Sandy Lowe and Radclyffe for all of your support and letting me be a part of the Bold Strokes team.

Barbara Ann Wright, your demand for more feelings rings through my mind and soul on a continuous loop making me a better writer and, quite possibly, a better person.

Every author should have a support system and I am forever grateful to mine: Finnian Burnett, Ona Marae, Nicole Disney, Millie Ireland, Avery Brooks, Cindy Rizzo, Jaycie Morrison, and Renee Young.

Michelle Dunkley is my first reader and one of the main reasons I continue to write; her praise and support is the best kind of motivation a writer could ever have.

Finally, nothing is more meaningful to a writer than their readers. Thank you all for reading my stories, writing the reviews, and getting lost in the worlds that would have been trapped in my head without your support.

Dedication

Forever Summer.

CHAPTER ONE

Mikayla Pierce involuntarily licked her lips as she watched the server walk toward their table. She sat up in her seat as he placed the pint glass of amber hard cider before her on the square coaster and another in front of Ashe, who pushed her wild mane of bright blue hair back and batted her boldly lined and lashed eyes at him.

Mikayla kicked her sister under the table but had a hard time being truly irritated at her, not while they sat overlooking the glimmering Pacific Ocean from the glassed-in patio of the Grotto, a restaurant situated on the cliffs of La Jolla, California. She was determined to wait until the server left before she lifted her drink and took a big sip. She didn't want to appear too eager. It wasn't the alcohol she craved but the memories it evoked. Her memories were bleak these days, and the cider reminded her of happier times. Sought-after happiness typically didn't come in a glass for her, but oh, the memories this one held.

"Thanks, Pete," she said, prying her eyes from the glass.

"No problem, Mrs. Duncan." He tucked the serving tray under his arm. "Will you be eating dinner with us this evening?"

"It's Ms. Pierce now, Pete, but how many times have I told you to call me Mikayla? We'll probably order something to eat in a little bit."

"Sorry. I forgot you said you were celebrating your divorce today. This first round is on me, ladies. I'll check in on you again soon."

She refrained from reminding him that Ashe had used the word celebrate, not her. She was definitely not celebrating. She had no idea *what* she was doing. Still numb from the shock of it all, she'd been avoiding her feelings and had only recently started to allow emotion into her world again. To her surprise, the expected devastation at the mention of the D-word didn't come. Maybe in time. She turned to ask Ashe how long it would take, only to catch her sister's eyes glued to the back of Pete's work pants as he walked back into the restaurant.

"He's not a pork chop. You can wipe the drool from your chin."

"I'm savoring the presentation," Ashe said, slowly turning her head back to Mikayla after Pete disappeared through the swinging kitchen doors. "That man is yummy."

"Jeez, Ashe. You're as bad as a man and almost twice his age. Try the cider." Mikayla buzzed with excitement to introduce Ashe to the new Julian Orchards Hard Fuji Apple Cider she'd discovered the last time she'd come to the Grotto. It tasted like a cherished memory, transporting her directly back to the winding drive up to the little mountain town of Julian with their beloved Grampa and Grandma James to pick apples. They'd died fifteen years ago, six months apart, he from a heart attack and she from a broken heart. She missed them as much now as she had back then. She wasn't going to let her sister's lechery spoil the moment. She needed this happy.

Ashe lifted her glass. "I'm certain he's a man who wants more than missionary sex. I have a rigid two-orgasm requirement. Life is too short for anything less."

Mikayla shook her head. "Whatever floats your boat, as Mom likes to say."

"Do not bring Mom into my bedroom." Ashe sipped her drink. She gave an impressed look at the glass. "This *is* good."

"Does it evoke any memories?"

"Now that you mention it…" Ashe closed her eyes, and thinking lines appeared between her eyebrows. As Mikayla watched, she smoothed the same spot between her own brows with a finger. Recent Botox had made it numb. "It reminds me of being slightly carsick, the odor of unfiltered Camel cigarette smoke, and…"

"Grandma and Grandpa James," they said together.

"Right?" Mikayla said.

"I miss them so much," Ashe said, taking another sip.

"I couldn't wait for you to try it exactly for that."

"I wondered why my wine-drinking sister all of a sudden got all hot for cider." Ashe laughed. "It's not often you surprise me, and you're such a sap for the good old days."

Mikayla sighed. "Things were uncomplicated back then."

"Well, we were ten and eight. Everything was uncomplicated."

Mikayla blew out a long sigh. "Yeah."

"Speaking of Mom, is she speaking to you again yet?"

Mikayla dropped her chin to her chest, blew out another big breath, then straightened, sitting tall in her chair. She trailed her finger through the condensation on her glass. "Dad says I should give her time to process. Apparently, it's shaken her to her core that Craig's going through with the divorce. As if it's up to me to fix it. Were you aware that divorced men have lower life expectancies? She's worried about *Craig*, and if I can't make my marriage work, no one can. She's already grieving the ocean views from our backyard and mourning our holiday gatherings." She didn't mention how their mother still hadn't asked her how she was holding up. Almost as if it had been *her* shattering *Craig's* hopes and dreams. Not the other way around. Craig would be fine. Mikayla? Well, that remained to be seen.

"You mean, she made it about herself? What a huge surprise." Sarcasm dripped from Ashe's voice.

Normally, having her sister say aloud what they both thought of their mother made Mikayla feel better, but this time, she only registered her mother's words. She'd always hated how overly servile her mother behaved toward her father. Actually, her *fathers*. Plural, since the man she presently called her father happened to be her second stepfather. Her and Ashe's biological father had died when they were seven and nine, and her mother's second husband had died when they were eleven and thirteen.

Daddy number three, currently still in the picture, had assumed his position by the time Mikayla turned twelve. They'd all been wonderful men, and she'd called all three of them Father from the deepest parts of her heart, but she absolutely hated how her mother made no apologies about putting them first and her two children second. So different than her mother's parents, Grandpa and Grandma James, who had always made them the center of their universe with unconditional love.

Both she and Ashe had spent years in therapy because of their mother's behavior, and while they now accepted their mom as she was, that didn't mean it didn't still hurt. Their mother simply needed a man in her life to complete her. Now, Mikayla had to come to terms with the fact that she and her mother were more alike than in just their genes, sharing similar light brown hair, mossy green eyes, an almost-dimple in their left cheeks when they smiled, long pianist's fingers, unmarked skin that blushed way too easily, and the exact same feet.

Mikayla had taken after her mother in the husband thing, too. She couldn't imagine herself not married. Being a wife, taking care of the house, planning everything for two people, making sure they ate right, exercised, wore their sunscreen, and possessed the perfect foyer table in their perfect house…she and her mother were good at and enjoyed all those things. Mikayla tried to remind herself how she wasn't as intently focused on the husband aspect but more on the whole package of what marriage entailed. Her career had been Cruise Director of her marriage, and she'd been fired. To make things worse, it took losing her marriage to realize she'd turned into her mother. It sickened her more than a little bit. She'd never set out to be *that* person.

Mikayla sighed. "Well, it's Mom. Maybe it's best for her to take time to get used to it. God forbid her emotions show."

Ashe laughed and held up her pint glass. "To Mom, her contained emotions and this amazing fucking cider. I may never drink wine again."

Ashe put into words what Mikayla had thought. She'd been coming to the Grotto at least weekly, and sometimes more, in the last several months, not exactly drowning her sorrows because she only ever drank one glass of wine—now cider—but she hated to eat alone. Ever since Craig had asked for a divorce, she'd been eating alone most meals. Thus, she found herself on a first-name basis with the waitstaff.

"To fresh horizons," Ashe said, tapping her glass.

"I liked the old horizons," she said, putting down her glass without taking a sip. Maybe it hadn't been such a great idea to come here on the day her divorce became final. Six months after Craig had asked for one and while she no longer felt like bursting into tears at the thought of the night her husband of twelve years had told her he'd fallen out of love with her, she wasn't anywhere near over it.

Ashe rubbed the top of Mikayla's hand where it rested on the table next to her glass. "I promise you. It gets easier. I have three times as much experience than you, so this is coming from an expert."

Mikayla appreciated the attempt to cheer her up, but it didn't. "You divorced all three of your ex-husbands, not the other way around."

Ashe snorted. "At least Craig didn't cheat on you."

Mikayla blew out a breath. "I think I might have preferred it. It probably wouldn't hurt as much as the fact that he couldn't stand my company any longer."

Ashe flapped her hand. "You know that's not true. It's because you can't give him children."

Mikayla glared at her. "Thank you so much for clearing it up for me."

"You're welcome." Ashe probably didn't register the glare or the sarcasm. She had always been one of those people who preferred directness and assumed other people did, too. It wasn't mean-spirited. Just the opposite, so she couldn't remain irritated with her.

Mikayla downed the rest of her cider without taking a breath and covered her mouth when she quietly burped. "I still consider it my fault, you know."

Ashe motioned to Pete for a couple of refills before responding. "What do you mean? Your inhospitable womb?"

Mikayla rolled her eyes. "I didn't want kids anyway."

Her sister reacted like she'd said she didn't like coffee, which would have been a surprising thing to reveal, considering the enormous amount she drank every day. "Do you mean you purposefully prevented getting pregnant?"

"It wasn't purposeful at all. I thought I wanted kids at first. Well, I didn't *not* want kids. I actually got caught up in Craig's excitement about finally starting a family after seven years of traveling and enjoying each other. I never took any precautions, and I tried to conceive…at first." She didn't mention how it didn't take long for her to realize she didn't want them. She'd figured it out when it had dawned on her that she'd be stuck with the lion's share of the work. Craig's career proved to be too demanding for him to help around the house, let alone with the raising of the kids thing. He mostly wanted them for the photo ops and Disneyland trips. Yep. Diapers and midnight feedings would all be on her. That wasn't how she wanted it to go.

"It still doesn't mean it's your fault. You tried. You didn't sabotage your uterus."

Pete swooped in, dropped off two new drinks, and Mikayla paused to thank him before responding. "But maybe I willed it not to happen. You know, putting out the bad vibes. Manifesting it?" Maybe she should feel guilty, but she didn't, at least not about not being able to have kids. Her guilt came from *not* feeling guilty. God. She was a mess.

"How come you never told me this?"

"Because he wanted kids so badly. I never tried *not* to have kids, at least until I found out about the inhospitable uterus situation." Those were the doctor's words, not hers. She shrugged. "It doesn't matter. It all came to the same end. The divorce is final. The house is sold. So it's real. I'm officially an ex-wife at thirty-five."

"You make it sound like a death sentence. Besides, you're *only* thirty-five, and you're a tasty slice. You won't be single for long. Mark my words."

Mikayla wanted to drop her head into her hands and wail, but she didn't. She sat up and didn't make a scene. "It feels like a death sentence. Who am I if I'm not a wife?"

"God, Mikayla, you sound like a nineteen-fifties housewife or—" Ashe stopped midsentence. There were certain things they never said to one another.

"It's gross, huh? I sound like her."

"That's not…well, kind of." She could always count on Ashe, to tell the truth…no matter how much it hurt.

"But seriously, I haven't worked in twelve years. My degree is in history, for goodness' sake. As soon as we got married, I stopped working."

"First, you work plenty hard. His success is tenfold what it would be without you. Second, you don't have to work, at least finance-wise. He made sure of it in the divorce, as is only fair."

"He offered me more today when he called to check in about the divorce being final. It's purely based on guilt." Sometimes, she wished he'd given her nothing. It made it impossible for her to hate him.

Ashe rolled her eyes. "Not one of my husbands called me the day our divorce became final. You two are something else."

Mikayla pushed her hair back with both hands. "Right now, I miss being a wife." She'd been obsessing over this all day, ever since the back-to-back calls from her lawyer and real estate agent telling her the divorce was final, and the house she'd lived in for the last twelve years displayed a sold sign now. Talking about it with Ashe made it real. It clobbered her. Every terrifying thing about being divorced that she'd kept at bay over the last six months flooded over her. Anxiety made her chest tight, threatening to choke her. "Oh God. Where am I going to *live*?"

"You have two other homes."

"They're not homes. They're vacation houses."

"Jesus, Mik, do you hear yourself right now?"

"Don't call me Mik. That's what he calls me."

"First of all, I've called you Mik all my life. Second, you can't dodge the obvious. You are absurdly privileged. You don't get to panic about where you get to live."

Mikayla rested her head on her arms. The anxiety remained, but now shame lived beside it. She needed the reminder. "I know," she said into the hollow of her arms. "I'm being overly sensitive. Believe me, guilt consumes me sometimes. I didn't do anything to deserve one house, let alone multiple."

Ashe stroked her hair. "You deserve it as much as Craig does. Jettison the guilt. You may be blind to your privilege, but your donations and volunteering help a lot of people. You're a good person. You're lucky to have two homes to choose from."

Mikayla lifted her head and straightened her hair. "Craig chose for me. He took the house in Mexico and told me to keep the house in London."

Ashe sat back in her chair. "He gave up the London house? He loves it there."

Mikayla shrugged. "Guilt." As much as she loved the London house, she'd give it all up if it meant she got to stay married.

"It's the least he could do. He'd be nowhere without you. You're the only reason he could throw all the froufrou parties and cocktail shindigs to woo his investors. For hell's sake, you made sure he got haircuts and cut his damn nails. He'd be shit without you and—" Ashe put up her hand and drained her drink. "I promised not to smack-talk him. I want you to get angry, not internalize *his* failures. He's given up the best thing he's ever had, and he's a fool to think otherwise."

"I appreciate your loyalty." Mikayla rubbed her sister's arm. "He's been more than fair. Sure, he's divorcing me, but a person can't choose to love someone they don't love anymore."

Ashe shot her a glare meant for him, not her. "I'll shut up about it. For now. But I still hate what he's done. And now he's forcing you to live in London? Selfishly, I don't want you to move anywhere far. I'd have to follow, and I adore the studio I'm working at. You can't find that vibe just anywhere. Maybe Sonoma. I could do Sonoma."

"I don't want to leave San Diego, either. I like it here. We were raised here."

"Are you sure it's not because Craig is here?"

Up until recently, his being there was a huge factor in her desire to remain, but now she refused to let his presence make her want to leave. "It's irrelevant. He's in Mexico. He might stay there." He lived there with Carmen, his new girlfriend, but she didn't explain. Ashe would try to make it into more than it needed to be.

"Probably for the best. Gives you space and time to regroup. Mix things up a little. Maybe get laid, huh?"

"As much as I don't want to mix anything up or get laid, you're right." A change sounded good. Something big, but not too big. There were limits to her threshold for change.

Ashe rested her chin on her fist. "I wish I could think of some bougie place to recommend to you. I'm more of a rent-a-room kind of person. Why don't you buy a place here in La Jolla? You love it here."

"Too close to Mom. I think I want to downsize, too. After all, it's just me." She loved the La Jolla house with its great views and location right next to the ocean, but it had always been too big for her and Craig. They'd bought it when they thought they'd fill it with kids. Now, it depressed her for the same reason. She'd been thinking about that since the call from the real estate agent saying they'd found a buyer who said they wanted it to grow their family. She'd said good luck before she could stop herself. Another trait she'd inherited from her mom: cynicism. She decided to work on that.

Before she'd left to meet Ashe at the restaurant, she'd been sitting on the top step of the grand staircase where she could see into many of the rooms and look out over the ocean. The afternoon sunshine had filled the large open spaces, yet the house had seemed vacuous. Sterile. Staged. As if no one lived there. As if their presence in the house over the last twelve years had left absolutely no impression on the space. Nothing. And they hadn't yet moved any of their belongings out. The movers were scheduled for the next day. Everything they'd brought into the house and their marriage remained inside it. Yet, it still felt barren. Like her.

"If not La Jolla, then where?" Ashe said, pulling Mikayla from her morose thoughts.

"I was thinking maybe North County. Carlsbad. Maybe Oceanside. Fallbrook would be cute, too, with their avocado festivals and art community. If only inland didn't get so hot."

Ashe snapped her fingers. "I have a place. But you have to promise to keep an open mind."

"Oh…kay," Mikayla said, recognizing the tone in Ashe's voice. She had an outrageous idea that Mikayla would humor but ultimately ignore.

"How about a house swap?"

Mission accomplished. Mikayla immediately discounted it.

"You mean trade the London flat for someone else's house? They stay there, I stay here? Like the reality shows on television?" Her sister was nuts. House swapping wasn't a real thing.

"Exactly. Just temporarily. Until you have a better idea of where you want to live."

A little tipsy after shotgunning the first one, Mikayla sipped her second drink slowly. "Very funny."

"I'm serious."

"God, no. They make reality TV because it's rife with drama. Scripted. Count me out."

"The drama is all staged. People actually do house swaps. What do you think Airbnb and VRBO are?"

"That's different. Those are intended as rentals. They're vetted."

Ashe petted her hand. "You sheltered thing. The world is full of wonderful and exciting things you are not aware of. I guessed you would say no." She sipped her cider and signaled for another.

It could've been the finality of the divorce causing her to reassess who she was. Maybe it took finally recognizing the sterility of the home she'd lived in for twelve years to make her ponder a change of scenery. Maybe her big sister, the artist who did anything she wanted without a care about who thought what about her, who made her crave a little more excitement and adventure in her life, played a part. But her sister, along with the whole world, perceived her as boring, and she was *not* boring, goddammit. Something stirred within Mikayla. She resolved to prove to her sister and the world that they were wrong.

"How would I find someone to swap with? I have two weeks."

Ashe put her empty glass down, sweeping her blue hair back, an excited expression on her face.

Oh no. What did she get herself into?

"That's the thing. My friend Brandi has a place in Oceanside and a contract gig in London for six months. She has to get out *tout de suite*. She's planning on renting a hotel room until she finds a place, but yours is perfect."

Doubt started to erode her resolve but she'd be damned if she'd show it. She. Was. Not. Unexciting. "You said gig. Is Brandi a musician?"

"Among other things. Mostly she's a multimedia artist. The gig is a graphic novel or video game or movie. She does it all."

Mikayla ran her finger around the lip of her glass. "It's weird thinking of staying in a stranger's house." More, having a stranger in hers, but she wouldn't say it. She. Was. Not. Unadventurous.

"It's no different from staying in a hotel room or an Airbnb. I'll take you up the day after tomorrow if Brandi is on board. She will be. She's up for anything."

"Maybe." Some of Ashe's friends were strange.

"I know that look. You're saying maybe when you mean no. Embrace life, Mikayla. Let it show you what's out there."

She almost decided to do it right then out of spite. "You make me sound like I have a stick up my butt."

Ashe lifted an eyebrow. "If the stick fits…"

"I don't have anything up my butt, thank you very much." She said it a little loud and Pete, waiting on the table next to them, lifted a brow. To her chagrin, Ashe silently egged him on with a thumbs-up. She smacked her hand. "Stop it."

Ashe returned her attention to Mikayla after letting her eyes roam up and down Pete's body. "You don't have to say yes, but at least look at it. Recognize there's a world outside of your bougie lifestyle. It's super cute."

She ignored the dig about her lifestyle. "Okay. I'll go see the place. I'm not promising anything. Make sure your friend Brenda knows it's not a done deal." She. Was. Not. Boring. If she didn't like it, she could always just not do it.

"It's Brandi, and you're going to like her and her fab house."

Mikayla wasn't convinced, but she sure as hell wasn't going to let the stick-in-the-ass comment define her.

CHAPTER TWO

Gem Helmstaad parked the golf cart right outside the closed front gate of Oceana Mobile Home Park and hopped out, following the landscaping crew along the stucco wall enclosing the periphery of the fifty-acre compound situated on the Pacific Coast Highway.

The nearby ocean glimmered in the mid-afternoon sun. With waves on the small side and long pauses between sets, they retained nice form, and the curl unfurling from jetty to jetty gave the scattering of patient surfers a nice long ride if they caught one. Most were lying on their boards beyond the breakwater, absorbing the warmth of the sun through their wet suits. Year-round surfers never expected much in April.

Gem remembered being one of them. Now, she worked. Besides, there were more great whites prowling the coast these days. She'd never thought of sharks when she was a kid, but as a grown-up, she couldn't imagine sharing the ocean while they were lurking in the depths below, trying to figure out if she was a delicious seal or an equally delicious surfer.

"We were thinking about planting them every ten feet. What do you think?" Devon interrupted her thoughts and pointed at the new bougainvillea vines, still in the plastic nursery pots, staged along the wall. "You said every six feet, but these are the big ones. They'll get huge with this direct sun. The new magnolias will be far enough forward to not block them for a few years."

Gem winced at the mention of the magnolias but nodded. She'd been forced to run interference between her father, who'd been harsh and argumentative, and Devon, who thankfully had a chill disposition. Her father couldn't explain why he didn't like the planned placement of the trees. "You're the expert. Do what you think best. We need some sort of coverage on this wall to discourage the kids from tagging it."

"The vines won't fill out until next year, but we'll install the lattice and spread them out enough to dissuade taggers."

"Perfect."

They spoke about the spring flower arrangements in the planters at the gate for a few minutes, then picked up a few scraps of garbage and pulled a few weeds. For the most part, their little town of Oceanside, California remained clean, but Gem kept Oceana immaculate, just like her father. He'd purchased the initial ten-acre community in 1972 and had added land and grown it to its present size, impeccably maintaining it, guaranteeing its success by differentiating it from the other mobile home parks. Occupants were inspired to keep their homes up when the premises were kept nicely. With the renters as conscientious as the homeowners, the community was a beautiful place to live, especially in April when the magnolias were blooming.

The giant white blossoms throughout the park caused Gem to think about her grandmother and the two giant magnolia trees that had once stood sentinel at the end of her driveway. They were now planted at the entrance to the park, and her father continued to plant similar trees to complement them. The scent of magnolia, lemony and floral, enveloped her now.

It was one of the few things she enjoyed about her job these days.

When she'd agreed to be co-manager alongside her father, she'd thought it would be for a short time while he recovered from a back injury. Now, four years later, his back had healed, but he'd started exhibiting signs of memory loss and confusion, and she'd been forced to take over most operations while he continued to "run" the community in name only. The facade was necessary because it would have crushed him if she and her sisters had taken over his dream. Gem's five sisters worked and took care of their own families, which left managing Oceana to Gem, the one unmarried daughter.

Initially, they'd chalked his confusion up to the pain pills, but he'd been off them for two years, and his confusion had grown steadily worse. Lately, he'd become argumentative, straining his relationships with residents, work crews, vendors, and recently, Gem. Now, she acted as his minder as well as property manager, a lot to deal with. Burnout plagued her on a regular basis, but she couldn't find a way out.

Her phone chimed, and her father's face filled the screen. She accepted the video call. "Hey, Pops. Perfect timing. I'm standing under Eloise, and she's putting on a show of elegant blossoms today." She turned her camera toward the canopy of the giant magnolia named after his mother. Several huge blossoms were scattered throughout the canopy, and she put her phone toward the closest one she could reach. As she did, a sleek, deep-blue BMW i8 convertible pulled up to the gate and keyed in the code. She wondered who in the park knew someone who could afford such a nice car.

Her father's voice brought her back to the call. "Gorgeous. The perfume of the blossoms is wafting throughout the property. How is my youngest daughter this Tuesday afternoon? I'm sorry for biting your head off earlier about the new trees. I forgot we put in that sidewalk. The spots Devon suggested are good."

"It's okay, Pops. Devon and the crew are planting the bougainvillea today. The small ones in the front so they don't block the view of the ocean through the glass wall and the big ones around the rest. Oh, and the planters are overflowing with pansies." She took a couple of photos and sent them to him.

"Ah, the red and whites this year. Your mother's favorites. So of course, I love it."

Her phone vibrated as a text from the front office came through. "Hey, Pops. I got a text. We're expecting a potential sublet this afternoon. Will you take them over to Brandi's place?" When she'd talked to him an hour earlier, he'd been at the house they shared, located behind the office and across the street from Brandi's place.

"I'm over at the new build going over plans with Tony. But you know I don't like sublets." He sounded cranky again, and she decided she couldn't inflict him upon an innocent sublet.

"You stay put, Pops. I'm around the corner. I'll make sure they're good people, and if anything even hints at being wonky, I'll give 'em the boot."

"Good. Keep me posted."

"I will. I love you, Pops. See you later."

Gem hopped into the golf cart, keyed the code to open the gate, and in less than a minute, pulled into the parking lot of the front office and noticed the fancy blue BMW parked near unit 1-B, Brandi's place. Brandi had only told her about the potential sublet the day before, but since she'd been called to London at short notice, Gem figured she'd let it slide. Brandi was a good tenant. Gem had no doubt she'd vet any sublet carefully.

Chapter Three

Mikayla would never have considered buying a faux-fur upholstered couch, but she adored the one currently enveloping her in Brandi's living room. It felt like sitting in a cloud, the soft fur surrounding her like a hug. She let out a long sigh as she sank into its comfort. Peering around the front room of Brandi Howell's home, Mikayla, who wasn't blessed with the same artist gene as her sister, didn't realize how starved for color she'd been all her life. Vivid paintings of people and animals in everyday situations decorated the walls, and small, colorful sculptures of sea animals filled most of the flat surfaces. Vibrant rugs and throw pillows added more color to the room, while the white furniture provided a sort of canvas for it, keeping the brilliant hues from overstimulating the senses.

The best thing of all had to be the big saltwater fish tank of seahorses sitting on a low bookcase and rising nearly to the ceiling, separating the dining area from the living room. Seeing the tank was worth the trip.

She'd almost canceled when her sister had flaked. She never canceled. But she'd fought the urge to turn around during the entire drive up the coast. To top it off, she'd been furious at her sister when she'd discovered she'd been sent to a trailer park. If the landscaping and buildings hadn't been meticulously kept, she would have driven past, but the magnificent magnolia trees near the gate had drawn her in. They were gorgeous, just like Brandi's home.

Brandi came back into the room and handed Mikayla a jean jacket. "Please tell Ashe thanks. I've been meaning to give it back since January when we went to the concert down in Pacific Beach. I'm forever underestimating how cold sixty degrees is in San Diego, even after living here for four years. I'm all, you're at the beach, Brandi, my girl. Flip-flops and tank tops? Yes, thank you. Then the coastal haze moves in, and it's like Siberia."

Mikayla loved the way she spoke. She came off as real and honest, unique in the way all artists seemed to be. But Mikayla could relate to her, which she couldn't say for most of her sister's friends. She'd felt comfortable with Brandi the moment she'd met her. "I've lived here all my life, and I still underestimate it. We don't own coats." Mikayla found it amusing that their conversation revolved mostly around the weather. "By the way, Ashe said she's sorry for not coming."

Brandi smirked. "No, she's not. She's with that trainer from the gym. She told me they were getting together last night. They're probably still in bed."

Heat rose in Mikayla's face. She'd long ago resigned herself to her sister's unreliable ways and was used to making excuses for her, but she found it embarrassing to be caught in a fib. "I wasn't sure. She told me she got tied up, and you'd understand."

"Tied up in more ways than one." Brandi winked. "Girl, she's been working on him for weeks. I don't blame her." Brandi leaned against the kitchen island and peered over a set of seahorse sculptures. "You got a sense of the place yet?"

"It's much bigger inside than it appears."

"Surprising, right? I had no idea mobile homes came with vaulted ceilings. I've lived in trailer parks…I mean, mobile home parks, all my life. The owners work hard to keep Oceana nice. So the house in London…"

Brandi let the sentence die right in the middle, and Mikayla realized she hadn't said anything about the house she would be swapping for. She got up and stopped on the other side of the counter, pulling up pictures. "It's quite boring compared to this, but here are a few photos." She pushed the phone across the granite countertop.

"So posh."

Mikayla wasn't sure if the comment meant she liked it or if it might be code for boring. She didn't appear disinterested or pleased. "The real draw is it's right in Brixton, which used to be a little sketchy, but it's now very popular. Lots of music at night and indoor markets during the day. It has a huge art scene, too. Ashe enjoys it there."

"She told me she loves it. How far is it from Peckham? I don't know the area, and that's where the studio I'm contracting for is located."

"Just a few minutes on the train, actually."

"I wouldn't need a car?"

"We never get a car when we go to Europe. There's public transportation unless you go to the country, and if you want a car, you can rent."

"I can't tell you how relieved I am to hear that. I'm a terrible driver. I can't imagine trying to learn to drive on the left."

Mikayla laughed. "Craig could never get the hang of it, but he refused to let me drive."

"He sounds like a real prince." Mikayla didn't miss the sarcasm in her voice and realized how controlling her story made him seem. "Is he your husband? Ex, I mean. Ashe gave me the highlights."

Mikayla nodded. "Yeah, my ex." It still sounded strange.

"Ashe said you were in a transition phase."

"You could call it that, I guess. It's still new, and I don't know how to be single." She wasn't sure why she'd said the last part. She hadn't specifically worried about being single. Lonely, yes. Single, not at all, and a huge ball of anxiety welled within her. Anxiety about her life, her future, about Brandi being there to witness it if she couldn't find a way to keep herself together. She sighed.

"You don't want to listen to all of this. Half of all marriages end in divorce. Mine isn't special."

"Every heart is unique."

The simple statement said so much, and it became official: she liked Brandi. Mikayla, for once in her life, wasn't compelled to ensure that everyone around her was comfortable at her expense. She focused on her own unique heart.

"I should tell you that everyone here knows everyone's business," Brandi said after a few moments of quiet. "Your neighbors will be extremely interested in anybody you bring home. Overnight guests are fine as long as you trust them, but you have to get front office approval if you have anyone stay longer than a week. And believe me, they will figure it out, regardless of how sneaky you are."

A light knock sounded, and a voice said, "You make living here sound like a gulag."

Mikayla jumped and looked toward the screen door.

Brandi laughed and waved the person in. A woman wearing a light blue polo shirt with the Oceana logo, a pair of khaki cargo shorts, and a white ball cap with the Oceana logo on it—her long brown hair pulled through the back—let herself in. Mikayla had seen her taking pictures of the flowers at the gate. An unexpected sense of anticipation washed through her.

The woman took off her mirrored sunglasses and held out a hand. "I'm Gem. I work in the front office." Her strikingly pretty blue eyes caught Mikayla's attention. Long dark lashes and shapely eyebrows made them pop. Mikayla could have gazed into them all day.

Brandi snorted. "Gem's family owns Oceana. Some of the nicest people you'll ever meet. We were about to talk about the neighbors."

"Have you decided to sublet Brandi's place, then?" Gem glanced between them, and those gorgeous eyes and lovely smile were hypnotizing.

"Well…" Mikayla began, feeling a little off-center. They hadn't talked specifics, but Brandi seemed as nice and trustworthy as Ashe had described. And the house, while small, had great energy and amazing charm. She wanted to downsize, and this would be a great chance to determine by how much.

Brandi left for England in two days, and Mikayla's house would be turned over to the new owners in a little over a week. Panic tried to set in just thinking about it. After months of numbness, she found all this more than a little overwhelming.

Gem grinned. "Did I jump the gun? You two seemed to have hit it off."

"We haven't gotten that far," Brandi said. "She showed me pictures of her house in Brixton. I have to say, I'd be getting the far better end of the deal. Check these out." She angled the phone so Gem could see.

"I don't know about that," Mikayla said. The house in Brixton might have been bigger and worth twenty of Brandi's house—not that either of those things factored into her decision—but the mobile home came with a much cozier atmosphere and a location right on the ocean, not to mention all the wonderful art. Everything about the place made Mikayla love it. "The house in Brixton doesn't have live seahorses. Do all of them swim in pairs?"

"They mate for life," Brandi said. "If one is taken away or dies, the other often dies of a broken heart."

"Mating for life is overrated." Mikayla heard the hardness in her voice and meant it, but she'd vowed to not become cynical.

"I hear you, girl," Brandi said, shaking her head, laughing.

"Well, seahorses or not, this is a beautiful house," Gem said, still going through the pictures on Mikayla's phone.

Brandi wore an amused expression. "Proof. I'm getting the better end of the deal. I mean, if we do the swap, which I'd be daft to turn down. Listen to me, already talking like a Brit." She handed the phone back. "The garden alone is gorgeous."

"Beyond gorgeous," Gem said.

Heat rose up Mikayla's neck. Gem might have been complimenting her with the way it affected her. "The garden is what made us buy it. Ironically, I haven't spent much time in it.

The weather doesn't cooperate when we go. I hope you like rain, by the way. You can watch the garden from the solarium."

Brandi's eyebrows rose. "Solarium. I rest my case. Any house with a solarium is swankier than a house in a trailer park."

Gem cleared her throat. "Mobile home estate."

Brandi laughed again. "I stand corrected. Mobile home estate. Don't worry, Gem. I'll be back after my contract. You can count on it. I may be drinking tea and eating crumpets with my royal pinky finger sticking out, but I'll be back. I love this place as much as I love the people."

"Tell me about the neighbors," Mikayla said.

Brandi turned to Gem near the end of the kitchen bar. Mikayla did the same, and those blue eyes captured her again.

"Tell her the story about when your dad bought this place," Brandi said.

"Oh. You want to go way, way back. I'll see if I can make a long story short," Gem said with a snort and leaned her elbows against the counter. "Let's see, my father got back from his tour in Vietnam in nineteen seventy and married my mom, but he and other vets found it hard to find jobs and places to live. Fortunately, the original owner of Oceana hired him as a handyman in exchange for a place to stay. When the owner sold it, my mom and dad bought it with my dad's VA benefits. They envisioned Oceana as a place for people looking to find their way, whatever that turned out to be. At first, they helped veterans separating from the service. Then, it included unmarried women who'd found it difficult to find places to buy or rent without a man's help. Over time, it's been a stepping-stone, a final home, a respite, a fresh start, a safe place, and a lot of other things. Most of the people who have lived here have a reason for choosing Oceana, other than its location."

"Your parents sound like wonderful people," Mikayla said, running her hands over the goose bumps on her arms.

"My mom passed away several years ago, but my dad still runs this place."

Mikayla noticed how soft her eyes got when she talked about her parents, and she wished she was as close to hers as Gem seemed to be. "Are you here to screen me?" she asked. It sounded as if some unseen power might have sent her to Oceana for the fresh start she'd talked to Ashe about.

Gem tilted her head. "I'm not sure I'd call it screening, but we do have a sublet policy requiring approval from the front office."

Mikayla hadn't anticipated being declined. She thought back to her sister's "privilege" comment. A small amount of shame rose in her, but she understood. "I've never done anything like this. What are the rules?"

"If the application goes through, you two can make a few adjustments to accommodate the nature of the swap in the rental agreement if you're curious about how to make this official." Gem grinned.

Mikayla grinned back and had a hard time prying her eyes away. "I'd like to take the evening to think it over, if it's okay."

They spoke for a few more minutes, and Mikayla took her leave, hoping she'd made a good impression. It would be awful to be rejected first by her husband and then by strangers over this house swap. She wasn't sure her fragile self-confidence could take it. God. What a totally unexpected situation to find herself in. She hadn't even thought of a plan B. Staying with her sister or parents was out of the question, and the idea of moving to a hotel or renting a house just depressed her. How had her life come to this point, where she was considering living among the possessions of a total stranger? Funny that the last prospect attracted her above all the other options.

CHAPTER FOUR

After work, Gem dropped by Brandi's, curious about the swap. Mikayla couldn't have been nicer or friendlier, and she came with a good recommendation from one of Brandi's closest friends. References didn't get much better than that. Moreover, Gem's gut told her Mikayla would be a great fit for the community.

Gem possessed a gift for sensing if people were a good fit for Oceana...or in general. Her father possessed it, too, a sort of sixth sense. They merely had to talk to someone for a few minutes to pick up on it. Sometimes, the sensations were more specific, and they got a sense of something indicating safety, compassion, friendliness, etc. They could also feel the opposite. Mikayla's energy, one of the most intense and specific Gem had encountered, screamed all the positive values and none of the negative ones. More specifically, kindness exuded from her stronger than any person Gem had known. She sensed something else there, too. It wasn't positive or negative, but it felt important. She couldn't put her finger on it, and she'd been trying to figure it out since the moment they'd met.

Without the sixth sense, Gem would have deduced the obvious aspects of Mikayla's life—the obscenely expensive car; the perfectly fitting, almost certainly tailored casual clothing; her formal posture; her impeccable manners—wealth, entitlement, and a propensity to value status over substance. But then, there'd been other signs indicating otherwise: body language, her quick smile, and warm eyes. When Mikayla looked at her, Gem felt seen in a way she normally didn't.

Having the benefit of her gift, Gem picked up something… interesting. Not in a bad way but something elusive and deep, keeping her wondering. A hard to define attribute, as if there was something more to Mikayla than she let people see, something far beneath the surface. A crackling kind of energy. Gem had a strong impression that Mikayla wasn't deliberately hiding anything, but maybe she wasn't aware of it herself or thought others wouldn't be interested in seeing the real her.

All of this had flashed through Gem's mind as she'd stood on the front porch listening to the conversation between Brandi and Mikayla. Mikayla was a mystery Gem wanted to solve.

When Gem knocked on the screen door for the second time that day, Brandi waved her in while talking on the phone and placing clothing in a suitcase. The conversation sounded like travel plans, which could go on for a while or be finished in minutes. Gem didn't have anything pressing, so she watched the seahorses. The big orange one, Othello, unhitched his tail from a strand of seagrass and swam to the front of the tank like he always did when she stood there. The others were close behind, including his mate, Desdemona. The recognition somehow validated her, as if they liked her beyond a Pavlovian response. She'd taken care of the aquarium several times and had sort of fallen in love with them. She'd spent hours watching them.

She fed them a snack of shrimp via the turkey baster Brandi kept near the tank, then she filled the food cup, placing it in the holder. They ate while she watched, and she was amazed at how they sucked food into their snouts and how Othello seemed to defer to Desdemona. They really did resemble horses if you ignored the twisty body past their necks. Their little faces never changed expression, always locked on a startled expression. Except for Othello. His eyes weren't quite as wide, giving him an appearance of intelligence that the others lacked. Yet another thing she liked about him.

Movement in the upper corner caught her eye; a few tiny seahorses bobbed in the water. Brandi called them fry. She'd partitioned the end of the tank off to keep them separate from the adults, otherwise, the bigger seahorses might eat them. These were the latest batch of fry from Othello and Desdemona, the only procreating pair. The other two pairs did the courting dance, but so far, were not breeding.

She counted about twenty fry, down from thirty-five the last time she'd counted. There had been hundreds after Othello had given birth, but Brandi had told her a good batch usually produced about five to ten survivors. Gem had convinced herself this would be bigger than a normal batch because the larger they got, the harder it was to see them die.

"They grow so fast," Brandi said, coming to stand next to her.

"When will they go to Scripps?"

"Rich will be by in a couple of weeks to get them. I think you were right. There might be about fifteen to twenty this time." She put a cube of frozen brine shrimp in with the fry, and the baby seahorses slurped up the tiny pieces floating from the cube.

"The fry eat like they're always starving."

"It's not even funny how often they have to be fed. I told Rich I was worried about leaving them for London, and he gave me a couple of timed feeders so they won't be such a pain in the ass. They only have to be restocked once a day. I wish I'd asked for them a long time ago. He'll come by a lot to check on them."

"So you don't need my help?" It never occurred to Gem that she wouldn't have access to the seahorses after Brandi left. It made her a little sad to think about.

"God. I couldn't put that on you. These fish are a major commitment. Not to mention, Othello is pregnant again. I never thought he and Desdemona would reproduce, and now they're putting out fry every other month."

"It wouldn't be putting anything on me. I love them. Going to London is throwing a bit of a kink into your dream of helping Scripps with their breeding program, huh?"

Brandi nodded. "I didn't foresee being gone for six months. I don't want anyone who stays here to get annoyed by them. If you're serious about wanting to help, I'd love it."

"I'm totally serious. It'll give me an excuse to watch them no matter who stays here. Has Mikayla agreed to the swap?" Gem trailed a fingertip along the front of the glass, and Othello followed. A little flutter of anticipation in her stomach accompanied the idea of seeing Mikayla again. When Brandi nodded, the flutter intensified.

"She called on the way home and said she's in if we are. We are, right?"

The news made the flutter in Gem's gut go nuts. "I'm sorry I rushed out before we were able to discuss it. The landscapers hit a sprinkler out front, and my dad wasn't being helpful. But, yeah. I liked her." She hated seeing the look of understanding pass over Brandi's face. The news about her father's mental decline had spread around the community.

The sprinkler episode didn't help. She'd arrived to see her father screaming at Devon, saying if he'd only placed the trees where he'd been told, they never would have hit the sprinkler. As if he'd forgotten all of their previous conversations about it. Gem gave Devon all the credit. He'd just stood there nodding until her father had finally run out of steam.

"I like her," Brandi said. "In some ways, she reminds me of her sister. In others, they're night and day. Ashe says she's having a hard time with her divorce."

Gem struggled to pick up the thread of their conversation. "Divorce?"

"I guess her husband asked for a divorce for the most effed-up reason: they couldn't have kids."

Gem sucked in air. "Yowch. That's harsh."

"Yeah. Ashe said their mother blames Mikayla for the failed marriage, like she should have done more to save it. She blames herself, and Ashe hates it. She wants Mikayla to get mad and stop turning it inward."

"Getting dumped for not being able to have kids would piss me off. I'd rather her be mad, too."

Brandi stared at her.

Gem mirrored Brandi's stare. "What?"

"You don't *get* mad."

Gem faked a scowl. "I do. In fact, I kicked the ground a little while ago when I found out we're on hold for planting until the county gets out here to mark the rest of the pipes."

Brandi scowled back. "But did you curse?"

"It didn't call for that."

Brandi rolled her eyes. "You proved my point. You don't *get* mad."

"Most of the time, there aren't many reasons to get mad. Still, I think I'd want to get mad during divorce. It seems appropriate. Don't you think? I mean, otherwise, why get one?"

"Being aromantic saves me from that kind of heartbreak." She shrugged. "But I guess a few breakups with friends broke my heart, so I see your point. Getting mad is a great way to distract yourself."

Gem watched Othello hitch himself to a branch near Desdemona. "I'm too busy to date, and none of my past relationships could be compared in the slightest to a marriage." She left out a big detail: her gift told her as soon as she met someone whether they were "the one" or simply "the one for now." Her father had known her mother was "the one" the minute he'd met her at the hospital where she'd volunteered as a candy striper. None of her sisters possessed it, just her and her dad. Everyone said her dad had a knack for sensing the essence in people, but she'd never told anyone but him. She'd become aware of it when she'd first gotten interested in social work, and by then, she didn't want to be known as the therapist who could determine whether a person behaved the way they did or thought the way they did because they were fundamentally good or bad. Life wasn't that simple.

Sure, she'd dated in the past. Even when a woman wasn't a match for her. She'd moved in with some, too. Like everyone, she got lonely. Just because someone didn't match with her didn't mean they couldn't be good company. She'd even fallen in love a couple of times. Hearts didn't care about "the one." They fell as easily for a "hell no" sometimes. However, these days, when it came to giving her heart, she no longer wanted to risk it unless she was certain she'd met her match. It didn't help that she hadn't felt like looking the last four years. She had enough going on.

She watched the seahorses and told herself to stop thinking about love.

Brandi paused in folding her clothes. "That's the first time I've ever heard you talk about dating. We've been friends for, what? Four years? I've bored you to tears about my aromantic asexual journey. Never once have I heard a single thing about your love life. I'm gonna mark this day in my calendar." She pretended to write in the air.

Gem laughed. Brandi always made things fun. It was ridiculous how much her love life didn't exist, and that was the only reason she never talked about it, not because she didn't want to. As far as her gift went, she didn't talk about it on purpose. Her father talked about his, and it had become part of the lore making Oceana the special place people knew it as. Somehow, she figured she'd be seen as more of a freak than a legend, so she stayed quiet. Besides, she mostly used hers to block people from sensing what was going on inside her. She was more comfortable that way. "As I said, there's not much to tell. And you never bore me."

"Remember, you can talk to me. I might be flying out in three days, but I'm a phone call away." She swiped Gem's hat and plopped it onto her head.

"Don't stay away too long. I'll miss you," Gem said as she stole her hat back. They talked nearly every day. She refused to think about not having Brandi to hang out with. At the moment, she let her new fascination with Mikayla occupy her mind. She could honestly say she'd never been intrigued with someone like this before.

CHAPTER FIVE

Mikayla had already made up her mind to do the swap with Brandi when she got into her car to drive home. Her house and Brandi's couldn't have been more different; from the community, to the people, to the sense of ease both Brandi and Gem exuded. She already imagined taking long walks on the beach and having neighbors dropping by for a cup of coffee without having to make plans days or weeks in advance. She'd always wanted to have drop-by-for-the-hell-of-it friends, as opposed to the plan-everything-down-to-an-inch-of-its-life friends who had disappeared as soon as the D-word hit the gossip circuit.

And all of the color!

It covered everything at Oceana from the ice plant blooming fiery red along the curbs to the orange hibiscus, the maroon bougainvillea, the multicolored pansies in the planters, and the purple Jacaranda. And Brandi's place felt more like home than her own house and was a stark contrast to the world in which she normally navigated. Her own house being a study in various shades of white and light gray. Her clothing, devoid of color. She peered at herself, frowning at her taupe shorts and white blouse.

I don't belong. I don't matter.

She sighed when the familiar refrain streamed through her mind. She did belong, and she did matter, but old ideas—in this case, ideas instilled as a small child trying to be seen by her self-absorbed mother beside her hellion of an older sister—were hard to erase.

The contrast between her clifftop house in La Jolla and Brandi's seaside house in Oceana reminded her of the difference between her artist sister and herself. All of her life, she'd admired her sister's vibrancy. She left a trail of creativity and light wherever she went, along with broken hearts and a fair amount of chaos. Mikayla was drawn to the same aesthetics as Ashe, but when she'd shopped to spice up her wardrobe or buy funky furniture to inject color into her life, she'd invariably come home with neutral purchases, the tasteful option. Hardly a mystery where that had come from. Her mother had never made a secret of how frustrating she found Ashe in all of her bohemian bedlam. Mikayla, younger by two years, had been her mother's hope for having a respectable daughter, a job Mikayla had excelled at until six months ago. At least, from all outward appearances. Now that she wasn't, she had no idea who she was, and she was finding out one painful change at a time.

What locked in her decision to do the swap were the seahorses. They'd always been her favorite animal. Other kids liked horses and monkeys. She'd liked seahorses. When she'd seen the tank in Brandi's house, she knew it was a sign.

The farther away she drove, the more anxious she grew about whether Brandi would agree to the swap. Before she hopped onto the freeway for the drive back to La Jolla, she stopped at a service station in South Oceanside to read the application and contract. Still surprised about the vetting, it gave her a sense of safety to know they were picky about who they let live there. She thought of Grampa James saying, "I refuse to join a club that would have me as a member," while wagging his eyebrows and pretending to hold a cigar.

Thinking about him gave her courage. She decided not to overthink, for once. Although she worried about coming off as too eager, she called Brandi ten minutes after she left. Thankfully, Brandi seemed as eager as she did, and they struck a verbal agreement. Brandi would leave on Thursday, and Mikayla would move in on Friday.

Excited about her decision, she looked over her half-organized house for the movers, whom she still needed to schedule. She and Craig had never talked about what to do with any of their possessions, and she didn't have it in her to initiate the conversation. She'd decided to put everything in storage and deal with it later. Most of it reminded her of her failed marriage. As far as she was concerned, she never wanted to see any of it again.

I don't belong. I don't matter.

Shut up!

She wanted to start new. Even her clothes. Now was her chance to be whoever she wanted. So instead of movers, she called a friend who did estate sales, arranged a virtual tour of the house, and scheduled the sale for the day after next. The whole lot of it would go to the highest bidder. The plan turned out to be easier and faster than she'd expected, and it included cleaning the house. One more thing she didn't have to schedule. It was such a relief, she wasn't sure what to do with herself.

She sat on the top step of the main staircase, something she'd found herself doing a lot lately, and gazed at the ocean. More than anything, she would miss this view. The huge windows gave her a one-eighty view over the cliffs above an ocean sparkling in the sunlight and up and down the coast. A few boats bobbed in the distance, and a few dozen surfers floated past the breakers. She'd always appreciated the view, but she couldn't see the beach or get to it from her house. She was removed from it.

If that wasn't a correlation to her life, nothing was.

Instead of the realization devastating her, as so many things did these days, excitement about starting a whole new chapter of her life filled her. She took a deep breath and smiled even as tears slid down her cheeks. She couldn't quite land on a single emotion.

Her phone buzzed quietly, and a glance at the caller ID told her it was Craig. The day their divorce had become final, she'd asked him to give her some space. However, there were things to discuss, such as the estate sale, and although she didn't want to, she'd called and left a message, asking him to call her back. The new chapter would start a little later.

"Hi, Mik. What are you up to?"

Oh, contemplating the wreck of my life. "Watching the water."

"Funny. Me, too. Wait, let me guess. You're on the terrace next to the fountain, and you have your feet propped up on Cupid's butt. It's a little early for wine, so you have an iced tea and lemonade. Am I close?"

"On the nose," she said. Much easier than correcting him, and she didn't want to guess where he was enjoying his view from. She didn't care.

"Totally called it." He said it confidently, no doubt thinking he knew her so well. "Hey, so the buyer wants to pay cash for the house."

"Sounds good to me. We get paid either way."

"On the condition we close escrow by the end of the week. It's a big ask. You'll have to find a place and get all the stuff out before then."

"Oh…kay." Good thing she'd set up the estate sale for Thursday. The speed of it took her off guard. Once the house closed, that would be it. Sadness and anxiety filled her stomach.

"I wouldn't consider it, but they've added an incentive. Ten percent over asking."

Always the financial planner. "What's their hurry?"

"No idea."

"That's a lot of money."

"It's all yours for the inconvenience. Half of the sale price and all of the incentive."

She sighed. It was all from guilt. "Craig. It's not necessary."

"I want to. It's only fair. You're the one who's being put out."

If put out means losing my marriage where I was under the impression that I belonged and mattered, you're right. "It's fine. I'll have everything out by Thursday. We can close on Friday." She told him about the estate sale, and he sounded almost as relieved as she felt.

"You're the best, babe. I'll let them know. I'm sure they'll be fine with it. They seem anxious to move in. Where will you stay? Maybe the Fairmont? How are you doing, by the way?"

You don't get to call me babe anymore. How am I? Devastated...wait, not devastated. Moving on. "I'm fine. I have a place already. It's fine."

"I'm glad. Relieved, actually. I hated to think about you scrambling for a decent place to live."

So glad you *feel better.* "How's Mexico?" She wasn't interested, but being the object of his pity was worse.

"It's good. I could stay here forever. Carmen misses home, though. We'll be back in a week or so."

She wondered where they would stay. She wasn't going to ask. In fact, she wasn't into doing small talk. "I have another call coming in," she lied. "I have to take it. Talk again soon."

She hung up before he said good-bye. Last time, when they were hanging up, he'd said he loved her. Probably from habit, like calling her babe. Still, she didn't want to hear it. Interestingly, she wasn't angry. Not this time. Anger at him came more out of habit now, and she didn't want to be that kind of person. If asked, she was more bored than angry and maybe inconvenienced. The realization made her smile. Maybe she'd processed the divorce more than she'd given herself credit for.

Her phone rang. This time, Ashe's voice bellowed from the speaker. She never bothered with greetings. "Brandi told me you two are going through with the swap."

Mikayla gave a laugh. "Word travels quickly."

"It does. You should have heard how excited she was. She can't wait to see your London place in person. She's going to offer you additional money to cover the difference in size and quality of the places."

Mikayla waved her hand. "I won't accept it. She's doing me a favor. I don't see myself traveling much for a while, and this way, it won't sit empty for so long. Besides, I love her place. It offers enough on its own merit."

"Isn't her place amazing? I know you like a more...sedate environment." She sounded pleased.

"Why do you say that?"

She laughed. "You're kidding, right?"

Her response rubbed Mikayla the wrong way. "Just because I don't decorate like Brandi...and may I remind you, she's an artist, and I'm not, but it doesn't mean I don't appreciate it."

Ashe chortled, literally chortled, which should have annoyed Mikayla but didn't. "I guess I misinterpreted the comment about wishing you'd worn sunglasses the last time you came to my place."

Mikayla wagged a finger, not caring that her sister couldn't see it. "Nope. You were staying with that Day-Glo performance artist. Tell me, why did you suggest the swap with Brandi if you suspected I'd be uncomfortable?"

"Honestly? I didn't think about it. I've always thought you'd like Brandi, and I took it as an opportunity to help two people solve a problem. It surprised me you even considered the swap, actually, so the rest occurred to me later. By then, you'd shockingly agreed to check it out, so I decided to roll with it."

"Well, I move in Friday."

"Do you want help?"

"It's two suitcases. I'll be fine."

"That's right. You're putting everything in storage."

"Nope. I'm getting rid of it all." Saying it aloud freed her soul. "Every last bit."

"Wait. Did you just say you're getting rid of *everything*?"

Surprising Ashe for a change satisfied her more than she ever imagined. "You heard right. It's all getting sold in an estate sale on Thursday."

"Wait. Wait. Wait. What about sentimental things? Jewelry? Pictures? Gifts from people?"

"All our pictures are digital. Important papers are in my computer bag with my laptop and Kindle. The only thing holding any meaning for me is the comforter you made me and Grandma James's rings, which I'll keep. Other than that, everything is just stuff. Stuff I have no attachment to. I'll keep some clothing, but everything else is getting sold. If there's anything you want, come and get it tonight. I'll tell Mom and Dad the same thing. She's always loved the blown glass stemware." Mikayla laughed. "I guess it's a fresh start. It's liberating."

"You mean it. You're getting rid of everything." She sounded stunned. Mikayla loved it.

"Yup. Fresh new start, fresh new me." Butterflies dashed around inside her.

CHAPTER SIX

S unlight glinted off the windshield of the BMW parked in Brandi's driveway when Gem came back to her house after work on Friday. Instead of driving the golf cart up her own driveway, she redirected and headed over to say hello. It had been a day of hand watering the foliage because the Call-Before-You-Dig appointment wasn't until Saturday, and the sprinklers all around the complex wall were still down. Despite being bone-tired, a buzz centered in Gem's stomach at the idea of seeing Mikayla again. As she stepped from the cart, Mikayla's head popped up from the other side of the car.

"Want any help?" Gem asked.

Mikayla's smile lit up her face. "Sure. If you don't mind bringing in the rest of the groceries." She nodded toward the inside of her car, her hands already full.

Gem came around the car and spied a box piled high with vegetables and fruit. "Looks like you just came from Costco."

"Brandi warned me about the handful of potentially expired condiments and the lone pitcher of lemonade in the refrigerator. Not only did I get food, I picked up a couple of books, a package of colored pens, and this weather station thing."

"Weather station thing?" Gem pushed the car door closed with her butt and followed Mikayla to the covered deck spanning the length of the mobile home. She'd helped Brandi build it two summers ago.

"It has a screen displaying the temperature, wind, rainfall, sunrise and sunset, and it connects to the local weather forecast. It gives historical weather information, the surf report, and issues alerts. I left one at the house I just sold, and since I used it all the time and it was on sale...Anyway, you don't need to know all that. I'll have to hire someone to install the sensor on the roof."

"I can do it for you, although I'm not sure why you want it. This is San Diego. We have an average temperature of seventy-two degrees, and it hardly ever rains."

Mikayla appeared surprised. "I couldn't ask you to install it, and it's for those days when it does rain. They always catch me off guard, and I'm always in the most inappropriate thing when they do."

"You didn't ask. I offered." Gem put the box on the counter, keeping the installation instructions. "I'm still in my grubbies, and it will take fifteen minutes."

"Are you sure?"

Gem thumbed through the instructions. It seemed simple. "I'll probably have it installed before you get all this washed and put away," she said, backing out the door. She returned in less than fifteen minutes with the screen programmed and everything working as it should. "All set. There's a warning feature. Wildfires, earthquakes, tsunamis, tornadoes."

Mikayla's shoulders slumped. "It seems like it's always wildfire season here, and ever since the tsunamis in Asia, I've been a little paranoid. I lived on the cliffs in La Jolla, which gave me some peace, but being at sea level...well...I have an overactive imagination."

It was cute. She came off as grounded and confident, but the admission was endearing. Gem decided not to tell her that the sandy cliffs of La Jolla were as much at risk during a tsunami as the lower elevations. Erosion definitely happened. "Well, you will be adequately warned by your new toy so you can evacuate to higher ground."

"You got that installed fast," Mikayla said. "I'm going to make veggie enchiladas. Can I repay you with food?"

"It took two minutes to install and the rest of the time to figure out how to program it." And she would have done it for any of her friends.

"Do you already have dinner plans, or do you not like enchiladas?"

"My plans for dinner tonight consist of canned soup. Enchiladas are one of my favorite foods. Veggie is a bonus, since I'm mostly a vegetarian who occasionally cheats for bacon." She took in the surprised expression on Mikayla's face and held up her hand. "I know. No one gets it, and neither do I, but it's a thing."

"It's settled, then. Would you like to eat here? Or I can drop them off at your place when they're ready."

"I'd be happy to eat here. Would it be okay if I took a shower first? I mean, at my place. Not here." She should tell her dad and make sure he ate something, too. Left to his own devices, he'd probably just fall asleep in front of the television.

Mikayla laughed. "Dinner won't be ready for about an hour. Take your time."

When Gem got home, she found her dad exactly where she thought he'd be, sitting in his recliner watching a true crime show with the volume turned up to excruciating. His eyes were closed, but as soon as she turned off the television, he sprang to attention.

"Hey. I was watching that."

"Through your eyelids?"

"I was blinking. A man needs to lubricate his eyeballs."

"My bad." She turned the television back on, only at a reasonable volume. "I'm going to eat dinner at a friend's house tonight."

"By friend, do you mean the new girl staying at Brandi's?"

"She's a woman, and yes."

"Moving fast, aren't you?"

"What do you mean?"

"You made a beeline to her as soon as you got home. I don't want you messing around with the residents."

Gem bristled at the implication. "What are you talking about? I eat dinner at Brandi's all the time."

"That's different. We don't want a replay of what happened with the Zepedas."

Morgan Zepeda. Gem had been twelve, and Morgan, fourteen, super-cool, and visiting her grandparents for the summer. They'd met at the Oceana community pool. Morgan could do a backflip, and nothing had scared her. Eventually, Gem had realized she didn't simply admire her, she loved her. However, she'd never mustered the courage to tell her, despite wanting to for more than half their summer together. The morning Morgan had left with her parents to go back home to somewhere in Northern California, Gem had given her a going-away present of a friendship bracelet, assorted candy, and a letter telling Morgan that she loved her. She'd hoped they'd write to each other. However, Morgan's grandmother had returned the small package to Gem's parents, along with words like, "bad influence," "pervert," and "sinner," and had soon moved out of Oceana, becoming the only residents who'd ever moved out on bad terms. Gem had hardly understood her own feelings yet, but the event had forced her to come out to her parents.

Her mother had cried, and her father had told her not to tell anyone about it. Even the parish priest had been dragged into it. They'd stopped going to church at about the same time, probably because she wasn't welcome. Once the shock over everything wore off, her parents had fully accepted and supported her, yet they'd never talked about what had initiated it, just that she shouldn't date residents. Fast-forward twenty years, Gem occasionally wondered how Morgan was, and she never dated residents. It didn't mean she hadn't had crushes a time or two, but she respected her father's wishes. She'd also developed an ability to block her father from seeing her true essence so he didn't worry about a repeat of what had happened with Morgan's family.

It surprised her that he was bringing it up now and with the same implication: she needed to be careful not to make the residents uncomfortable and move out. Logic told her his admonition came from whatever was going on with his memory, but her child's heart screamed into her pillow, and the shame of being told to hide rushed right back, almost as strong as if it had happened yesterday. This time, she refused to hide who she was.

"Oh my God, Dad. You're seriously bringing up something that happened when I was twelve?"

He wagged a finger at her. "Don't use the Lord's name in vain, Gem. You know your mother doesn't like it."

She dropped her chin to her chest and breathed deeply. He sounded exactly like he had back then, trying to protect her mother's sensitivities. She tried to remember this wasn't him, at least, not the supportive father he'd become. She cleared her throat and straightened her back. "Do you want a BLT or some soup with those crackers you like?" She gave two choices instead of asking what he wanted. Otherwise, he'd say he didn't want anything.

"I fixed a sandwich when I got home." A couple of months ago, the statement would have sent her flying to the kitchen to check for fire, but she'd shut off the gas to the stove after he'd left one of the burners on without a flame for several hours, causing the carbon monoxide alarm to go off in the middle of the night. Now, they only used the microwave, and she'd locked up all the sharp knives in the back shed. Cutting up all of the produce ahead of time so he could make his sandwiches was a pain in the ass, but it was worth the peace of mind, and it gave him a semblance of autonomy.

"Okay. I'll get our vitamins, and after that, you can watch TV all night if you want."

She ducked into the kitchen to get his medicine and her vitamins and returned to the living room where they took their "vitamins" together. Her previously neat-as-a-nun father had left a mess in the kitchen, yet it appeared as if he'd actually eaten most of his sandwich, a fair trade. She hated the nights he argued about eating. Mostly, she worried about his nutrition, but his late-night snacks also resulted in an absolute mess she didn't want to deal with the next day.

After he took his pills, she slid off his slippers before spreading a blanket over him. He'd be out in minutes and sleep there all night. He rarely slept in his bed anymore. Surprisingly, mornings were usually his best time. He'd wake up sharp, fix breakfast, and read the paper until she came into the kitchen to eat and chat about their day. Saturday mornings were her favorite because they were less about work and more about hanging out together.

"Enjoy your date tonight, Gemmy. Remember. Not a minute after eleven o'clock. I'll be waiting up." He'd already forgotten his previous warning, and his eyes were closed. The last part came out in a mumble.

He'd said it to her many times in high school, and it caught her between feelings of nostalgia and irritation. It didn't matter. His finger already rested on the volume control of the remote.

After her shower and another quick peek in on her father, Gem remembered her mother's advice about not arriving at another person's home for dinner without a gift, and she decided to bring some flowers from her own flower bed. The gerbera daisies and daffodils had been showing off their loveliness for a few weeks, so she put together a colorful bouquet in a jelly jar.

Halfway to Mikayla's, she started to have doubts about the flowers. She almost threw them in the garbage when she passed the community dumpsters tucked behind their ornate metal screens, worried Mikayla might read into them.

"Are you all right there, Gem?" Mikayla leaned over the deck.

Gem wondered how long she'd been standing there. Embarrassed, she grinned and shrugged. "I was overthinking bringing flowers."

Mikayla held open the front door. "I watched you from the kitchen window for a few minutes, wondering if you'd turned to stone. Are they from your garden? I noticed the flowers this morning."

"They are," she said, explaining her mother's advice.

"Just gorgeous. My mom says the same thing. However, her advice is specific to wine." Mikayla bit her lip and accepted the flowers. She put them in the middle of the dining room table and admired them.

Gem tried not to stare at how sexy she looked biting her lip and then told herself to stop leering at the residents. "Do you want wine? I have a couple of bottles at my place."

Mikayla rested a hand on her arm before moving around the kitchen. "I have wine."

"Did you get moved in okay?"

"Having two suitcases and groceries made the move fairly simple." She checked on the enchiladas. The food smelled amazing, making Gem's stomach rumble. "Dinner will be a few more minutes."

Gem gazed around the tidy space strewn with art. It still felt exactly like Brandi's place, but it was weird being a stranger in a house she'd always felt comfortable in. "There isn't much room for more furnishings, anyway."

"I like it as it is. I've never been somewhere so vibrant. The colors, textures, patterns…it should be chaotic, but there's a…" She paused as if trying to think of a word.

"Harmony?" Gem suggested. She took a seat on one of the barstools in the kitchen.

"Yes. That's exactly it. It all exists in harmony. I love how it grounds me." She leaned her elbows on the counter.

The answer couldn't have captured the essence of Brandi and her house better. "Brandi is probably the most harmonious and balanced person you'll ever meet."

"She seemed relaxed for someone who hadn't figured out her living situation three days before moving to a different country. I had stress dripping from my ears, and I only moved thirty miles."

"I can't believe she did the swap."

Mikayla appeared surprised. "Oh? Why is that?"

"It's just that Brandi is standoffish until she gets to know someone. I think you being Ashe's sister had a lot to do with it, but it was still out of character. She liked you from the start. She told me."

Mikayla laughed. "I liked her from the start, too. I'm terrible at reading people. I would have guessed a swap was nothing to her."

Gem guessed Mikayla brought people out of their shells. "Brandi's more of a listener than a talker. It takes her a long time to warm up to people."

"I'm glad she felt comfortable with me, then."

Gem had only seen Mikayla around one other person, but her gift for reading people told her Mikayla presented herself as the same person no matter who she was around. The same sense said she always saw the best in people.

"She said you reminded her of your sister." Gem had met Ashe through Brandi, and she didn't see it. They bore a slight resemblance in their facial structure and maybe a few gestures, but she found it hard to believe the two of them were related at all. Ashe was intense and erratic energy, and Mikayla was gentle and steady. There was a pull about her, drawing one in, the very definition of arresting. Gem couldn't think of a better way to describe the unseen power pulling them together.

Mikayla huffed. "That's the first I've ever been told that I reminded anyone of my sister."

"Is the comparison a good thing or a bad thing?"

"Good. Everyone loves Ashe. She's warm and outgoing. Compared to her, I'm a stick-in-the-mud. She doesn't let anything get to her. She lives and loves with passion. She also knows when to move on. I'm always worried she'll be lonely, but there's something to be said for moving on when the time is right. I'd like to be more like her."

"Well, I don't think you're a stick-in-the-mud. By the way, I'm not like my sisters, either."

"How many sisters do you have?"

"Five. Ana is the oldest. Then Leticia, followed by Gabriela, Adriana, Silvia, and then me, the youngest. Twelve years separate me and my youngest sister. I was a surprise." Gem's sisters were more like aunts to her. Most of them were already living their own lives by the time she was old enough to understand what being a sister meant.

"Twelve years is a big span." Mikayla searched through the cabinets, opening a couple before she found plates and glasses. "It's just me and my sister. Any brothers?"

"Just us six girls. My mom wanted a big family. And a boy. She would have kept trying for a boy until she got one, but after Silvia, she stopped getting pregnant until I came along."

"Your name is different from them. Is it a nickname?" Mikayla set the table after a brief search.

"My given name is Francisca, but no one calls me that. My dad called me Angel from the start. But my niece Rose called me 'Agem' when she first started to talk, and it stuck."

"That's sweet." Mikayla stopped with a handful of silverware. Her gaze penetrated all the way to Gem's bones, as if she was being seen for the first time. "I have to say, Gem fits you better than Francisca. Not that I know you well." She put the silverware next to the plates.

The memory of Mikayla's gaze on her still warmed Gem's skin. She cleared her tight throat. "It could have been worse. Do I come off as a Fran or Franny?"

Mikayla studied her again, and Gem would have given almost anything to see what she saw. "I like Angel."

It took a second to figure out she was teasing. Her subtle sense of humor was unexpected. Gem couldn't help a smile. "My dad's the only one who's ever called me Angel, but I'll let you if you want."

"I'll take it into consideration. What's your dad like?" Mikayla found a spatula in a drawer.

The question was a loaded one. Her dad now was so different from the dad she knew and loved. She'd always love him, but he was becoming more of a stranger every day. She decided to stick with generalities because anything more threatened to break her heart. "His parents are Danish, and he wasn't raised in a big family. He went along with whatever my mom wanted. Dad was always happy when my mom was happy."

Mikayla tilted her head. "You said she's been gone for several years?"

Gem was surprised when a pang of grief hit her. "Ten years ago from breast cancer."

"I'm sorry to hear that." Mikayla's eyes overflowed with compassion, and Gem's memories of her mother, all good, flooded her mind. Mikayla's presence somehow allowed her to relax, letting in emotions she usually reserved for quiet alone times.

"They always say it gets easier with time," Gem said. "I don't think it does. Life just keeps happening, but the pain is still there, getting integrated into all the other distractions and other memories."

"Sounds like you miss her."

"So much. My sisters are good mothers because of her. Of course, my dad had something to do with it, but everyone knows who ran the house. Now, my sisters and I are like his wives, making sure he eats right, goes to the doctor, and all that." Gem laughed because it was true, except for the doctor part. Not from lack of trying. She dreamed about how much easier it would have been with her mom here to help. She always knew how to guide him, and he needed it so much now.

"Did you live in London long?" she asked, changing the subject.

Mikayla looked confused. "London? I'm from here."

"I assumed because you have a house in London, you must have lived there."

Mikayla shook her head. "It's a vacation house. My husband spent so much time in London for work, and I often accompanied him. I got it in the divorce."

So much for a subject change. Gem searched her mind for a less touchy subject, and as a result, the pause drew out.

"The subject of divorce kills conversations." Mikayla grimaced. "It's not off-limits. Or we can totally change the subject."

Gem laughed, probably a little more than the comment warranted. "Whatever's comfortable to you. Or we can meet in the middle and talk about the swap with Brandi. If the divorce comes up, so be it."

"Great idea," Mikayla said, and Gem saw her shoulders relax.

"The whole concept is interesting to me. It's obvious why Brandi did it. As usual, she waited until the last minute. Things always magically work out for her. Although, I wonder why *you* chose to. I may be wrong, but you probably have the means to live anywhere. Why here?"

"I've been wondering the same thing," Mikayla said, and then her eyes got comically big. "That came out wrong. Oceana is a beautiful place."

"I didn't think you meant it any other way." She didn't seem to be a very judgmental person, as far as Gem could tell so far.

"I truly didn't. The simple answer is, my sister suggested it when my old house sold faster than expected. The longer answer is, the divorce just became final." She cocked a brow at Gem, who thought it was cute. "There it is again. Anyway. Six months ago, I was happily married, living in the house I'd lived in for twelve years, with a husband who loved me. Everything seemed like it would be the same forever. I never envisioned the structure of my life collapsing so completely. One brick fell out and *bang*. Now I have to figure out how to rebuild it." She pushed her hair back. "And the thing is, I don't even know if I *like* brick anymore. Maybe I like flagstone, marble, or glass. I couldn't figure out where to live. Who I wanted to be. When I came to see Brandi's place, peace flowed into me."

She paused, and Gem didn't try to fill the silence, so they just hung out until Mikayla let out a breath.

"It's stupid. I came here because my sister thinks I'm boring. She didn't think I would. And honestly, I had no intention of swapping. I'm anything but an impulsive person. It's funny. I stepped into this house, and it seemed safe. Not only safe. Inspired. I honestly can't explain it, but the idea of staying here for a while seemed like the right thing to do. So here I am."

"Wow. That's a lot." In effect, she was starting all over again. Gem guessed that in six months, Mikayla would embark on yet another new adventure, leaving Oceana behind. A little surge of envy hit her at the idea.

"I'm sorry for the emotional dump." Mikayla fidgeted with the napkins. "Dinner finished cooking a while ago, but I've been blathering. I promised to feed you."

Gem reached for the napkins, worried that her comment about it being a lot had come off wrong. "Don't be sorry. I was just absorbing what you said. It's who you are. We should all be so insightful and be the person we want to be." Gem caught a glint of something that might be gratitude in Mikayla's eyes. "Do you mind if we eat out on the deck? It's perfect outside, and the sun will set in a little while."

Some of the tension left Mikayla's stance. "That sounds amazing. I'll bring the food out."

Gem picked up the plates and silverware and went out to the deck to set the table.

"You'll have to forgive me," Mikayla said, following and setting out the food. "It's just enchiladas and salad. I forgot to start the rice when we were talking. I never do that."

"Enchiladas and salad are perfect. If it tastes anything like it smells, it's delicious." Gem went back in to get their drinks. When she returned, Mikayla was watching the sunset. A few boats floated close to shore, and a large ship inched across the horizon in front of the sun hanging just above the edge of the ocean. A slight breeze ruffled their hair, making it a perfect evening.

"This is beautiful," Mikayla said.

Gem took a bite and tried to keep from moaning. "And this is delicious."

"Thank you." The pleased expression on Mikayla's face made her smile.

"Hey, Gem," a familiar voice yelled from the street.

"Hey, Shia. How were the sets?" Gem called back.

Shia carried a short surfboard under her arm, her wet suit draped over it. She wore swim shorts and a sweatshirt with the hood pulled over her head, and Gem guessed she'd just gotten out of the water. She paused at the base of the stairs. "Mostly mush and no juice from the onshore winds."

"It'll be better in the morning."

"Hope so. I'm dropping off my board and headed to the hot tub to warm up."

A smidgeon of shame brushed through Gem. She liked Shia and normally enjoyed her company, but right now, she wanted her to leave so she could get to know Mikayla a little better on her own. The pause became a little uncomfortable.

"Have you met Mikayla?"

"Nope." Shia rested her board against the deck and stepped up. "You're eating. Sorry to interrupt. I'm Shia. I live next door." She offered her hand.

Mikayla stood as she took it, mirroring Shia's wide smile. "I'm glad to meet you. Are you hungry? We have plenty."

Disappointment washed through Gem. *Don't say yes. Don't say yes.* Gem was positive Shia couldn't read her mind, but she still felt bad for wishing she'd go away.

Shia glanced between them. "It smells good, but I'm all about rinsing off and hitting the hot tub."

Gem let out a relieved breath.

"Brandi told me a lot about you. I've never met a professional surfer before," Mikayla said, and Gem tried not to be too impatient for Shia to leave.

"There are probably a half dozen of us in Oceana and a hundred rec surfers," Shia said. "We should have a bonfire so you can meet everyone. Not all the surfers, just the neighbors on our street."

"That would be nice," Mikayla said.

"I'm freezing my tits off." Shia put a hand over her mouth. "Sorry. I'll figure out the bonfire and let you know. My date with the hot tub awaits. I'll see you around. If you need anything, gimme a knock." And with that, she retrieved her board and disappeared around her house.

"Did Brandi tell you we have a pool and hot tub?" Gem asked, hoping her relief wasn't obvious.

"I'll definitely use the pool. I used to swim in the ocean but lost the habit. Maybe I'll pick it up again living here."

"Shia swims the jetties most mornings. I'm sure she'd love a buddy." Gem pointed to two dark lines made of piled boulders that jutted out into the ocean. The waves started building right about where they left off. "They're about three-hundred yards apart."

"Do you swim with her?"

"Nope."

"Is it the cold?"

"*Jaws*." Ridiculous but the God's honest truth.

Mikayla snorted. "The movie about the shark?"

"Don't make fun. I watched it at the harbor float-in on a big screen several summers ago. They show movies throughout the summer and rent kayaks, paddleboards…all sorts of floating devices, so people can watch the show from the water. It's like a drive-in on the water. I made the mistake of watching that damn movie. It's insane how the people in tubes could let their body parts dangle in the water." She shivered even as she knew how ridiculous she was. "It's irrational how the movie made me afraid of deep water, where sharks or other very large carnivorous creatures can hide. I'm good with lakes and rivers and all that. I'll even play in the waves, but forget about the ocean."

Mikayla looked amused. "I would have never guessed."

Gem shrugged and continued eating.

"I can't wait to meet more of the neighbors. Tell me more about the people on our little cul-de-sac." Mikayla took a last bite.

"Well, you just met Shia from next door."

"Brandi said she's a bit of a loner. Very sweet. And if you aren't around, I can go to her for help with small fixes around the house, and she accepts baked goods for her trouble."

Gem laughed. "A very accurate assessment."

"She seems so young."

"She's twenty-two." She didn't offer anything about Shia's past spent in the foster system. It was Shia's story to tell. "She's got a good head on her shoulders, and she's a phenomenal surfer. I think she's doing well for herself." She pointed at the double-sectioned mobile home past Shia's. "Next door to Shia is Alice. She's been here going on twenty-five years. She'll no doubt be over in the next day or two with a plate of cookies. I think she lives off coffee and cookies. She works up at the mission. She's religious, which you'll probably notice right away. I only say that so you can make an informed decision if you decide to curse or something in front of her. My dad says she came from a convent. I have my doubts. I think it's because she usually carries a rosary."

"It doesn't matter to me one way or the other," Mikayla said. "My mom was raised Methodist, I think, and my biological dad was Jewish, but the rest of my family isn't religious. We've never gone to church or temple except on the odd religious holiday."

Gem took a sip of water. "My mom was *super* religious. We went every Sunday and to other Masses during the week, depending on the occasion. We did all the Catholic things. The whole shebang. A couple of my sisters picked it back up after Mom died, maybe out of habit. My dad only ever attended on holidays." She didn't want to get into how she'd quit going to church when the priest had preached about the sin of homosexuality after the whole Morgan thing had happened, but it remained heavy on her mind as she pointed at the house next to Alice's. "That's Harper's place. They work on our landscaping crew and is usually quiet at block parties. But they're funny when they open up a little."

"They? Is it a family?"

"They and them are Harper's pronouns."

"Gotcha. Thanks for telling me."

"Next to Harper is Eight."

"Like the number?"

"It's a nickname. She told me it's from having lived eight of her nine lives. Like a cat. She used to be a stuntwoman. You'll probably like her. Everyone does. She's got a story for every occasion, all of them funny, most of them harrowing." Gem stood and gathered their plates. "And those are the people of Oceana Place, our little oasis."

Mikayla picked up the dishes. "I wasn't friendly with any of my neighbors at my old house. Not one. All the houses were hidden behind gates and walls." She paused in the gathering of dishes. "I lived there for years, and here, on the first day, I'm having dinner with you. Impromptu, no pretenses, no putting on of airs, just you and me, some food, and a fabulous sunset. This. This is real." She breathed deeply, as if taking it in.

Gem absorbed those words as they continued to chat, and she helped with the dishes before she said good night. The sincerity of Mikayla's words sat with her, along with the knowledge that Mikayla had enjoyed their time together. She'd enjoyed it, too, and it wasn't because she didn't have neighbors to have dinner with. She did. There was something else. They seemed to click. When she left, she wasn't ready to go, but she didn't want to overstay her welcome.

As she walked across the quiet street, the damp sea air carrying the sweet perfume of star jasmine, Gem allowed herself a moment to ponder what it would be like to date Mikayla. She told herself it was just hypothetical because her dad had brought it up, but she knew deep down that it was way more than that, and she should curb even theoretical situations. But dang, Mikayla's essence was so…so captivating and still so different than any essence she'd encountered. They'd only just met, and they were so different, but it didn't matter. Gem wanted more dinners, more everything.

The therapist in her kicked in, telling her she'd made peace a long time ago with the no-getting-romantically-involved-with-residents situation, so it was fortunate that Mikayla's recent divorce meant she needed time to work on herself. Gem knew it was the right thing to do, but she was surprised at her thoughts. In the last four years, she hadn't entertained anything romantic with anyone. Sometime between dinner and the dishes, through no fault of her own, she'd developed a little crush on her new neighbor.

It was nice to know she still had the capability to dream of romance, but Gem was good at boundaries and had plenty of reasons to respect this one, mostly her responsibilities to her father.

However, she couldn't discount the true danger here. Gem would fall way too fast into deep waters if she let her crush on Mikayla have free rein, which sounded scarier than coming face-to-face with a real-life shark.

CHAPTER SEVEN

A different kind of quiet greeted Mikayla when she woke up, and for a moment, she didn't know where she was, but a quick look around settled her. She waited for the paralyzing depression that always came with her first waking thoughts: the memory of the day Craig had upended her life. It didn't come. Nor did all the questions about what she could have done to make him stay. There were still fears about what she was supposed to do now, but the memory and the familiar lead blanket of failure and depression never came. Something else had moved in. A sense of joy she'd thought she'd lost filled her heart.

But what was different?

Everything. She'd purged, she'd moved, she'd met knew people.

Thinking about the last, she rolled onto her back and stretched. The evening with Gem had gone better than expected, not that she'd expected anything. Her biggest talent was entertaining. Being the wife of the president of an investment company meant she could do it in her sleep, and so many times, she almost had. Craig's business was the definition of boring. All the dinners bled into one.

Gem was a refreshing departure from the elitist and stuffy posturing of Mikayla's old social circle. She was charming and interesting. She loved her family, and she seemed to genuinely care about the people around her, including her neighbors, who seemed more like family than friends. Mikayla could have spoken to her all night.

Sighing, she forced herself from her reverie, tossed aside the blankets, and sat up. There were seahorses to tend to. They were fascinating creatures. Last night, she'd left the front door open to let in the gentle sea breeze and had watched the seahorses. Brandi had left a laminated page of information, and she'd already studied the feeding regimen, which was intense. The adults required feeding at least three times a day with frozen blocks of shrimp, and the babies had to be fed every two hours.

Thankful for the automated feeders, Mikayla only had to make sure the squares of frozen shrimp were loaded into the chilling chambers in the feeders each morning. The seahorses would be fine for the rest of the day, and someone from the Birch Aquarium at Scripps Institute would come once a week to check on the tank.

Othello and Desdemona, the largest and brightest with their deep yellow coloring, were swimming with their tales curled together. When Brandi had described how they mated for life and how they did the little swim-dance, Mikayla had to admit she'd had a cynical response, but she watched avidly, enjoying the signs of affection. Proof that her bruised heart had healed a little.

When the feeder cycled, filling the feeding tray, Othello and Desdemona joined an orange-reddish colored pair named Bonnie and Clyde, as well as Will and Grace, who were a tan and black couple with stripes on their tails. Enthralled, Mikayla spent the rest of the morning learning about the odd fish.

Two hours later, a knock on the door roused her, and she hadn't even fixed her first cup of coffee. She got up to answer, still in pajama bottoms and an old T-shirt. She threw on a hoodie, unconcerned about not having her makeup on, a thing the old Mikayla would never have done. She'd decided on a natural appearance while she stayed in Oceana, and so far, it felt comfortable, although it hadn't even been twenty-four hours. It didn't mean staying in her pajamas all day, however, so it was going to be a work-in-progress.

Shia stood on the deck and waved shyly. "Hi. We met last night?"

"Shia, come in. I was about to make a cup of coffee."

She entered and headed straight for the fish tank. "Yes! She kept the seahorses. Will Rich be helping you?"

"He'll come on Mondays," Mikayla said, joining her. "I've been doing research all morning."

Shia watched for a minute more, then plopped on the furry couch, sinking her fingers into the long white upholstery. "I live for those seahorses. Brandi lets me come over all the time to watch them."

"Come by any time you want," Mikayla said. It wasn't like her schedule was particularly full, and Shia seemed nice. She stepped around the island to make coffee.

"How do you know Brandi? Have you been friends long?" Shia asked and then laughed. "I told myself not to be nosey, and here I am. Brandi's my Oceana mom. She told me she was going to London for a few months, but she never mentioned a house sitter until, like, a day or two before she left. Did you know she's going to work on graphics for some superhero movie? She's so cool."

"She's working on a movie?" Mikayla asked. "She told me she's a graphic designer. I didn't ask for details. Maybe I should have." It struck her, once again, how little she knew about Brandi, and still, they'd swapped houses. It wasn't something she would have guessed she'd be doing just a week ago, and that gave her a bit of a thrill.

"She does contract work for all kinds of companies."

"I met her for the first time Monday. My sister introduced us. She needed a place in London, and I was looking for a temporary place here, so we sort of swapped."

Shia got up from the couch and stood on the other side of the counter while Mikayla waited for the coffee to brew. "That's cool. I never would have imagined people could swap houses like that. You're from London? You don't have an accent."

Embarrassed to keep explaining her vacation home, she didn't. "I'm from here. I wanted a place to stay while I figured out my next move, and my sister told me about Brandi's house."

"That's kind of how I came to Oceana. I have to live close to the beach for obvious reasons. I couldn't afford it, but my social worker helped me get some grants since I wanted to go to college, so…" She waved a hand dismissively. "It's a boring story. I'm glad Gem and her dad let me stay here. I have no idea where I would have gone." She said it as if being homeless wasn't terrifying, and Mikayla wondered how someone so young could possess so much self-confidence. Used to people telling her their stories, she took it as a compliment Shia trusted her.

"The coffee's done. How do you take yours?"

"Do you have milk and sugar? I just started liking coffee."

Mikayla took their cups and fixings to the kitchen table. She found coffee a great way to get to know someone, another thing that reminded her of Grandma James. She'd been thinking about her grandparents a lot lately, taking comfort in the memories. Grandma James had always enjoyed the small things, like having coffee with a neighbor.

"Did Gem tell you about me being a foster kid?"

"She only said you've lived here for about as long as Brandi," Mikayla said, taking a sip.

Shia nodded, spooning several heaps of sugar into her cup. "Yeah, we moved here in the same month, except I brought a backpack, and she rolled in with a truck full of furniture and whatnot. When she found out I didn't have a bed, she gave me her futon and a few other things. She took me to thrift stores and helped me get settled. I was completely clueless."

"I see why you call her your Oceana mom."

"Yeah. She helped me so much. For someone who planned to live on the beach if it came to it, I was lucky."

"You were going to live on the beach?"

Shia shrugged. "I didn't have a lot of options. But with the grants and Alice—she's the neighbor on the other side of me—she got me into a program through the mission, and I was able to swing it. I'm starting to get sponsors from surfing, which is how most professionals make a living, so maybe I'll be able to do it on my own. I never dreamed I'd be able to surf professionally." She looked so happy to have what she did, but the story touched Mikayla's heart.

An unexpected sense of protectiveness welled up within her. "It must have been hard."

"Which part?" Shia asked, and Mikayla didn't think it was cynicism, which she had a right to, but against all odds, didn't seem to.

"All of it. Being in the foster system in the first place and everything after that. It's unfair."

"I don't think fairness is a real thing. Some people are given awesome parents, and I was given Sharon the meth-head and some john she probably did for a pack of cigarettes. It's the luck of the draw, you know? It doesn't matter what you were given to start off with. It matters what you do with it." Her eyes grew unfocused, as if she were thinking about something. "If you can find a way to survive until you have some control over your own life."

Her last words made Mikayla shiver. "Your caseworker told you about Oceana?"

"Brandi's friends with my caseworker and told her about the cul-de-sac of misfit souls, and my caseworker said I should check it out."

"Misfit souls?"

Shia laughed. "It's what Alice calls Oceana Place, our little street. It's sort of caught on."

"I haven't met her yet."

"She's been here forever. You should hear the stories she tells. The Helmstaads have always been here when people needed a safe place. Like people who get discharged from the service. Lots of other people live here, too, but when someone is going through a rough patch or something else, especially women, there's always an opening on this little street. Alice calls it divine intervention, like, maybe God is involved. Brandi thinks it's the law of attraction. Gem says her dad has a sixth sense for finding the right people. Whatever it is, it's almost mystical. Do you believe in that kind of thing?"

Mikayla was used to people sharing personal information. Her sister said she must have been a priest or therapist in a previous life. She figured she was just a good listener. Either way, she always felt like people expected her to share her innermost secrets, too, but she was a private person. She'd had her husband to confide in before, and her life had been fairly charmed. So she hadn't had worries to share.

Of course, now her husband didn't love her and her so-called friends had all but disappeared. A wave of regret hit her, but she couldn't stop it. Having never confided in her friends, their disappearance hadn't really been a big loss. She mostly missed the book club. But now she wondered if her friends had been like that because she hadn't *let* them in. The last six months had been lonely, and she not only missed being the person people confided in, but she recognized the void that had opened when she'd lost Craig as a confidant.

Shia's trust meant a lot to her. It made her want to answer Shia's question thoughtfully, even if the subject made her uncomfortable. Was it just a coincidence that her sister knew Brandi, someone who needed a place just like she did?

"I don't know if I believe in a power that makes things happen for people. I feel lucky I'm here. If that's what mystical means, I guess so. Do you think we're all misfits?"

"Kind of. I can't speak to your situation, but I mean, I think I am. In a good way. Whatever I am, Gem and her dad let me move in without a deposit or references. No way would I have qualified for an apartment anywhere close to the beach, even with a social worker vouching for me."

"And here you are, a professional surfer."

Shia nodded. "I started a little late because I didn't have a board until I was sixteen. One of the kids in the group home I lived at left one when they moved out, and I taught myself to ride, and now people pay me to do what I love."

"It's wonderful that you have sponsors." Mikayla was impressed. Shia was a real professional surfer.

She nodded, and although Mikayla had just met her, her success didn't appear to be going to her head. "I've won a lot of local competitions and a few up the coast, which brought in a few offers. Most of them are smallish except one well-known brand." She pointed to the logo on her T-shirt. "Sometimes, I'm not sure it's real, you know?"

Mikayla loved how humble she was. "Gem told me you swim the jetties."

"It's not very far, but the currents and chop make it hard some days. I actually hate the swim, but it's part of the job. The surf is brutal sometimes, so I have to stay strong."

"That sounds like fun along with a lot of work."

"It's mostly work. Especially at six in the morning when the water's like ice. I can't complain. It's a great job." She shook her head with a smile Mikayla was sure attracted a lot of attention. "Dang. Sometimes, I forget there's more to life than surfing. I almost forgot what I came over for. The bonfire. Tonight. It'll be the first fire of the season. You in?"

Mikayla was tickled to be invited. "Sure. How could I miss it?"

"It'd be hard since it's pretty much in your backyard." Shia looked delighted.

"What should I bring?"

"Maybe a snack and something to drink? It's totally casual."

Mikayla couldn't remember the last time she looked forward to a gathering. She wondered if she was truly considered one of the misfit souls now.

CHAPTER EIGHT

Although operating Oceana was a twenty-four-hour, seven-day-a-week responsibility, Saturday mornings were generally quiet, and Gem enjoyed spending them with her father. She liked to be around him at his sharpest and when they weren't talking about work. It reminded her of a more carefree time, when she wasn't so worried about his declining health. On Sundays, her sisters took turns bringing him to their houses to hang out with the kids, and Gem was grateful for the break.

They were sitting outside on the garden patio, he with his newspaper and she with her sudoku book, enjoying the morning and drinking coffee. She tried to concentrate on her puzzle, but her mind kept wandering to Mikayla. She couldn't remember being as at ease with someone so quickly. Her gift of sensing a person's true essence usually told her why she felt a particular way, but while she could tell a lot about Mikayla, she couldn't say exactly why she'd been drawn to her so strongly.

"Did I tell you Alice came by Thursday afternoon?" her father asked, turning the page of the paper. "She brought cookies and a pack of cards with the big numbers so I could see them. We played hearts." It was a good morning for his memory.

"Where was I?"

"You were dealing with the broken pipe and told me a man of my stature in the community is too important to be mucking around in the mud, but in truth, you wanted me out from under your feet. Sulking, I puttered around in the garage, and then Alice came by to beat me handily at cards."

"Not true. You weren't under my feet," she said, although he had been. She hated how he saw through her, but his memory impressed her. Most days, he couldn't remember anything he'd done.

"You don't have to sugarcoat things, Gem. I'm getting in the way more often than not these days."

She had to choose between his pride or the painful truth, or she could change the subject. The whole family ignored the obvious and continued to dance around the decline in his mental acuity. No one talked about it directly. It was hard enough to think about dementia, let alone say it. Had the time come? Should she broach the subject now? More than anything, she wanted to get him to a doctor, but he refused, gun-shy from all the time he'd spent going to appointments for his back four years ago.

He lowered the paper. "Your reaction tells me you don't want to step on my toes." She felt called out. Had he learned to get around the mental barriers she'd put up to avoid him seeing her emotions? That would be awful. She didn't blame him, but she had no life because of him, and she never wanted him to know how unhappy she was. "I've given it a lot of thought, and I think you should take over full oversight of Oceana. You don't always do things my way, but you do them well, and I have to respect that. You've earned it." He put the paper on the table. "I think it's time for me to retire."

"Retire?" Something beneath the words about being underfoot and retiring made her wonder how aware he might be of his decline. As a therapist, she'd seen how cognitive dissonance could make the most apparent things invisible to those who were not equipped to handle them.

"Dad, we should—"

He held up a hand. "It's yours, Gem. As of now, you have full authority around here. I won't get in your way. I'm looking forward to playing more cards. I might even take up golf or something."

But she didn't want it. Panic seeped into her. "Dad, that's not what I'm—"

"You don't need to ask. It's good." He beamed, exuding pride. "You've been doing a great job, and you make your old pops proud. Before you came back to work here, I was beginning to think I had no choice but to hire a property manager, and it hurt my heart to think about letting an outsider in on the family business. It wouldn't be the same. They might ruin what we have. I don't think I want to be alive to see it happen." He gazed around with a loving expression. "Our family spirit is in this place, and it attracts good people. You know. You have the eye for picking good people, just like me. Bringing a stranger in would kill that. I'm grateful you found your way back. You, of all my girls, understand what makes Oceana special. You've renewed my hope."

His words should have eased her concerns, but instead, they trapped her. Even worse, they forced her to acknowledge his decline as inevitable. She was proud of Oceana. She wanted it to continue to be the special place he'd created but not with her at the wheel. She wanted her life back. She wanted to take him back to the idea of hiring a full-time property manager, except he'd made it clear he wanted the place to stay under family control.

She continued to die on the inside. "It's a lot, Dad."

He patted her hand. "Of all my daughters, you understand how much Oceana means to me and your mother. What it means to all of the residents. Not just anyone can manage it. Your mother and I will always be here to keep an eye out, but it's yours to run, Angel. You'll make the family proud. You already do."

A heavy weight settled over her. He wasn't aware that Oceana had become her prison. And she'd never tell him, not unless she wanted to break his heart.

Later, when he went inside to watch television, Gem took a walk to the harbor, her favorite place to think. Oceanside Harbor was fairly large, and most of the boats docked there were pleasure craft. There were also a few working fishing boats, as well as a handful of commercial excursion craft for deep-sea fishing and whale watching.

With most of the commercial boats out to sea for the day, the place was subdued, only a few tourists and a handful of boat owners puttering around. Come midafternoon, the lobster and halibut boats would be back with their catches, and the excursion boats would unload their passengers. For now, she leaned on the railing and watched a couple repaint the trim on their little cruiser and a playful pair of seals swim between the rows of slips, begging for food.

All of this nautical chill sat in the background of the problem with Oceana. She loved it. She really did. She'd grown up there, and she'd watched her parents take care of it. She understood her father's concern and didn't want to turn it over to someone else, either. Her father's exacting attention to detail had been drilled into her, and although her crews exceeded expectations, she continued to point out how to do things better. They didn't always see the missing screws, the just-beginning-to-flake paint, the fraying screens, all the small things that could make a place appear worn down. A stranger couldn't see all of that. She called it the Tripp Helmstaad way. He'd shown her how to help people take pride in their work.

But he had Oceana, and she had social work.

She wanted her life back.

Her former colleagues often checked in and asked when she would be back. After all, she'd only taken a leave of absence. But a few months had stretched into four years. She'd put in her time, and she hated thinking of it like that.

The gulls squawked over something at the water's edge. She pushed away from the railing and walked up the sidewalk to the little coffee shop. Thankfully, there weren't a lot of tourists, and no one she knew worked the counter. She wasn't in the mood to talk. She wasn't in the mood to think anymore, either, since she couldn't figure a way out of her situation. She ordered an iced hibiscus tea and lemonade and walked down to the jetty to sit on a rock and watch the waves wash up on the beach.

To distract herself, she replayed dinner with Mikayla, which had been an unexpected pleasure. How could she not have developed a crush? They'd never run out of things to talk about, and Mikayla had been the perfect host. At one point, Gem had envisioned her among her wealthy friends, proper, put together, flawlessly presented. She had a feeling Mikayla hadn't relaxed much in those settings, but she'd been relaxed last night, and Gem had gotten the impression she'd seen an unvarnished side of her, a side most people never got to witness, and she took it as a compliment that Mikayla let her see it.

She enjoyed her secret crush and the little stomach flutters it brought and hoped to spend a lot more time with Mikayla while she was there.

Of course, her crush would remain secret.

CHAPTER NINE

Mikayla stood in front of the fish tank, looking forward to the bonfire. Shia said she could join whenever she liked. As a person who usually made definitive plans, she found she liked the idea of just letting things happen. To her, it personified beach life, something more apparent at Oceana than at her old house. She and Craig had paid a lot to live near the beach, but being on the cliffs was different from being across the street, and she'd hardly ever gone. Living in someone else's house brought a certain sense of disorientation. It felt like a vacation. Like her real life had been put on hold. She had to remind herself this *was* her real life now.

She needed to stop thinking like that. It was *all* real. Her life before had been happy once, and it could be again. Now was the time to determine the next phase. Now was everything. She had to stop looking back, enjoy the now, and look forward to her future.

She consciously relaxed her shoulders and shook out her arms. The evening couldn't come fast enough. She wanted to meet more of her neighbors. And she hoped Gem would be there.

It seemed silly how much she anticipated it, but she couldn't remember the last time she'd met people who weren't clients or colleagues of Craig's. She was so nervous, she'd changed her clothes a few times before she'd settled on a pair of khaki capris; a flowy, sleeveless white top; and a thigh-length oversized cardigan. She'd missed her last pedicure appointment, so rather than show off her unmaintained toe polish, she'd put on a pair of canvas slip-ons, reminding herself that her vow to be more natural was a work in progress.

With time to spare, she thought about tidying up, but Brandi had given it a thorough cleaning before she'd left, something Mikayla would have done, too. She ended up wandering into the back part of the house. Other than during the initial tour, she hadn't ventured into any of the back rooms except the guest bedroom and bathroom. Brandi had made a point to tell her she could explore to her heart's content, promising nothing too personal or off-limits would be left on display.

Both back rooms were art rooms, set up with industrial shelves neatly filled with various materials, tools, and pieces of unfinished art. All the supplies gave Mikayla an itch to do something creative, a sensation she rarely ever felt. Even when she did, she usually didn't pursue it. After a lifetime of Ashe being the artist in the family, Mikayla had learned to ignore most of her creative urges. She had a passion for art, though, and truly appreciated it. In fact, on the rare occasion she put a little effort into creating something, she usually did well.

She remembered in sixth grade when she'd won the Judges Choice award at the county fair for a painting she'd done of her mother and friends playing bridge. Her mother had hated the picture it had been based on, irritated at how unflattering it was, and she'd despised the painting. It had showed her mother with her head thrown back in laughter. That was why she'd painted it. But when she'd brought it home, her mother had barely looked at it and had slid it into a drawer, telling Mikayla she should stick to pastimes that actually showcased her talents, adding that one artist in the family was enough. It had stung, but her mother hadn't shown much interest in Ashe's artwork, either. That was the moment she'd realized her mother had other plans for her.

Mikayla had never seen the painting again. She hadn't taken another art class, either. Instead, she'd focused her creative impulses on interior design, homemaking trends, and how to plan the perfect event for any occasion, focusing on "tasteful," which usually meant white and monochrome themes, allowing the personalities in the room to take center stage.

The problem was, most of the personalities had been as bland as the color schemes. Even the guests had chosen demure clothing, khaki, white, or black, as if every occasion was formal.

A sense of ennui settled over Mikayla, its weight heavy across her shoulders. The emotion was gray and morose, and it penetrated all the way through her. But when her eyes landed on a vibrant coral reef drawing pinned to the wall, she shook off the heaviness of her past, letting in the lightness of the piece. She realized she'd been taking shallow breaths and intentionally took a deep one, filling her lungs, allowing the residual darkness to evaporate and the color to flow in.

However, when she spied the pencils lying next to a sketch pad open to a fresh piece of paper, practically inviting her to draw something, she turned away. There was only so much introspection she was willing to do in one day. Instead, she appreciated some of the stained glass haphazardly stored on a shelf, along with stacks of tiny paintings of ocean creatures, all of it showing her how devoid of color her life had been until now.

Exploring farther, she stood in the doorway of the master bedroom, and a blast of yet more color greeted her. Bright tapestries adorned the walls, and a rainbow comforter covered the bed while a sensory explosion of textured, multicolored pillows piled against the headboard. Like the rest of the house, there were paintings and small sculptures on most of the surfaces, and it gave her a shiver of excitement to continue seeing different aspects of Brandi's psyche. After two days in her space, she felt like she knew her better than she knew herself. She didn't want to even guess what Brandi was getting to know about her through the London house, certain it was the polar opposite of what she was experiencing in Brandi's sensuous world. For the countless time, she told herself she got the better end of the deal.

Amid the prism of color that was Brandi's bedroom, she spotted a black acoustic guitar on a stand next to the door. She ran her fingers across the strings. They were in tune. Brandi probably played regularly. Mikayla enjoyed the idea she and Brandi had the guitar in common, even if she hadn't played much after she'd married Craig. A pang of regret seared through her for letting her guitars go in the estate sale.

A stack of books on the table next to the bed caught her eye, and she approached them, feeling a little like a voyeur despite Brandi telling her to explore as much as she wanted. *Asexuality and the Aromantic Heart.* She flipped through the pages and found words written in the margins. Human sexuality fascinated her, mainly because she'd had very little exposure to anything other than her and Craig's relationship, which, if she was honest with herself, had been underwhelming, maybe even boring. She felt a little guilty summing up the last twelve years with him like that, and it was a bit of a surprise that "boring" had come to mind so quickly and with such certainty, but she didn't feel like gilding the memory of a marriage her husband had so easily tossed aside. It seemed timely to learn about life outside of a beige relationship.

She flipped through the book without seeing it. Having taken off her rose-colored glasses and looked at her marriage, it wasn't a huge leap to examine other facets of her life.

She was aware that asexual was part of the LGBTQIA+ community, and she considered herself progressive. Most people didn't know that about her. She never talked about politics. She'd been raised to think it impolite. Even Craig avoided it. Her sister, on the other hand, was quite outspoken, but Mikayla's own knowledge was insufficient to have a political discussion. How a book about sexuality led her down this path of thinking, she wasn't sure, but the simple idea that she'd suppressed an interest in a subject that she'd considered to be a human issue and not a political one made her want to know more about it.

A sense of treading on forbidden ground titillated her, and she took the book into the living room, flipping through pages filled with handwritten notes as she curled up on the chair next to the aquarium and began to read.

She'd finished the introduction when a knock at the door roused her. When she answered, a middle-aged woman stood there holding a plate of cookies. An image from an old sitcom flashed through her mind, and she wasn't sure if she'd ever experienced such a wholesome situation.

"I'm Alice. You must be Mikayla. Shia suggested I tell you we're about to start the fire. It's still light out, but some of us"—she pointed at herself in a comedic way—"go to bed early. Anyway, I insisted on meeting you before the crowd congregates."

Mikayla returned her smile. Alice appeared exactly how a person who worked at a church might look, from her demure skirt and cardigan to her sensible shoes. Her lively eyes sparkled beneath her bangs. Mikayla immediately liked her. "It's a pleasure to meet you. Gem gave me the rundown on all the neighbors."

"I would have been over yesterday, but it was Good Friday, and I went to Mass and had to bake cookies for sunrise services tomorrow." Alice held the plate out. "Chocolate chip and coconut. These are for you. I made more for the bonfire."

No one had ever given her fresh cookies before, and the neighborly act gave her warm fuzzies. "Thank you. I adore coconut."

"You're welcome." Alice turned to leave. "I'm going to head over to the park now. I want to soak up as much fun as I can before bed."

"Do you mind if I go with you? I sort of dreaded arriving by myself. Traumatic memories of first days of school, and all that." She laughed, but the old Mikayla would have never asked to tag along with a person she'd just met. Alice just put off a comfortable vibe and Mikayla instinctively knew she would be a great conduit to meeting the other residents. Still, her stomach knotted up in anticipation of Alice's answer.

Alice turned back. "I'd be delighted."

Relief trickled through her. "Let me grab the wine and charcuterie board." She left the cookies on the coffee table, grabbed her hoodie, and went into the kitchen for the platter and bottle.

"Charcuter-what?" Alice said, stepping inside.

"It's just a fancy word for a meat and cheese board, except I don't put meat on mine, and there are other snacks like nuts, spreads, grapes, and berries."

"Sounds delightful, except I like meat, and I don't like nuts. Also, I'm somewhat lactose intolerant. I'm sure the grapes and berries will be wonderful," Alice said, leading them toward the flickering light of a blazing fire. "Off we go. Time to par-tay!" She pumped a fist in the air, and Mikayla laughed nervously while she scanned the half dozen people already gathered. Disappointed, she noticed Gem hadn't arrived yet, and she recognized Shia but none of the others. Uncertainty made her wonder if she was stepping too far out of her comfort zone too soon.

"Do you know everyone here?" she asked.

"I think so, unless Shia invited people outside of Oceana, which I wouldn't put past her. She's a bit of a celebrity, don't you know. I pretty much know everyone in the park."

"That's a lot of people."

"I've lived here twenty-five years, and I'm a nosey lady."

Mikayla loved how eccentric Alice turned out to be. She wasn't anything like the drab woman she'd imagined or even how she'd appeared when Mikayla had first set eyes on her. She suspected there was a lot going on under the subdued exterior of the interesting person Alice revealed one comment at a time.

CHAPTER TEN

Gem walked back to Oceana after spending the afternoon at the harbor. Going after her father's surprise declaration about handing everything off to her had been a good decision. He'd definitely thrown her for a loop. She should have anticipated something like that happening, even as she tried hard not to think of his continuing decline.

She hadn't figured out how to deal with his declaration, but being next to the ocean had calmed her mind, helped her understand the importance of the hurdles in life compared to the constants of love and family, which were more important than anything else. She didn't need to have all the answers now. It didn't mean she wouldn't have them at some point, but her time of reflection had recharged her as it usually did, reminding her that she needed to be patient, to keep on doing what she'd been doing, and trust in her decision to be there for her father, who had always been there for her. Struggling against her fears and focusing on the negatives guaranteed she'd end up filled with anger and frustration or worse, resentment. She didn't want to poison the time she had left with her dad, an extremely sobering thought.

She made her way up the main drive and keyed in the access code to the pedestrian gate. The golden light of sunset bathed the front entrance, making the Oceana sign look like something from a postcard, helping to lift her mood. Maybe the universe was giving her a sign, both literally and metaphorically.

The dancing light of fire caught her eye, and she spotted most of the residents of Oceana Place gathered around the firepit, plus a few stragglers from elsewhere in the park. Shia hadn't wasted any time coordinating the first bonfire of the season. Gem could already taste Alice's cookies. Although the breeze off the ocean chilled her bare arms and legs with the sun going down, she headed straight for the gathering rather than go home to change.

"Gem! I saved a spot for you." Alice waved. Happily, Gem saw Mikayla, too, and when she neared, Alice patted the empty spot at the picnic table between them.

Gem was more pleased about being able to sit by Mikayla than she should have been. She'd been thinking about their dinner together all day between bouts of mulling over the conversation with her dad, and as much as she chided herself for enjoying her time with Mikayla, the little excitement of her secret crush made for a pleasant distraction from real life.

"Is it okay?" Gem asked, gesturing toward the seat, barely enough room for her.

Mikayla took her hand and tugged, setting off a fluttery poof of excitement in her stomach. "Of course. Let's keep each other warm."

Gem squeezed in with Mikayla's words echoing in her head. She probably didn't mean them as flirty, and that only amplified the hotness. The excitement morphed into a thrill scattered throughout her body, and she became hyperaware of their thighs pressed together.

Alice patted her knee. "See? Plenty of room. I knocked on your door earlier to tell you about the fire. Your dad said you were out."

"I went to the harbor and stayed for the sunset."

Alice continued to pat her leg. "Sunset at the harbor is a blessing. Your dad is at the top of my prayer list."

Alice hadn't said why, but Gem knew. The community had mostly caught on. "We appreciate it," she said.

"He's worried about his memory, so I gave him some ginkgo biloba."

"He told you?" Shocked, Gem said it a little louder than intended. He'd never mentioned his memory issues before. Maybe this meant she could finally talk to him about it.

"More like confirmed it. He left our card game earlier this week to get a cup of tea, and I found him sitting at the kitchen table drinking his with mine sitting on the counter. I reminded him we were playing cards, and he said he'd forgotten and wondered why he'd made two cups. He said it might be lack of sleep. I suggested he visit his doctor. He blamed it on age and didn't want to, thus the ginkgo. Compromise is a powerful tool."

Alice and her dad were an unlikely pair as far as friendships went. Outwardly, they were so different. However, on the inside, they shared a devotion to helping people; her father through Oceana and Alice through her work at the mission. Her dad said that Alice had come to Oceana at twenty-one from a convent. Gem's mother had helped get her a job teaching and then later at the mission. Alice often said she considered Gem's parents the parents she wished she'd had. But how much did Alice know of her father's struggles with his health and memory? It was hard to imagine anyone not seeing it, but Alice had never mentioned it, and Gem hadn't known how to bring it up. It would be nice to talk about it with someone other than her sisters, who minimized it so much, the conversations were more frustrating than comfort.

Mikayla shifted, and Gem had an unexpected desire to confide in her. A yelp from Shia near the fire caused all of them to look and interrupted her train of thought, frustrating her.

"Goodness, am I going to have to add Shia to the prayer list as well?" Alice got up and marched over to Shia, who'd added more wood to the fire, causing an inferno.

"Is your father ill?" Mikayla asked.

Gem hid the shiver Mikayla's breath against her ear caused. "He's just getting older. It's how it goes." Gem stared into the fire. It occurred to her that talking about it made it real. For all the complaining she did about her sisters not facing it, she didn't enjoy talking about it, either. She wished she found it easier to share her feelings, but it was easier to give help than receive it.

"Getting older beats the alternative," Mikayla said. "That's what my dad says when he justifies taking a cart rather than walking the golf course."

"Your dad has a good point."

"I think it's accidental wisdom." Mikayla chuckled, and Gem liked being the cause of it. "It's easier to carry his whiskey and Coke."

Gem laughed and watched Mikayla wipe her cheek, smearing a streak of ash under her eye, one of the hazards of bonfires. Unable to resist, Gem gestured at it. "You have a bit of…do you mind?" she asked as she lightly wiped the mark, and at the same time, noticed the specks of brown dancing in Mikayla's pine-green eyes. "Your eyes are so—"

"There you are, Gem. Your mother has been looking all over for you. I told her you were probably with your friends, and here you are."

Gem peered over her shoulder to see her father standing on the other side of the picnic table with his hands on his hips. Several emotions hit her at once: disappointment at being interrupted, relief at being interrupted, sensing she'd done something wrong, embarrassment for being chastised in front of her friends, but primarily, shame for the pity she felt aimed at her and her father because her mother was gone, and everyone knew.

"Hey, Dad," she said, standing. "I came here directly from the harbor. Sorry I didn't check in."

He flapped a hand, an expression of uncertainty shading his face. "It's okay. We were…I mean, I was wondering where you were."

She froze, unsure how to react. The few people gathered by the fire couldn't help but witness the interaction, and embarrassment for him swept through her like a river of lava. Her father, although not an overly proud man, was used to being in charge and at the center of things. Now he literally stood on the outside, unable to carry on the friendly conversations he'd always enjoyed.

When she glanced around, everyone seemed like they were trying to not watch, and the expression of uncertainty passing over his face prompted her to walk around the table. "Do you want to join us? Or do you want me to walk home with you?"

"I don't know." He peered at himself. He wore the same khaki pants and Oceana polo he'd been in earlier, but he'd changed from his work boots to his house slippers. Normally, he'd never wear his slippers outside.

She rested a hand on his shoulder. "It's chilly. Why don't we go back to the house and get our jackets, and you can decide once we're there?"

"You haven't introduced me to the pretty lady you were talking to." He walked around the table and stood before Mikayla, who rose. "Gem doesn't bring a lot of friends around. I'm her dad. Most people call me Tripp."

Mikayla's pleasure to meet him appeared genuine, and Gem was grateful. "I'm Mikayla. I'm staying at Brandi's place for the summer."

Her father's expression transitioned from goodwill to confusion and back to a smile. "Any friend of Brandi's is a friend of mine." He gazed around. "Where's Brandi? Is she planning to attend this soiree?"

Gem came up alongside her father. "Brandi's in London, Dad. Mikayla's staying here while she's away."

"Oh. The sublet." The friendliness vanished from his voice, and everything in Gem clenched. This whole thing could go in any direction, and she didn't want to deal with her father blowing up, especially at or because of Mikayla. He squinted, shifting his gaze to Gem and then back to Mikayla again. "She passed the sniff test?" he finally said without taking his eyes from Mikayla, who continued to smile warmly under his scrutiny.

"She did," Gem said, hoping this would be the end of it.

Like a snap, his friendliness came back. "Well, then. How do you like Oceana?"

"It's beautiful. The magnolias are gorgeous, and everyone has been so warm and welcoming."

He beamed, and Gem wanted to kiss Mikayla. She'd won him over. Everything in Gem relaxed even as she longed to get him away from everyone, especially before he remembered his warning not to date Mikayla from the day before.

He shook a finger at Mikayla and glanced at Gem. "I like this one. She has good taste."

"She certainly does, Dad." She slid her arm around his. "I'm chilly. Let's go get our jackets." She started to lead him away.

"Sounds good. You kids don't want an old fuddy-duddy like me cramping your style. I'll probably stay home and watch CSI."

"I love CSI," Mikayla said.

He stopped and probably would have turned back to discuss the intricacies of the show because, like everything else, he held some very strong opinions about it. "Come on, Dad. I'm turning into an ice cube." She locked eyes with Mikayla, hoping she picked up on the thank-you in her gaze.

"We can talk over coffee sometime, Mr. Helmstaad."

"Tripp. Just call me Tripp," he said with a wave, and Gem led him home, mulling over the unexpected connection she'd just witnessed between her father and Mikayla, a person who'd just met him but who had known exactly how to interact with him. Gem's secret crush just got bigger.

"I know what's missing," Alice said, coming back to sit on the bench after Gem had left with her father. "Brandi and her guitar. Shia, are you up for a little playing tonight?"

Shia groaned and covered her face. "I've only taken a couple of lessons from Brandi before she left. I suck so bad."

"Practice makes perfect," Alice said and turned to Mikayla. "You don't happen to play, do you?"

"I do." As soon as she said it, Mikayla wished she hadn't. It had been years since she'd played, and she'd never been comfortable playing for others, including Craig, who'd heard her play maybe a couple of times. Too many nerve-racking recitals with people who were headed toward places like Juilliard. She could have gone, but classical guitar wasn't her passion, and it showed. She'd done better with contemporary music because she liked it, but her mother wouldn't let her "waste her time" on it very often. Still, she managed to acquire a passable competency, but she was never as good as she wanted to be and playing for herself wasn't very fun.

"Mikayla saves the day," Alice said, delighted. "No bonfire is complete without campfire songs."

Mikayla got up to get Brandi's guitar and wondered what she'd done, hoping she wouldn't disappoint. When she returned, there were a couple of new people in the group whom she'd never met, and Alice introduced her to Eight and Harper. While it was nice to meet them, her performance anxiety multiplied. Someone switched the radio off, and she self-consciously took a seat and asked what they wanted to hear.

The group suggested a few songs, few of which she'd ever played, so she brought her phone out and put her earbuds in so she could pull up the songs and play along. It was a bit of a cheat but the best she could do on short notice. Fortunately, she could usually pick up the melody by ear and replicate it well enough to recognize, thanks to the magic of the pentatonic scale.

Part of her was thankful Gem had to leave. She would have been too nervous to concentrate. As it was, a little tingle remained after Gem had wiped the ash off her face. The sight of Gem's face so close in the dusky light of sunset, how the fire had reflected in her eyes…damn, she needed to concentrate, and letting herself get distracted by a person she'd just met was so not like her.

"Please sing along. It's been a while since I've played, and your voices will cover up my mistakes." She laughed, but she was mostly serious. Alice gave her a thumbs-up.

The lyrics started to scroll on the video she'd chosen, and she started to sing. One by one, the others joined in, and soon enough, they were all singing. By the end of the next song, she felt more comfortable performing and played a few more before her fingers, unused to playing, started to hurt.

She announced the end of the sing-along, and a few people groaned, which she took as a sign that they liked her playing.

Before someone turned the radio back on, she noticed clapping behind her, and when she turned, Gem gazed back at her with a big grin. Scorching heat climbed her neck and cheeks, and it wasn't from the bonfire.

"You were fantastic."

"Thanks," Mikayla said, unable to meet her gaze.

"I've always been impressed with musical people," Gem said. "You have a nice voice."

"Thanks," she managed again, focusing on the table. The charcuterie board sat unsampled while the cookies, chips, and hot wings were almost gone. She pulled the clear wrap off it and put a little bit of everything on one of the small paper plates someone had brought.

Shia followed her lead. "I've been waiting for someone else to dig into this. It's so classy, I didn't want to mess it up."

"Is that why no one was eating it?" Mikayla asked, glad to have the spotlight off her.

"I wasn't about to be the first to befoul this work of art," Alice said, picking up a plate and joining Shia.

Gem came to stand with them. "You must be thirsty from singing. Would you like me to pour you a glass of wine?"

"Wine sounded good before, but right now, I'd kill for something cold."

"You got it." Gem opened the cooler. "Beer or Coke?"

"A Diet Coke would be perfect if there are any."

"You're in luck." Gem cracked one open and handed it to her. "How long have you been playing?"

"I was ten when I switched from violin to guitar, but I haven't picked one up in several years."

"You fooled me. This is going to sound corny," Gem said, "there's something about musicians. I get all fan-girly and crush on them."

The comment made a spark of excitement erupt in her stomach. Of course, Gem hadn't meant a crush on *her*, though. "I wouldn't call myself a musician."

"How'd you know all those songs?"

"I cheated by pulling up the tablature and words on my phone."

They sat in their previous seats, backs to the table, eyes on the fire. Alice was busy supervising Shia as she added more wood, and Gem hadn't moved over. The heat of their thighs together contributed to the fluttering in Mikayla's stomach.

"I couldn't have done that," Gem said.

"Do you play?"

Gem shook her head. "I've always wanted to. But we were talking about you. You play guitar, and you sing. What other talents are you hiding?"

"Oh, jeez. Talents? None, really. I barely manage the piano. I've forgotten almost everything I learned on the violin…um, I have a pretty strong backhand in tennis, I guess. Other than those fascinating facets, I'm the most uninteresting person," Mikayla said, biting into a sweet pickle, internally rolling her eyes. Seriously, could she be any more boring?

"You're far from uninteresting. What kinds of things do you like to do?"

Mikayla's stomach flipped a little at Gem's assertion. She didn't believe her, but she liked thinking Gem liked her enough to try to make her feel better. "I enjoy a lot of things, but I wouldn't say I have an innate talent at any of them."

Gem waved her hand in a "give me more" gesture. "Which are…"

Mikayla considered. "I love to cook."

"I can attest to your exceptional proficiency in the kitchen." Gem gestured for more.

Exceptional, huh? The comment gave her a boost of self-confidence. "I'm a whiz at sudoku."

Gem nodded. "Something we have in common."

That information made her happy. "I like sailing and scuba."

Gem made a face. "Too many sharks, thank you."

Mikayla laughed. "I love to organize things and do research. Oh, and I can read all day and night. I love to read. No sharks there."

"Much better. What else?"

The pressure was getting to her. She'd run out of ideas, and now she was once again leaning toward dejection about her beige life. The only thing keeping her from wallowing in it was the little buzz she felt being near Gem. "That's about it. Nothing remarkable."

Gem narrowed her eyes. "I think you're either being humble or underestimating yourself."

Mikayla shrugged. "Just being truthful. What are your talents?"

Gem stared at the night sky as if thinking. "I'm good with people."

"I agree," Mikayla said with a tilt of her head as she picked at her food. "You make everyone around you feel...I don't know... seen? Yeah, that's it. You're a good conversationalist but also a good listener." Although she'd only known Gem a couple of days, she already knew these things firsthand.

"I think people are fascinating. You have a gift with people, too."

Mikayla waved the compliment away. Any skill she had with people was drilled into her by her mother. "Mine is practiced, and yours is innate. I've spent my entire life making people around me comfortable."

"You have a natural way. I'd love to hear why you think yours is practiced and why that's a bad thing." Gem said, popping a stuffed sweet pepper into her mouth.

Mikayla admired what appeared to be her effortless, relaxed nature. "Well, first of all, being raised with an older sister who cares nothing about what people think about her and says people are responsible for their own comfort, I had an obligation to make up for it to my mother. I love my sister, but she's a handful. Also, the sorority I pledged to in college put an emphasis on hospitality and entertaining." As soon as she said it, she heard how pretentious and utterly without a backbone she sounded. She actually envied her sister's independence and refusal to be anything other than herself. Mikayla wondered what it would feel like to not care about what anyone thought of her.

Gem seemed to be studying her, and she wished she could take back most of what she'd just said. "Are there really sororities like that still around these days?"

Mikayla nodded. "My mom was in it when she attended school and wanted me to follow in her footsteps." Gem's polite expression made Mikayla wonder if she was masking disappointment in what some might consider a step backward for women. She wanted to make sure Gem knew it was because she'd enjoyed it, not because she had to. "I liked it, for the most part. It could be a bit much what with the formals and teas, but aside from the white-glove requirement, I actually liked all of the pomp and circumstance. I liked that I was carrying on a family tradition. Plus, being married to Craig, I used all those skills in real life, throwing dinner parties and working the floor at business functions, helping Craig land big clients. Most people think I'm an extrovert, but I'm such an introvert, it's painful sometimes. The sorority taught me how to turn my social butterfly on and off."

"Social butterfly, huh?" Gem laughed.

Mikayla tilted her head. "The life of a business owner."

"What kind of business did you two own?"

"Craig owns an investment firm. He didn't want me to work. I took care of the houses, scheduled his trips and our vacations, managed the finances. A little of a lot of things."

Gem scowled. "Sounds like a lot of work."

Mikayla blew out a breath. She wasn't explaining it well. She'd been happy doing it. "It was. It gave me purpose. Anyway, there you have it. How I learned to be good with people. But I'd rather be at home reading."

The scowl disappeared, and Gem's eyes held a sort of kinship. "I hear you. I love reading, but I can't remember when I spent more than fifteen minutes doing it at a time."

"I just picked it up again." They fell silent for a moment, and Mikayla wondered if Gem thought she was dull. The extending pause made her uncomfortable. "You were impressive with your dad. I'd think you were a counselor or something."

Gem squinted, and a corner of her mouth twitched. She glanced away. "I used to be, before becoming a property manager of a trailer park."

"Mobile home community." Mikayla bumped her shoulder, teasing her.

Gem grinned. "Adaptable domestic sanctuary."

"Habitat for movable domiciles," Mikayla offered, enjoying the game.

"Sanctuary of diverse humanity."

"Oh, I like that one." Mikayla grinned. "So you're a counselor?"

"A social worker, actually. At least, I used to be."

"A huge difference from, what do you call what you do? Property manager? Do you like it?"

"Counseling or property managing?"

Mikayla tipped her head to the side. "Either."

Gem appeared to think it over. "I like them both," she finally said. "Social work is satisfying when you make a difference in a person's life. Property management is definitely not my calling, but it's our family business, which means a lot to me, and there's the community aspect. I love those things about it." It looked like she wanted to say more, but she didn't. She also hadn't responded to the comment about being good with her dad, who seemed to have dementia. If Gem didn't want to talk about it, Mikayla wasn't about to push it.

"I see why you love this place," Mikayla said instead.

They were quiet for a moment, and it seemed the others had paused in their conversations as well. In the silence, the rushing of the nearby surf crashing against the shore filtered up from the beach.

"It's nights like this that make everything appear magical," Gem said.

Her words described exactly what Mikayla was feeling. Her heart was full, something she hadn't felt in a very long time. For a second, she thought she might cry.

"I guess now would be a bad time to ask you about a loose handle in my shower," she said to avoid embarrassing herself by showing her swinging emotions.

Gem laughed. "Not at all. Shall I grab my tools?"

Mikayla meant it as a joke, but something about Gem's response—whether it was the immediate acceptance or the idea of a person who could confidently use tools—gave her a little flutter of excitement. Gem had admitted she grew crushes on musicians and singers, and she supposed the feeling she currently had was what Gem had been talking about. Regardless, the confidence definitely did something to her. She patted Gem's arm. "It can wait until you have the time."

Gem's eyes sparkled in the firelight. "If you wait until I have time, it might be a while. How about I come by tomorrow?"

Mikayla agreed. It wasn't much longer before the little gathering began to break up, starting with Alice blowing kisses good night and literally dancing home. As much as Mikayla didn't want it to end, she was also a little overwhelmed by all of the emotions the little bonfire had elicited in her.

As she drifted off to sleep shortly after getting home—and, yes, she already felt at home in Brandi's colorful house—she couldn't remember having had such a good time. The last thing she remembered thinking before sleep took her was how much she looked forward to seeing Gem when she came to fix the shower handle.

CHAPTER ELEVEN

Gem helped Shia spread the fire to put it out, and once the flames turned to embers, she slid the metal lid over it so the wind wouldn't blow anything from the ring. The aroma of damp salt air and eucalyptus wood reminded her of countless nights at the beach, most of them as a kid, footloose and fancy-free, as her dad liked to say. They used to make a fire in an indent in the sand on the beach and cover it when they finished. How many times had she or her friends walked through one of those the next morning and burnt their feet? Of course, everything had been different then. They could park directly on the beach. Times were simpler, more dangerous but simpler.

Now, she was meticulous at her job, just like her dad. He'd taught her that loyalty and attention to detail were the most important qualities to have. No embers to walk on, no burnt feet.

After everyone dispersed, Gem went home and prepared for the next day. It was Sunday, but still she had tasks to do, especially since they'd fallen behind with the spring planting because of the broken sprinkler pipe, which had caused maintenance tasks to pile up, which had caused other things to be put on hold. One issue had a cascading effect that would impact them for the next few weeks. At least the pipe had been repaired, and they could finish planting the bougainvillea, and the taggers would leave the wall alone.

A quick peek into the living room found her dad fully reclined in his chair, snoring. She pulled a blanket over him, kissed his forehead, and turned off CSI, wondering if he dreamed of crime procedurals.

With the house quiet and dark, she dropped into the chair in front of her computer and pulled up her schedule for the next day. There were three maintenance calls to make…actually four, with the handle to fix at Mikayla's house. She knew exactly what to do there. She'd fixed it twice before for Brandi. The cold-water handle had stripped threads. Plumber's tape had worked for a few months before it had worn down. She should replace the entire apparatus this time. A slightly bigger job, but it would prevent future work. She'd use some of the hardware from the units they were renovating and order a new one. They were a few weeks out from installing the fixtures there anyway. She made the order while she had it on her mind.

It reminded her of a few weeks earlier when her father had wanted to help and had ordered sinks for the new units. Gem had puzzled over the out-of-balance budget for two full days before she'd figured out there were twice as many sinks as they needed.

Normally, she would have returned them; however, they'd been custom fabricated and non-returnable. It wasn't the first time he'd messed up an order. He'd mixed up the bougainvillea last week, the pool chemicals the week before, and he'd sent the pest control guys away last week, too, thinking they'd already been there and that they'd come back to "screw him over." Some of them she'd been able to fix without additional charges, but some—like the sinks—had cost them money, and every situation had cost them time.

The idea of seeing Mikayla gave her something nice to look forward to. Her peaceful and positive ways elevated Gem's mood. Even better, she could enjoy the little buzz in her stomach without constantly analyzing every look or touch because they weren't dating and never would. In a way, this secret crush thing was kind of cool.

She needed to think in terms of friendship. That was all.

She opened her email. No new maintenance orders. Breathing a sigh of relief, she opened a thread she'd been exchanging with an old work colleague, Margo, who'd become a friend. She kicked off her shoes. There was a thirty-year age gap between them, but it didn't feel like it, not with Margo participating in Ironman competitions and running a half dozen marathons each year, compared to Gem's favorite exercise of walks on the beach. Of course, Gem's job was fairly manual at times, so she didn't feel like a slacker.

The first part of the note from Margo was a continuation of a discussion about work-life balance. Gem had once mentioned how she was getting burnt out from being on call at all hours at Oceana, and Margo had decided to be her pseudo life coach to help Gem figure out a solution. Gem listened but rarely took any of her advice, not that it wasn't good advice, but because it meant challenging her father, who was the source of most of her work trouble. Additionally, in her mind, working at Oceana had always been short-term, and she didn't have the emotional fortitude to acknowledge that short-term no longer meant her father would take control back. In fact, that morning, he'd told her just the opposite.

Fortunately, Margo didn't go there. Instead, she wrote about her own work issues with staffing shortages making balance difficult for her. Not for the first time, she asked if Gem knew anyone qualified for the job.

Hint. Hint. Gem, I'm thinking about you, Margo wrote with a string of emojis.

Gem sat back in her chair. *Wish I could,* she typed before deleting it and replacing it with, *What does me working there look like to you?* Didn't hurt to dream, right? Then why was her heart racing?

She breathed out. No way could she leave Oceana now. She sighed and read a few more emails—mostly subscriptions to various lists—and was about to shut down her computer when a response from Margo dinged in.

Whatever you want it to be. A couple of days a week. Three? A few half days. Weekends only? You tell me.

She'd never considered that there might be a way to do social work outside of traditional hours. Part-time? Weekends? Compelling. Something resembling hope bloomed in her chest and just as quickly withered. Reality hit her like a cold shower. She already worked after-hours, weekends, and holidays. Things came up at all hours in a community like Oceana. Still, she couldn't bring herself to say no. *Sounds interesting. Never considered part-time. I'll think about it.* Followed by laughing emojis when she felt like crying.

A different tone sounded on Gem's computer. Margo had switched to instant messenger. *Take as much time as you like...as long as you get back to me immediately. Just kidding. I'm so glad you haven't stopped considering, even if it's a small possibility. You're a damn good social worker, Gem. Let's meet for coffee to talk about it.*

Was Margo in her head?

We should have coffee regardless. In the meantime, I'll keep you posted if things change, or I find a way to make the part-time thing work.

Perfect! Margo replied.

Gem leaned back in her chair again. She was leading Margo on. She already worked seven days a week. ...Unless she could figure out a way...

She shut down her computer and decided to take a long bath. She did her best thinking soaking in hot water with a scented bath bomb.

CHAPTER TWELVE

M ikayla woke on Sunday morning thinking about the night before. Spontaneous and easy, something she hadn't experienced in years. As an adult, she'd lost all sense of spontaneity. Gatherings were more formal, with advanced scheduling and planning. Simply meeting for drinks or going to brunch with her tennis partners meant planning. Every meetup required a sync of calendars and at least a week's notice. Going out with her sister didn't count. They almost always met up spur-of-the-moment, especially in the last several months while the divorce played out, but Ashe had never operated like others. Usually, the opposite. Plans made in advance with her sister were always broken, and last-minute suggestions usually worked out.

But this wasn't about her sister or her old tennis partners. This was about her new life.

The last-minute bonfire, including getting talked into playing and singing for everyone, had turned out to be fun. She'd had no time to get spun up with nerves. The more she thought about it, the more she began to believe it had everything to do with how relaxed she'd felt among the people who'd been there. In contrast, most of her adult life had been a never-ending series of obligations requiring her to be *on*, putting on a front, acting like someone or something she was not. Simply being herself last night had filled her with a sense of freedom. She hoped for more evenings like it.

For so long, everything she'd done had been connected to Craig's work. Dinners, drinks, parties, even tennis was connected to Craig's coworkers and clients, including their significant others. Vacations weren't even free from his work, and therefore meant work for her. She'd been the boss's wife. All of the training her mother insisted on giving her had been about how to be the hostess with the mostest. And she'd been the *best* at it. But in the end, she'd merely been a functional accessory to her husband's dreams. Brainwashed into thinking she enjoyed her role, that she was important. Away from it now, she realized she'd dreaded almost all of it: listening to investment strategies, portfolio diversification, hot stocks, and money markets. It wasn't outside of her knowledge, just boring. *Bo-ring.* The judgment and gossip in their circle, along with uninformed political-but-not-really-political rants because that would be unseemly, were even worse. In contrast, the small group at the bonfire had seemed to be close-knit and kind, and there wasn't a hint of gossip. People interacted as if they genuinely cared about each other, and not a single topic discussed had bored her. She'd left wanting more.

Excited about Gem coming over, she got dressed and attended to the seahorses. She didn't have to do much, but it gave her a lift when the fish swam over as if they were excited to see her. She suspected it was a learned response, but she didn't care. Taking care of them gave her a sense of purpose.

After they ate, Othello and Desdemona swam around the tank doing their dance, being all beautiful and sweet, and she got teary-eyed about the show of affection.

Several minutes later, Mikayla still stood at the tank, baster in hand, her thoughts having moved from seahorses to the idea of a sense of purpose. She'd never questioned her purpose until recently, and as she'd done quite a bit lately, she wondered what she was going to do with herself. It came down to identity as much as purpose. If she wasn't a wife, who was she?

Her entire life had revolved around Craig. His work, his interests, his time off. Without him, she couldn't come up with an answer, and it terrified her. Sure, she was a daughter and a sister, too, but she had to face it, the daughter thing did little for her *or* her parents, who were busy with their own things until an event or a situation called for the appearance of the entire family. As for being a sister, she didn't see much of Ashe. Hell, she wasn't even a good friend. She hadn't done much to nurture her friendships before the divorce or to reach out afterward. The way they'd so quickly retreated after the news was as much her fault as theirs. As it stood, she didn't miss any of them, and they probably didn't miss her either. She was left with a whole lot of time on her hands. She needed to know what her next steps were, or she was going to lose it.

She'd always known her next steps.

Get good enough grades to get into a good school. Check.

Graduate with honors. Check.

Get a job. Check. With the help of her stepfather at his financial company and the hope of her mother for her to meet Mr. Financially Right.

Marriage. Check. Within a couple of months, she'd started dating Craig, and soon after they'd married, he'd opened his own financial management company.

Support Craig's dreams. Check.

They'd been her dreams, too. As a team, they'd pursued his success. She knew without a doubt that her support had given him all the time and emotional strength to successfully build his business. She'd downplayed her role, but Craig had needed her, and she'd been entitled to everything she'd received in the divorce. It irked her when people talked about what a great guy he was to "give" her "so much." It wasn't "great." It was fair. And while it had shocked her to the core when he'd asked her for a divorce, she didn't blame him. He'd told her he'd wanted kids from the start. So her purpose had been to enjoy her marriage and support Craig until kids, at which time, her purpose would be to become a mother. She'd tried to have kids. For him.

Become a mother…not checked.

They'd tried until the doctors had said she couldn't. Craig had believed her to be as upset as he was, and she hadn't corrected him. She'd even suggested adoption or surrogacy, but he hadn't wanted to explore those routes. He'd built an idea of parenthood in his mind, had gone about it like he'd done with his career. She'd get pregnant. They would celebrate, and he'd hand out cigars, pamper her, go out for midnight grocery runs to satisfy her cravings, take before and after photos, coach her through delivery, all the things that came along with the "perfect" portrait of parenthood.

The day they'd received the news about her inability to carry a pregnancy had given her immediate relief about being spared a life sentence. The tears she'd cried had been real, but she could never tell him they were from relief. How was she to know he'd end up divorcing her for having defective reproductive organs? For fuck's sake, she'd tried.

She took a deep breath. Getting angry wasn't the answer.

Othello followed Desdemona through the tank, and they anchored on a piece of coral, snuggled together. It was ironic how excited she was about them having babies. Watching it wasn't anything like her situation. Or was it? In a way, she'd been a spectator to her entire life.

The realization made her shiver. After thirty-five years of being what everyone else had expected her to be, she needed to figure out what *she* wanted. But she didn't have a clue what that was.

One thing she did know: she didn't want to be taken care of, nor did she want to take care of someone else. She wanted to take care of herself. Irrationally, the nicer Craig had acted, the more she'd resented him. She hated how he continued to check on her. It seemed hypocritical, and she wanted to refuse his kindness just to hurt him. It wasn't about the money. She deserved that. It confused her. She wanted to hate him, but she couldn't bring herself to do so. Illogically, she was embarrassed for allowing her situation to get to this point: a divorced woman with no kids, no house, no job, nothing to make her life meaningful.

A knock on the door pulled her from her rapidly spiraling thoughts. Gem's face through the glass brought her out of her morose musings.

"I wasn't sure what time to come by, so I waited until ten. Is this a good time?" Gem said as Mikayla stepped aside to let her and her tool bag in.

"I get up around six most mornings," Mikayla said, still a little foggy from her dive into the lake of deep introspection. As she followed Gem into the living room, she shook her head to break free of the fog.

"Even on Sunday?" Gem asked as she set her tools on the counter.

"I've always wanted to be the kind of person who slept until noon, but I can't do it."

"If I didn't have so much to do, I'd probably still be sleeping. I love a good lie-in. Unfortunately, I don't get to do it often."

"For some reason, I was under the impression you'd be an early riser."

"You have mistaken me for my father. He gets up at four a.m. every morning. I only get up at six-thirty for work."

"Now that's just wrong," Mikayla said with a laugh.

"Agreed." Gem snorted. "He also falls asleep by six or seven each night. So there's that."

Mikayla loved her authentic and upbeat energy.

"Do you need running water for the next ten minutes?" When Mikayla shook her head, Gem reached under the sink and turned off the water main.

Mikayla followed her to the hall bathroom. "Looks like you've done this a time or two."

"A couple of times." Gem slid open the glass shower door, jiggling the hot and cold handles. "Is it leaking at all?"

"Nope. Just loose. I have to push on it to get traction. Sometimes, it takes a bit of futzing."

"Futzing can be frustrating. I've tightened it before, so I'm going to change the hardware so we don't have to do this again in a couple of months."

Mikayla understood, but it would have been a nice excuse to see Gem again. She'd have to find another reason. The idea that she had to make up a reason surprised her. Why would she have to make an excuse? She lived next door.

Gem removed a piece of hardware from a package and placed it on the soap dish before she popped off a little metal disk on the end of the knob, revealing a screw, which she loosened, and in less than a minute, the handle and the inside of the knob were removed. She then wrapped some plumber's tape around the end and put on the new hardware. She did the same to the other knob and then the showerhead, and in less than ten minutes, the whole set had been replaced. She went back to the kitchen and turned on the water.

When Mikayla tested it, it worked without a bit of futzing or leaking, and she realized she could have done this by herself if she wanted to. "That was quick."

"I've probably repaired or replaced a hundred of these in the last four years."

"How many homes are in Oceana?"

"We're zoned for nine-hundred and six. Currently, there are five-hundred, with another twenty being set up in the northwest corner. A good section of the community contains units over fifty-years old. They've been refurbished and upgraded a few times, so the plumbing and electrical aren't old, but they all need care and maintenance."

Mikayla hadn't gone any farther into the community than the little building housing the mailboxes. She decided to explore more of it soon. "You certainly have a knack for keeping things in good shape."

Gem tapped a wrench against her thigh and shrugged. "I'm just doing what my dad taught me. 'Take care of things, and they'll take care of you,' is one of his favorite sayings."

Mikayla liked her humble response and watched her wipe down the wrench, pliers, and screwdriver. Respect washed over her. Along with something else. She remembered what Gem had said to her the night before.

"You know how you get crushes on musicians and singers?" Mikayla said. "I get them on people who fix things. You know, people who can use tools proficiently." She fibbed a tiny bit when she said people; it was really only Gem.

"Oh, yeah?" Gem gave her an amused grin. An emotion Mikayla wasn't ready to think about flashed through her. A strange pull, almost attraction. Her interactions with Gem so far weren't like any she'd ever experienced. Maybe it had to do with meeting new people, doing things she wasn't used to, and living in a new place. Or maybe it was specifically Gem, which was the thing she wasn't ready to think about. She remembered a dream from the night before where she and Gem had been walking on the beach holding hands. Simple, sweet, friendly. However, her intentions hadn't been exactly friendly in the dream. They'd been anticipatory and exciting. A shadow of it rose inside her now it, but she couldn't explain it. Instead, she wiped imaginary crumbs off the counter.

"Craig can't fix anything. He's terrible with tools." Mikayla shook her head. "Couldn't. Wasn't." She blurted it, filling the silence, not wanting to delve into what she'd just experienced.

Gem zipped her tool bag closed and gave her another amused grin.

"What?" Mikayla asked.

"What what?"

"What are you grinning at?"

Gem appeared to consider. "You know I'm a lesbian, right?"

"Actually, I didn't." The feeling she didn't understand bubbled a little more intensely inside her. She tried to never assume, and she'd been focused on herself lately, so embarrassingly enough, Gem's sexual orientation hadn't crossed her mind. Now that it had, the bubbling became more like a low boil. While Mikayla enjoyed it, it scared her, too. And now she wondered what kissing Gem would be like. So random but so important all of a sudden. And scary.

"But you suspected."

She almost didn't hear in her preoccupation. "I didn't think about it at all."

"Come on. Seriously? I mean…Never mind." Gem smiled and shook her head, a mix of disbelief and surprise on her face, a super cute look for her. Vulnerable and real. "Some of us think women using tools is hot, especially when there's a toolbelt involved."

To Mikayla, it sounded like an inside joke she wasn't in on.

Gem must have guessed. "How do I say this? Okay, so, some lesbians—not all of them, but many—like tools. Either using them or watching someone else use them. It's also a sexual reference. Tools. Toys. Toolbelt. Toy belt, usually called a harness…and… well…" Gem stammered with a bright red face. "Anyhow, it's not as funny if you have to explain the joke…so…"

Mikayla had caught on but didn't let on, partially out of lack of knowledge of the subject, but mostly because she was having fun watching Gem get flustered. "Toy belt?" she asked, trying to suppress a smile. She knew what that meant, even if she'd never seen one in person.

Gem adjusted the bill of her cap. "Well, no one calls it that. It's a harness, and toy belt seemed more effective to link the concepts."

She appeared so earnest. It wasn't fair of Mikayla to tease her like this, but it had been so long since she'd teased anyone. "Harness as in, the kind you put on a dog lead?"

Mikayla thought Gem's cheeks were already as red as they could get. She was wrong. "Sure. There are those kinds of harnesses. People in the BDSM community wear them. There is an array of harnesses, not necessarily exclusive to the BDSM community. In fact, the ones I referred to earlier are meant for holding toys in place."

"I'm not sure I'm following. Holding toys? Like attached to a backpack or something like that?"

"Um, no." Gem gestured with both hands at her waist and hips. "More like—" She breathed out, seeming to be at a loss for words. "It's a belt with straps and—"

Mikayla couldn't keep her laughter in any longer. "I'm sorry, Gem. I'm being mean. I know what a strap-on is."

Gem let out a huge gush of air. "Oh God. Thank you. I was... hey. You already...and you were making me..." Gem growled, grabbed the dishtowel, and threw it at her.

Mikayla bent at the waist, laughing so hard she couldn't breathe, and when she stood, she realized she'd made a huge mistake and ran toward the bathroom. So close to peeing her pants, she made it to the toilet with no time to spare and yanked down her shorts, still chuckling.

"Are you okay?" Gem's voice preceded her appearance in the doorway, and then she jumped back. "Oh, sorry!"

It only made Mikayla laugh harder, and she couldn't answer. She finished on the toilet, pulled up her shorts, flushed, and washed her hands, all while laughing and struggling to breathe. She glimpsed her face in the mirror over the sink, and she looked a fright with her hair tied up in a messy up-sweep on the back of her head and her face blotchy and tear-streaked. No time to fix any of it, she needed to apologize.

She found Gem still at the kitchen counter, gathering her tools.

"I'm sorry. I couldn't resist," Mikayla said. "As you can see, it gave me instant karma."

Gem waved a hand, her face pink. "And I'm sorry for barging in on you in the bathroom."

Laughter spilled from both of them.

"You had me going," Gem said, adjusting the collar of her shirt.

"You were so adorable, trying to educate me."

"So you knew all along?"

"No. But I *have* heard of sex toys, so…"

"Ah…" Poor Gem seemed to be at a loss for words.

"Seriously. I haven't laughed so hard in a long time," Mikayla said. More erupting again just remembering. She wiped her eyes.

"I'm glad I amuse you," Gem said, cracking a smile.

A silence fell between them, and Mikayla wondered what she could do to keep Gem there a little longer. Truthfully, the shower handle could have waited. But now, when Brandi came back in six months, her home would be little more in order than when she'd left.

"You said you have a few other things to do today? On a Sunday? Do you ever have a day off?" Mikayla asked as Gem finished zipping up her tool bag.

"I normally take Sunday off and only handle urgent issues on Saturday, but we're a little behind. Just a few small things for today. A new sheet of fiberglass on a storage shed in one place and reattaching the chain on a sink stopper in another. The most complex thing is installing a new garbage disposal. Nothing too difficult, merely time-consuming. We're backed up because of the broken water line last week. Had to pull the maintenance crew to help the landscaping crew hand water the newly planted vines."

"Installing a garbage disposal seems complex to me. Isn't it plumbing?"

"Not really. The hardest part is getting all of the crap people store under their sinks out of the way. I ask the resident to do it before I get there, so I don't have to worry about it. In fact, Serg and Amy are waiting for me now." Gem turned to leave and stopped, turning back. "You want to come along? There might be people wielding tools," she said and winked. "But I'd love to show you how easy it is to replace one. It's a good skill to have. Kind of like changing a tire."

"I don't know how to change a tire, either."

"We'll have to address that." Gem grinned for a second. "I mean, unless you don't want to. Not everyone is the handywoman type."

"Let me get some shoes on. I do want to be a handywoman type. I just didn't know until now." Excitement flared within her. She wasn't going to lie, a big part of it had to do with getting to spend time with Gem.

CHAPTER THIRTEEN

Gem had parked the golf cart in Mikayla's driveway next to her shiny BMW, close enough that Mikayla had to climb over the driver's seat to get in. Gem shouldn't have stared at her ass or her legs with their long muscles and smooth skin, but they were right there. Still, not cool, so she sidestepped to the back of the cart and concentrated on putting her tool bag away. Something had subtly shifted between them when Mikayla had teased her about harnesses, and maybe there'd been a little bit of flirting. Out of practice and probably reading too much into it, Gem decided she should probably stay clear of the flirting thing for both their sakes. Keep it on the friend level.

She legitimately liked Mikayla and could totally see them as friends. She was smart, funny, and a good listener who could carry on a great conversation. Both charming and real, she seemed to genuinely like making people happy. Gem had seen her discomfort about playing and singing for all of them, but she'd done it, and Gem couldn't stop thinking about it. Mikayla's gentle confidence was a majorly attractive quality that Gem really, *really* liked to be around. She needed to stop staring at her ass and let friendship take its course.

She jumped into the driver's seat. "The storage shed is on the way, and it should only take a couple of minutes, so I'm going to swing by there before heading to Serg and Amy's."

"Sounds good. I'll go to all the calls if you want. I'm glad to be out of the house." She rested a hand on Gem's thigh. It was a surprise but a nice one. "Not to infer I'm going with you because I have nothing better to do. I'm glad to spend time with you." Mikayla patted her leg and removed her hand, and Gem struggled not to rub the spot where it had been. *Stop it!*

"What were your weekends like before you moved here?" she asked, still thinking about the warmth of her hand.

"My routine is chaos since Craig and I split up, so the last six months have been…" She seemed to think. "A blur. A big boring blur of me feeling sorry for myself." She shrugged. "I honestly don't remember much. I stayed at home, avoiding my friends and parents. Nothing notable. Before that, my Saturdays were usually either spent on the boat or playing tennis if we weren't on a trip. Sundays are Craig's golf days. Or were. I have no idea anymore. He would golf, and I would visit my parents or my sister or go shopping. Sometimes, I'd lie by the pool and read. I loved having the house to myself. It's funny, when Craig moved out and I had it to myself all the time, I couldn't stand to be there." She peered up at a palm tree they passed. "I don't know why I miss it now."

"The marriage or the house?"

"Not the marriage." Mikayla gasped and put a hand to her mouth. "I can't believe those words just came out." She sounded surprised. "It must be true. I miss the idea of being married, yet I don't miss our marriage." She kept her hand to her mouth and seemed to be thinking. "I don't miss being married to Craig. It's not that I don't love him. I do. But I'm not sure I was ever *in* love with him. God. What a thing to have realized. You must think I'm a complete…what? Fool? Bitch? Foolish bitch?"

"You are not a bitch or a fool. You sound like you're taking stock of your life." Gem slowed to a stop and turned slightly to face Mikayla, who looked and sounded like she'd come to a huge realization. "I'm a good listener if you want to talk about it. Or do you want to be alone with your thoughts? I'm good either way."

Mikayla gazed at her with a contemplative expression. "I'd rather hang out with you. I think I want to mull this over privately when we're finished, but in the meantime, I'd like to continue tagging along if it's okay."

"Well, let's go fix a shed roof, then." Gem was adept at reading her clients when they were working through issues, and she was pretty sure she had an idea about what Mikayla was going through. Coming to terms with some of the emotions and or truths that revealed themselves after a major life event was sometimes as traumatic as the event itself. Gem liked to think about life as a sort of river that mostly just flowed along, but when the river got rough, diverted, or dammed up, the riverbed sometimes revealed unexpected items. She wondered what items Mikayla was just now seeing. But Gem was good with boundaries, at least when they didn't relate to her father, and Mikayla had asked for privacy. In the meantime, Gem was just happy Mikayla wanted to hang out with her.

She started up the cart again and a few minutes later, stopped next to a storage shed behind a single-wide in a section of the park where single-wides lined the street on both sides. It was the short-term rental section. There wasn't much room between the units, none had porches, and the rent tended to be lower. They were mostly used by tenants who needed something cheaper until they got back on their feet; however, a few residents stayed there longer. She and her dad still made sure the area was kept as nicely as the others, and Gem spent more of her time in this area keeping it up than any other section.

Dean, the renter of this particular unit, came out to greet them. Gem liked him. A good guy and a hard worker, he took care of his mobile home, which was neat and orderly. Her father would approve. "Hey, Gem. Thanks for coming by to fix the shed. I'd have done it myself, but I have an inner-ear thing, and getting up on ladders isn't a great idea." His gaze shifted to Mikayla, and his grin widened. "You got yourself an assistant. Hi there, the name's Dean." He stuck his hand out.

Mikayla shook it and introduced herself. "I'm just along for the ride."

Gem caught Dean checking Mikayla out and gave him the stink-eye. She knew the exact moment he noticed her glare and dropped the macho attitude. Her gift saw him for what he was: harmless and insecure, thus the attitude. He was a tall man, though, and could come across as intimidating. She didn't want Mikayla to feel uncomfortable.

"Let me show you the shed," he said.

Gem took the ladder from the roof of the cart and hefted it onto her shoulder, following him. It surprised her when Mikayla came up beside her with the sheet of corrugated fiberglass and her tool bag. "Hey, thanks," she said as she put the ladder in place.

"Happy to help. Do you need anything else?"

"I think it's all in the bag."

A few minutes later, she'd already loaded the ladder back on the cart, and they were headed to Serg and Amy's for the garbage disposal.

"I wasn't quite sure about Dean at first," Mikayla said when they pulled away.

"He can be a little intense," Gem said.

"I didn't like the way he sized me up. But then it disappeared, and I wondered if I imagined it."

"You didn't. He acted the same with me at first, staring and then asking me out until I told him I'm gay. Now, he's just friendly."

"Do you think he took me for…you know…"

"Gay, too?" Gem was surprised by the tickle of anticipation the thought of Mikayla being gay gave her. Until now, she'd considered her secret crush as completely one-sided.

"Like, maybe he thought I dated women, maybe even you, when I said I was your friend."

"Maybe." Gem wanted to ask if the possibility bothered her, but Mikayla beat her to it.

"If it keeps men from leering at me like I'm a steak, I'm all for it."

"Do you deal with it a lot?" Of course she did. She was beautiful. Gem would give anything...*Stop*, she told herself.

"Men treating me like I'm a piece of meat?"

"I guess. I mean, if that's what it makes you feel like."

Mikayla shrugged. "It started with my father's colleagues, then horny classmates, then students and teachers at college. I expected it to stop when I got married, but my husband's friends and clients joined the clique. It's repulsive and never-ending." She turned in her seat. "You must get it, too. Before men realize you're a lesbian. Or maybe in spite of it. Wait. Do you prefer gay? You've referred to yourself as both."

"I'm good with whatever, lesbian, gay, queer. Some people have a specific preference. Some don't want to be labeled. As long as it's not said out of anger or meanness, I'm fine with any of those."

"Do my questions bother you?"

"Not at all. I'd rather be asked than have assumptions made. I'll tell you if I don't want to talk about something." When Mikayla didn't answer, Gem glanced at her just in time to see her mischievous smile. "I think I may have misplaced my trust."

Mikayla laughed. "We just met and everything, but fair warning, I'll probably nose into your love life at some point. You've been warned."

"It's nonexistent, so you're up to speed. Boring, party of one." She raised her hand while a tingle made its way through Gem. Mikayla showed a little more of herself each time they were together, and the more Gem saw, the more she liked. She had a feeling she'd tell Mikayla anything she asked.

"No girlfriend?"

Gem paused. Not because she didn't want to answer, but because she wondered *why* Mikayla wanted to know. Part of her, the part that kept forgetting that it wasn't a good idea to date Mikayla, hoped it was because she was interested, but the reality was probably simple curiosity. Disappointing but probably best, she told herself. "My last relationship ended four years ago. I've gone on a few dates since. None have gone past the first." She guessed Mikayla would want to know why. "My first year back here, I busted my butt trying to live up to my dad's standards, and I wore myself out. He'd hurt his back and couldn't do physical work. His pointing finger worked very well, however. What a tough year. Then he came back to work under orders to take it easy, and we got into a routine. I was getting ready to go back to my regular life when he started forgetting things."

She remembered the day when it had dawned on her that the increasing frequency of frustration and out-of-character anger coming from her father weren't him simply being ill-tempered about his physical limitations. He'd walked out of the bathroom holding the ends of his belt, confused about what to do with them. He'd started to forget how to perform basic tasks. Prior to that, she'd been fighting impatience and had snapped at him for joking around too much. When she saw the belt ends in each of his hands, she'd understood, and shame mixed with fear had rolled down her body. That was when she'd known she was losing him before her very eyes.

Just remembering it made her want to cry.

She cleared her throat. "I tried to convince him to hire a property manager or an assistant, but he struck that down in a hurry. And about a year and a half ago, he went to renew his driver's license and couldn't pass the written test. I'd noticed his confusion getting worse, along with his memory. He began barking orders at everyone, as if the louder he got, the less we would notice or something. I have to monitor him all the time as well as run this place. Between all the hours at work and my own low-grade depression, it's just hard to date." Great. She hadn't meant to say so much. Especially about the depression. It was situational but still, something she normally didn't disclose to people she'd just met. Mikayla was just so easy to talk to.

In the ensuing silence, Gem watched the road, sensing the weight of Mikayla's gaze. Surprisingly, she felt better for having said it. She wanted… No. She *longed* to share this. Her gift had told her how spectacularly *kind* Mikayla was. The rest of her personality sort of wrapped around that intrinsic kindness and merged everything together. Some people were like that, with each aspect of their core essence supporting the main one. Her father was like that. All of the aspects of his core essence integrated with his devotion to helping others, although fear had become a little more prevalent recently. Even his deteriorating health didn't change it; it was just that, like other basic tasks, he'd started to lose his grasp on how to use his own gift. Other people's essences were often more random than her father's and Mikayla's, switching from emotion to emotion.

With Mikayla, she felt like she was wrapped in an infinite blanket of kindness. It was what had initially attracted her, although, at the time, she hadn't seen it as a romantic attraction. It was still a wonderful feeling, but it was unlike anything she'd ever experienced, and in this way, it was much different than what she felt with her father. It was more of a mist around Mikayla that pulled them together.

Something in her resisted thinking too hard about their unique connection. She'd gotten used to her gift telling her if people were compatible with her or with each other. It just happened. And it wasn't like it gave her a specific yes or no, she just knew. But because the way Mikayla's essence was so different from anything she'd experienced before, she didn't have a clue what the all-encompassing, wrapped in mist thing she got from Mikayla meant. This was entirely new to her. Could this mean... No. She was not going to assume anything. It was probably because she'd never met anyone like Mikayla before.

"Now that you run everything, are you planning to hire an assistant?" Mikayla asked.

The question pulled her from her thoughts. Wow. She'd really gotten lost there for a bit, but they hadn't driven too far, and Mikayla didn't seem to notice. "My father vetoed it. 'No one can or will run this place like our family.' Now he says he's retired, and it's mine to run as I please, but he made it clear he doesn't want outsiders coming in. It's frustrating, and I feel kind of stuck."

She didn't mention how he'd yelled at her. He'd never been violent, but the venom in his words had felt worse than a physical blow. She never wanted to go through that again.

Mikayla rested a hand on her arm, and the mix of comfort and desire to be close to her made Gem forget some of her frustration. They'd arrived at the next job, anyway.

She stopped the cart near Serg and Amy's place, grateful for the distraction of Mikayla's company. Now wasn't the time to let her emotions run loose about her father. She had work to do. So she did what she was good at: she stuffed it down.

CHAPTER FOURTEEN

The steam from Mikayla's coffee rose into the ocean air as she sat on the deck and gazed out over the water. She loved the gentle coastal breeze first thing in the morning and watched the waves marching in an endless parade toward the beach. They seemed subdued in the gray morning chill, which would mostly burn away like it did every morning when the sun fully rose.

She noticed an upstairs light in Gem's house flicker on. The kitchen light had been on when she'd woken. She took a sip of coffee and returned her focus to the ocean, imagining Gem getting ready for her day. In a way, she was envious. Gem had tasks to do, people to see, places to be. Mikayla had no tasks, no people, no places. There were the seahorses, but they had the auto-feeder and were still sleeping, their tails curled around the grasses in their tank.

The upstairs light in Gem's house switched off, and a few seconds later, a figure moved in the kitchen window. Mikayla imagined Gem making coffee and wondered what kind of things she liked for breakfast. Mikayla rarely ate breakfast. Unless coffee counted. Currently on her second cup of the morning, she'd been awake for a couple of hours. But not by choice.

She'd had another dream featuring Gem last night. Much like the one from a couple of nights ago, she and Gem were walking on the beach, but this time, the water unexpectedly receded, leaving a treasure of shells on the smooth wet sand. Awestruck, they walked onto the drained seabed to investigate. Several yards from the shoreline, they realized a tsunami was coming, and they stared at each other, waiting for someone to tell them what to do. That was when she'd woken up, heart pounding. At four thirty and still dark. She'd gotten up, had wrapped a blanket around her shoulders against the damp night air coming in from the bedroom window, and made her first cup of coffee. Two hours later, she'd moved from the breakfast table to the deck, but the dream kept coming to mind. Obviously, she'd dreamt about Gem because she'd been spending time with her. But why the underlying fear?

She drained the last of her coffee and rose to get another. This time, she took a couple of to-go mugs from the shelf above the coffee maker. She set it to brew and went to her room to change into a pair of jeans, a T-shirt, and a worn UCSD sweatshirt. When the coffee was in the cups, she poured a little half-and-half into each, along with a skosh of pure Mexican vanilla. She told the seahorses she'd be back and left the house.

Her intention was to say good morning, give Gem a cup of coffee to take along on her day's work, and head out for a walk. She hadn't gone down to the beach since she'd moved in. Her plan to take a daily walk would begin today.

Coffee in hand, she walked to the door on the side of Gem's house where all the lights were on. Slightly nervous, she took a deep breath and knocked. Gem opened it almost immediately. Her face went from neutral to a smile, which made Mikayla smile in return.

Without a word, Gem stepped back, inviting her in as if they did this every day. Mikayla stepped into the kitchen, breathing in Gem's freshly showered scent. Two empty cups already sat on the table, and the sound of a morning news show played extremely loudly from the front of the house.

"Sorry about the volume," Gem said. "He won't wear his hearing aids. I'm about to load stuff into the cart."

"My dad does the same thing." Mikayla held one of the cups up. "I'm going for a walk and noticed your lights were on and wanted to stop by with a cup of coffee you can take with you."

"That's sweet of you." Gem accepted the mug and took one sip, then another, closing her eyes. "So good. I'm stopping by your house for coffee in the morning from now on."

Mikayla used to like her mornings to herself, or at least, she had before being by herself all day. It would be nice to start her day with Gem and coffee. She tapped the sides of her mug and rocked on the balls of her feet. "I'm always awake. Come on over whenever you want."

Gem pointed at her with a wink. "Just remember, you offered." She took another sip and hummed with pleasure.

"I won't forget," Mikayla said, basking in the appreciation of such a simple thing as coffee.

"Did I hear another voice?" The television noise ceased, and Gem's father appeared in the doorway. He smiled when he saw Mikayla and approached her with his hand out. "If we've met, I can't recall your name. I'm Tripp."

Mikayla took his hand. "We did. Briefly, at the bonfire Saturday night. There were a lot of people there. I'm Mikayla."

"You're a friend of Gem's, then?" He glanced between them.

"She's a friend. She's also subletting Brandi's place," Gem said.

His eyes narrowed before returning to normal, and Mikayla wondered what had caused it. "Well, I'll get out of your hair. It's nice to meet you, Mikayla." He turned to leave.

"Hey, Dad? What are your plans for today?"

He turned back around, rolling up his sleeves. "I'm going to take a walk up to the new section. Make sure Tony and the boys don't cut any corners like they did under the counters last time. I don't care if people don't usually notice under there. I want the finishing pieces I asked for."

Gem looked confused.

"What?" he asked, putting his hands on his hips, clearly irritated. "Don't go defending him, Gem. We don't stand for cheap work here."

Gem glanced nervously at her, and Mikayla wondered if she should step out to let them talk. But Gem returned her gaze to her father. The smile didn't reach her eyes. "I agree with you, Dad. No cheap work. But they already did it, and it looks great."

"It's not signed off on until I say so."

Gem shrugged. "Sounds good."

His scowl returned to a more amicable expression. "Of course it does. Your old man sets the bar high." He turned to Mikayla. "It was nice to meet you, M…m…m'lady," he said, apparently giving up on remembering her name as he left the room. The ensuing quiet was thick, allowing for the clear sound of the front door opening and closing a few seconds later.

Mikayla pretended to concentrate on her coffee, wondering how to gracefully leave. Before she had a chance to say anything, Gem pulled her phone from her pocket and selected a number. She glanced at Mikayla as she did it and lifted her brows as if in apology.

"Hey, Tony. Are you onsite yet? Not yet? Well, Dad is on his way over…I think he's walking. He's focused on the finishing pieces under the counters…I know…You did…Super focused… Just let him say what he says…Yeah…I appreciate it, Tony…give him the delivery sheets from Friday. We already went over them, but you don't have to tell him. Cool. I'll come around in a little bit. I'll wait a while. Otherwise, he'll think I'm checking up on him… Yeah…Yeah…you always do. Thanks, man. You're the best. I owe you."

Gem slid her phone into her back pocket and rested a hand on her forehead for a few seconds before turning toward Mikayla, her lips in a tight line. "Sorry about that."

"There's nothing to be sorry about," Mikayla said.

"You wanna go for a ride with me? Just around the grounds."

Surprised by the invitation, she happily accepted. A few minutes later, they were riding in the cart, sipping coffee and watching the sky lighten into true morning.

"This is my favorite part of the day," Gem said. "It's quiet. The air is extra beachy, and there's something about it making me want to slow down and experience the moment."

Mikayla watched the tension melting from her face. "That's a great way of describing it."

Gem drove them to the back of the quiet complex. A few cars went by, and they passed a few early morning joggers and dog walkers. Gem waved and called a greeting to each one. They drove by a few small parks like the one next to Brandi's place, each of them well-groomed, with a covered area big enough for a couple of picnic tables, a barbeque, and a firepit. An expanse of grass and a square of sand for a volleyball court, along with a big shade tree and a little flower garden completed the area. Gem stopped at one and hopped out.

"DJ took today off, and since yesterday was Easter, all the parks were full, so I'm on trash duty today." She pulled on a pair of latex gloves and jogged over to the garbage can and back. "Looks like someone already took care of it."

Gem pointed at a low sign next to the trunk of a tall magnolia tree. The sign said Ana's Park, with a date under the name. "This is the park my dad built for my oldest sister, Ana. He planted the tree the day she was born."

"It's gorgeous."

Gem pointed to the flower garden on the other side of the small park. Bordered by a colorful array of pansies were four rose bushes. "The flowers won't bloom for another month or so, but when they do, they'll be white long-stemmed. He gets them from a nursery in Carlsbad near the flower fields."

Mikayla smiled. "I go there every year to go strawberry picking."

Gem glanced at her. "We should go. It's been a few years since I've gone."

"I'd love to," Mikayla said, and butterflies took off in her stomach as she recognized that their friendship was growing. It reminded her of when she was younger, when friendships seemed more vibrant and meaningful. Aside from Craig, her adult relationships seemed…uninspired and dull in comparison, and she was starting to reevaluate how much joy her marriage had actually given her, too.

They rode to another park. The garbage had been neatly bagged up already, and Gem simply threw the bags into the small trailer they pulled behind the cart.

"I'm sensing a pattern here," Mikayla said.

"Yeah. The residents are pretty awesome. They make my job easier."

"I was talking about the park. Your father made one for each of your sisters?"

"Ah, yeah. This one is for Leticia. He plants rosebushes for each of the grandchildren."

Gem took her through the rest of the community, pointing out the other signs with the rest of her sisters' names until they were next to the park behind Brandi's house where the bonfire had been, Francisca and Grecia Park. She remembered that Francisca was Gem's given name. Both names had the same birth date under them, but the date was repeated under Grecia's.

"Was Grecia your twin?"

Gem nodded, and Mikayla took note of how Gem often took a moment to respond to some things in a conversation, especially when the topic leaned a little heavier. So different from Craig, who filled silences with words.

Gem cleared her throat, and Mikayla sensed she was about to share something personal which, again, made her aware of their growing friendship…a friendship that in such a short period of time had become meaningful to her. Gem was quickly becoming someone who mattered to her. Gem lifted her hand from the steering wheel, and Mikayla thought she was going to rest it over hers, but after a slight hesitation, Gem laid it in her own lap. A stirring of disappointment caught Mikayla by surprise.

"This will sound a little weird, but you have a quality about you that's very unique," Gem said. "I saw it the moment I met you. Your…essence expands and sort of absorbs the energy of the things you appreciate, things that matter to you. Like the parks. It's a connection with significant people and things, but it's more than a connection. Something in you gathers around and sort of integrates with it." She closed her eyes and shook her head. "I don't know if it makes sense."

Mikayla knew Gem just shared something that was more than just personal. Her response mattered, but she wasn't sure she understood. She took Gem's hand, hoping it conveyed her desire to understand. "My essence?"

"The best way to describe it is, it's the core of the energy that makes you, you. I see it. Not with my eyes but with my own essence, so I feel it, too." Gem let out a self-conscious laugh. "I told you it would sound weird."

"It sounds a bit New Agey, but I don't think that's weird. I believe you see and feel it. Some people are more empathic than others. You described my…essence the way I've felt it to be all my life but never had words for." The sense of their friendship growing was even stronger.

Gem appeared to relax a little, and something like relief shone in her eyes. "It's a little more than empathic, but that's a good way of saying it. You don't think I'm crazy?"

"Maybe I do. But I guess I'm crazy, too."

"My dad has it, too. He calls it our 'gift.'"

Mikayla was intrigued. "You sense this kind of thing with everyone?"

Gem nodded. "I get a sense of who they are, whether they're good people, kind, smart, bad, mean, etc. My dad's pretty open about it, but I don't tell people I have it. I don't want that kind of scrutiny. He thinks the twin thing has something to do with it because he lost his twin, too. His brother." Gem stared into the canopy of the magnolia in her park. "I told you it was going to sound weird."

They were quiet for a moment, Mikayla absorbing what Gem told her, and Gem probably paying attention to her special sense to see how she reacted to it. Mikayla surprised herself at how easily she accepted this new information. She believed that a big part of it was that she'd felt a kind of ease with Gem from the very beginning that she'd never experienced before. It made it easier for her to trust what Gem said was true.

"It's not weird. I've sensed a unique connection with you." Mikayla gazed into the canopy, too, because looking at Gem felt almost too personal. "Thank you for telling me about it and sharing your parks. Yours is different than the others."

"There's star jasmine because I don't have any children, but I'm an aunt to many, so the tiny flowers represent them."

"It's very sweet."

"My mother's idea, actually, and I love it. All of it."

"I like the way your face lights up when you talk about your mother."

"I miss her every day."

"Is there a park named after her?"

Gem tilted her head toward her house. "The tree next to the house is named after her. Guadalupe."

"It's beautiful." Mikayla inhaled the scent of the flowers. "Francisca. It's a beautiful name, too, but Gem suits you better."

"I think so, too."

"And now I know your birthday."

They grinned at each other.

"I like hanging out with you," Gem said. Her shoulders dropped like she'd been holding them up, waiting for something to happen. She turned to face Mikayla, her grin fading. "You saw my dad the other night and today. His mental health is…sometimes, he's almost like he's always been, and then sometimes, he's almost unrecognizable. Thankfully, he's himself more often than not, but it's slowly getting worse. He didn't remember you this morning. He might remember you next time, or he might not. He gets argumentative. That's why I called Tony. He deals with it, but I worry how much more he'll take. My dad spends a lot of time in the new builds, so Tony is used to his…moods."

"Is it dementia? What do the doctors say?"

"He won't go to the doctor. I suspect it's dementia, maybe Alzheimer's. Once, he went outside the gate to pick up litter and couldn't remember how to get back in. He tried to climb the fence and fell on his way down. He broke his wrist. Luckily, it wasn't worse. When we were in urgent care, the doctor asked what had happened, and my dad said he got confused and couldn't remember how to get back in, and the doctor started to ask questions like how long, how bad, did he think he might need assistance? All of the normal follow-up questions, and my dad clammed up. He's refused to go to the doctor since. He even cut the cast off himself. It's like he's afraid they'll lock him up or something. He makes comments about his memory not being the same but won't talk about it anymore than that and gets angry if one of us brings it up. A good thing about it is there's no worry about him wandering away. He's terrified of leaving the park unless he's in a car with one of us."

"This must be hard for both of you."

Gem nodded. "I'm more worried about him, and I keep waiting for something to happen that's beyond my capabilities." She blew out a breath. "Anyway, now you know if he keeps asking your name and repeats things."

Mikayla didn't want Gem to worry about her with so much else to deal with. "Don't worry about me. What do your sisters say about it?"

"They don't like talking about it and shut me down when I try."

"That's interesting."

"Right? I'm a social worker. I talk about everything. When Dad nearly broke his back four years ago, we talked about it obsessively to figure things out. But they refuse to talk about this. Classic avoidance. If they don't mention it, it'll go away."

"My mom's like that. How are they helping you?"

"They all have jobs and kids to take care of but drop by when they can. Between the five of them, they take him to lunch a few times a week, and they trade off on having him come over for a family day every Sunday."

"But you take care of him the rest of the time?"

"He mostly takes care of himself. I have to remind him about things more often and sometimes mediate interactions with other people. Mostly just the employees and vendors. You witnessed the Tony thing. He's always professional with the residents, at least."

"That's still a lot to deal with."

"Sometimes."

Mikayla got the impression Gem didn't want sympathy but probably wanted someone to share her troubles with. She was honored to be the one she trusted. She looked for something to keep the discussion going, to show her interest. "How is he with everyday tasks? Is he good to cook?"

"I disconnected the gas stove after he burnt a few things, and I put all the knives up out of caution. He uses the microwave. He's terrible about cleaning up, so I have to do most of it, but honestly, it's not bad."

"I watched you the other night at the bonfire. You were good with him, and it's obvious that he listens to you and trusts you."

Gem's eyes grew soft. "He does."

Mikayla rested her hand over Gem's and squeezed. "Thank you for trusting me enough to talk about this."

Gem tilted her head. "Thank you. I'm usually the helper, not the helpee."

Mikayla sensed how uncomfortable being the helpee made her, and selfishly, she wasn't ready to stop hanging out with her. "Can I ask you a favor?"

"Sure. Anything."

"Can I tag along with you again today? I don't think I can stand sitting in the house all day."

Gem looked surprised. "I'd love the company. Just promise me you'll tell me if you get bored, and I'll take you home."

Mikayla was pretty sure hanging out with Gem promised to be far from boring.

Chapter Fifteen

Gem glanced at Mikayla as they drove through the property. Talking about her father had released something inside her, as if she'd been slowly suffocating for a long time, and now, she could almost breathe again. Almost. Talking about it didn't make her worries go away, but at least she wasn't alone anymore. She, of all people, should have known talking about it with someone would help. Even therapists needed to be reminded sometimes.

She'd asked Mikayla to go on the drive through the park to blow off the stress her father had stirred up and ended up giving Mikayla a tour of her family history. She'd also talked about her gift, something she never did. Instead of feeling exposed and vulnerable, she felt...seen...accepted...relieved of being the only person who knew her heavy load of responsibilities and worries. God. That was a lot. Typical Gem would have wanted to be alone with her thoughts after all of that, but she was glad Mikayla had asked to ride along. Her lack of expectations and abundance of calm was a comfort.

The day had definitely not turned out like she'd thought it would when she woke up, and it wasn't even mid-morning. She'd expected the knock on the door to be Harper asking her to keep her eyes open for her cat, Rico, who had a habit of darting out the door when he was supposed to be an indoor cat. Mikayla had been a pleasant surprise. "What made you come by this morning?" she asked. "I mean, other than wanting to spoil me with good coffee?" Gem asked taking another sip.

She drove along the path encircling the mobile home park, taking the long way to show off the beautiful landscaping. Her father had put it in so the residents could get some exercise whether they walked, ran, biked, or rode their skateboards. Her contributions, aside from the bougainvillea and additional magnolias, were the archways draped with star jasmine and honeysuckle. She was proud of how pretty they had turned out and how they complemented the tangy scented pepper trees every fifty feet or so with their drooping branches overhanging the path. It was almost romantic, especially with the intoxicating scents mixed with the damp marine layer and dew.

"Impulse. I noticed your lights were on and wanted to brighten your day. Also, selfishly, I didn't have any plans, and I couldn't bear to spend a day without hearing another person's voice."

"What did you do yesterday afternoon after I dropped you off?"

"I went to the grocery store to get out of the house. Pathetic as it sounds, I didn't need anything. I just wanted to be around people, even if it was only to exchange dull pleasantries with the cashier. Unfortunately, I was thwarted."

"That's a good word. Thwarted."

"Isn't it? The grocery usher person took note of my meager selection, obviously intended for one person, and waved me over to use the self-checkout lane. He moved on to the next person before I had a chance to say thanks. I considered going through the drive-thru at Angelo's to talk to the window clerk, but fast food and I don't get along." Mikayla dropped her forehead into her hand. "I was trying for off-handed and funny, but I just make myself sound pitiful, didn't I?"

Gem laughed. "You were funny. But what's the deal with you and fast food? Don't tell me it's some sort of diet. You're perfect." Oh, jeez! Had she said that out loud?

"I love it, and it punishes me. I'd rather go to solitary for a week than live with the consequences of a delicious burger, tostada, or chicken nugget." She slid down in her seat. "And now I insinuated diarrhea. Kill me now. Please put this thing into turbo and push me out? Preferably next to a tall cliff. With cactus at the bottom and broken glass. Lots of broken glass."

Gem laughed so hard, she had to stop the cart, which made Mikayla nearly curl up into a ball. She laughed a lot with Mikayla, and she loved it. "Detail logged and don't worry. I have twenty nieces and nephews, with two on the way and two grand-nieces. Diarrhea is a frequent topic in my social circle, second only to farts and vomit." She got Mikayla to sit up and laugh, the best sound in the world. She started the cart again. "What are your plans for this morning, other than taking this tour around our palatial estate?"

"Well, I've learned all there is about seahorses, so I planned to finish a book I found at Brandi's about aromantic asexuality. Oh, speaking of Brandi's house, I have to be back by this afternoon because a guy from Scripps will be here to check on the seahorses."

"That would be Rich. He's a nice guy, even if he's a total geek about marine life. I understand only half of what he talks about. Sounds like you're making your way through Brandi's bookshelf. She teaches classes at the youth center. About aromanticism, not seahorses."

"Interesting. I can see her being a really good teacher, based on the little I've been around her. I found the book on a table. The subject is new to me."

"I'd never heard about it, either, until I read about it. I'll bet you're reading the same book she loaned me." She liked to think about Mikayla holding the same book she'd held.

Why on Earth would she care about something like that? She told herself to stop.

Mikayla didn't seem to notice. "It reminded me of how much I don't know. There's so much truth in the saying, the more you learn, the less you realize you actually know."

"I hear you. I used to learn all kinds of new stuff from my social work clients. I miss how much wider my worldview was back then. Now, I barely have time to glance at news on my phone. There's no rest for the wicked, or so my father likes to say."

"He's a funny guy."

"He was on a roll yesterday. He came back from my sister Adriana's house with some terrible dad jokes. In fact…why did the man stop telling flatulence jokes?"

Mikayla squinted, and Gem second-guessed the joke. Too late now. "I have no idea."

"Someone told him his jokes stink."

"Just like your joke." Mikayla pushed her shoulder, and the cart swerved. They both squealed. "And your driving."

"Hey, someone pushed me."

"Then it's official. Your joke nearly killed us, and you are hereby forbidden to tell dad jokes."

"I think the punishment's fair." Gem laughed and stopped the cart near the work crew. "Be back in a few." She jumped from the cart to check in with Devon, who let her know they were back on schedule. When she returned, Mikayla was taking pictures of flowers with her phone.

"Updating your social media feed?" Gem joked as they got back into the cart.

Mikayla grimaced. "I abandoned social media when all this with Craig started. Who wants to read morose updates from a jilted housewife?"

Gem whipped a glance at her. "Is that how you see yourself?"

Thankfully, Mikayla laughed. "You look like I just told you I planned to end it all or something."

Gem was embarrassed. "Sorry. I don't want you to police your comments. But come on, there's a lot to unpack in your statement."

Mikayla appeared to consider it. "Nope. I am, indeed, a jilted housewife. No one wants to read posts of a person going through the seven stages of grief."

"Divorce is hard. I won't negate your feelings."

"I know I might seem pretty happy, but a therapist once told me divorce is like death." She held up seven fingers and started ticking them off. "You have shock, pain, anger, and depression before you start to see happiness and then start working on acceptance and hope. I'm somewhere in the depression phase, I think."

"I'm familiar with that process. Still, *so* much to unpack there. I just met you, and I am certain there is much, *much* more to this woman"—she gestured at Mikayla in a flourish—"than a jilted housewife."

Mikayla tilted her head and smiled, which made Gem all warm inside. "You're so sweet. I know what you're saying. I even agree. However, it truly is the extent of what I am right now. At this moment."

Gem could tell from the steady eye contact that Mikayla honestly believed it. Instead of turning toward the entrance of the park, she steered the cart onto the bike lane going into town. "Do you like scones?"

"Am I being kidnapped? Next to cherry and cream cheese Danishes, they're one of my favorite things. But not chocolate chip. Chocolate chip scones are too much."

"More for me, then. We're going to Seaside Café, and I'm going to introduce you to the wondrous delight of a beach plum scone and my niece, Rose, if she's working."

"Sounds yummy. The scone, not the niece, although I'm excited to meet more of your family. I've never heard of a beach plum."

"They grow on the east coast. Originally from Maine, the owners brought their scones and their coffee to Oceanside five years ago, and for that, I forgive them for buying the building I'd dreamed about making into a bed and breakfast since I was a child."

"You want to run a bed and breakfast?"

She shook her head. "Too much work and I prefer social work. It sounded like a fun way to meet a never-ending string of travelers."

"A source of endless new friends?"

Gem gave her a sly grin. "Something like that."

Mikayla's expressive face revealed her confusion and then understanding. "Oh! *Lady* travelers."

Gem laughed and parked in front of a two-story, Victorian-style house facing the ocean. She'd brought Mikayla here for two reasons. First, she wanted to talk about the jilted housewife thing. There was so much more to Mikayla than that. The other thing was that she wanted to show Mikayla she had interests outside of her work. And maybe she needed to remind herself of that, too.

CHAPTER SIXTEEN

Gem looked up at the colonial-style house that stood out from most of the houses and stores around it, or in Southern California, for that matter, which tended toward uniform architecture and stucco siding.

"It's interesting, huh?" Gem said, leading Mikayla to the stairs rising up to the wraparound porch. The doors were propped open to the chill morning air, and the scent of coffee and freshly baked goods wafted out. Inside, the café looked warm and cozy.

Mikayla gazed around. "I already love it."

"Just wait until you sample those scones. Their lunch menu is fantastic, too."

The line to order stood four people deep, so Gem watched Mikayla take in the shop, trying to see it from her point of view. There were pieces from local artists on the walls, small price tags dangling from them. Event posters covered the wall behind the condiment counter, and a shelf near the register hawked T-shirts, hoodies, mugs, and dog bandanas with the café logo on them. Mikayla soon zeroed in on a sign promoting live music on Friday nights.

"Looking for a place to take your act?" Gem asked.

"God, no." Mikayla snorted. "I just love live music."

"Hey, Auntie Gem." Rose approached the counter from a back room. She tilted her head at Mikayla, who was examining jars of beach plum jam a few feet away, then leaned over the counter to whisper, "She's awfully cute. A new girlfriend? Please say yes."

Gem shook her head. "Just a friend.

Rose lifted her eyebrows like she didn't believe it. "Bummer because she's smokin'."

"And recently divorced. From a man. So there's that."

"It wouldn't stop me." Rose giggled, then became serious. "Um, hey. Speaking about stopping..." She grimaced. "I quit school. I wanted to talk to you about, well..."

"You want your job back?"

"If it's still available." Rose peered around as if to make sure no one could hear. "I love it here, but it's not a career, you feel me?"

"I feel you, niece, I feel you. Come by the park, and we'll talk." The hopeful look on Rose's face made her happy. Family took care of one another. And a little louder, she said, "Mikayla, come meet Rose."

Mikayla came closer with a smile, lifting her eyebrows and chin, which Gem now recognized to be her polite "meet and greet" face. "It's nice to meet you."

"Any friend of Auntie Gem's is a friend of mine," she said, sounding just like her grandfather. "I know what *you* want, Auntie," Rose said, standing tall behind the counter as the line brought them to the register. "What can I get you, Mikayla?"

"If you have a spicy chai latte, I'd love a medium, please," Mikayla said. "Gem says I must try the beach plum scone, too."

"They make a wonderful spicy chai latte," Gem said. "Make it two of the scones and a bag of ground coffee." Gem pushed away Mikayla's hand holding her card and grabbed a bag of coffee from the display. "Put it on my account."

"Got it." Rose called for the other barista to make the chai and Gem's hazelnut latte while she collected the other items and placed them on the counter. "I'm only charging you for the coffee beans."

"Whatever," Gem said, leaning forward. "Give your favorite auntie a hug." When Rose leaned forward, Gem slid a twenty into the front pocket of her apron.

They chatted while the chai and latte steamed, then Gem and Mikayla found a table. "I love this place," Mikayla whispered as they settled.

"Why are you whispering?"

"I don't want to come off as a tourist in my own town."

Gem laughed. "Fair enough. Try the scone."

Mikayla licked her lips and moved her hair back before taking a small bite of the crumbly sweet bread. She hummed her appreciation. "Yum."

"Glad you like it." Gem tried to ignore how much she enjoyed watching her enjoy the food.

Mikayla pointed at the scone. "Like doesn't begin to describe the depth of emotion evoked by this scone. I'm inspired to write sonnets about it. Also, I thought you said Rose was your niece. You can't be more than a year or two older."

Gem sat back in her chair, used to the reaction. "She's twenty-six. The oldest of Ana's kids. I'm only six years older. It weirded me out when she called me Auntie when were kids, but I'm used to it now." She lifted her coffee, gesturing to Mikayla with it before taking a sip. "Let's talk about the jilted housewife thing." Mikayla seemed to accept being a castoff. Gem wanted her to see she was anything but.

Mikayla's face registered surprise, as if she'd already forgotten about the conversation. "What's there to talk about?" Then, she smirked. "Oh wait, are you trying to therapize me?"

Gem chuckled. "I'm trying to be a friend. One who wants to get to know you better, someone you can talk to about things if you want to. You know, help you find your way? Maybe this is why you came to Oceana. Have you considered that?"

"Like, predestination? I didn't move here for any other reason than to have a few months to figure out what's next. My sister suggested it." She tapped Gem's hand and pointed at her. "I'm glad I came."

Gem loved the little touches Mikayla sprinkled into conversations. She decided to go out on a limb since Mikayla had responded well to the discussion about her "gift" and might benefit from the conversation. She seemed so lost, so disconnected, so Gem cut straight to the point. "I'm not surprised it wasn't your idea. People don't move to Oceana purposely. They usually just wind up here. They find whatever it is they need, and along the way, they play a part in helping another person. I don't know how it works, but I've witnessed it time and again."

Mikayla didn't react like she doubted that, but she did look amused. "Shia mentioned something like that. You all believe in a mystical force at Oceana, don't you?"

Gem contemplated for a moment. "I know it sounds crazy. But isn't life just a chain of mystical experiences? People generally get what they need, even if it isn't what they want. It sounds incredibly shortsighted when we have so much suffering in this world, but in its small way, Oceana seems to help people find exactly what they need at the time they need it. I see it in how people naturally take care of the park and each other. I think it's extra strong on our little street, Oceana Place."

Mikayla tilted her head. Gem sensed her puzzlement but not any real pushback. "I have to admit, it does sound a little woo-woo, and truthfully, I usually change the subject when this kind of stuff comes up, but I think this matters to you." She leaned forward. "I personally don't believe in fate, but I do believe in a sort of universal energy. I would guess you and your father's gifts are part of it because you somehow connect to it. I think it connects people together in various ways, some more closely than others, and everyone is part of it."

Even as Gem's sense of being accepted and seen increased, she sensed a big "but" coming up.

"But Oceana being a magical place? Well, I hate to say it because I don't want to offend you, but I think it's probably wishful thinking that seems confirmed when good things happen to the people who live here. Good things are gonna happen. Bang! Proof. So are bad things. That's life." She grimaced. "I don't want to dismiss something obviously important to you. Do you hate me?"

Gem chuckled. "Not at all. You're being honest. Maybe in time, you'll believe. I'm willing to wait."

"Good to know. Has it helped you? You've lived here most of your life."

Gem considered. "I've seen it at work several times." She shrugged. "Other than being able to pick the right people to live here, I haven't been part of anything directly."

Mikayla tapped her hand again. "I like the idea. I really do."

Gem felt the tap with her entire body and hid a shiver. "Let's get back to the jilted housewife thing," she said. "I may have been a little quick to make a judgment about your comment. I heard you ask why anyone would want to interact on social media with a jilted housewife, and I assumed you meant yourself."

"I did."

"As a whole?"

Mikayla laughed. "No one is just one thing. But in this moment of my life, it's what I am, mostly." She said it so matter-of-factly.

It hurt Gem's heart for such a kind woman to distill herself down to what someone else had done to her. "Why?"

"It literally is all of my identity now. I don't have anything meaningful attached to my existence. No one counts on me. When I visit my parents, they regard me with pity, and in my mom's case, blame. When I visit my sister, she sees me as someone to save, which only proves my point. She wants to take my mind off it. She devises ways for me to move on, get revenge, and forget my sorrows. Her advice is to sleep with a hundred people, the way she got through her three divorces."

That last part about screwing a bunch of people bothered Gem more than it had any right to. Mikayla didn't seem the type, but Gem had seen lots of people go wild after a nasty breakup. Mikayla seemed to be doing the exact opposite, isolating herself. Was it any better? "You still haven't convinced me. How about your friends? Do they make you feel like you're one-dimensional?"

Mikayla spread her hands stared at them. "I've sort of taken a break from most people."

Yep, she was isolating. "Why?"

"Because I'm tired of talking about my divorce. I'm single, and they aren't. They can't perceive me independently from Craig. We don't have similar interests aside from tennis, and there's only so much tennis I can play or talk about."

"You must have people in your life you interact with as something other than a wife, let alone a jilted one. And by the way, let me be clear, there's nothing wrong with being a jilted housewife as long as it's not all you think you are." Saying no negative self-talk would truly sound like she was therapizing.

Mikayla's smile didn't make it to her eyes. "I seriously don't want you worrying about me or worse, pitying me." She pushed her hair back in what might have been frustration. "I couldn't bear it if you pitied me. I didn't want to say it because I didn't want you to think I was a cold person, but I have never been remotely close with any of the women in my social circle. I don't mind letting those friendships fade away. And as much as I thought I loved being married to Craig, none of it truly reflects who I am. None of it. It sounds shitty, but I'd rather you think of me as cold than pity me."

Gem took her hand and waited until she met her gaze. "I do not pity you, and you are the furthest thing from cold. I'm sorry. I heard you diminish yourself, and I reacted too strongly. I just failed the listening class in therapy school."

"You're a great listener."

"There are four rules for listening: reflect back on what you hear, validate feelings, questions over answers, and don't give advice until it's asked for. I broke every one of them."

Mikayla appeared amused. "So you *are* psychoanalyzing me, Doctor?"

Damn. She'd been called out. "You can take the therapist out of the practice…I'm not a doctor, but I am sorry. I swear, I'm not analyzing you, just being a friend."

"We are friends. Certainly better friends than any of the people I called friends in my old social circle."

The comment caused a warm sensation to spread through her. "I consider us friends, too."

Mikayla dropped her gaze. "You were right as a friend and a therapist. I was diminishing myself. At the risk of abusing our new friendship, what free advice would you give me?"

"Everyone heals differently," she said. "My advice would be to be kind to yourself, and when you find you're focusing on negatives, remind yourself of the positives. You're kind, funny, smart, warm, gorgeous, and sexy, along with a lot of other wonderful things. Try to remember that." A wave of heat blossomed on her face. Gorgeous and sexy? That was not how she typically described her friends.

Mikayla laughed. "I'll remember."

"For what it's worth, I know it's not easy to focus on the positives when you're going through a brutal divorce. Don't beat yourself up if you have a hard time with it."

Mikayla took a long sip and sighed. "I'm not going through a divorce. It's over. Done. And probably the most civil event the North County Courthouse ever processed." She let out a derisive huff. "My lawyer actually apologized for having to charge me the minimum hourly retainer. Mediation entailed us showing up, my lawyer asking for a fifty-fifty split, Craig's lawyer giving a counteroffer giving me much, *much* more than my request, us accepting, and finally, signatures. We were in and out within twenty minutes, and we all went to lunch together, courtesy of Craig's attorney. We then endured the six-months before it became official. Craig moved from our house into a rental about half a mile away, but he's down in Mexico now, living in the vacation house he and I bought shortly after we married. He's considering making it his permanent address. *Their* permanent address."

"Was he cheating?" Gem couldn't imagine any man finding another woman more compelling than Mikayla.

"I'm absolutely certain he wasn't."

"Sorry. You said *their* address, so I figured…"

"Nope. He isn't a cheater. He's actually a good guy. I said their house because he started seeing someone a couple of months after we separated. One of his clients set them up. She's nice. I've met her."

"And you like her?" Gem found it surprising how Mikayla had accepted her ex-husband's new girlfriend. Aside from the comment about being a jilted housewife and going through the stages of grief, Mikayla didn't appear to be grieving her marriage very deeply. She could have been holding her emotions close to her chest, but Gem noticed that kind of thing as a therapist, even on top of her "gift." "Was the divorce a long time coming? It sounds like you were ready for it, or at least, weren't surprised by it."

"A complete surprise. I mean, every couple goes through ups and downs. Love is kind of like the tides. Sometimes it's high, sometimes it's low, but it's always there. At first, I was shocked. After that, I didn't believe it. In fact, I'd almost convinced myself that the conversation hadn't really happened. Then I got angry. I cried, which made him cry. I told him to leave, then begged him to stay. I was positive I was going insane, feeling one way one moment, then the exact opposite. We talked. And talked. So much. He said he felt the same way, and I believed him. You don't live with someone for twelve years and not know them. Every time new emotions came up, we'd figure out how to move forward." She sighed and paused, staring into the middle distance. Then, she seemed to pull herself back. "Eventually, we split as friends. At first, it was nice to have him there if something happened. It was the day the divorce became final that I realized I needed time and space to get used to being on my own."

"When did it finalize?"

"A couple of weeks ago." Obviously, she was sad about the breakup but not devastated.

"You said you were surprised when he asked for the divorce. In hindsight, are you still surprised?"

Mikayla shrugged, a sad, accepting gesture. "He wanted kids, and I couldn't give them to him. It never occurred to me that he'd leave."

Brandi had told her that much. Gem had never wanted kids, but all of her sisters had big families. None of them would have divorced their husbands if they couldn't have had kids, though. "Tell me more."

Mikayla pushed her hair back. "Well, *Doctor…*" Gem grimaced, which resulted in another huffy laugh. "I never wanted kids. I was ambivalent. I assumed they were an inevitability. 'When you have kids…Once the kids come…Your kids will make you see, blah, blah blah.' It's the natural progression. Meet. Marry. Kids. Empty nest. Grandkids. Retirement. The expected way of things. Our mothers asked about it every time we were around. It became a joke." She half laughed.

Gem felt the weight of the expectations placed on Mikayla and wished she could go back and remove the damage it had done to her self-image. She knew firsthand how painful it was for a person to have expectations foisted upon them. There wasn't a clear-cut way to make the fear of disappointing people go away. So she just listened.

"We talked about it before we got married, but it seemed years away, and we both expected them in this nebulous way. At first, we didn't have time with him starting his business. It was seven years before he suggested we start trying. We figured it would just happen. Two years raced by. It came up once in a while, but we were too busy to think about it. I loved being able to pack a bag and go on vacation or buy a boat or new vacation home." She closed her eyes and shook her head. "God, I sound pretentious. Anyway, about two years in, we talked about how we should get a little more intentional about the baby thing. I took supplements, temperatures, tracked ovulation, monitored my weight, my diet, what positions we did it in, everything. We finally got fertility drugs, which caused a lot of pain because of endometriosis. Later, when I went through procedures to control it, they found fibroid tumors. Because of both conditions, I ended up having a uterine ablation, which ended my ability to get pregnant."

Gem had the sensation of being on a roller coaster. "Wow. That's a lot. How did you feel when you found out?"

Mikayla stared at her hands with a faraway look. "I felt bad for Craig. When he sets his mind to something, he invests everything in it. *Everything*. So when I came home from the doctor and told him, he broke down. I'd never seen him cry. It broke my heart."

She'd asked Mikayla how it made *her* feel, and she'd focused on Craig. The therapist in Gem diagnosed cognitive dissonance, disassociation, or an off-the-charts amount of empathy. Maybe all three. Gem didn't blame her. Her life had been irreparably affected by her diagnosis and treatment. As a friend, Gem wanted to hate Craig. Despite all his wife had gone through, he'd decided to divorce the best thing that had no doubt ever happened to him. It seemed especially unforgivable to think about Mikayla dealing with the loss of fertility and also undergoing a major medical procedure at the time. Good people didn't leave people they supposedly loved when they needed them the most. Mikayla deserved so much better.

Gem tempered her emotions. "I understand you have empathy for him. How did it make *you* feel?"

Mikayla sighed and dropped her chin to her chest before straightening again. "Relieved."

Shocked, Gem tried to mask her expression. "Can you expand on that?"

"First, I didn't have to keep trying to get pregnant. Also, I didn't have to deal with my god-awful periods anymore. Mostly, the whole ordeal made me realize how much I didn't want kids. I wanted them for Craig." She paused. "I don't *not* like kids. They're fine. And I would have been a good mom, I suppose, so I had major guilt because my husband really, *really* wanted them, which devastated him."

It was official. Gem really, *really* didn't like Mikayla's ex-husband. "How did he respond? Did he blame you for not being *able* to have kids or because you never *wanted* them?"

"I never told him how relieved I was. But deep down, I think he knew."

"Why do you say that?"

"My reactions. He'd be so disappointed each month while I shrugged it off. It would have been disingenuous for me to act upset. He commented on it once, said he understood how I had to compartmentalize it, how I had to stuff it down every month. I never corrected him. I think he tried to convince himself of my devastation because he couldn't fathom otherwise."

So many questions ran through Gem's mind. "Would it be too intrusive to ask if you considered adoption or surrogacy?"

"Full surrogacy wasn't an option. My ovaries were scarred from the endometriosis. But even partial wouldn't do. He wanted the whole experience. The emotional high of finding out we were pregnant, the cigars, the midnight cravings, baby's first kicks, pampering me during the whole pregnancy, being together in the delivery room." She grinned as if the manufactured dream scenario was cute and sweet and not the setup for a psychological thriller.

"I'm sorry, but he sounds like a selfish asshole." As a friend, she got to be snarky. Craig sounded like a narcissistic scumbag who'd manipulated Mikayla into worrying more about his happiness than hers, not to mention all of the mental, emotional, and physical pain she'd undergone because he didn't get what he wanted. And then he divorced her for her failure to become pregnant.

Mikayla shook her head, appearing amused. "Everyone has the same reaction. If you met him, you'd change your mind. All of this occurred over several years. He's not to blame for the divorce. If anyone is, it's me....or at least, my body. He was never a bad husband. He loved me. Having kids was just more important to him. I can't blame him for being honest. It tore him apart."

Gem blew out a disdainful breath. "I'm sure he felt awful." A disease might have kept Mikayla from getting pregnant, but it wasn't her fault, nor was the divorce. But right now wasn't the time.

"He'd been very clear about wanting kids all along. Please don't hate him."

Gem tried to let go of her anger. She didn't want to inadvertently hurt Mikayla any more than she'd already been hurt. She deserved to be protected as much as she protected her ex-husband.

Chapter Seventeen

A t any given moment, Mikayla counted at least seven hummingbirds whizzing around the feeder hanging from the far end of the porch of Brandi's home, sometimes more. There were also a couple of feeders at the end of the porch, and a few finches were visiting the sock feeder. Mikayla enjoyed watching all of them, but the tinier, green-headed hummingbirds were her favorite.

The shorty wet suit she'd worn for her first swim with Shia much earlier that morning hung on the railing to dry, and a book about modern-day pirates lay open and facedown on the glass-top table next to her. She sipped coffee, her bare feet propped up on the chair beside her, and for once, she didn't feel like she was a loser for having nothing to do all day. Probably because of the endorphins she'd created during the brisk swim. Thinking about getting up to make a sandwich for lunch, she heard steps on the deck behind her. She turned to see Gem's father coming up the stairs. Not the Helmstaad she'd hoped to see, but she was pleased to see him.

"Hi there, Mr. Helmstaad," she said, standing and meeting him near the front door.

A friendly expression lit up his face. "Ah! Gem's friend. I remember the face. Your name escapes me. Please forgive an old man's Swiss cheese memory." He tapped his temple cheerfully before offering his hand.

Puzzled by his visit, she shook his hand. "Mikayla. How are you doing today?"

"Just dandy on this beautiful day," he said, gesturing to the day at large and peering around. "I've been wandering around the park today, enjoying the various flowers and topiary. He tipped his head toward the end of the porch. "I see you have a swarm of black-chinned hummingbirds at your feeder. It's nesting season. They like to build their little nests in the honeysuckle. You have to look close, though. They're no bigger than a Ping-Pong ball, and the eggs are smaller than the nail on my pinky." He held up his little finger.

"They're lovely. I've been watching them all morning. I'm going to fix lunch. Can I make you a sandwich?"

He waved a hand dismissively. "I couldn't put you out. I wanted to ask Brandi if I could watch the seahorses. Is she around?"

She took his arm and showed him into the house. "She's not here right now. Othello's ready to have the babies any day. Rich came by yesterday and confirmed it."

He stood before the huge tank and watched the fish. His eyes were so much like Gem's with their clear blue color. "They're amazing. Such unexpected creatures. They don't swim well, so they're easy prey. They use their ability to change colors to camouflage themselves. Truly amazing animals."

"I agree," she said, gathering bread and other ingredients. "I can't get enough of watching them. Are you sure you wouldn't like a sandwich? I'm in the mood for a grilled cheese. It isn't any trouble."

"You've convinced me. Grilled cheese sounds delightful. The trick to the perfect grilled cheese is to butter both sides of the bread, inside and out. It's how my wife Lupe makes them." He mimicked holding a piece of bread and using a knife to spread butter. "A layer over the entire piece, top and bottom. The kids eat every bite and ask for more." He kissed his fingertips as he continued to watch the fish.

"I've never put it on the inside of the bread. I'll give it a try."

He winked at her. "You won't be sorry."

She gathered the things for the sandwiches and watched him watch the fish. Like Gem, it appeared he'd been there many times before. He used the baster to feed them individual shrimp and seemed enthralled, talking about how they were paired up and how Scripps had caught them in the wild for their breeding program. She learned quite a bit while she cooked lunch.

"Sandwiches are ready. Would you like to eat on the porch or in here?" she asked as she plated their food.

"Out on the porch is good. We can watch the birds and enjoy the breeze."

He helped her take the food and iced tea out to the glass-top table, and they began to eat. One bite in and she was hooked.

"Yum. Butter on both sides of the bread is definitely the trick. This is good."

He beamed. "Lupe is a fabulous cook. There isn't anything she can't cook."

"Gem brags about her cooking, too."

His eyes grew soft. "Gem. My Angel. Our surprise baby. Her and Grecia. They were so tiny when they were born. No one imagined they would make it, and Grecia didn't." His eyes watered as if he might cry. "My Angel, she's a fighter. What a wonderful woman she's grown into. We're so proud of her. Did she tell you she's a social worker? She helps so many people, and now she's helping me. In a different way, of course. She manages this whole place and does a wonderful job, too. I don't think there's anything she can't do."

Mikayla was sure her parents had never talked about her with such pride. She wished Gem could hear her father now. "She's an amazing woman."

"How long have you known her?" he asked before taking a long drink.

"I met her last Monday when I came to talk to Brandi about staying here while she's in London. So just over a week."

"How do you like Oceana?"

"I love it here."

The pleasure on his face was infectious. "Our Oceana is a special place. It may sound like I'm a crazy man for saying this, but Oceana makes people want to be better people. It's always been this way. I sensed it from the beginning. Lupe did, too. I always wondered where the energy came from, as if we're on ley lines or sacred ground. You know, like in Sedona, Arizona? People say there's a confluence of energy there. Something generated by the Earth. I think there's something like that here. Some people feel it, and some people don't. Even if people don't, they benefit from it. Do you feel it?"

Unlike the almost apologetic manner in which he'd arrived, he sounded like an ancient mystic when he spoke about Oceana, so confident and sure. Mikayla marveled at the contrast as she considered his question. She couldn't tell if she'd felt the energy he spoke of. She did know she felt happy here and had been comfortable from the moment she'd arrived. She felt lighter and more grounded, too. Then, there was the snap decision to stay without hours of deliberation as she normally did. Was it the place? She remembered the skepticism she'd responded with before. Was it still as strong? "I'm not sure. I feel different since I've come here, but I'm not sure if it's because I've met some incredible people or because I'm starting new."

He nodded. "You're aware of it, then. You don't need to explain it to know it. Good things happen, and ultimately, it's about wanting to be better and becoming better. Not necessarily in a physical way. More in a general way. I can't explain it." He finished his sandwich. "You said you came here to start over? What were you leaving behind?"

"My marriage. I recently got divorced, so I needed some time out of my normal life to figure out what I want to do." She usually hated talking about her failed marriage with people she *did* know, let alone people she didn't. Here she was doing it for the second time in just a few days. Gem's father exuded something familiar. Maybe because he and Gem were family.

"Have you figured it out yet?"

She laughed. "It's only been a week."

"I don't sense deep despair in you. Not the kind that comes from losing a relationship, anyway. It seems like you might have figured something out, even if you haven't figured everything out."

As when talking about the energy of Oceana, he said it confidently, and he wasn't wrong. She realized she was less sad about losing Craig, and even more interesting, she was sadder about not being married rather than not being his wife, a surprising enlightenment.

Gem had said she and her father had a knack for sensing the essence of a person and she was pretty sure now that she could feel the awareness of *their* awareness. At least, she did so with Gem. She accepted that her understanding of it wasn't perfect, but both Gem and her father seemed to know her overall disposition before she did. It seemed she was in need of a little introspection.

"Hey, Dad. I went home for lunch, and you weren't there."

The new voice kept her from going too far down that path, and she turned to see Gem mounting the porch steps. Despite the deep thoughts a moment ago, a little buzz of pleasure passed through her.

"I'm having lunch with Mikayla. She's staying at Brandi's house. Have you met her yet?" Mikayla noticed how quickly he'd gone from asking her how *long* she and Gem had known each other to *if* they knew each other.

As if sensing what was on her mind, Gem gave her a sad little smile and then returned her gaze to her father. "I have. What did you two have for lunch?"

"She made grilled cheese sandwiches like your mother makes them."

"Sounds delicious." Gem came up behind her father's chair and put her hands on his shoulders. He patted one. The display of affection made Mikayla wish she had a fraction of it with either of her parents. Gem mouthed, "*Is everything, okay?*" and Mikayla nodded discreetly.

"Would you like a sandwich?" she asked. "It would only take a few minutes to make."

"Thanks. It's tempting, but I've already eaten. Can I borrow my dad? I have some work stuff to talk to him about."

He stood. "It seems work calls, Mikayla. Thank you for letting me watch the fish and for lunch. I can't wait to tell Lupe you tried her grilled cheese secret."

"I enjoyed chatting," Mikayla said to Gem and put a hand on his arm. "Drop by any time, Mr. Helmstaad."

"Thank you, Mikayla, but please call me Tripp."

She agreed, and Gem and her father left. Mikayla cleaned the dishes, thinking about how much she'd enjoyed his dropping by, but if asked, she'd have said she enjoyed Gem's very brief visit even more.

Walking home with her father, Gem realized her little crush on Mikayla was getting stronger. Finding her father there had activated a set of emotions she didn't even know she had hiding in her. Gratitude and admiration didn't come close to explaining. All she knew was that it meant a lot to her that Mikayla had looked past his confusion or occasional strange behavior and offered kindness.

"You two have a thing going on, don't you?" he asked, studying his watch.

"What do you mean?"

"I could see it."

Gem wanted to ask whether he *saw* it, which meant it was really strong, or had just sensed it. She wasn't sure she wanted the answer. "We're just friends."

"For now, maybe. You know my rule about dating residents." He looked at his watch again.

She sighed. Why had he decided to bring up something from decades ago? She couldn't discuss it, either. She'd lost that kind of access to him, and she grieved for it. The contrast between this old pain being resurrected and the flare of warmth she'd experienced moments ago set up a potential tinderbox, and she had to very consciously contain it or risk saying something she regretted. "Why do you keep checking your watch?"

"I have almost ten thousand steps in already. I want to hit it by the time we get home so the spies at the watch factory don't think I'm slacking."

She laughed at the rare glimpse of his silly humor while a little stab of sadness still poked her heart. Gem had given him the smartwatch for his birthday. More than a gift, it was a way to remind him to take his medication and for her to keep track of his whereabouts. Aside from the one time he'd become disoriented outside the gate, he'd never displayed any other issues with remembering where he was, but for his safety and her peace of mind, she'd given him the watch because she could track his location any time. That was how she'd known he was at Brandi's. Afraid he might be bothering Mikayla, she'd come to check in.

"How'd you manage to wrangle a lunch invitation from Mikayla?"

"First, I stopped by Alice's place. She wasn't home."

"She works during the week, Dad."

"It's hard to keep track of the days when you're retired." He chuckled. "I'm going to have to get a hobby."

She shoulder-bumped him. "You'll figure it out."

"After I left Alice's, I took a walk." He stopped and patted his pockets before he removed a small notebook and handed it to her. "I took a few notes about things I noticed that need a little attention. Nothing major or urgent. Just minor repairs."

She scanned the items. A loose skirt on one of the units, a section of walkway where tree roots were lifting it, a window screen missing on the mail building, and a host of minor things, most of which she already had workorders on. "Thanks, Dad. I'll give this to Tony. You still haven't explained how you managed a lunch invitation from Mikayla."

He laughed. "Oh, yeah. When I came back from my walk, I wanted to see the seahorses, and Brandi wasn't there, but Mikayla was. I like her. She has a calm way about her. She watches the hummingbirds. Anyone who likes to watch nature is a good person in my book."

"I'd have to agree with you," she said.

"It doesn't mean you should date her."

They'd gotten to their door, and Gem paused. His statement, while said casually, grated her already thin skin. There were so many other reasons why dating Mikayla might be a bad idea, not discounting her father's insistence about not dating residents. But it wasn't up to him to tell her who she could and couldn't date. "Can I ask you why you keep bringing this up?"

His brows knitted together. "I don't keep bringing it up."

"Yes, you do, Dad. You said it the other night when I had dinner with her. And the night of the bonfire. Just a few minutes ago and again now."

He looked confused. "I don't remember those other times."

She tried to keep the irritation from her voice but couldn't help a big sigh. She opened the door, and they went inside. "It doesn't matter. She might not even date women, Dad. Not to mention, she's getting over a painful divorce and probably needs time to heal. Besides, I have my hands full and don't have the time or energy to date. We're friends. I'm allowed to have friends, aren't I?"

He put his hands on her shoulders, and she felt like a teenager again. "Of course. But I know *you*, my Angel. You're interested in her. I can also see how strongly she loves and how quickly it shifted. I don't want you to get hurt when she moves out."

His statement rushed through her like a bullet. "You're protecting *me* from being hurt?"

He stroked the side of her head. "Of course. I like Mikayla, but you're my daughter. Your heart comes first. Always."

Her eyes blurred with tears. All this time, she'd assumed his concern was for other people. "I thought you didn't want to upset residents."

"Why would you think that?"

"Because Morgan and her family and the letter I wrote to her."

He hugged her. "Oh no, honey. We were never upset with you. We were upset at them and how they reacted to an innocent declaration of love. I was wrong about them. I should never have let them live here."

A tsunami of mixed emotions rolled through her, starting with the release of pain she'd carried for years. First, the crushing disappointment she'd thought she was to her parents, and then, the belief of being responsible for the one and only time a resident had left Oceana out of anger. So much had balanced on those assumptions: damage to Oceana's otherwise perfect reputation, making it her responsibility to make sure it never happened again, and reinforcing her father's belief that the management of Oceana had to stay within the family to protect it. Her professional training and her social work practice had demonstrated time and again how the impact waves of childhood trauma influenced her clients in a myriad of ways, but she'd never applied it to herself in quite this way.

She felt the realization like a physical blow.

The thing that bothered her the most was that she had put up a barrier between her and her father that had muted his ability to see her true essence. She felt robbed of that special connection, while at the same time, she was grateful that he couldn't fully sense the tumult currently raging within her, nor the terror that his declining health caused her.

CHAPTER EIGHTEEN

Mikayla stayed up late reading, and by the time she prepared for bed, the big yawns had hit. Looking forward to sleep, she turned off all of the lights and stopped by the fish tank to say good night, as she did every evening.

Othello hadn't eaten earlier when she'd given them all snacks, so she gave him a few, but just as before, he seemed disinterested. He looked fine until he turned just right, and she noticed a tiny hole above his belly.

Concerned, she remembered reading in Brandi's books how extremely fragile seahorses were and how their skin damaged easily. With his belly distended in pregnancy, she wondered if his skin had split, or maybe one of the other seahorses had bitten him. She considered calling Rich, but it was late, and she wondered if she should wait until morning. The injury didn't appear irritated. So instead of calling, she snapped a picture and sent it to Rich and Brandi, asking if she should be concerned.

Wide awake now, she peeked down the street toward Gem's house and saw a light on the second floor and decided to call her. She'd feel awful if something happened to the seahorses on her watch.

When Gem answered, relief flooded through her. "So sorry to call you this late. Something's wrong with Othello, and I'm not sure what to do. I considered calling Rich. What if it's nothing, and

I get him worried and he comes all the way up here, and—" She stopped herself. "Would it be possible for you to come over and look at him?"

"Sure. I'm not sure I have the skills to determine if a seahorse is okay, but I'll be happy to check it."

"Thank you."

Relieved to have Gem coming over, Mikayla hung up and anxiously pulled one of the chairs closer and continued to watch the fish who, aside from Othello's wound, all appeared fine. She gnawed at her thumbnail, a habit she'd broken long ago, and took it from her mouth, sliding it under her thigh to keep from putting it right back in.

When she answered a knock on the door, Gem stood there looking casually gorgeous in basketball shorts and a threadbare University of San Diego T-shirt, indicating she had lost no time rushing over. She'd probably been in bed when Mikayla had called. The idea elicited a tremor of pleasure she didn't examine.

Gem's eyes swept down her body and back up as she stepped past. She turned almost in a circle as she caught Mikayla's gaze. "You look amazingly cute in your jammies."

"I could say the same of you."

Gem peered down and shrugged self-consciously. "The height of Oceana sleepwear this season."

Mikayla laughed because she wasn't sure what else to do. Her body reacted to Gem's presence in a way she hadn't experienced since the time she'd woken up in college and had caught her roommates, Kate and Lori, having sex in the bed across the room. The streetlight outside their dorm window had allowed Mikayla to see everything. She'd never been so turned on. It had been the most erotic moment of her life, and even now, when the need arose, she could get herself off in minutes simply by thinking about it. In fact, she'd spent most of her marriage fantasizing about that night while having sex with Craig, often finishing herself off after he'd fallen asleep because he wasn't the most attentive after he was done.

Now, with Gem in her living room looking like sex in basketball shorts, an ache of arousal pulsed through her core, tightening her nipples and igniting a ball of desire spreading throughout her body. Heat pulsed between her legs just as hot, if not hotter, than when she'd watched Kate and Lori make love, and she wondered if Gem could sense it. She definitely *saw* it, because her eyes focused on Mikayla's chest. She didn't need to look to see how her nipples made small tents in the thin fabric of her T-shirt.

After a moment of openmouthed staring, Gem turned toward the tank. "Um. Right. Othello."

Mikayla quickly joined her next to the blue-lit tank, more aware of Gem than the crisis. She pointed behind the big piece of coral among a thick patch of algae. "He's been hanging out there most of the night."

Gem walked around to the other side. "Boy, his little tummy is big. Where did you say the injury was?"

Mikayla gestured a big belly on herself and pointed to the top between her breasts. "Right here."

Gem's gaze followed her gestures and remained on her chest for a couple of seconds before she quickly redirected her gaze to the obscured form of Othello. Mikayla's pulse beat like a drum, and she tried to focus on the fish.

"I think he's getting ready to have his babies. What you described is the top of his pouch where the fry come out. Has he eaten today?"

"They're on automatic feeders, and I didn't pay close attention, but he didn't rush to the food with the others. He also ignored the last two times I gave them snacks. Normally, he's a little piggy. His color is lighter, too. More yellow than orange."

"Yeah. I think it's almost time. Did Rich tell you what to do?"

"He told me labor can last an hour or three days, and if he goes into labor to let him know. He'll come up after the babies come and separate them from the adults. He did say it was optimal if Othello gave birth in the nursery section, but he couldn't tell how long it would be or how long labor could be, and he didn't want to separate him and Desdemona. Do you think it's okay to move him now? Will it mess up his labor?"

Gem appeared to think it over. "I don't know, but I think we should move him to the nursery. I've helped Brandi during tank cleanings. Rich and Brandi scoop them up in their hands. But maybe we should use a container? We wouldn't actually be handling him, and you won't have to stay up all night waiting if they don't come until tomorrow or later."

"Sounds good to me, as long as it doesn't hurt him."

Mikayla trailed after Gem into the dark kitchen and found a clear plastic bowl. "I'm so glad you're here. I wouldn't know what to do. Rich said I could call him day or night, so I sent a text with a picture."

Gem grinned. "We can handle this. I mean, seahorses have babies in the wild all on their own, right? This isn't even Othello's first rodeo." They both washed their hands and returned to the tank, and Gem set up a folding stepladder she found tucked in a corner.

"Already, you're helping. I had no idea she stored a ladder there. I would have used a chair."

"You're easy to impress." Gem opened the top of the tank, and Othello chose to swim out from the plants. The hole above his belly had grown bigger, and he was moving in a jerky, rhythmic way. Mikayla picked up her phone and snapped a picture. "I watched some videos, and I think those are contractions. I'm sending these to Rich and Brandi."

Gem looked serious as she got ready to reach into the tank. "I never expected to become a midwife to a seahorse."

Mikayla laughed and took a picture of her, too. She looked so cute holding her arms out over the tank, like a doctor ready for surgery.

"Here goes." Gem plunged her arms into the tank as if she'd done it a million times. The tank was almost as deep as she was tall, and she ended up submerging her entire arms to get to Othello, who thankfully, wasn't all the way at the bottom. In one try, she scooped him up in the bowl and carefully released him into the nursery tank.

"Is there anything you can't do?" Mikayla asked, thoroughly impressed.

Gem laughed as she pulled her hands from the tank. "Apparently, I can't plan ahead. Otherwise, I would have had a towel ready." Still holding her dripping arms over the tank, Gem stood straighter, revealing her drenched shirt, which was now see-through. Even in just the light of the tank, it looked as if she was standing there topless, Mikayla could see her breasts in perfect detail. And when she thought perfect, she meant absolutely perfect. Small, round, pert—

"A little help here?" Gem's voice pulled her from her trance.

"Right. One towel coming up." Embarrassed for being caught staring, Mikayla ran to get a clean towel. "Here you go."

Gem took it, hugging it as she jumped off the stepladder. "You were totally checking me—"

"Oh my gosh! He's doing it. He's having babies." Mikayla couldn't contain her excitement. She moved next to Gem, and they stood shoulder to shoulder watching as Othello jerked, and a bunch of blurry little specks shot from his pouch opening. He did this over and over, and finally, his movements produced no more specks. He gave a few more, and then he slowly sank into the seagrass in the nursery tank, where he anchored himself to a stalk with his tail.

"He must be tuckered out," Gem said.

"There are so many of them. If you squint, they're miniature replicas of their mom and dad."

Gem stared back with a wide-eyed grin. "That was amazing."

Mikayla didn't think about it, she hugged Gem tightly, nearly vibrating with excitement. "I can't believe we got to watch him have the babies."

Gem's arms slipped around her, and she realized what she'd done. And she didn't care. Gem's warm body against hers woke her spirit. She molded her body to her and sank into the embrace, nuzzling her cheek against Gem's neck. She breathed in the fragrance of her hair and her skin and the overall warm scent of her.

It had been so long since she'd hugged another person like this. It made her dizzy with elation and, yes, desire coursing through her.

"I'm making your clothes wet," Gem said quietly but didn't let go.

Mikayla didn't move. "I don't care. This is nice."

Gem tightened her arms and nuzzled the side of her head.

A minute or so later, self-consciousness took hold of Mikayla, making her wonder if she should let Gem go, as much as she didn't want to. She gave a squeeze, loosened her hold, and shivered.

"Sorry," Gem said.

"It's my fault. You warned me."

Mikayla blushed as she gazed directly into Gem's lapis-colored eyes. Unable to hold Gem's gaze, she glanced down. Mikayla found it hard to breathe. She wasn't sure who reached for who first, but it didn't matter. The press of their bodies together sent an avalanche of sensations through her. She sank into Gem's arms once again, which tightened around her.

She lifted her head, singularly focused on Gem's lips and how much she wanted to kiss them. So she did. When their lips met, Mikayla couldn't believe how soft they were, how tender, how warm. And while she remembered all of her previous first kisses with others as being tentative and unsure, this kiss wasn't tentative. It wasn't unsure. They seemed to have jumped right into the kind of kiss that sent her senses reeling, her blood rushing, and certain body parts pulsing.

Mikayla buried her hands in Gem's hair and held her head as she branded a kiss upon Gem's lips, claiming them. Mikayla's body could not be her own because it already knew how to move against Gem, fit tightly into position, filling the dips and swells as if they'd kissed a million times, their unfamiliar but perfectly matched contours melding. Gem's hands moved, one to Mikayla's lower back to rock her pelvis forward and bring their lower bodies together, and the other to cup her jaw, stroking the tender skin behind Mikayla's earlobe. The teasing of that fingertip sent tingles all the way through her.

She could not get enough of Gem's mouth, her lips, and now, her tongue, the air she breathed.

Mikayla slowly and gently pulled away, dumbfounded by her ability to stand upright. Her senses were completely overwhelmed by their incredible kiss and everything it did and continued to do to her body. When she opened her eyes, she imagined that if an expression could display exactly what was going on in a person's mind and body, Gem wore it.

"It's late," Mikayla said. She had no memory of thinking those words before they tumbled from her mouth, but there they were, and Gem nodded, looking as struck as Mikayla felt.

"Way past my bedtime."

Gem handed over the towel she'd given her, what? Ten minutes ago? An hour? Three and a half days ago? And while Mikayla's lips pulsed, aching for more kisses, Gem backed out of the house, and before Mikayla could think of the words, "good night," Gem had disappeared out the door, and Mikayla stood there, holding a damp towel and wondering what just happened.

One thing for sure, she didn't have to imagine herself watching anyone have sex to make herself come that night. The sensations that flooded her body while kissing Gem were still coursing through her body, craving Gem's touch. She fell over the edge almost immediately, after which, she fell into a fitful sleep.

❖

Gem barely noticed the chill night air, nor did she take more than a distracted note of the moon hovering above the ocean, setting silver auras on the homes, flowers, and trees around her. What she did notice were the tingles of electricity still flowing across her thoroughly kissed lips and the flavor of Mikayla's mouth still lingering on her tongue. Oh, and the warm body she'd held against her, creating a longing so fierce, she'd had to leave or she would have initiated more kissing and probably some touching, which would have led to acts of undressing and—

God, her brain short-circuited at the idea of undressing Mikayla and exploring every inch of skin before diving completely into her.

Inside her house, she ran upstairs, kicked off her boots, and threw herself on her bed facedown, sinking into the soft duvet, her mouth wide open in a silent scream, her body coiled with tension from the arousal coursing through her blood.

She'd been milliseconds away from sinking to the floor with Mikayla, ready to tumble into blind ecstasy when Mikayla had broken their kiss.

God. That kiss. Never in her life had she kissed or been kissed so thoroughly, where the entire world melted away, and only Mikayla existed in her arms, the exquisite joining of their mouths transporting them to a galaxy where everything revolved around the supernova building between them. But it was more than heat and lips and arms and mouths. Her entire body was involved. Every movement rippled across her body, and where her fingertips came in contact with Mikayla, the ripple spread through her fingers and into Mikayla's soft skin. Mikayla's fingers were doing the same to her, as if they'd completed an electrical circuit when they touched, and the energy they created cycled through each other, fueling their desire.

No one kissed the way Mikayla did.

Gem hugged a pillow, allowing her memory to sweep her away with thoughts of kissing Mikayla again.

CHAPTER NINETEEN

Despite having gone to bed later than usual and forgetting to set her alarm, Gem woke the next morning at six twenty-six, her accustomed time to wake up, four minutes before her alarm. But instead of bounding out of bed like she normally did, she lay there thinking about kisses and seahorses, both of which had taken over her dreams the night before. She let herself float in the sweet comfort of those dreams for several minutes before she rose, and when she did, she had far more energy than she should have had for a person who'd gotten less than five and a half hours of restless sleep.

Before she turned on her bedroom light, she peeked out the window at Mikayla's place. The lights were on, and Gem's stomach fluttered to find Mikayla sitting at the dining room table, holding a cup of coffee. From the distance, Gem wondered if she'd also had trouble sleeping and if her dreams consisted of the out-of-this-world kiss they'd shared. Did Mikayla keep reliving the kiss like she did? Did she hope for more? Did she crave the response of her body?

Gem tried to conjure how Mikayla had looked when they'd said good night.

It hit her. She'd simply left. No good night. No see you soon. Just an exit.

What did Mikayla think had happened? Was she thinking Gem had run away?

She'd never simply left before. It was so unlike her to run from anything. Hindsight told her it hadn't been the best choice, and now she felt a little sick to her stomach wondering what Mikayla might be thinking. In her defense, she couldn't find words, and something told her if she'd stayed without any words, they might have done something they would have questioned in the morning. She wouldn't have regretted it, but a kiss like that deserved some time to settle, a little room to marinate. A kiss like that was explosive and dangerous and required careful handling. She didn't have words for what had happened, merely emotions and sensations surging through her when she remembered.

Gem couldn't pry her eyes away from Mikayla, and her heart nearly beat out of her chest when Mikayla adjusted her gaze slightly so it appeared she looked her way, and a physical sensation swept through Gem when their eyes met. With sunrise still over an hour away, the darkness of Gem's room and the deep gloom outside probably made that impossible, yet Gem couldn't move. The unyielding gaze held her in place until Mikayla sat up slightly, her posture relaxed, and she resumed her previous pose, eyes on the ocean, cup between her hands, elbows on the table. The very definition of pensive.

Gem wished she knew what Mikayla was thinking.

The knock on the door wasn't a surprise. Mikayla had watched Gem leave her place and head toward her house. She wasn't sure Gem would come after what had happened. A thin thread of panic bloomed within her. What would they talk about? The kiss? She'd been thinking about it since it happened, but she wasn't sure if she could talk about it.

She was glad she'd changed out of her pajamas and into leggings and a gauzy, oversized button-up with a white tank top underneath. Thinking about pajamas, she remembered the see-through shirt Gem had worn the night before, and a tremor ran through her. Now, as she sat at the table, she steadied herself before rising to answer the door.

What would she say to the woman who'd unleashed such a tumult of desire in her?

"Good morning," Gem said with her usual tone and expression, friendly and warm, saving her from making the first coherent sentence between them since the kiss that could melt steel.

Something else lurked there, something simmering beneath Gem's calm exterior. Mikayla might have been imagining it. She caught a hint of…she wasn't sure. Was it expectation? Not exactly the right word but close enough.

"Good morning. I wasn't sure if I'd see you today. I definitely didn't expect you so early, what with how late we were up."

"My internal clock is set at six thirty on weekdays. It doesn't matter how late I stay up. I saw your lights on," Gem said and glanced at the tank. "I wanted to help move Othello back to the main tank before he starts to eat his young."

"I moved him this morning. Seeing you do it gave me confidence. It went off without a hitch."

"I have no reason to be wearing my swimsuit under my clothes, then?"

The joke released some of the tension wrapped around Mikayla's chest as uncertainty, confusion, and arousal continued to battle within her. Nothing was as strong as her desire. Now that it had been freed, it consumed her.

She gestured to the tank, hoping all of her emotions weren't nakedly displayed on her face. "Don't let me keep you from taking a dunk."

"I'm just kidding. That's not what I'm here for."

Mikayla's heart skipped a beat until she noticed Gem holding up a to-go mug. Disappointment sucked every bit of oxygen from the room. "One cup of coffee, coming up," she said, turning toward the kitchen.

"Wait." Gem's voice stopped her, but the hand on her wrist spun her around and into Gem's arms again. The kiss from last night did not compare to the eruption of sensation Mikayla experienced with kiss number two. Short and not the least bit sweet, the kiss insinuated sexy activities, if only they weren't fully clothed, and its brevity did nothing to limit how tantalizing it would be if only they remedied the clothing problem. When Gem let go, Mikayla's body reacted as if she'd stepped in front of a speeding train, and Gem had pulled her back. Her adrenaline raced, her heart hammered in her chest, and she questioned how kisses could render her unable to think.

Trying to regain her bearings, she caught the tail end of something Gem said to her.

"Huh?" she asked. Not, "Can you please repeat what you said?" or "Pardon me?" or "I'm sorry, I am having a hard time hearing you because it seems all the blood in my body has moved to one central location, rendering my ears useless. Please repeat what you said or kiss me again." None of that. Just "Huh?" Apparently, this was what a short-circuited brain did.

"I said, I wanted to make one thing clear," Gem said.

"Clear?" Maybe not short-circuited, perhaps broken.

"About last night."

"Last night?" Beyond repair.

"I left kind of suddenly. I should have waited to make sure we were on the same page. I should have checked in and asked how you felt about it. One minute, we were doing seahorse things, and the next, we were kissing and it…it…I can't explain it. I liked it, and I wanted to do it again, but instead of saying any of this, I kissed you again and—"

Mikayla put a hand over Gem's mouth. Still reeling from the kiss, her words continued to escape her, but she knew exactly how to respond to Gem's rapid-fire summary of what had just happened.

She slid her hand to Gem's cheek and kissed her again. This time, she went slow. She leaned in incrementally. First, she slid her arms around Gem and felt the same; then, she pressed closer, and Gem pressed right back, her abdomen flattening against Mikayla's, their hips and thighs…all the way to Mikayla's bare toes resting on the firm toe of Gem's boots. Mikayla slowly and deliberately kissed her. While this kiss still filled her body with arousal so strong it stole her breath, she found a desire to do more than consume Gem. She wanted to make it very obvious how extremely okay the kiss from the night before had been. And the one a few minutes ago. Even the one now. More importantly, she wanted to make it abundantly clear that she wanted more kisses. An endless parade.

Only a lack of oxygen could part their mouths, and when Mikayla pulled back ever so slightly to gaze into Gem's eyes and see if she'd effectively communicated what she needed to, it seemed she had, at least as far as Mikayla could discern from the half-lidded, soft gaze and goofy grin Gem wore. It seemed they might be on the same page. She still couldn't make her words work, but she could kiss, so she did. There was nothing broken about their kisses.

After Mikayla made coffee, they sat at the table, the corner of which separated them, and half faced each other as they gazed through the window in the dining area. Their knees pressed together under the table, Mikayla's right knee to Gem's left, and a world of sensation flowed through them.

They quietly drank coffee, the light in the sky gradually growing brighter. Gem had things to do today, but she wasn't ready to leave yet.

She turned toward the tank. "How many babies do you—"

"You're the first woman I've kissed."

Gem turned her gaze on Mikayla. She wasn't surprised by her declaration. After all, she'd just gotten out of a long-term marriage with a man.

Mikayla stared at her cup as she put it on the table and sat back. She shoved her hair back and crossed her arms, uncrossed them, crossed them again, and then pushed her hands under her thighs.

A few responses went through Gem's mind. Mikayla was going through something, and Gem wasn't about to ignore how kissing a woman for the first time could be a major event for anyone, let alone a woman who'd been married quite recently to a man. Gem had no doubt that if she ever found herself attracted to a man, she'd question the shit out of it. And that was probably what Mikayla was doing. Gem wished she wasn't a therapist for once because the last thing she wanted to do was spoil the crazy wild feelings she was experiencing by analyzing them. But here she was, flipped upside down, inside out, and every way to Tuesday. In other words, overwhelmed.

"Tell me what's going on in your head," she said.

"Just what I said. You're the first woman I've kissed. It's a fact. I'm not particularly surprised. I imagined kissing you the day you fixed the shower. I think the thing getting me worked up is how fucking incredible it was. I mean, damn, talk about toe-curling, mind-blowing, staggering, and ridiculously amazing kisses. There are feelings going on inside me lacking sufficient definition to describe them. I'm sitting here on my hands because all I want is to do it again. I can't begin to describe what kissing you does to my body. It's metaphysical. Astounding. Truly stupefying. You reduce me to trembling liquid."

Gem absorbed her words, even the curse words she'd never expected, but which were like bolts of electricity for their unexpectedness. All the overthinking she'd been doing in the past seven hours…had it been more? Time had become elastic, depending on what emotion bombarded her. All the overthinking was ludicrous. Toe-curling? Metaphysical? Trembling liquid? She wanted Mikayla to get off her hands. Express that poetry with a kiss.

It took everything to remain where she was, her knee against Mikayla's, pressing more firmly with each word. However, the visible parts of her hopefully appeared calm. "You're not alone. I feel it, too, although I couldn't find those perfect words for it. It's like my first time all over again." Gem studied Mikayla's face. She appeared to be barely holding herself together. Was it the surprise and newness? Possibly fear? Or was something deeper going on? "Are you okay?" The question sounded insufficient and weak. "I mean, obviously, you're processing. It's a lot to deal with. Can I help?"

Mikayla's eyes softened. "Believe me, you're helping me want to do it again. And again. And maybe again. Definitely again."

Gem dipped her head. "I'll assume that's good."

"Oh, very good. Very, *very* good."

"Is it? Or am I stirring things up? It's okay to say so. You stir me up, and you aren't the first woman I've kissed."

"I'd already guessed as much. You are an amazing kisser."

"Thank you. If I'm amazing, you are infinitely amazing." Gem's body grew hot thinking about it.

The corner of Mikayla's mouth twitched as if she was about to say something, but she dropped her eyes. For someone who gave great eye contact, it was unusual.

"What?" Gem asked.

"Just thinking about your kisses is making me a little lightheaded. I experience new and incredible things when I'm kissing you. Things with no adequate description."

Gem realized she sat on her own hands now, unconsciously mirroring Mikayla's posture, slightly leaned forward, shoulders a little hunched, almost as if they were trying desperately not to do something they very much wanted to do. Interestingly, their faces were only inches apart now, and all Gem had to do was—

Mikayla's mouth pressed against hers. With nothing other than their mouths engaged, the experience was even more sensual, more intense. Every bit of concentration was directed toward the soft, sensitive flesh of their mouths. No hands moving to distract them, no breasts heaving to think about, no body heat to divert them. Gem took in every detail. Mikayla's plump lips, the bottom slightly larger than the upper. The corners of her mouth, where the soft skin of her lips met the slick skin of the inner cheek. The warm tongue, at once exploring and inviting, a tantalizing host and visitor. Gem gently bit Mikayla's lower lip, sucking it into her mouth, eliciting a soft whimper as Mikayla pressed more firmly into her, telling Gem she liked it. Gem nibbled her lip for a few seconds and released it, gently licking the places where her teeth had been. This time, a moan flowed from Mikayla's throat, a deep, impassioned sound that drew out, tickling the places where their mouths barely touched.

Needing more, Gem leaned in, and the motion made her chair slide the other way, which abruptly ended the kiss. They both blew out sounds of frustration before they realized what had happened, and the frustration turned to laughter.

Mikayla's gaze bored into Gem. "I could probably kiss you for several hours."

Gem wanted to take her up on it, but the kisses would most certainly turn to other things real fast. Her mind tried to figure out how to push her morning work off until the afternoon.

A knock sounded at the door.

Mikayla didn't react like she noticed. Her eyes were on Gem's mouth, and she looked as if she wanted to pick up where they'd left off.

"Someone's at the door," Gem said.

"Huh?" Mikayla seemed confused and shook her head. "Rich, maybe? I sent pictures to him and Brandi last night. Brandi's beyond excited, by the way. A little bummed to have missed the event. The birth, not the kiss. I didn't tell her about that."

Another knock sounded, and Mikayla answered the door while Gem pulled her seat back into place and remained sitting. Her coffee was cold now. A glance at her watch told her she'd already missed meeting with Devon at seven thirty. He didn't call, which meant things were okay.

Mikayla let Rich in, and they stood on the other side of the tank for a few minutes, talking about the birth and how the babies were doing. Gem used the time to pull herself together. She chuckled, thinking it wasn't only Mikayla who needed to process things.

Gem had it bad. Like, really bad. Unable to be alone with her thoughts with the object of her desire so near, she got up and met

Rich as he came around to the back of the tank. "Hey, Rich," she said.

"Oh, hey, Gem. I hear you finally got to see a birth."

"I did. It was amazing."

Rich focused on the tank. All business, he climbed the stepladder and took the lid off the nursery side, glancing down. "Ah. They're a bit bunched up. I'm going to feed them and take them back with me."

"I noticed the bunching. You said not to handle them, so I left them alone," Mikayla said.

He nodded. "They get a little confused and will try to anchor to anything, including each other. They stop soon enough, but if you don't get them un-bunched, they'll starve."

Gem moved closer to the nursery tank. "Brandi usually keeps them here for a few weeks."

Rich placed a net bag in the water with a few frozen cubes in it. It floated on the surface, and as the cubes melted, tiny particles started drifting from it, and the babies slurped them up. The bunched ones started to detach, and Rich gently helped a few others separate. "They're pretty high-maintenance for the first month to six weeks. Brandi and I decided it would be best if I took them all down to Scripps." He studied the little fish. "This is a healthy bunch. I'd say there are thirteen or fourteen hundred and not too many expired. A good number."

Gem turned to Mikayla. "This will probably take a little time." She glanced at Rich, who intently observed the seahorses. "I have to get to work. I'd like to continue our conversation later if it's something you'd like to do."

Mikayla looked disappointed. "I would. Very much. Do you want to come over after work? I can make dinner."

They made plans, and Gem said good-bye to both Mikayla and Rich, wondering how she would get through her day without doing something stupid because of her distraction.

CHAPTER TWENTY

A couple of hours later, after Rich collected the fry and took care of the maintenance on the tank, he left with all the geeky science intensity he'd arrived with. The day creeped by quietly, allowing Mikayla to float in a dreamy fog, her thoughts anchored on Gem, her kisses, and the warmth of her body. Lost in a tumble of sensations holding her mind and body captive, she sat at the table and replayed every moment of every kiss. For once, she appreciated her habit of overanalyzing because it allowed her to remember every sexy detail.

Mikayla floated in a cloud of anticipation and impatience, waiting to see Gem again. She tried to figure out what to do with all of the time until then. She picked up her phone and sent a text: *I can't wait for dinner tonight.* She didn't usually use emojis, but she sent an emoji with stars in its eyes.

She'd barely hit send before Gem responded, and a little bubble of excitement popped in Mikayla's stomach: *Me either. Should I bring anything?* Followed by a bunch of flowers, a bottle of wine, and a question mark.

Just yourself. And maybe the outfit you were wearing last night. She hesitated before she sent an emoji with the eyes popping out.

Shorts and a tank? O wait. I see what you did. A little devil emoji followed.

Mikayla typed out a variety of responses of varying degrees of salaciousness but deleted each one before she sent: *You have no idea. Tell me about food preferences-limitations.* The emojis were getting her a little worked up, so she didn't send one this time.

O I have some idea. Followed by a winky face and a pause while the dancing ellipsis indicated she had more to say: *No limitations and I currently have a certain craving.* A kiss emoji. More dancing ellipsis. *I'm easy to please and sure anything you make or do will make me happy.* A little angel emoji.

Mikayla guessed she wasn't talking about food. *Those are high expectations. I'll figure something out and hope you'll enjoy it.* She wanted to add a million kiss emojis, but she didn't.

I'll be happy with stale bread and a glass of tap water as long as you're there. A simple smiley face this time.

Sweet talker. Now get back to work. I have shopping to do. She added a grocery cart only because she'd seen it when looking for the previous emojis.

Laughing, she washed their cups and grabbed her keys, phone, and wallet before she headed out the door. She'd no sooner turned the car on and backed out than her phone rang, the caller ID displaying Craig's name. A flash of irritation went through her, and she let the call go to voice mail. He was the last person she wanted to talk to right now or any other time, if she was honest with herself. She wanted to float on the high of whatever was happening between her and Gem, not be the object of guilt-driven check-ins from her ex-husband. She'd asked for a break, and the call violated that boundary. Irritated, she rolled down the window of her car, found an upbeat song on her satellite radio, and cranked it up.

The short drive landed her in the parking lot of the store when the phone rang again, this time with Ashe on the caller ID. She popped her earbuds in and answered as she walked toward the door. "Well, if it isn't Ashe the Flash," she answered, using a childhood nickname.

"What's it to you, Mik the Stick?" her sister replied as she had so many times when they were children, although it had been years since she'd last said it.

"That brings up memories."

"You're telling me. It just came out like I've said it every day since we were kids." Ashe's voice sounded nostalgic. "How's it going, Sis?"

"Good, actually. How about you?"

"Still waiting for the gallery to tell me if I made the summer schedule. I've been thinking if they don't pick me up, I might go out to the UK and hang out with Brandi for the duration of her gig out there. I could use a reboot of my creative engine."

"You'd pick up and move to England? What about your job?"

"It's jobs, Mik. With an S. One's a shitty job doing face painting for a second-rate amusement park, and the other is not as shitty but still shitty, tearing concert tickets and stamping hands at the Tavern. There are a million other jobs like those. I've saved a little from a few pieces I sold. I need a change of scenery. Brandi said she'd love it if I came out there. She's a little homesick, and I love it over there. I'm just thinking about it. We'll see how the gallery thing goes."

Mikayla was used to her sister's wandering ways. In fact, she was surprised she'd stayed in San Diego as long as she had. Going on three years, she'd been there longer than most places. "Have you told Mom yet?"

"Hell, no. Not until I decide for sure. Enough about me. Tell your crazy ex to stop calling me. He thinks I'm some sort of Mikayla Duncan news source."

"Pierce. I switched back in the divorce."

"Whatevs. He said you aren't answering his calls."

"He called once. Just minutes ago. He knows why I don't answer. What did he want?"

"Just to hear how you're doing. I think he thinks you're languishing in your heartache."

"What did you tell him?"

"I told him you were frolicking in the Caymans with Rodolfo."

"Tell me you didn't. Actually, I don't care what you told him. It's none of his business."

"You're damn right it isn't. I told him to wait until you were ready to take his calls. He pressed, but I didn't say anything at all about you. He seemed frustrated."

Mikayla blew out an exasperated sigh. "Is that all you two spoke about?"

"I don't speak Wall Street, and he doesn't speak human, so we had nothing else to say."

"You didn't cuss him out again, did you?"

"Does one word count as cussing? Because I might have said something about him being a myopic piece of shit for divorcing a woman who was better than anything he would ever find again and how you were blessed to be rid of him."

Mikayla pinched the bridge of her nose and barked out a laugh, startling the woman standing next to her near the tomatillos in the produce section. "Thank you for always being on my side."

"You're welcome. You sound different."

"What do you mean? I'm in the grocery store, so I'm trying not to be the person who broadcasts their conversations."

"Nope. There's something different. Something not all Eeyore about you. You sound almost…happy?"

"What are you trying to say?"

"I'm not *trying* to say anything. I *am* saying you sound happy. Are you, my sister, happy, perchance?"

"As a matter of fact, I am. I think the change of scenery has been good for me. I feel better. Lighter." She wasn't about to tell her sister about Gem, at least not yet. Ashe had a habit of making too much out of things, and she wasn't ready to deal with it.

"You deserve some lightness in your life. It sounds good on you." Thankfully, Ashe didn't dig deeper. It would probably come later, but for now, Ashe let it go, and Mikayla enjoyed her new happiness.

"I have to go now. I'm at the checkout, and I refuse to be the kind of person who stays on their phone, ignoring the cashier."

They rang off, and Mikayla paid for the makings of dinner, a bunch of fresh flowers, and a bottle of wine.

Two hours later, Mikayla sang along to Dua Lipa and checked on the *puerco con chile* simmering on the stovetop when there was a knock on the door. She wiped her hands on a dishtowel and answered, thinking it had to be Gem. Her happy expectation faded when she found Craig standing on the porch.

"Hello, Mickie. I was in the neighborhood so..." He let the sentence fade, obviously waiting for her to invite him in. He craned his neck to see into the house through the screen door. When his eyes met hers again, he raised his eyebrows, and she couldn't help it, she fell into her old hostess mode and opened the door. Shock at seeing him on her doorstep rendered her speechless.

He only took a couple of steps inside the threshold, which crowded her as she latched the screen. She had to shrink to get around him, and she nearly screamed from the literal parallel to their old life. He lifted his arms as if to hug her and then dropped them, slipping his hands into his pockets when she didn't walk into them. His blond hair hung over his eyes, causing him to toss his head to move it to the side, and his skin was bronzed and tan, making him appear a decade younger than his fifty-one years. He'd always been attractive, one of the fortunate men who kept getting better looking as he aged. She'd always considered it appealing how he seemed not to notice, and he actually didn't. He'd often made comments about wanting to be more like men much different than him, as if his California frat-boy looks were unappealing and weak. However, he'd never sunk to self-deprecation, and she'd disagreed. His unassuming and genuine personality were attractive.

But none of it affected her like it used to. There was none of the longing that had plagued her for the last six months. The effect was both a revelation and a letdown but mostly a relief. A tightness she'd been holding in her chest seemed to break free.

"It looks like a normal house on the inside," he said, gazing around. "Bigger than it does on the outside. I've never been in a trailer home before."

"Mobile home," she corrected, slipping away to turn down the music.

"It's colorful. I love the fish tank. Are those seahorses? Did you know the males carry the babies? I think they call them ponies."

She didn't bother to correct him. "I'm subletting from a friend." She didn't want to tell him Ashe had introduced her to Brandi. He'd dismiss Brandi as frivolous, like he'd always done to Ashe, something she'd never noticed before she'd started to spend more time with her sister after she'd moved back to San Diego. He'd dismissed her as flakey and irresponsible, which she was, but only Mikayla had the right to say such things. "How did you find out where I live?"

He pushed the hair on his forehead back. "You ask as if you were trying to keep it a secret."

"It's not a secret. But I didn't tell you, so I wonder who did."

"Deirdre."

"My mom?" Typical. Her mother liked Craig better than she liked either of her daughters.

"Why do you sound so incredulous, Mickie?" He sounded truly surprised.

"I told you I needed time and space. But you're calling and talking to my mom and sister, and now you're here. I am a little surprised. You're usually more respectful."

"I respect you more than anyone I know, Mik." He appeared truly concerned by what she'd said. Craig had always been a what-you-see-is-what-you-get person. "I'll bet Ashe called you as soon as we hung up. She wasn't very pleasant to me. I don't blame her. You have no idea the guilt I carry. I only called her because I had a weird feeling you weren't doing well. I would never have come here otherwise."

"I'm doing fine."

He peered around again. "Are you sure? This is one of the last places I imagined you'd be, not when you have more than enough to make you comfortable. I couldn't believe it when I googled it. Your mom thinks it's a spa or something. The name Oceana has that vibe. I didn't correct her. I don't want her to worry about your state of mind."

"State of mind?"

"You haven't been yourself." He sighed and sat on the arm of one of the living room chairs. "It's my fault. I admit it. My selfishness upended your life and—"

"We've been over this. You hate how your happiness is at odds with my happiness, but it's not up to you to fix, Craig. I can handle it."

"By moving to a trailer park?"

"Mobile home community," she countered once again.

"Call it a seaside resort, but this is a far cry from La Jolla, Mik. You can see why I'm worried, right?"

"I never took you for a snob, Craig. I expect it from my mother. I like it here. I've met all my neighbors. Aside from cursory waves, I never met a single one where we lived for twelve years."

"I'm not saying this is a bad place. In fact, it seems safe and not at all what I pictured of a trai…mobile home park. I have this specific image about these places. I think most people do."

"It's a mobile home *community*."

"Same difference."

She decided it wasn't worth it to argue. "Well, you've seen it. I'm safe. I like it here. I'm still trying to figure out what my next steps are, and I'd like to do it among the people I've met here than behind iron gates and ten-foot walls. It's nice to be a part of a community. I find it very…healing." A picture of Gem's face right before they kissed was emblazoned on her mind.

"Well, at least there's that."

"Last I knew, you were in Mexico." She wondered if he'd come back for this.

"I love it there, but I guess like you, I have a hard time with the isolation."

Before, she might have wondered where isolation came in if Carmen was there with him, but it wasn't her business, and she honestly didn't care, which was a nice change.

"Are you back for good or a visit? By back, I mean in California, not here, *here*," she emphasized.

"I'm staying in the rental in our old neighborhood. I'm not sure where I want to settle. It's strange not being tethered. It's lonely."

He seemed to be dropping hints. About what, she didn't know. Or care. "What about Carmen?"

"It's complicated. I think I jumped into a relationship too quickly after us. We're still seeing each other. It's casual, though. I have room to figure things out." She couldn't help being curious, but she wasn't going to ask. He seemed to sense her discomfort, and he chuckled. "You know what I miss?" Afraid of what he'd say, she shook her head. "Your coffee. I've watched you make it for years. It never comes out the same when I make it."

"Would you like a cup?" she asked, regretting it because it would keep him there longer.

"I hoped you'd ask."

The eager expression on his face tugged at her heart. It reminded her of all the times he'd been excited about something or engaged in whatever they'd been doing, whether they were in a new city, going to a museum, or just watching a new television show. He had a gift for being fully present and fully himself. He'd never been anything else, as painful as it could be at times, like when he'd let her know her inadequate uterus didn't factor into his life plan. As much as she wanted to be free of the complicated emotions of the past several months, being reminded of why she'd loved him gave her some peace. She could say good-bye to the pieces of her that she had to leave behind.

It wasn't particularly revelatory. More like an acceptance of her feelings for Craig, which were probably never going to be fully understood and would never go back to what they once were. She could continue to love him without wishing to remain married to him. With that, her impatience and any of the annoyance accompanying his appearance at her door mostly disappeared. It would be nice to have coffee with him. She didn't expect Gem for another hour or so, and she'd still have time to finish making dinner.

"I'll make it."

"Do you happen to have a throne for me to sit on?"

She rolled her eyes. It was code for when he had to go to the bathroom, and it wasn't the standing up kind. She pointed him to the guest bath and went to make coffee. As she stirred vanilla into the cups, a light tap at the door drew her attention.

Gem's presence automatically filled her with excitement, which only increased when Gem stepped in, wrapped her in her arms, and kissed her. The kiss reignited all the heat from earlier. Mikayla forgot everything as she melted.

The muffled flush reminded her about Craig, and she mustered all her will to step away. She gave Gem an apologetic smile when the bathroom door opened.

"Hey, Mik, I used the last of the toilet paper."

"Craig dropped by for a surprise visit," she said quietly and headed toward the bathroom, passing Craig and barely suppressing a glare at him. She fixed the toilet paper situation and hurried back to the front room to introduce Gem but found Craig already with his hand held out.

"Craig," he said. "Mikayla's husband."

"Ex-husband," Mikayla said.

He ducked his head. "Ex-husband. Sorry, habit."

Gem took his hand. "Gem. Mikayla's neighbor…friend. I'm her neighbor-friend."

"Nice to meet you, Mikayla's neighbor-friend." He pumped Gem's hand once.

Mikayla backed into the kitchen. "I'm making coffee."

Gem followed. "Um…I'm early. I finished work, so I came by. I could come back later."

Mikayla wished she could explain Craig's unexpected visit. "Stay. Dinner will be ready in about an hour. We can have coffee while it cooks." Mikayla didn't wait for Gem to say yes; she just started fixing her a cup. "So you got off work early. How was your day?"

Gem walked into the kitchen. Mikayla's anxiety lowered quite a bit just being near her. When she gazed into Gem's eyes, she remembered kissing her just minutes ago. "We're finally done with weaving the bougainvillea through the new trellises."

"That's great," Mikayla said. "I can't wait to see it."

Craig leaned against the island counter on her other side, pushing his hands into his pockets. His closeness annoyed Mikayla as he peered over her head at Gem. "So you're in landscaping?"

"I do a lot of things. Today, I did landscaping. Tomorrow, I'll be installing skirting on some units in the back. I'm the property manager for Oceana."

"Sounds like a lot of hard work," he said.

"Her family owns the park, and she's helping her father out. She's also a social worker. There's nothing she can't do." Mikayla handed Gem a cup, sneaking her a private wink.

Gem winked back, and the gleam in her eyes returned. "Thanks." She sipped it and nodded.

Craig took a cup from the two left on the counter, and Mikayla might have imagined it, but he looked irritated when she didn't hand him the first cup, as she always used to do as a little sign of affection when they had guests over. "She's always made the best coffee," he said before taking a sip. "Speaking of, I stopped in at the café at the club and ran into Libby, Renee, and Trish. They wanted me to tell you they miss you and would love for you to come down for doubles. You're still on the membership."

He had never cared for her tennis partners. Bringing them and the club membership up was a power play, she guessed. She wondered if he sensed something between her and Gem. The idea almost made her chortle, and she was not a chortler. "I'll send them a text," she said.

"If you're interested in coming, the charity golf tournament is next weekend. Carmen doesn't golf, so I could use a partner. Your name is already on the roster since I registered us last year at the post-tournament banquet."

She gave him a long look and hoped he picked up on her displeasure. "I think I'll pass."

Gem remained unusually quiet, and Mikayla wouldn't blame her for being uncomfortable. It didn't help that Craig kept bringing up things about their past life.

"Why don't you two take a seat at the table? I'll get some chips and salsa." She lifted the lid of the pan and stirred the simmering food.

"Do I smell *puerco con chile?*" Craig asked.

"You do." She replaced the top on the pan, rinsed the spoon she'd used to stir, and laid it back on the counter before getting a bowl for the chips.

"It's one of her best dishes. I used to beg her to make it all the time," Craig said to Gem.

Mikayla peeked at Gem, who winked at her, telling her she was good with the weirdness.

"I'll send some home for you and Carmen," she offered as she sat at the table next to Gem. They were in the same places they'd been that morning, and she pressed her knee to Gem's, seeking out their connection.

"Carmen is still down in Ensenada. She decided to invite a few girlfriends down. She'll be back up next Monday. I'd be happy to stay for dinner. I don't have anything going on."

Mikayla tried to think of a way to respond without being rude. A lifetime of being uncomfortable so others were not almost won. No. She wasn't going to do it. She'd been looking forward to dinner with Gem all day, and she wasn't going to give it up because Craig had showed up unannounced. In fact, he'd been the rude one for inviting himself to dinner.

"I'll send you home with some, Craig. Gem and I have dinner plans."

Empowering. That was how it felt to not care more about Craig's feelings than her own. She'd accepted it as part of her role as his wife and her mother's daughter, but wife no longer defined her.

CHAPTER TWENTY-ONE

Gem cleared the coffee cups, rinsed them, and left them to dry beside the sink. She enjoyed handwashing dishes. It helped her think. And right then, it gave her time to think about the little glimpses into Mikayla's life she'd gotten in the brief time Craig had been there. He'd mentioned tennis clubs, charity events, London houses, Mexico houses, his Porsche, her BMW. How could a woman accustomed to those things be happy living in a trailer park?

"I am so sorry about Craig." Mikayla came in after seeing him out. "He dropped by, and I asked him to leave, and somehow, he talked me into making coffee, and then you got here, and all I wanted was for him to leave. Ugh." Mikayla leaned heavily against the counter.

Gem took her hands. "If you're worried about me, don't be. Are *you* okay? It sounds like you were dealing with a lot internally. Should I have left? Would it have been easier for you?"

Mikayla pulled her hands from Gem's and cradled her face. "You were invited. Not him. I'm glad you stayed." Mikayla gave her a kiss. "I don't know if I'm technically okay, but I'm so much better now with him gone and you here. I'm just a little scattered at the moment. I wanted to have dinner all put together before you got here so we could enjoy a glass of wine while it finished cooking. Now it's all out of sync."

Gem glanced around the kitchen. In addition to two pots on the stove, a bag of flour sat next to a bag of rice on the counter. "Tell me what you have going on here. What do we have to finish making? Rice? Were you planning to make tortillas?" She washed her hands.

"The puerco con chile can keep simmering, along with the black beans. So, yes, some cilantro and lemon rice and tortillas."

Gem rolled up her shirt sleeves. "It just so happens, I'm quite the tortilla maker. So why don't I whip up the dough while you pour us some wine and turn up the music?"

Mikayla appeared unsure. "I'm supposed to be making *you* dinner."

Gem chuckled. "Making dinner is a family affair. At least, it always has been in our house."

While Mikayla opened the wine, Gem pulled out the wooden cutting board and spilled out a small mound of flour and rubbed it over the surface. She then piled flour onto the middle of it and circled her finger in the top of it to make a crater. She sprinkled a little baking powder and salt into it and started to pour a little water, folding the flour over it and mixing it up into first a paste and then a dough as all of the flour got mixed in.

"You don't happen to have a little lard, do you?" Gem asked as she kneaded the small mound.

"I use olive oil."

"So much better for you. Damn those trans fats." Gem shook her flour-covered fist and laughed. She mixed a couple of splashes of olive oil into the dough, continuing to knead until the consistency was right. After which, she formed it into a mound and left it on the board to rest for a few minutes.

"I like how you did it directly on the board without measuring cups or anything," Mikayla said, handing her a dishtowel after Gem washed the flour from her hands.

"Why dirty more dishes? My mom always did it this way. She'd sing a little thing about it that goes through my mind every time I make them. I've made so many tortillas, I could do it in my sleep. It's more about how the dough feels than about the perfect measures of ingredients, anyway."

"What's the song?"

Gem clapped her hands in time with the lyrics:

"Make a little mountain.

Poke a little hole.

For a great tortilla.

Without a dirty bowl."

Mikayla was clapping along by the end with a gleeful bounce. Gem enjoyed sharing a happy memory from childhood. She took the cast iron skillet from the hanging rack above the kitchen sink and put it on the stovetop. Next to her, Mikayla put water and rice into the pot and turned the flame on, then set a timer. Gem leaned against the kitchen island and accepted a glass of petite Syrah. They tapped the rims of their glasses together and took a sip, after which, Mikayla put her glass on the counter, doing the same with Gem's.

Gem watched her with amusement. "Why do I get the sense you plan to do something to me?"

"Because I do. Turns out, I get crushes on tortilla chefs who sing." Mikayla put her hands on the counter on either side of Gem. "I find it makes me quite happy and...other things."

Mikayla moved her face slowly closer; her eyes pierced Gem's, who held her breath, waiting for Mikayla to kiss her. Instead, Mikayla put a finger on Gem's lips and watched as she slowly traced the contours. The contact sent sparks throughout Gem's entire being, and she fought against wrapping her arms around Mikayla to pull her closer.

Mikayla's mouth curved into a half-smile. "You have perfectly defined lips. The round sweep of your lower lip and the perfect arches of your upper. They're soft, so very, exquisitely soft. So warm and full." She sounded and looked a little dazed. Gem could barely breathe. "I've been thinking about them all day." As she said the last, she pressed her lips against Gem's.

For a few seconds, Mikayla's lips and fingers teased her, and when Mikayla opened her mouth, gently pressing her tongue forward, fingertips brushing the skin, the fingers were withdrawn, and they were kissing deeply, wrapping their arms around one another, their torsos pressed breast to breast. Gem inhaled, breathing Mikayla's air and molded herself to her.

Gem switched their positions to have Mikayla against the counter and slid a leg between hers, trying to get closer. The heat of Mikayla's center rested on her bare thigh, and Gem grazed the skin along Mikayla's thigh until a shiver ran through both of them. Mikayla moaned into Gem's mouth and surged into her, and they were grasping at one another, moving in a sort of rhythm. Gem slid her hands under the bottom edge of Mikayla's shirt and flattened them against her back, relishing the soft planes and the warmth of Mikayla's skin. She imagined running her hands all over, letting her desire mount—

The timer on the stove started to ding.

Reluctantly, Gem disentangled herself before she ended the kiss, and when their lips were no longer together, she finally opened her eyes. The sight of Mikayla, breathless and flushed, eyes hooded and unfocused, became the most erotic thing she had ever seen. Her center pulsed as Mikayla ran her fingers through her hair.

"Holy shit." Mikayla's voice, low, almost a growl, caused another pulse to cascade through Gem. When their eyes met again, Gem mustered every bit of control not to turn off the stove and lead Mikayla to the nearest bed.

She pulled a hand down her face, tearing her gaze from Mikayla's, and spun toward the annoying sound of the timer and turned it off. "Okay, what do we have here?" Her voice was tight, so she cleared her throat. She checked the rice, covered it, and turned the flame to a low simmer, barely aware of her actions, the awareness of Mikayla behind her stealing most of her attention. She focused on the food, lighting the flame under the skillet because if she looked at Mikayla, things might start up again, and her hunger no longer focused on food but the woman who moved around her, ran a hand across her shoulders, and hummed along with the song on the radio, the woman who distracted her more than she'd ever been distracted before.

Gem held the counter and took a moment to breathe before pinching off pieces of the rested dough and rolling them into balls before smashing them flat into six-inch disks. She didn't have a rolling pin, so she used a floured drinking glass. She tossed the flattened disc into the heated pan and kept an eye on it as she rolled out the second one. With the second flattened, she waited for a few air bubbles to form in the first, flipped it with her fingers, and tossed the second one next to it. She made a dozen tortillas in about fifteen minutes, just when the rice timer chimed.

Mikayla stirred the puerco con chile and beans, set the table, moved their wine, then moved behind Gem at the stove, loosely wrapping her arms around her waist and peering over her shoulder.

The embrace distracted her but in a very good way. She relished the heat of Mikayla's body against and the occasional nuzzle on her neck. She was disappointed when the last tortilla came out of the pan, and she turned the fire off.

Mikayla picked up the plate and led her to the table. "That was an impressive display of tortilla making. From the volcano song to the assembly line cooking."

"You should watch me and my sisters make tamales."

"I'm almost afraid for you to try my puerco con chile."

Gem slid into a chair. "Why? It smells perfect."

"I get the impression your cooking is a lot more authentic than mine. And here I made you Mexican food both times I cooked for you."

Gem laughed. "I might have an unfair advantage. My mom and dad were both fabulous cooks. My mom was Mexican, and my dad is Danish but picked up cooking from everywhere he traveled while in the Marines. Both loved to cook, so we all learned a variety of dishes."

As they'd been talking, they had dished up their food, and Gem took her first bite. "Oh, my heavens," she nearly moaned.

"This is delicious." She covered her mouth and swallowed. "I'm sorry I spoke with my mouth full. Damn, it's good."

Mikayla covered her full mouth. "Thank you. I can't tell what's funnier, the expression on your face when you apologized, which reminded me of a little girl, or the fact that you actually said, 'Oh, my heavens,'" she said after she'd swallowed. "Who says, oh, my heavens, anymore?"

Gem laughed. "Honestly, it just came out. I had no control over it, it's so good."

"I'm glad you like it. I wanted to ask if you wanted something else before I made it, but I got distracted by...things."

Gem's brows rose, knowing exactly what those things were. "I probably would have said this is more than perfect, even though I'm usually a vegetarian."

Mikayla put down her silverware, looking abashed. "Oh God. I completely forgot. I am so sorry."

"Don't be. When I cheat, it's almost always with pork. Usually bacon. This is well worth it."

"You don't have to eat it. I'm sincerely sorry."

Gem placed a hand on Mikayla's arm. "And I am sincerely okay with eating this. I'm not a strict vegetarian. I'm kind of an accidental one. I don't make a conscious effort to not eat meat. I just generally don't. I eat it about four or five times a year, and there is no rhyme or reason, except for my mom's tamales. If I didn't want this, I wouldn't eat it. And to warn you, I'll probably have seconds." She scooped some up in a fresh tortilla and popped it into her mouth.

Mikayla appeared a little less shattered, and they continued to eat.

Several minutes later, Gem wiped her mouth and took a sip of wine. "I'm so full. I shouldn't have taken thirds."

Mikayla rose and began to clear the dishes, and Gem got up to help. Mikayla stopped her. "I'll take care of the dishes later. Let's put the food away and enjoy our wine."

"Your wish is my command," Gem said. The glint in Mikayla's eyes promised more than just wine, and her heart beat a little harder. Her mind drifted back to the kiss before dinner. If it indicated how things might go once they'd let their dinner settle, Gem couldn't wait.

"I'm glad you got off work early." Mikayla put the last of the leftovers in bowls on the counter to cool before putting them in the refrigerator, and Gem rinsed the pots and pans and piled the other dishes neatly in the sink to wash later.

"I decided to put a few things off until tomorrow. Between being excited about dinner with you and a little conflicted about an email I received from Margo, I wasn't accomplishing much anyway."

They sat at the table again, and Mikayla poured the remainder of the wine into their glasses. "Margo is the woman you used to work with, right?"

Gem nodded. "She's desperate for me to take the part-time social worker position at the hospital. It's gotten to the point where she won't have time to train someone new. She wants someone who can hit the ground running."

"Are you going to take it?"

"I don't think I can. Timing wise, I could probably reshuffle some of the work here, but I have to be here for urgent issues." Gem knew Mikayla understood she was talking about her father.

"What if I help you?"

Gem was stunned. "Thank you. Seriously. But, no. You'd quickly regret signing up for it."

"I've been tagging along with you for almost four weeks. I'm pretty sure I understand what I'd be getting into. I don't want to make a career of it, but let's see how it works out, and if and when I want to stop, I'll give you plenty of notice so you have time to get someone else. Maybe even a full-time property manager while you go back to social work."

More tempted than ever, Gem still wasn't convinced. "I have to be honest, Mikayla, I saw Craig's face when he mistook me for the landscaper. He wonders why you chose to live here. It's obvious you're used to a more opulent lifestyle."

"I don't—"

Gem laid a hand on hers. "I'll admit, his judgment rubbed me the wrong way, and you have never acted that way. However, I did notice you were quick to tell him I wasn't just a property manager. The thing is, this is what I am. It's my family's business. I won't apologize for it."

"I wouldn't ask you to."

Gem stroked her arm. "It doesn't change that you lived a very different life than this. It might look interesting right now, but I promise, when the novelty of it wears off, it's just a job. As much as you want to help me out—which I absolutely appreciate more than I can adequately express—I don't think it will take long for you to wish you hadn't."

Mikayla was quiet for a minute, staring at her wine, and Gem worried she'd made her mad or worse, hurt her feelings.

"I understand what you're trying to say." Mikayla finally glanced up. "You said it rubbed you the wrong way when Craig revealed his judgment. I'm wrestling with the same thing now. I spent twelve years as his wife. Those twelve years were happy. I had purpose. He wouldn't have risen in his career if I wasn't doing everything else. He would never have opened his own investment firm. I'm proud of what I did to support him. Now, I'm not his wife. I do nothing important. I'm in the middle of an identity crisis. I crave having something important to do. Oceana is important. It's home to several hundred people. It's a family business. It's an oasis to people when they need it. Keeping it functioning *is* important. If it's a matter of you thinking I'm not qualified or competent to take some of it off your shoulders, that's one thing. However, if it's my 'stature in the community' causing you to exclude me, well, I'd like you to reconsider." She made air quotes to emphasis how much she seemingly hated the idea of being judged.

Shame washed through Gem. She took Mikayla's hand. "I'm sorry. None of what you mentioned occurred to me. I think I've been too preoccupied with my own frustration, and I didn't try to see it from your perspective. For someone who bases much of her practice on telling people to trust what others tell them, I've neglected to do it with you. You told me you'd like to help, and I shrugged it off. For all the talking I do about how important Oceana is to me, my family, and the community, I sure haven't been acting like it. I'm sorry." Gem was embarrassed for having been so quick to brush Mikayla off when she was right. She'd assumed a few things and made a decision for Mikayla based on faulty evidence.

"You told Craig I can do anything. But it's you who can do anything." Gem sighed. "I should have started this monologue by telling you I have no doubt how capable you are of doing the job. In fact, I'm pretty sure you could do it better than me. If you're serious…wait. Let me rephrase it. I'd love for you to do it, to see if you like it. I have space on a cloud server with most of the work detailed. I started it before my dad put the kibosh on hiring a property manager." Gem pushed a hand through her hair. A sense of relief washed over her about Mikayla's interest in taking on the work. Even if it was temporary, it would give her some space to really assess the possibility of going back to social work.

Still, it was hard to believe there actually was a chance. It would be painful to find out it wasn't possible. Maybe that was her issue. "I've been having a hard time pulling the trigger on this because my dad is adamant about it remaining under the care of the family, and part of me is reluctant to admit the hard truth. He will never come back to work. I've been aware of it at some level for a while, and I still haven't absorbed it. God. I probably would have been frozen like this for the next ten years if we hadn't had this conversation. I should thank you for forcing me to face it. More than anything, I don't want you to doubt yourself or how capable I think you are."

Mikayla's face revealed a parade of emotions, but by the end, she wore a smile. "Then it's settled. Tomorrow, we'll figure out the best way to help you out, and we'll give it a try. Tonight, we'll enjoy each other."

Gem's stomach fluttered. Several scenarios played in her head. They hadn't moved beyond kissing, and she didn't want to rush things, but the idea of enjoying more of Mikayla did pleasurable things to her body. Between that and the mental and emotional calisthenics they'd just gone through, she felt raw and exposed, but it wasn't an unpleasant sensation. In fact, it made her feel close to Mikayla on so many levels. She wasn't sure she was ready to let her know, but Mikayla had the power to make her do anything in that moment. Gem had never let that happen before.

And she liked it.

CHAPTER TWENTY-TWO

The energy between them crackled, and Mikayla panicked. Where had the phrase, "Tonight, we'll enjoy each other," come from? Like someone a whole lot smoother than her had said it. She wasn't smooth. She was just trying to breathe. The expression on Gem's face, although subtle, said she'd been surprised by it, too. And now here she was, expected to live up to words she had no idea how to fulfill.

"How do you feel about a walk on the beach?" It was all she had.

"Sure. I don't go on enough nighttime walks on the beach." Gem pushed a strand of hair from Mikayla's brow, giving her goose bumps.

"I love it, and I keep meaning to go, but I've read one too many Stephen King books to go by myself at night." Why was she so nervous?

Gem gave her a mischievous grin. "Did you just admit to being afraid of the dark?"

"I'm not afraid of the dark. I'm afraid of what's in it. Like, vampires swooping from the night sky. Common things, you know?" Great. Now she was nervous *and* a little creeped out.

"Fair enough," Gem said, laughing. "I'd love to stroll and keep the monsters away. It might help digest all the food I ate."

Mikayla playfully punched her shoulder and went to get sweatshirts. Something had shifted between them. Something good. A bubbly sort of anticipatory energy filled her body.

The walk to the beach was uneventful, and the sense of anticipation followed them, erupting in laughter and looks between them that made heat spread through her. Streetlights helped to illuminate the path and settle most of Mikayla's unfounded fears, but once the pavement of the street ended, so did the lights, and they found themselves carefully picking through the line of erosion-preventing boulders put in place to protect from tidal surges. Concentrating on the path kept her fears at bay, and even her nervousness faded somewhat. A band of smooth ocean rock was easier to walk on, if not a little slippery, and they giggled, holding hands, trying to stay upright. Mikayla no longer thought about vampires, just the warm hand in hers and how they gently bumped against each other as they walked.

After walking through the wide swath of dry sand and jumping over the line of fishy-smelling kelp, they found themselves on sand left smooth by the receding tide, reminding Mikayla of her dream. Once beyond the street, light still illuminated the beach from the moon. The continuously rolling waves drowned out the sounds of civilization. Mikayla slipped out of her sandals and breathed deeply of the cool sea air. They were still holding hands as she picked up her shoes, and they began walking along the shore. The cool air creeped through her sweater and long linen pants.

"Are you sure you're warm enough?" she asked Gem, who wore shorts and a hoodie.

"I love this kind of spring night when the nights dip down. It's chilly but a good kind of chilly. The hoodie you loaned me is perfect."

The tide washed up nearly to their feet, and the white foam almost glowed in the light of the moon. A million air bubbles erupted in the sand as it receded, evidence of tiny sand crabs living at the water's edge.

"Can I ask you something?" Gem asked after a few moments.

"Anything," Mikayla replied, meaning it.

"You told me I'm the first woman you've kissed."

"Yes."

"That implies you have never dated a woman, I assume."

"Also yes."

"I suppose I should check in about how all this kissing is going for you."

Mikayla peered at her through her lashes. "I'd say it's going very well for me."

"I suspected as much, but I wanted to make sure."

"I imagine you have other questions, too?"

"I do."

Mikayla pushed back her hair blowing across her face and held it at the nape of her neck. "Let me see if I can head some of them off. I've never been romantically involved with a woman, either, at least anything reciprocated. When I think back on it, some of my friendships as a girl were crushes, but once I started dating boys, I got swept up in the social expectations. It wasn't until college I realized an attraction to women as well as men. I developed a huge crush on a classmate my senior year. Initially, I confused it with curiosity more than real attraction, but eventually, I knew it for what it was. God, I had it bad for her. I finally worked up the courage to tell her, and she wasn't interested. She let me down easy. I was still embarrassed, so our friendship, which wasn't very deep to begin with, faded away. I still wonder about her."

"Was she straight?"

"I never found out. She simply told me she was flattered but was too busy with school to date." She'd also given her a hug, reducing the embarrassment. It only made it harder to be brushed off.

"She had to be straight or ace or something. There's no way she wouldn't have been interested in you."

Despite the cool night air, heat spread across her face and neck. "Speaking of which, I just finished that book I found at Brandi's about asexual aromanticism."

"That's how Brandi identifies."

"I sort of assumed. She has several books on the subject. Maybe my friend was, too. All I know is unless someone tells me, I don't want to assume. I've been assumed to be straight all my life, and now I'm trying to navigate life outside of my straight marriage."

"I can only imagine."

A few steps later, Gem stopped walking, and still holding her hand, Mikayla turned back, and what she saw took the breath from her. The moonlight illuminated Gem's face, distinctly shading the plains and valleys in a study of contrasts; the valleys were dark, the plains appeared as if they were liquid silver, and her hair moved in the wind like it was dancing. She'd never seen a more lovely sight. She stepped closer and caressed Gem's face, pushing her fingers into her hair. She could stand there and stare at her forever.

Gem rested her hands on Mikayla's hips. "I don't want to rush you into anything you're not ready for. It's probably too soon to be talking like this, but I'm kind of into you, if you haven't figured it out by now. If you want time or space to work through things, I'll back off. It'll be hard, but I'll do it until you're ready."

"You aren't rushing me. I love every minute I'm around you. I especially like the kissing minutes. I don't need time or space. In fact, I want more. A lot more. I always thought I wouldn't have a clue what to do if I dated a woman. But I think I do now. I've been thinking about it since the first kiss. I guess you could say I'm into you, too. Very, *very* into you."

Gem opened her mouth as if to speak and closed it. Mikayla decided to put her out of her misery and kissed her. In the moments leading up to it, she'd imagined the kiss would be searing hot due to all the pent-up desire and emotion, but when their lips met, a tenderness deeper than any she'd ever experienced inspired her to slow down and savor the warmth and gentleness of Gem's mouth.

When their bodies came together, breast to breast, thigh against thigh, Mikayla ceased to acknowledge the wind, the roaring of the waves, or the night wrapped around them. Only her and Gem, standing on the edge of something she longed to explore. Her natural instinct to cautiously move forward disappeared, leaving her to fall headlong into the soft warmth of Gem, and she was ready to go wherever passion took them. When Gem's hands slid under her sweater, beneath the cotton shirt, and along the bottom edge of the tank top, her skin begged them to move higher, to slide forward and cup her breasts. Her nipples ached for it, and her back arched. The only thing keeping her from pulling her clothing over her head to give Gem unimpeded access was it meant stepping from Gem's embrace, and she loved the feel of Gem's arms holding her.

Gem's mouth trailed along her jawline and down the column of her throat, and Mikayla noted the fluttering fingers caressing her back, the cool air sneaking in under the bottom of her sweater, and Gem's hands moving up her bare sides, stopping below the swells of her breasts. Her nipples responded with an even tighter ache to be touched. In her mind, she begged Gem to cradle her breasts, dying for the warmth of her hands.

"I could kiss you all night standing here," Gem said against the skin of her collarbone, eliciting a pleasant tickle.

"Let's do it, then. We'll watch the sunrise."

"Sounds perfect."

Mikayla had a change of heart, however. She wanted to be able to concentrate on what they were about to do, but sand had a tendency to stick to wet places, and she was as wet as she'd ever been. "I have a better idea. Why don't we go back to my place where it's more comfortable?"

"The couch *is* more comfortable than damp sand."

"My bed is more comfortable than a couch."

Gem's mouth stopped moving for a beat, and her hands grew still, then she continued kissing up her neck and back to her mouth where the gentle kisses became insistent until they slowly pulled away. "It's incredible how much restraint it's taking me not to run back to the house while pulling you like a kite."

Mikayla laughed. "Let's walk. My bed will still be there."

Gem took her hand, and they began walking back, their pace a little faster. Mikayla's heart pounded, and she squeezed Gem's hand. She couldn't remember a time she'd been amped up more. She'd always waited for someone else to initiate sex, and she'd surprised herself by even insinuating they would have it. So much of this was new to her, giving her a wonderous, expectant elation.

They were almost to the point where they would have to walk through the loose sand and then the rocks when Mikayla stomped on something squishy. Repulsion rushed through her before fire enveloped the bottom and the sides of her foot. She must have pulled her hand from Gem's, because she couldn't balance on one foot, and she fell back onto the sand with a yelp of pain. Excruciating, fiery, pain.

Gem was at her side in a flash. "What happened?"

"I stepped on something. Glass or fire or both."

Gem shined the phone flashlight on her foot, and she expected it to be mangled with the pain that radiated from her ankle to her toes. Unbelievably, it appeared unharmed, just with agony wrapped around it.

"I can't believe there's no blood. I promise, I'm not usually a wimp. God. It burns. I don't think I can walk." She tried not to whine, although she heard it in her voice.

"I think you stepped on a jellyfish. I know it hurts, but it's not life-threatening unless you happen to be allergic. Let's get you home and put vinegar on it." Gem helped her up and pulled one arm over her shoulder, wrapping an arm around her waist. "Any trouble breathing or swelling of your throat or tongue?"

"No." Mikayla swallowed to make sure. Her throat worked fine, but now, in addition to her foot feeling like she'd stepped in lava, she was worried about having an allergic reaction. She'd never even been stung by a bee. "How long does it take?"

"If you're the bad kind of allergic, you'd know by now. Those purple-striped jellies wash up all the time. I've stepped on a few myself. Once, my cousin flung one at me, hitting me in the neck. It was small, so the sting wasn't as bad as it could have been."

Mikayla walk-hopped with Gem's help, which took her mind off some of the pain because she thought they'd never get back. But they did, and by the time they got to Brandi's house, Mikayla flopped, exhausted, into a chair. The stinging had gone from fiery to a hot burning sensation that had started to itch, and there were raised red stripes going from the bottom and up the sides of her foot.

Gem brought a bowl of vinegar, and when Mikayla put her foot in it, the stinging stopped. It itched like crazy and still burnt a little, but the relief was dramatic.

"So much better." She breathed out, lying her head against the back of the chair.

"Your foot's not swollen. Just a few welts. I think it's going to be fine."

Mikayla felt like crying. It was probably the adrenaline rush receding. "Thank you for helping me."

Gem grinned. "As if I would have left you there. 'Sorry about the jellyfish. Gotta skedaddle.'"

Mikayla couldn't help but laugh. "Not at all. You were calm and collected, got me back home, and showed me the vinegar trick. You were perfect. Craig would have called 9-1-1."

"For a jellyfish sting?"

"I cut my finger once on the sharp edge of a patio chair. To his credit, it bled a lot. Before I got a chance to wash it off to see how bad I'd cut it, he'd already called. So embarrassing. They wrapped it up and told me to go to urgent care. It didn't even require stitches. I seriously think they bandaged it because they figured a Band-Aid would have been anticlimactic with all the drama Craig flung about."

"Some people panic at the sight of blood."

"I'll bet you don't," Mikayla said.

"Adrenaline keeps me sharp in most emergencies. It's afterward that wipes me out."

"I get it. After the adrenaline rush, it's nap time." Mikayla yawned.

"Are you trying to tell me you're tired now? Because I am."

It looked like she tried to suppress a yawn, and Mikayla chuckled. "Part of it was hopping all the way back to the house, but yeah, I'm a little wiped out."

"Nothing like a vicious jellyfish attack to kill the mood," Gem said with a laugh.

"Come here and kiss me good night." She held up her arms, and Gem slid into them as gracefully as a person could when standing while the other was sitting. Mikayla gave her a lingering kiss. "I demand a raincheck on tonight."

"You got it. Do you need anything before I leave?"

Mikayla could think of a thing or two but restrained herself. "Nope. I'll sit here for a few more minutes soaking my foot and then take a shower if I'm still awake. There's sand in my underwear from falling down. And to think, I was considering being somewhat naked on the beach for a minute or two."

Gem opened her mouth, maybe to say something, but slammed it shut and waved good-bye. Mikayla laughed and couldn't be angry for not getting another kiss.

Chapter Twenty-three

Wanting to check in on Mikayla and hoping for some coffee, Gem didn't waste time getting to her house the next morning. The days were lengthening, and the sky turned lighter earlier every day. This morning featured a bright blue sky, meaning it would be sunny and without the usual marine layer to burn off. Soon enough, the June Gloom—which, despite its name, started in May and often went until July—would be in full effect, and the coastal cities would have to wait until nearly noon to see the sun most days. But today, being in the bright morning sunshine with memories of kissing Mikayla in the moonlight on the beach, Gem felt almost effervescent. Part of her wondered how different the morning would have been if the jellyfish incident hadn't occurred. Some of the possibilities that passed through her mind made her blush. She bounded up the porch steps and knocked on the door.

"It's open," Mikayla called.

Gem peeked around the screen door before walking in. Mikayla sat in her pajamas at the dining table with her foot propped on the chair next to her. Still beautiful, even if she'd obviously rolled right out of bed. Gem longed to run her fingers through that slightly messy hair, but she settled for adjusting the hood of the zip-up sweatshirt Mikayla wore as an excuse to touch her. She wanted to kiss her, too, but they weren't quite at the kiss-upon-greeting phase yet.

"Thanks. I'm a mess. I was up all night with an itchy foot."

"You're adorable," Gem said, eliciting a playful scowl. "How is it now?"

"Much better. Still a little itchy. I researched it last night when it got so bad, I wanted to scream. Google told me to take an antihistamine and put aloe on it, and it's doing okay now."

"You look high."

"It's the antihistamine. Knocks me for a loop every time."

Gem checked out her foot before she assessed the coffee situation. Mikayla's cup was empty. "More coffee? I can't guarantee it will live up to yours, but I'll try."

"I'll walk you through it."

Mikayla provided detailed instructions, and Gem took a seat, sliding Mikayla's cup to her and taking a sip of her own. "Not as good as yours but drinkable."

"Thank you. Look at them," Mikayla said, picking up the cup and cradling it between her hands. She nodded at the aquarium. Othello and Desdemona were floating away from all the plants, their tails entwined, slowly turning. "It's like a dance. They've been doing it all morning. They're so cute."

"She's going to pass her eggs to him if she hasn't already," Gem said.

"He just had babies, though."

"They don't waste any time between births. Since they came of age for reproduction, they've been having a new batch every one or two months. Much like my sisters." Gem slapped a hand over her mouth. "I shouldn't have said that. It's true, but they'd hate me saying it to someone they haven't met."

"I won't tell." Mikayla winked.

Gem liked how comfortable they'd become with one another. "I knew there was a reason I liked you so much."

"I thought it was for my enchiladas," Mikayla said, her eyes sparkling with humor over the cup.

"Well, those are up there, too."

"It must be the coffee."

"That's near the top of the list, for sure. You still haven't guessed my favorite thing."

"If it's not my enchiladas and it's not my coffee, I have no idea."

"Let me give you a hint," Gem said, leaning forward and placing a soft kiss on Mikayla's mouth. She let her lips linger for a moment and started to pull away when Mikayla slid a hand behind her neck and pulled her back in. The searing kiss that followed made every nerve in her body come alive and, somehow, they stood, and her hands were under both Mikayla's sleep shirt and sweatshirt, caressing her smooth back, and Mikayla's hands were thrust into her hair, holding her there as she kissed the living hell out of her. She didn't have a clue how they'd gone from sipping coffee to making out so quickly, but she was definitely on board with it, and when Mikayla slipped a hand down her back into her shorts, she nearly exploded.

The sound of Mikayla's phone pulled her back to reality, reminding her she had a job to get to at some point. She pulled away slightly and tried to catch her breath. The warm air from Mikayla's gasping breaths blew against her neck, and she let out a shaky laugh.

"That was...unexpected," she said as the phone continued to ring, and she took a small step back, nearly toppling her chair. Her hands slid from Mikayla's back, along her soft sides, and finally out from under her clothes.

"My God. What just happened?" Mikayla whispered, looking dazed.

The phone stopped ringing, and they stared at each other. Gem wondered if Mikayla was thinking what she was: whether she should just take her into the bedroom. Only Mikayla's hurt foot kept her from doing it.

Mikayla looked around as if she needed to get her bearings. Miraculously, both their nearly full coffee cups were sitting on the table without a drop spilled. "I'm so smooth. I can't get enough of kissing you. I was seconds away from pulling you into my bedroom."

Gem pushed her hair back, her heart still racing. "What stopped you?"

"I've stripped all the bedding off. I should have taken a shower last night. Sand was all over the bed from me falling on the beach."

Gem's mind filled with images of Mikayla in the shower, causing heat and moisture to erupt between her legs. She sat and picked up her coffee in what she hoped appeared to be a natural manner, trying not to let her thoughts show on her face and struggling with ideas on how to get them back to neutral territory. "All righty, then."

"Indeed," Mikayla said, sitting, too.

"What were we talking about before you attacked me?" Gem asked, holding back a laugh as she took a sip. Why did she play with fire?

Amusement shone in Mikayla's eyes. "Before we played twenty questions about what you like about me, you were telling me how we'll probably have another batch of seahorse babies in a month or so."

"Oh yeah. When the other two pairs start reproducing, it will be fry city in there."

"The other night when Othello had the babies wasn't a big deal for you?"

"It was my first time, but I think it would've been magical after seeing it a hundred times." Just like what had happened after the babies were born. Had it only been forty-eight hours ago? So much had changed between then and now. Especially all the kissing. And Mikayla's misty, all-encompassing essence was now more complex, a dense fog of kindness and comfort mixed with desire, excitement, and so many other emotions, she had trouble defining them.

"I could sit here and watch them dance around the tank all day," Mikayla said.

Gem chuckled. "This coming from the woman who said she didn't believe in mating for life? Is this the antihistamine talking?"

"I admit, I'm a little aslant this morning, and the antihistamine is only part of the reason," she said, looking through her lashes. "I believe in love. I talk a good talk, but deep down, I'm a sappy, all in kinda girl. Don't tell anyone." She took a sip of her coffee and grinned at the seahorses. "Aren't they miracles?"

Their conversation paused for a moment while they watched Othello and Desdemona dance among the seagrass. Finally, Mikayla broke the silence. "I browbeat you into letting me help you, and there's nothing I'd like to do more today than spend it tagging along with you, but I think I should take today off to keep applying aloe to my foot."

Gem was processing the part about Mikayla being all in on love and while disappointed about her staying home, she actually needed a little time to think. It wasn't like she was ready to declare anything, but having been under the impression that this thing with Mikayla would never happen, Gem now wrangled a mix of hope and fear that made her stomach tremble.

The phone rang again. Mikayla looked at the caller ID and sighed, silenced the ring, and put it back down.

"Someone calling to talk to you about an extended warranty?" Gem joked.

"It's Craig. So much for the time and space I asked for."

"He probably just needs reminding." Gem tried to sound casual. She didn't have a right to it, but she felt slightly uncomfortable with his and Mikayla's relationship. He clearly had expectations of maintaining a closer relationship than Gem was comfortable with. All his talk about their previous life had felt like he'd been proving his claim on her. It was probably her insecurity either way, but now with Mikayla admitting to being open to love, she worried that the boundaries with him weren't as clear-cut as she wished it was. As a therapist, she had seen people say one thing with conviction one day and the exact opposite the next and mean it both times. It was what made people fascinating. It was what made them frustrating, too. People were enigmas.

All this made her anxious and insecure, two things she'd never spent a lot of time being. To top it off, she'd already developed some fairly serious feelings for Mikayla, and she had to figure out whether she was willing to help Mikayla figure out what she was willing to put into a relationship so soon after divorce.

She'd become the rebound girlfriend she'd never intended to become.

❖

Later, while Gem visited one of the units being remodeled, excitement flared within her to see Mikayla walking up the street. At first, she guessed it was wishful thinking because she'd been thinking about her all day. But when she confirmed that Mikayla wasn't a figment of her imagination, she went out to meet her. They walked together into the unit, where Gem made sure they were alone before she gave her a kiss. Not a kiss as smoldering as the one earlier but still a kiss that promised to melt the newly applied paint from the walls if they let it go on for another five seconds.

"I didn't expect you to be walking around today." She looked at Mikayla's flip-flop-clad feet. "You're not even limping."

"My foot is surprisingly almost back to normal. Just a little red around the sides. I got a little antsy and decided to take a walk. I dropped by for lunch with your dad. I think I might have to learn how to play rummy. He keeps asking me to play cards."

Gem loved how Mikayla and her father had hit it off. "What did you two have?"

"I brought him some of the leftover puerco con chile. He said he'd been planning to heat up some soup your mom made last night. I love how he speaks about her like she hung the stars. It must be beautiful for him to believe she's still around."

As Mikayla spoke, her eyes filled, which made Gem's eyes fill. She'd become used to her father talking about her mother as if she was still with them, however, it had always been in a sad way. It had never occurred to her that sometimes in his mind, she was still alive, and that brought him such happiness. She didn't check if anyone could see them this time before she gave her a kiss. "Thank you for being my dad's friend."

"It's far from a burden, I promise you." They stared at each other for a long moment, smiling, until Mikayla seemed to shake herself from her thoughts. "I wanted to stop by and check out the renovations. I'm not stalking you, per se. It just looks like I am. Is it annoying?"

"Well, we *were* supposed to work together today. And by the way, I don't think you could ever annoy me."

"Oh, give me time," Mikayla said with a tinge of pink in her cheeks. "How's your day been?"

"It got infinitely more interesting when you arrived, making a good day even better. I ate lunch, which is always a plus. The afternoon's been busy. I'm checking the progress here. Oh, and Rose came by today. We've been talking about her taking her old job back."

"The Rose I met at the Seaside Café?"

"That's the one. She's been working here off and on since she turned sixteen." Gem explained how Rose had worked there until she'd decided to try school again. "My dad keeps encouraging her to get a degree. But she isn't cut out for school. She barely graduated high school. Not because she isn't smart. She excels at things she's interested in. It took her a lot to come here today, though. She doesn't want to disappoint her grandfather, and it's making it hard for her to figure out what she wants to do with her life, and making coffee isn't it."

"What's she into?"

"She likes to be outside, working with her hands. She's better than me at fixing almost anything, including cars, and she can build almost anything, too. She's really good with the residents. DJ, our head of maintenance, is kind of gruff, so the residents like working with her."

"Sounds like a good property manager to me."

Before she could respond, Tony, the head building contractor, came into the unit. "Mikayla. Just the person I wanted to see. Some of the hardware for the bathrooms is back-ordered, so I have to order something else. Gem and I have narrowed it down to two.

Which one do you think we should go with?" He held up his phone to show her.

Gem enjoyed watching Mikayla work, and it only took a few minutes for her to pick out the replacement hardware. Ever since their talk the night before, Gem had felt a new sense of internal peace, like she'd finally accepted her role at Oceana. Even if property management wasn't her passion, she had fun with Mikayla around.

Her phone vibrated in her pocket, and when she checked the caller ID, she didn't recognize the number, so she let it roll over to voice mail. Probably just another salesperson. Seconds later, her phone rang again. This time, it was her sister Ana. It wasn't normal to get a call from her in the middle of the day, so she answered.

Ana spoke before Gem finished saying hello. "Thank God you picked up. North County Regional called saying they have Dad. They couldn't tell me anything else. They asked me to come down. What happened?"

A wall of shock swept through Gem. It wasn't possible. Mikayla had just seen him. Her intuition didn't respond. "What are you talking about? I'm back in the renovations. He's fine. He's at home."

Mikayla and Tony were watching her now.

Her sister's sigh sounded worried and harried. "All I know is, he arrived at the hospital via ambulance, and they found the 'In Case of Emergency' card in his wallet and went down the list."

She remembered the previous call she hadn't answered. "Hold on." She pulled up the location app on her phone to check where her father's watch was. The pin showed him about five miles away. The shock caused her to go numb. She met Mikayla's concerned gaze. "How long ago did you leave my dad?" she managed to ask.

"About half an hour, maybe a little longer. Why? What's going on?"

"He's in the hospital. How did he look when you left the house?"

"Good. He ate well. He was in good spirits."

Ana interrupted. "I'm in the pickup line at school. I'll drop the kids off at home and go straight to the hospital. I'll call the others while you get down there." She didn't even ask if Gem could go.

"What's going on?" Mikayla stood close, holding her arm when she got off the phone.

"They didn't tell Ana anything other than an ambulance brought my dad to the hospital. Oh God. I heard the sirens. I thought they were just passing on the highway. I have to go." Her lips didn't want to form words. She should have been running to her car, not just standing there.

"Do you want me to drive you?"

"I do, but could I ask you to stay here with Tony and the others to lock up?" She took some keys from her pocket.

Mikayla rubbed her arm. "I can do both, but are you okay?"

Either Mikayla's touch or her words got Gem's brain going again, and she roused herself from the shock. "I can drive. I'll come back if anything comes up."

"Can you forward calls to me so you don't have to worry?" Mikayla asked.

"Sure, but I don't think—"

"I promise to call you if anything comes up that I don't think I can handle. Just forward everything. I'm not asking. You have to focus on your family."

Gem's heart raced, and anxiety held her chest in a vise. Mikayla's take-charge attitude was exactly what she needed. She had everything under control. She was resourceful and confident, and she provided a comfort Gem had never felt in the four years she'd been managing Oceana. With work in safe hands, she could concentrate on getting to her father's side.

CHAPTER TWENTY-FOUR

Tired didn't begin to describe the weariness that had Gem in its grasp. Three straight days at the hospital sitting at her father's bedside had made time seem inconsequential. Her whole concept of space had narrowed to a twenty-by-twenty room on the fourth floor overlooking a busy highway. Occasionally, she'd ventured to the first floor for food, but mostly, she stayed in her father's room, sitting in an upholstered chair that converted into an uncomfortable narrow bed. She didn't expect comfort, and she didn't get it. What she did get was time with her father and to hold his hand while a steady stream of visitors and medical staff flowed in and out of his room.

He had suffered a stroke while preparing a cup of tea. His smartwatch had automatically dialed 9-1-1 when it had detected his fall. She'd activated that when she'd set it up for him, hoping it would never be used. Now, she was certain the watch had saved his life.

At least one of her sisters stayed at the hospital with her each day, but it was just her and her dad at night. He slept most of the time, yet, for some reason, he became wakeful at night, and while his speech slurred due to what they hoped was temporary paralysis on his left side, they had good conversations. His temperament had always been kind, save for his difficulties in the last few years, but now, he possessed a new kind of sweetness.

He spent much of the night talking about her mother and telling her about their recent conversations, how Gem looked more like him than her sisters but acted the most like her mother, with her kind and loyal soul. It comforted her hearing she'd inherited most of her mother's mannerisms. She gained a sense of closeness to her family that she'd always felt was missing and felt less like the oops baby she'd always considered herself to be. It also gave her a stronger link to her mother, who she missed so much, it ached sometimes.

When it came time for her father to be discharged to Sierra Vista—a skilled nursing home near Oceana, where he would get physical therapy until he recovered enough to go home—she'd been desperate for rest, but she didn't want to abandon him. It helped when Annabel, the facility manager, gently mentioned that he'd need time to get used to his new routine, so it would be best if she and her sisters limited their visiting time. They agreed to a rotating visitation schedule and forced Gem to go home for a couple of days until her turn came around again.

When Gem pulled up to her house Saturday evening for the first time since Wednesday afternoon, she found herself walking to Mikayla's. As she climbed the stairs, music caught her attention, and Mikayla sang along. Gem loved the sound of her voice and stood outside just listening, her muscles relaxing for the first time in three days. She knocked when the song ended.

The instant she walked in, Mikayla took her in her arms, and Gem sank into them, savoring the comfort. She'd been on constant vigilance in the hospital, wanting to be there for her father and always on alert for the nurses and specialists who dropped in at all times, day or night. With her guard down, exhaustion caught up to her, and all she could think about was falling into bed and sleeping for days.

After a few minutes, Mikayla led her to the couch, and she dropped onto it, grateful for how soft it was. Mikayla perched next to her, holding her hand. "When's the last time you ate something?"

Gem tried to think. All the days blended together. "This morning. Ana brought me a breakfast burrito. Oh, and I ate a granola bar from the vending machine sometime today, too."

"How does a BLT sound?"

Not as good as sleep. But her stomach seemed to think differently because it growled loudly. "It sounds wonderful," she said through a yawn. "I can't promise to stay awake to eat it."

"I'll wake you up if you doze off."

Gem meant to answer, but the next thing she knew, Mikayla was stroking the side of her face.

"Come over to the table and have at least a few bites."

Gem did as she was told. "How's everything around here?" she asked between bites. Nothing had ever tasted so good in her life. "I'm sorry I abandoned you. Did anything come up? I sensed you were trying to keep my mind from work in our daily calls."

Mikayla sat next to her, drinking a glass of water as she stroked Gem's arm. "Everything went well. There was only one thing I didn't tell you about. The afternoon you left, Tony stepped off one of the porches and fell into some materials stacked next to it, cutting himself pretty badly. One of his guys took him to urgent care, and they stitched him up."

"Is he okay?" As tired as she was, Gem planned to call him as soon as she finished eating.

"He's fine. Back to work the next day, although I suggested he take a day or two off."

"That's Tony. He's as stubborn as my dad. It's the first time anyone's gotten hurt enough for a doctor's visit in the time I've been back. I'm going to have to find out what we're required to do."

"His company is bonded, so it's all covered by his insurance." Mikayla stroked her arm again, calming her.

"Are you sure?"

"One hundred percent. I talked to his office, and they verified it. A while back, we put an addition on our house, and one of the workers carrying a couple of sheets of steel mesh for the foundation slipped, and a piece of it pierced his leg near the shin and came out the back of his calf." As exhausted as Gem was, the visual still made her entire body clench. "I went through all the legalities, but because they were bonded, their insurance took care of everything. We're fine."

"Thank you." Gem appreciated it more than she could say, but her hunger took top billing. She finished her sandwich, and Mikayla pushed a glass of water toward her.

"I'll bet you didn't drink much water in the hospital."

"You would win that bet," Gem said before she downed half of it. Water had never tasted so good. "I thought I was too exhausted to eat. Thank you for taking care of me and everything around here."

"You are more than welcome." Mikayla stroked the side of Gem's face, and her eyes closed in pleasure.

"I had no idea how hungry I was. What did you put in it to make it so good?"

Mikayla shook her head. "Just a regular BLT. Nothing special."

"Oh. It's special." Gem pushed her plate and glass away and folded her arms on the table before dropping her head onto them. Mikayla played with her hair, and she almost purred.

"I met Ana. She's really nice," Mikayla said.

"Thanks for letting her into the house to get my things. It's incredible how wonderful a change of clothes and a toothbrush will make you feel."

"Did your dad settle into the new place okay?"

Gem nodded as best she could with her head still resting on her arms. "The doctors gave us the rundown of what happened as part of the discharge to Sierra Vista. They're fairly sure he had a series of smaller strokes a while ago before the one on Wednesday. They think they contributed to his memory issues. They aren't sure how much permanent damage he has, but after they administered the meds, his signs of dementia faded. Not completely but quite a bit. His left side is weak, so they'll work on getting him to walk again and use his left arm. His face already seems to be bouncing back, and he's not slurring as much as he was. It's mostly muscle coordination. They couldn't estimate how long he'll be in Sierra Vista, but they're hoping for less than two weeks." Gem shivered. It was hard to think that this stroke, which had nearly killed him, had ended up correcting memory issues he had dealt with for so many months.

"You sound hopeful."

"I am." The food and water were exactly what she'd needed, and she could barely keep her eyes open, but she had to tell Mikayla how relieved she was. "I'd already accepted everything as being inevitable. I have my dad back." Her voice cracked at the last, and she took a few deep breaths as Mikayla drew closer and rubbed her back, her touch was better medicine than the food. Gem wanted nothing more than to curl up inside her arms. She wiped her eyes. "Sorry. I'm just tired."

"Don't be. What a gift," Mikayla said.

Gem nodded, still overcome with emotion, and leaned toward Mikayla, who shifted her chair to hold her. The comfort and safety were unbelievable. "I realized something else while I mostly watched him sleep."

"Oh yeah?" Mikayla stroked the side of her face.

"This one isn't as wonderful, but it does come with a weird kind of relief." She paused before going on, trying to find the right words. "I finally realized I've been living in a weird limbo state between waiting for something to happen to allow me to go back to my old life and staying here, managing the community my dad built."

"Oh yeah?"

"I've accepted my future here. Even if my dad gets better enough to come home, he can't go back to running this place. It runs me ragged, and I'm a third his age."

"Is it what you want?"

"To be a property manager? Not in a million years. But to keep Oceana in the family and running at the level it does? It's important to me. My dad's right. The magic of this place wouldn't be the same under a person who doesn't love it like the family. My place is here. Knowing my sacrifice will protect it is enough to free me from my limbo."

"Have you talked to your father about this?"

"I could never. It would break his heart."

"What about *your* heart?"

"I have my father back. He's worth it. Am I sad? Yes. But it's just the end of my social work career. I have my dad back." Mortified, Gem realized she was crying. She wiped her eyes. "Sorry. I'm tired. It's been a long week."

Mikayla squeezed her tighter, and she relaxed. "Don't apologize. You've been through a lot. Is there anything I can do to help?"

Such a simple question. Hadn't she been helping since her arrival at Oceana? "Just keep being you," Gem said and sat up. God, Mikayla was beautiful. "You being here helps. So much. I don't just mean helping while I stayed with my dad, which I can't thank you for enough. I like being around you. And when you're not here…" She patted the center of her chest in the rhythm of her heartbeat. "…you're right here. Is it okay to say that? Did I already say it? I'm so tired. I came here before I went to my own house. Just to be near you…I'm not making sense."

The warm sound of Mikayla laughing made her happy. "It makes plenty of sense, but you're barely keeping your eyes open," Mikayla said.

"I don't need my eyes to make sense, and I'm not ready to leave."

Mikayla squeezed her hand, and she squeezed back. "Let's at least get you into a comfortable bed." Mikayla stood, and Gem reached out, not wanting to let her go.

"Don't go. It's nice right here."

"Come on. You don't have to leave. Follow me." Mikayla helped her up, and Gem walked with her eyes closed because they wouldn't stay open. When she ran into the side of a bed, she blindly started to crawl onto it. "Wait. Let me turn down the covers." Gem stood, swaying, while Mikayla adjusted the covers and then guided her in, sliding her shoes off. Nothing ever felt so good. The veil of sleep lowered as Mikayla tucked her in.

"Snuggle with me? Don't worry, they let me shower at the hospital. They had…" were the last words she remembered saying, and the most delicious comfort wrapped around her.

❖

Mikayla slowly woke, slightly disoriented, loving the comfort and warmth of the arms wrapped around her from behind. She sighed dreamily when she remembered how Gem had pulled her back every time she'd shifted away. She'd never been much of a snuggler. Sometimes, she had nestled in the crook of Craig's arm to go to sleep, but the position had always led to a crick in her neck, or his body heat had become oppressive, or his snoring had kept her awake, so most of the time, she'd slept on her side of the bed and he on his. But last night and this morning, it seemed as if she couldn't get enough of being nestled against Gem.

Wide-awake in the misty dawn light, Mikayla relaxed into the warmth, enjoying the luxury. An hour later, her bladder finally forced her from bed, and once up, she had to restock the seahorse feeder, and as much as she craved the warmth of Gem's arms, she didn't want to risk waking her afterward. Gem needed uninterrupted sleep to make up for the long days and nights in the hospital.

Quietly, Mikayla settled in the living room with a book about the local mission, San Louis Rey, and a cup of coffee. The clock said eleven thirty when Mikayla heard movement down the hall. She was curled up on the couch with the book and enjoying her third cup of coffee when Gem shuffled into the living room.

"I can't believe how late it is." Gem plopped on the couch near her.

"You needed the rest. You've been asleep for almost sixteen hours."

"I feel underwater. Maybe I slept too much. Sorry for conking out on you last night." As she said it, she pulled her feet onto the couch and curled up against Mikayla's side. Mikayla lifted her arm, inviting Gem to snuggle more closely.

"Don't be sorry. Your sister Ana called about an hour ago. You left your phone out here, and her name came up. I watched it just in case something seemed urgent. She didn't try again or text, so I let you sleep."

Gem didn't lift her head. "I'll call her back later. My phone would light up with all kinds of calls and messages if anything had happened."

A warm sensation spread over Mikayla's chest, and she realized Gem was yawning into it. The poor thing was still worn out. "Are you going to check on your dad today?"

"Uh-uh." Gem yawned again. "It's Ana's day. We're rotating. I'll see him again in a few days."

"Do you want to go back and lie down again?"

"I like it right here." Gem snuggled into Mikayla's chest. "Am I bothering you?"

Mikayla smiled and played with her hair. "Definitely not. I like having you here." She did. She *really* liked having her there. Maybe more than she should. The house didn't feel as empty.

Gem relaxed more. "I like being here, too. I'm tired but not enough to sleep. This is nice. Tell me about your last few days. Have I told you how much I appreciate you handling things while I stayed with my dad?"

"Only about a thousand times." Mikayla stroked her hair. "Let's see. They finished planting the perimeter and started on the new garden by the renovated trailers. Tony says the renovations are on schedule. DJ managed all the work orders without issue, including outside vendors like pest control and the arborist. Other than that, one person gave a thirty-day notice."

"Unit forty-two?"

"Yes. She said she'd already told you."

Gem nodded. "She's a marine and expected orders."

"That's what she said. Oh, and a woman named Anna said she would be late on the rent."

Gem nodded. "Annabeth. I took care of it."

"Oh good. I told her I would check into it and get back to her."

"Mm-hmm."

"I'll send an email to you with a few other things."

"Mm-hmm."

Mikayla wasn't surprised when Gem's breathing became steady and deep, so she spread one of the soft blankets from the arm of the couch over them, then settled more comfortably into the corner so Gem could stretch out.

CHAPTER TWENTY-FIVE

Gem woke gradually, enjoying the fuzzy in-between place of sleep and awake, particularly enjoying it with Mikayla lying next to her on the sofa. Thoughts of holding her through the night sent waves of pleasure through her, the kind that wound within her like silken sensuality and cradled her in a sort of comfort she'd rarely known except in dreams. She allowed gravity to mold her into perfect alignment with Mikayla. A low simmer of arousal stirred when she shifted, and Mikayla's warm and pliant body shifted perfectly with hers, their legs entwined, Mikayla's thigh warm against her center. Not wanting to break the tenuous spell in which she still floated, she held still. With only awareness to fuel her growing arousal, low pulses began to rise and gently flow outward from between her legs, along their length, and through her torso, a lazy whirlwind of desire spinning higher.

Fully awake, barely breathing, suspended in rapt attention to the sensations washing through her, she noticed Mikayla's breathing become shallower, and Gem tightened her muscles in an effort to remain motionless. One slight move and a host of new awareness assailed her. The first was her arm draped across Mikayla's body, under her shirt, one hand lying limp over the soft mound of Mikayla's bare breast. The firm nipple swelled against her splayed fingers. The second was the pulsing between her legs as she fought the urge to grind against Mikayla's leg.

Gem sucked in a breath, and it seemed to initiate the release of their suspended motion. Mikayla took a long shuddering gulp of air. Gem cupped her breast firmly. Mikayla's thigh pressed between Gem's legs, and Gem moved higher, kissing her all in one seamless motion.

All their kisses until now, as amazing as they'd been, didn't come close to the intensity of this one. Nuclear fusion, atomic explosion, atoms colliding, the implosion of a star—none of these described the melting of Gem's brain as Mikayla's lips claimed her while their bodies danced against each other. And it *was* a dance. Gem couldn't call it anything else. The surge and the ebb of their bodies, the swoop of their smooth hands as they explored, the hum of voices as they gave sound to the emotions flowing over them like music. Nothing in Gem's experience had ever approached this sensation of being so in tune with another person while new emotions charted unexplored regions of her body, mind, spirit… the totality of her existence. Every word and emotion described it, yet nothing came close to expressing the depth of what she was experiencing.

As her mind tried to grasp the experience, her body continued the dance. She brushed her fingertips along the smooth planes of Mikayla's back, stomach, breasts, shoulders, sides, thighs, and, oh…the heat radiating from her center drew her in. Like a drug, it overtook her, and she peeled the shorts down Mikayla's legs. In the past, where she'd been impatient, she took her time now, relishing the experience, discovering new landscapes.

The numinous blue light from the fish tank bathed them in soft light. Gem had her own T-shirt halfway off when the presence of mind struck her to check in with Mikayla to make sure the spell of desire was a mutual thing. She pulled her T-shirt back down and kissed her neck. "Are you awake?"

Mikayla's heavy breathing broke into a laugh. "More than I've ever been in my life." Her voice was low and sexy, eliciting goose bumps on Gem's skin.

"I wasn't sure."

"Well, now we've cleared it up, can you finish taking off your shirt? I saw a glimpse of paradise before you pulled it back down."

Gem accommodated, enjoying the rush of passion Mikayla's gaze added to the motion, feeling the skin tighten around her nipples. She cupped her own breasts.

"God, you're hot." Mikayla rose up on her elbows, and a flash of arousal ignited Gem's core. Still straddling Mikayla's thigh, her clit throbbed. All it would take was for her to grind down, and she'd come. Two or three thrusts would do it. Just thinking about it almost took her over the edge. She didn't want to come that way. She wanted Mikayla to make it happen.

She stood and slid her shorts down and helped Mikayla sit up and out of her shirt. With Mikayla sitting before her on the sofa, she again felt the power of her gaze trailing electric paths across her body, and when Mikayla's hands joined the erotic sensation, she became impatient to touch her in intimate ways. She sat beside Mikayla and pulled her onto her lap facing her, and Mikayla slid so their fronts were pressed together, the soft warmth of skin on skin, breast against breast was exquisite, setting off explosions of need.

Their lips met, a kiss eclipsing all the previous kisses. Their bodies surged together, and they explored each other's mouths with an urgency causing a sensory overload, making Gem tremble. She caressed Mikayla's breasts, enjoying the gasp of pleasure when she gently pinched her nipples. Kissing Mikayla made her lightheaded. Instead of coming up for air, she made a trail of kisses to Mikayla's chin, along her jaw, and then down her neck, leaving a path of light nibbles and gentle bites. When she made her way down to Mikayla's breasts. Mikayla arched as Gem explored the warm skin before taking a nipple into her mouth, cupping the other breast, and Mikayla voiced her pleasure.

Gem slipped her other hand down to the curve of Mikayla's ass, caressing, running slow circles around it until she skimmed the inside of her thigh from behind, followed by the crease of her leg. Emboldened by the sounds Mikayla made, she lightly grazed the extremely wet, very swollen flesh between her legs. Gem switched breasts and hands, sucking her nipple and teasing her opening while Mikayla rocked her hips. Each time Gem's fingers glanced across her center, Mikayla emitted a half moan, half whine, triggering a waterfall of shivers down Gem's spine.

Mikayla leaned back, holding Gem's shoulders so tightly, her nails threatened to break the skin. "I don't know what it is, but I need it now. Whether it's inside me, outside, your hand, or your mouth. I need it now, or I'll be forced to touch myself."

Her words caused a hot sensation to pour down Gem's body, coalescing around her throbbing clit. The slightest contact or her legs squeezing together would make her come so hard, it would shatter her. A wave of tingling pleasure roared from her center to the edges of her body, where it crashed and washed back through her. The thought of watching Mikayla touching herself stirred a beast within her. She was tempted, so very tempted, to ask her to do it, but she wanted to hold her when she came, be inside her. She wanted to experience the wonder of making her quiver and quake. She stood with Mikayla in her arms and laid her on the sofa, lying beside her.

Mikayla's eyes bored into hers, and with their eyes locked, she ran a finger from the dip at the base of Mikayla's throat, down her chest, between her breasts, along her torso, around her belly button, along the slight swell of her belly, through tight curls, and into slick folds. Mikayla's hips rose. Gem made a circle around Mikayla's clit, and her eyes bored even deeper into Gem's. Mikayla had gone beyond teasing. She needed relief, and Gem gave it to her. She slipped one finger and then another into her, and Mikayla bit her lip, her gaze unwavering. Gem let her set the pace with the tempo of her hips, and it wasn't long before Mikayla shuddered beneath her.

When Mikayla's orgasm subsided, Gem removed her fingers and gently pulled Mikayla to her, kissing her soft lips until Mikayla nuzzled her neck. Slowly, Mikayla's body grew limp, and Gem continued to hold her. She wanted to ask how she was, what she felt, but words seemed insufficient, so she held her and stroked her back, basking in the connection between them that had become infinitely closer.

"Is it just me, or are the places where our skin touches kind of…how to explain it…zippy?" Mikayla's voice tickled Gem's neck, and she pulled back a bit to keep from laughing. She didn't want to break the moment. When she peered into Mikayla's eyes again, they were so soft, her expression so open, Gem found it hard to concentrate on anything else. "Do you feel it?"

She did, but she attributed it to her ability to sense people on a deeper level. The astonishing thing was how Mikayla felt it, too. Maybe it was a pathway between them opened by their lovemaking. It was there, a layer of space between their skin passing something back and forth: electrons, atoms, energy, spirit, lo…wait. It was too soon. Way too soon. Right?

Mikayla's eyes widened. "It got zippier for a second."

Gem cleared her throat. She'd experienced it, too, but the possibility she might be…she couldn't think it. For a moment, she couldn't breathe. "I felt something, and yes, zippy describes it perfectly."

Mikayla settled back into the circle of Gem's arms. "No one has ever held me like this after…after…"

"Sex?" Gem asked.

"That wasn't just sex," Mikayla said. She said it so matter-of-fact that it didn't become the weird thing it could have been in other circumstances, those where Gem had almost called it…the other thing. The one that started with the big L. It *was* something big. A significant something big.

"You're right. It wasn't just sex. And I can't believe no one has ever held you like this afterward. You should bask. Savor. Luxuriate."

"Is this how it always is? I mean, between women?"

Gem squeezed her. She almost laughed. Not even close, she almost said. "Not always. It's like anything else, it depends on the situation. There are certainly other"—she cleared her throat—"positions. And sometimes, it's urgent, and other times, it's slow. It depends on the situation."

"I didn't mean *that* kind of way. Of course, those things can all change depending on the situation." She laughed. "I meant the intensity."

Gem honestly couldn't say because she'd never experienced this particular kind of intensity before. She'd been in several relationships, all with women, some of whom she'd loved. She started to think she might be in trouble because whatever they had, this thing zipping between them, it was definitely more than anything she'd ever experienced, even with women she'd loved. Logical reasoning meant this was more than love, which was scary, which meant…what?

Oh, she was in trouble all right.

CHAPTER TWENTY-SIX

A lone at Brandi's, Mikayla couldn't help herself. She picked up the phone she'd been staring at all day.

With a sigh, she pushed her hair back, hit the number, and leaned against the granite counter, listening to the ringing on the other end. Regretting her weakness, she'd have hung up if it weren't for the damn caller ID on the other end. She tapped the toe of her sandal against the floor. Five rings was enough. She started to lower the phone when Gem's voice replaced the ringing.

"Hello, beautiful."

Mikayla's voice left her. Well, words left her.

Gem's laugh carried across the line. "I can hear you breathing. Is this a butt dial?"

Mikayla snorted. "Sorry. Nope, I called you on purpose."

"Just so you know, I would have taken the butt dial. I miss you. I know it's only been a few hours, but I'm not ashamed to admit it."

Mikayla heard the smile in her voice, and it broke the tightness in her chest that had clamped around her since she'd hit the dial button on her phone. Around mid-morning, after hours of sex, Gem had received a call from her father, asking her to bring some sweats and shorts to the hospital, and she'd reluctantly left.

And Mikayla couldn't stop thinking about her.

"You're quiet. Are you thinking about this morning in the shower when I came in your mouth? Because I am."

Mikayla had just exhaled, so when the breath was sucked from her lungs by Gem's words, it made her a little lightheaded. She slid down to the floor with her back against the kitchen island, and still, she couldn't respond, at least verbally.

"Okay, I heard you gasp. At least I know you're there. It wasn't fair, but I like surprising you."

"You have a knack for it." Mikayla finally got the words out after managing to take a deep breath. "I miss you, too."

"Good. Because I'm at your front door, and I'm about to walk in. Are you decent?"

Mikayla's head swiveled toward the squeak of the screen door. When she stood, Gem was in the living room and in a few strides, stood before her. Mikayla still held the phone to her ear. The air stood still. She set the phone on the counter, and when Gem kissed her, she became feral, all earthy desire and animal instinct.

All of the frantic desire from the night before surged through her, and she wanted to rip Gem's clothes off, but she settled for taking Gem's head in her hands and kissing her back with all the emotion she held, melting into her. Gem gathered up the skirt of Mikayla's sundress, lifting it until her hands rested hot against the skin of Mikayla's lower back, then slid into the back of her panties.

The next thing she knew, Mikayla had her back against the counter with her panties off and Gem's fingers deep inside her. Even sore from all the previous sex, she was ready to wrap around Gem's talented fingers and take the thrusts that were perfectly measured, exactly hard enough, and breathtakingly deep enough to make her ache for release. Just when she needed it, Gem dropped to her knees and continued to fuck her as she pulled her clit into her mouth, making her come, and finally, keeping her mouth on her and her fingers inside until the last pulse rippled within her.

Gem rose, wiping her mouth on the shoulder of her T-shirt before kissing Mikayla again. She took her time, and Mikayla savored the mix of sated physical desire—at least for now—mixed with unquenched emotional need. Drunk on it and dizzy, she was glad Gem held her to keep her from falling.

"What were you doing down there?" Gem asked.

"I believe it was you down there." Mikayla grinned.

"Your wit is something I dig about you, you know." Gem laughed and kissed her again. "You were on the floor when I came in."

"Yes. I was and speechless." When she remembered why, her knees grew weak again. "Because of you. Sometimes you do or say something, and it literally knocks me off my feet."

Gem drew back with a puzzled expression, and then a slow smile stretched across her face. "I knocked you off your feet? Like, really? From standing to sitting on the floor? Just like that?"

Mikayla nodded at every question, laughter bubbling in her chest. "Just like that."

"What did I do or say?"

"The comment about the shower."

Another puzzled expression started to emerge on Gem's face, and then the smile returned. No, a grin. A mischievous grin. "I'd like to try it again."

Mikayla's knees went weak, but she held on to Gem this time. "I think it can be arranged."

Gem's expression changed.

"You look so serious all of a sudden."

"I have a serious decision to make. Shower or dinner? One is way more fun than the other, but the other is a necessity."

"Have you eaten today?" They hadn't taken a break to eat the night before. And while she'd made herself lunch after Gem had left for the nursing home, she'd done more daydreaming than eating. Her stomach growled loudly.

Gem shook her head. "Just a candy bar from the vending machine at Sierra Vista."

"What do you want to do about it?"

"Are you asking me if we should eat or shower? Because I for sure have a preference. So be it if I starve to death in the process."

"We can't have that. Let me fix us something because I'm hoping to keep you busy for a while tonight."

❖

Gem pointed at the sandwich from which she'd just taken a bite. "How is this vegetarian? It has the flavor and texture of a real crab cake." She took another bite, already thinking she would have seconds.

"It's chickpea and artichoke with some seasoning. It's probably the kelp flakes making it taste like real crab."

Gem shook her head. "It doesn't matter how I prep chickpeas, they always come out as mush."

"That's the artichoke. I'm glad you like it. How was your dad today? I'm sorry I didn't ask sooner."

"Totally my fault. I kind of attacked you as soon as I got in the door." Gem tried to put on an apologetic face, but she wasn't sorry at all. "He's doing well. Better than expected, the doctors say. His left side is still weak, but he has almost full range of motion for a man his age." She put her sandwich down. "And I can't believe how much of his cognitive function has been restored. He has a few blank spots from the last year and a half or so, but there's no indication of continuing short-term memory issues. It's way too early to tell, but it's like I have my dad back again." The sting of tears caused her vision to blur for a second, and she tried to blink it back. It was hard to think about how much she'd missed him.

Mikayla pushed Gem's hair behind her ear and stroked her cheek. "I'm so happy for you. I'd be the same way about either of my parents. I'm not as close to them as you are with your dad, but our parents are a huge part of our lives."

"It's weird to be in the house without him."

"I'll bet. You've spent most of your life there with family. Are they still saying a few weeks?"

Gem shook her head and swallowed another bite. "Maybe the end of this week, optimistically. But so far, he's exceeded all the estimates. He won't be back to full strength any time soon, if ever, so he'll have to take it easy. Although, they said that a routine with purpose would be helpful for exercising mind and body."

"That's fabulous news. Have you given any more consideration about Rose as a possible protégé? It would keep the property management in the family."

Gem shook her head again. "She couldn't manage the park and watch my dad at the same time. At least, I wouldn't ask that of her. It's too much for one person. And if I'm going to be here to watch him, I might as well manage the park." She saw the look on Mikayla's face. "I'm used to it."

Mikayla rubbed her shoulder. "I know. I want to visit him this week if it's okay."

Gem's chest swelled with emotion. "He'd love it. He sleeps a lot. The doctors say it's because his body is mending. When he's not sleeping, he's doing therapy. Lunchtime is the best time to catch him."

Gem's phone chimed with the tone she'd set up to identify work orders, and she grimaced. It was Sunday, her one day off, but she still monitored the queue for emergency notifications. A quick glance and a sigh of relief later, the list told her it could wait.

An email had come in from Margo, too. The subject said, *Part-Time Clinical Social Worker Requisition*. Procrastinating about telling Margo she couldn't do it wasn't going to work out. It had been fun to dream about it the last few weeks, but her father's health had given her a cold dose of reality. Her future entailed managing Oceana. Forever.

Mikayla tipped her head toward the phone. "Bad news?"

Gem could almost see Mikayla's thoughts flying behind her eyes, and she wondered what was on her mind. It never seemed to rest. It happened to be something she loved about Mikayla. If she wasn't actively engaged in something, she had a book to read or research to do.

Gem explained the note from Margo and her obligation to Oceana. "We have a lunch date later this week. I'll talk to her then."

"That makes me incredibly sad for you. I can tell you're upset."

"There's no way around it now. In a way, I have my dad back, and it's reminded me of what's important. My life is here."

She hoped the wave of sadness and loss would get better over time.

CHAPTER TWENTY-SEVEN

When Mikayla arrived at Sierra Vista after a short walk, including a stop at Seaside Café to pick up an afternoon treat of coffee and scones, she was thoroughly invigorated by the sunshine and clear skies, and she turned around to take in the view. The slight change in elevation opened up the horizons, and San Clemente Island rose out of the ocean to the north. Days like this reminded her why San Diego continued to be her home.

She stopped at the front desk to sign in and followed a nurse down a long, carpeted hallway with ocean-themed watercolors displayed along the walls. They looked familiar and upon closer inspection, she found Brandi's signature on each.

"How do you know Mr. Helmstaad? Are you family?" the nurse asked.

"I live at Oceana. I'm friends with his daughter, Gem."

"Ah, Gem. She lives up to her name, such a sweet girl, and she just dotes on her daddy. All his girls do. He's a lucky man." She stopped at door 127, which stood slightly ajar. "Enjoy your visit."

Mikayla knocked on the door. When she heard the strong, "Come in," she could already tell how much better he felt.

"Good morning, Mr. Helmstaad," she said, poking her head inside. He had a lovely room that looked more like a nice hotel suite than a hospital room.

He waved. "What am I going to have to do to get you to call me Tripp? My father wasn't even Mr. Helmstaad."

"Oops. Bad habit. Tripp," she said, happy that he seemed to remember her.

He watched as she placed the items from the café on his bed table. "Pull up a chair. I hope you don't mind if I stay in bed. Therapy after lunch still has my legs shaking." He laughed. "Here I was longing for Seaside coffee. And if I'm looking at a beach plum scone, I might ask you to marry me."

She winked as she pulled a chair closer. "I'd say yes if I didn't have my eye on another suitor. I hope it doesn't mean we can't be friends."

"I suspect I know this other suitor, and I'm not terribly disappointed," he said with a wink of his own. "I was worried about my Gem for a little bit. She's lost so much of her natural sparkle over the last couple of years. She seems to have regained much of it, and it coincides with your arrival."

"Does it?" The idea she might be responsible for Gem's sparkle made Mikayla inordinately happy, even while the bit about Gem having lost it in the first place made her sad. "She was unhappy before?"

Tripp accepted the coffee and cradled the to-go cup, appearing to think. "For a while, I thought it was loneliness because she'd broken up with...I can't remember her name. My memory is shot, but Gem didn't bring her around much." He snapped his fingers as if trying to remember before he gave up. "I can't remember. She was with her right before she moved back home. When I asked if that was the cause, she said it wasn't, that she didn't date because of the long hours at work. It makes sense. She doesn't know how to take a break."

Mikayla wanted to tell him the truth about Gem missing her social work career, but it wasn't her place. This was not her situation to fix, although every cell in her body wanted to. "You think she's happier lately?" she asked instead. It made her almost giddy.

He nodded in a preoccupied way. "She's got a kick in her step again. I caused some concern because of this," he said, gesturing to the room, "but once she rested, her kick returned with a vengeance. She was fairly bubbling yesterday when she brought my clothes."

"Was she?" Mikayla struggled to keep her smile from turning into something that would give them away.

"She certainly was, and it was nice to see. Did she tell you I'd been struggling with my memory? Turns out, I'd already had several strokes without knowing it. Can you imagine?" He snapped his fingers again. "I still can't remember the woman's name. The one she lived with. Drives me crazy. I can't tell how much is from the stroke or just getting old. It messes with you, not being able to trust your mind."

"Are you thinking about Angela?"

He snapped again. "Yes. Angela. Not nearly as pretty as you." Heat rose up Mikayla's neck, but thankfully, he kept talking. "I never got the impression they were particularly sweet on each other. More like just spending time. My Gem deserves more. And it didn't help to see her struggle at her job. So I asked her to come back home to help me. Not only did it help her with the job burnout, it gave her a good excuse to move on from that Angela." He shook his head. "Why am I telling you this? I woke up worried about her. She's my youngest. I'll always have a thing about protecting the baby. Not that she needs it." He frowned. "I have big holes in my memories over the last few years, and I think I lost the protectiveness for a while, but it's come back."

"Protectiveness must be a trait shared by your whole family. Gem has it, too."

He smiled. "It's why I worry about her. She takes on the weight of the world sometimes. I was so happy when she gave up social work. It had started eating her up. You look surprised."

Mikayla regretted that her expression gave her away. "She told me she loved social work. The fact that it's hard at times only makes it more rewarding. She said she'd love to go back, actually."

"Tell me. I think there's more to this than I realize, and maybe I did realize it at one point and forgot, or maybe I'm just not perceptive about my daughter." His eyes glistened with tears, and he shook his hands next to his ears. "It makes me crazy to think I'm not being a good father."

Mikayla suspected it to be a little of everything, and his confusion and concern pulled at her heartstrings. It reminded her of how he'd looked the night of the bonfire, so vulnerable and confused. He'd trusted Gem, though, which had been everything.

She felt caught. She didn't feel comfortable telling Gem's story, even to her father. She also didn't want him to think she was hiding anything. "I don't know much more. Some of the sadness you sense is her mourning her career. However, you're more important to her." She wasn't about to tell him how much of Gem's stress had been from watching his mental health decline. "Her old boss asked her to return, which I think stirred up some emotions. She wouldn't have done anything differently, given the choice. She loves you very much. Oceana is important to you, and she's willing to make the sacrifice."

His expression turned from worry to shock. "Sacrifice? I would never ask for that. I wouldn't have asked her to come back if I suspected any of this. She loved social work when she started, but it became so difficult, and when the docs told me I had to have the back surgery a few years ago, it seemed like the perfect way to give her an easy out. She seemed happy to come home to help." He looked devastated, and Mikayla wished he hadn't brought any of this up.

"She's happy when you're happy," she said.

"I want her to be happy for herself. It's all I've ever wanted."

"She knows. She's proud she can be here for you. Her family is everything to her. She told me the other night that having her dad here has reminded her of what's important in her life."

He rested his rough hand on her arm. "You've answered all my questions, young lady, and have given me a lot to think about. Thank you."

She was happy she'd helped him. When she left, she couldn't wait to talk to Gem about it. However, she'd promised her sister they'd meet up at the Grotto, so it would have to wait. She planned to confess to sleeping with Gem, a big deal, so her mind quickly moved on to different things, especially how her mother would react to the news. Both dread and a little glee swept through her at the prospect.

❖

Gem's watch read almost midnight, way past her normal bedtime on a weeknight. She sat at the kitchen table, nursing a now tepid cup of chamomile tea. Her father's words from when she'd gone to visit him for dinner kept circling through her mind. She desperately wished Mikayla was home to talk to, but she'd gone to dinner with her sister and wasn't home yet. Gem had been staring out the window toward her house for the last couple of hours. She wasn't sure why; she wasn't about to run over there as soon as the car pulled up. It would be pretty pathetic, no matter how much she wanted to. Yet, it made her feel better to know she could.

She drank the dregs of the cold tea and got up to rinse out the cup and try once again to sleep, doubting it would be possible while her father's words rang in her head.

Even with her back to the window, she knew when Mikayla pulled up. She couldn't hear the quiet car or see the lights, but the atmosphere changed to one of anticipation. When she turned to look, Mikayla's car sat in the carport. Her nearness was comforting, but Gem still wasn't going to go over there. She had to show a little restraint.

A knock on the door should have startled her. She hadn't seen Mikayla walk over, but she knew it was her. Much of the tension in her tight shoulders and clenched jaw melted away when she opened the door, and the object of her longing stood on the other side. In one step, Mikayla walked into her arms, and the apple-flavored kiss erased all her worries. All her fractured thoughts became background noise.

"You're still up," Mikayla said when their lips parted.

"I couldn't sleep."

"Too much coffee today?"

"There is no such thing as too much coffee. However, I only drank the cup you gave me this morning. I can't sleep because of a weird conversation with my dad tonight." She pulled out two chairs at the table.

"Oh, yeah? He seemed in a good mood when I left this afternoon."

"He mentioned that you came by. He likes you."

"Well, I like him, so it's mutual. What was weird about your conversation?"

"First, tell me how dinner with your sister went."

"Ashe was Ashe. She broke up with her boyfriend, who happens to be one of the servers at the restaurant."

"That sounds awkward."

"He wasn't there, thank goodness. But while we were there, she hit on a different server. At some point, the restaurant is going to ban her for preying on their staff."

Gem shook her head. "She and Brandi are opposites in many ways. Sometimes, I wonder how they can be such great friends."

"Ashe is the opposite of most people. Craig couldn't stand her."

"Oh, really?"

"She couldn't stand him either, so it worked out, even if it kept me from seeing her as often as I wanted. I'm glad to have her back in my life more frequently." Mikayla paused. "I told her about us."

Gem had wondered if she would. She'd imagined Mikayla would want to talk about it with someone other than her. "And?"

"She's understandably surprised."

"Because it's too soon after the divorce? Because I'm a woman? Because it's me?"

"Probably everything you listed." She rolled her eyes in a lighthearted way. "Honestly, I think it's because she has a hard time thinking of me having sex."

"She obviously doesn't know you how I know you."

"She *definitely* doesn't know me how you know me." Mikayla gave her an impish smile. "She asked me if I'm a lesbian now."

It hadn't occurred to Gem to wonder. "What did you tell her?"

"That I'm probably bisexual."

Hearing Mikayla say it as if it was an ordinary thing gave Gem a rush of something resembling anticipation, like maybe what they had wasn't doomed. Her gift still didn't help with determining if they were a match. She sensed Mikayla's essence as a thick fog of kindness that expanded beyond her, touching everything, only now there was that zippy sensation of energy that seemed to flow between them. "Did she have a reaction?"

"Mostly surprise. I've always been the straight and narrow sister. Pun totally intended. She's the one who experiments. She's tried being with women, but it's not her thing. She sounded disappointed. I'm not sure if it's because she'd rather be with women—and I don't blame her—or because she doesn't like how I'm encroaching on her job of being the shocking and eccentric sister." She chuckled before a long pause.

Gem wondered how well she was managing this new aspect of herself. This time, a definite rush of anticipation struck her when Mikayla said she didn't blame her sister for wanting to sleep with women. Gem allowed a little more hope to creep in. "I should have asked you before now. You don't seem to be…" Gem struggled to find the right word.

"Flabbergasted? Gobsmacked?" Mikayla asked with a chuckle. "Because I am. Because it's amazing…you're amazing… and not because I'm surprised I'm sleeping with you. I'm not surprised. I'm ecstatic." Her eyes shone with intensity.

"Good to know." Gem took her hand. "I feel the same way. Just to check in, are you comfortable about being bisexual?"

She stroked Gem's face. "I'm comfortable being whatever it is as long as it means being with you. Whether it's bisexual, demisexual, or some other label. All I know is I really, really, *really* love having sex with you. I mean, *so* much. Maybe it makes me a Gem-sexual."

"I like that idea."

"Me, too." Mikayla brushed the tip of her nose against Gem's, and something big filled her up. Something significant. And her entire body felt like she'd stepped into a plasma ball; every hair stood up. It took a moment for her to realize Mikayla was still talking. "…and I'm glad my mother and father are in Europe for the next six weeks because I don't think I want to deal with their input right now."

"Sometimes, a little time is all anyone needs."

"My sentiments exactly." She ran a hand along Gem's arm, and it amazed her there wasn't a sting or a pop of static electricity because she distinctly felt that energy running through her. "Tell me about the weird conversation with your dad."

Gem was still thinking about Mikayla saying she loved having sex with her, so it took her a second to catch up. When she did, some of the hurt and confusion from the conversation with her dad resurfaced. She tried not to let it bleed into their conversation. "His memories are coming back, and he's having a hard time putting them into context. It occasionally makes him flustered and irritable. At least he isn't directing it at other people anymore."

"He mentioned that it causes him to get a little scattered. He seemed thoughtful about it but otherwise fine."

Mikayla's comments made her wonder if she had overreacted. "Well, I think he's feeling more like himself. It feels like he might be jumping forward a little too fast."

"What do you mean?"

"Did he tell you he's got a thing for one of the nurses?"

"No." She looked amused.

Gem would have preferred concerned, but maybe that was part of her overreaction. "He probably wouldn't mention it to you. I think the strokes scared him. He mentioned wanting to try dating before it was too late, and then he kind of danced around how uncomfortable it would be with me living there and asked me if I planned to find my own place." She watched for Mikayla's reaction.

"You'd think he'd want you here because of his health issues."

"Me, too," she said, glad they were on the same page. "But he said he might ask one of the nurses to go out with him." She ran a hand down her face. "More concerning, for some reason, my dad wants to run Oceana again."

"Wait. The last we spoke about it, he was all about retirement."

"He was. Now, he's flipping everything on its head, taking the doctors' advice to heart about creating a routine, including both physical and mental exercise, and he wants the house to himself in case he starts dating. He's making all these decisions without thinking about how they affect others. Namely me, since all I've been doing is…" She held her hand up, stopping herself from going down a path she didn't want to, at least not now. "This is about him. I'm just trying to process it, and I definitely have some major feelings about it."

"It's a lot to take in."

Gem was still confused about why he'd brought it up out of the blue. "He kept justifying it by saying this would be good for both of us and how unhappy I've been."

A look of understanding came over Mikayla's face. "He mentioned to me you were unhappy, too."

The words hit Gem like a blast of arctic air. "Wait. You talked about me being unhappy with my dad?"

"He asked if I had noticed it."

"What did you say?"

"Mostly, I just listened, but when he brought up how much you'd wanted to quit social work, I told him I was under the impression you actually loved social work."

Dread washed over Gem. "You told him about our conversation?"

Mikayla shifted in her seat. "I answered his questions. He'd already been thinking about it before I got there. What are you uncomfortable about?" She rested a hand on Gem's arm, and Gem almost moved it away. She needed a little space.

"I wish you wouldn't have talked about our private conversations with my father."

Mikayla looked confused. "I didn't…he asked me—"

"You didn't have to confirm that I'm unhappy. I'm not sure why you talked to him about it at all. You should have just let him talk. Isn't it obvious he's not thinking clearly and shouldn't be making decisions right now?" She heard how she sounded, but she couldn't help it. She'd been walking a tightrope for so long, and she'd just gotten her dad back. Now things were all screwed up.

"That's not how—"

Gem sat back in her chair. "It makes sense now."

Mikayla leaned forward. "What does? Did I do something wrong?"

Betrayal, already stinging and sharp from her father, pierced her again when she realized Mikayla's role in it. "He told me to call my old boss and get my job back. I wondered why he specifically mentioned my old job. You told him I've been talking to Margo, didn't you?"

"Not in those words."

That confirmed it. Her heart broke. Mikayla of all people knew how fragile everything had been with her father. She'd never dreamed Mikayla would insert herself into her and her father's relationship like this. "You didn't have to. He's making assumptions based on incomplete information."

Mikayla's expression changed from confused to resolute. "I wonder if you both are."

"What's that supposed to mean?"

"Nothing. Forget I said it. I think there are some crossed messages going on here. I didn't bring anything up to your father that he wasn't already thinking about."

"You said you told him I missed social work. But let's not get caught up in specific words. It only blurs the core of the discussion. The net result is my father now thinks I've been unhappy working here and has made up his mind to go back to work against his doctor's advice and…" Her head swam with so many thoughts, most of them revolving around worry about her father pushing himself too hard too soon and now betrayal from both him and

Mikayla, which was something she never would have expected. It was all too much to think about. "I need time to think about all of this."

A pause drew out, and Mikayla looked as if she was trying to figure out what to say. Gem desperately hoped she wouldn't say anything. She didn't want to be mad at her, however, anger and hurt had a stranglehold on her, and she couldn't aim any of it at her father when he needed to recover.

Mikayla rested a hand on Gem's arm again, and this time, she did withdraw it. The look of hurt on Mikayla's face before she steadied her expression would have normally made Gem ashamed, but it did the opposite. She felt vindicated. This conversation was about Gem's hurt, not Mikayla's.

"This obviously isn't how you envisioned any of this going." Mikayla sounded reserved. "Aside from being taken off guard by your dad's announcement, isn't this what you wanted?"

Gem couldn't believe Mikayla had just minimized her entire life. She actually loved that Mikayla's default setting was optimistic, but it was almost too much to bear after four fucking years of taking care of her father only for him to dismiss everything she'd done, which caused conflicting emotions because she'd never sought acknowledgment. It had always been about what her father needed, making sure he could maintain some of his autonomy before it wasn't possible anymore. Her whole purpose in life had been to keep her father out of a memory care facility for as long as possible, to keep from losing her dad as long as she could. God. Her thoughts were racing all over the place.

"What *I* want? For my father to think I see him as an invalid? For him to fire me and kick me out of my home? You think that's what I want?" She heard her voice getting louder, but she couldn't help it. Mikayla hadn't raised her voice at all, but every word from her mouth just made Gem angrier, as if she didn't care what she'd done. To top it off, it made Gem mad to see Mikayla so composed when she was losing it so epically.

"Not at all." Mikayla's composure seemed to have morphed into steel, infuriating Gem even more.

"Well, it happened because of you."

"Me? How do you figure I had anything to do with it?"

"You told my father things he didn't need to know. Things I specifically didn't tell him because he's incapable of dealing with them. I can't believe you did this, Mikayla. You of all people. You got involved more than you have any business to, and I can't imagine why you did. You don't appear to understand how this affects...affects *everything*. You're not invested. You've been here, what, six weeks? You have a fucked-up sense of boundaries. I should have noticed when you didn't think it was weird when your ex-husband showed up at your house, and you couldn't tell him to leave."

Gem knew as soon as she said it that she shouldn't have brought up Craig. It was way out of bounds, and now Mikayla's eyes, always so open, were dark and closed off. "You have no idea about my boundaries."

"Because you don't have any."

Mikayla's cold eyes now filled with tears, and Gem couldn't find it in herself to back off. Mikayla took a few steps away. "That's not...you know what? Never mind. I don't have to justify myself or my marriage or my boundaries to you. I'm going to leave before either of us makes this worse."

"That's a very good idea." Before Gem had finished the sentence, Mikayla had gone, and while Gem feared they had gone beyond the ability to repair the rift they'd opened, she was relieved. If Mikayla hadn't gone, Gem might have continued to unleash all the emotions she'd bottled up for so long. And there were a *lot* of them.

CHAPTER TWENTY-EIGHT

Mikayla tossed and turned after she left Gem's. She'd thrown herself into bed, and as she lay there in the dark, replaying the argument, she asked herself how such a good day could have ended so badly.

She couldn't think about the fight with Gem without her guts tying themselves in knots. Every time, an unbearable sense of loss and anger and confusion filled her, and she slammed the trapdoor against the debilitating emotions. How had things spiraled into such a poisonous exchange? Never in her life had she felt so... ambushed. She would have never imagined Gem as so unreachable, so unyielding, and so...*mean*.

It was the meanness that hurt the most. Gem hadn't even tried to listen. She'd launched into attack mode, and having come from a life where displaying anger had always been considered bad taste, Mikayla didn't know how to handle it. So she'd done what she'd done her entire life: she'd imagined herself as a pillar of stone. She'd endured Gem's anger and left, keeping the stone in place because if she'd let it go, she might dissolve into a million pieces.

The moment she'd found herself alone, she'd crumbled. She'd thrown herself on her bed and had cried until she'd ached and finally slept.

The dim illumination starting to leak into the room and the now-familiar objects around her reminded her she wasn't in her own space. She didn't have her own space anymore. At some point in the night between fits of sleep, she'd started to think her life was empty and vacuous. And waking in a room that wasn't hers, in a home that wasn't hers, in a community that wasn't hers, was pathetic, just like her. She'd fallen asleep repeating two phrases in her mind:

I don't belong. I don't matter.

And they were still streaming through her mind when she woke. They were the backdrop to all of her thoughts. Ones like: How would she fill her day? There were no true friends to spend time with, no one to look forward to seeing first thing in the morning, no one to invite to dinner. No Gem.

I don't belong. I don't matter.

The words she'd repeated to herself throughout the divorce from Craig. This time, she stopped. She would not go through it again. And she wouldn't let Gem discard her as Craig had. She would not lose herself in someone else's life. She would not go back to feeling like she didn't matter. For once, she'd done the leaving. Now, she was angry.

She fixed her coffee and took a seat at the table, staring out over the water, refusing to glance toward the house she'd nearly run from the night before, refusing to diminish herself for her failures. This time would be different.

She'd just finished her second cup when Shia walked past in her wet suit, carrying her surfboard, and an idea came to her. Too tired and too sad to explore it, she watched Shia walk down the street as the idea percolated in her mind, even with her heart torn and hurting, reminding her of all she had lost in the last several months. She had no idea how she would pull the pieces back together this time. One thing was certain: she wasn't going to let her relationship to another person define her worth. As much as she loved Gem, she needed to take care of herself.

Love?

A physical pain gripped her heart. Yes, love.

❖

After spending most of the day online researching her idea, Mikayla took a glass of iced tea and sat on the steps of her deck, watching the colors of sunset start to stain the sky. It wasn't long before Shia walked up from the beach carrying her surfboard.

"Hey, Shia. How were the waves?"

Shia leaned her board against the deck. "Small but long."

Having done a bunch of research about surfing, Mikayla knew the phrase meant the waves weren't very tall, but they kept breaking for a long time and gave a long ride. "Do you still swim in the mornings?"

"I've been switching it up a little. Sometimes in the morning and sometimes in the afternoon. Why?"

"I want to give it another try. I got distracted with other things after the first time we went, but I'd like to go again."

"I'm going tomorrow morning. Want to come with?"

"Sure." The idea gave her a flare of hope in her otherwise bleak mood. A mood she hoped would change soon since she might have found a purpose, at least for now. "I also wanted to talk to you about your sponsorships. How's it going?"

Shia shrugged. "It's not, to be honest. I still have the ones I told you about, but I haven't talked to anyone about others. I have a list, but it's hard to beg money so I can play at the beach all the time, you know?"

"Would you like an agent?"

Shia tossed her head. "Yeah, right."

"I'm serious."

"I've never even won a big competition."

"You've placed, though."

"Yeah. Just local stuff. Nothing major."

"Why do you surf?"

Shia paused, and a dreamy expression came over her. "There's a moment when you're on a wave, and it's perfect, and it's holding you in place. You're in the right spot at the right time, and there's a sort of rush you get. It's awesome when you're in the curl. It can happen on smaller waves, too. It's like you and the ocean are connected. The sweet spot."

"I want to be your agent. I want to support you because of what you just described."

"How long have you been a sports agent?"

"I'm not."

"Do you surf?"

"I took a few lessons as a kid, and I've played around a little. However, I'm not in any sense of the word, a surfer."

"Why, then?"

"I've watched you carry your surfboard back and forth from the beach twice a day for weeks. You're more dedicated to your job than most professionals. You deserve a chance at what you love. It's quite possible nothing will come of this. We won't figure it out if we don't try, right?"

"There's no money in it. None. The big events have a decent payout, but there are few of them, and only the top six women get a cut."

"It's not about winning competitions. It's about doing what you love. Most athletes make their living from sponsorships, anyway. You told me that."

"What about you? What's in it for you?"

That was the question, wasn't it? Not just with this, but what did she get from relationships in general? She'd never given it thought, and look where it had gotten her.

But she had an answer.

"I love helping people. That's where I get my rush. I like to support people who have a passion for something. It's not business for me." It never had been, had it? "As far as the business end, if I land a sponsorship, I get a cut. Honestly, the money isn't the main thing for me." Mikayla saw the look of suspicion. "Really. I'm comfortable. I don't need the money. But to make it a balanced partnership, I would take a cut."

"Why me? Have you ever seen me surf?"

"No. And I guess I should. However, I recognize passion, and you have it. I play tennis. As a kid, I wanted to become a professional tennis player. My mom told me how ridiculous my dreams were. Maybe they were. I wasn't a top player on any of the teams I've been on. I never had encouragement, either. Actually, quite the opposite. Playing tennis was specifically a social thing." Mikayla thought about her art, guitar, marriage, tennis…her life had been a series of doing everything everyone else wanted her to do but rarely what she wanted to do. That had changed recently, and she liked it.

"Something in me always wondered how things might have been if I'd been supported," she continued. "I'd like to be your support person. You figured out a way to keep doing it when it was difficult. I'd like to watch how your passion blooms, given encouragement. I can get sponsorships from companies. I've run charity events asking for donations, taking sponsorships, and giving advertising opportunities. Companies set aside money specifically for things like this. A lot of it goes unused simply because no one asks. I'll make a deal with you. We try it out. Either one of us has the power to walk away at any time. No questions asked. And if either you or I get into a position where one of us thinks you need an agent who's more qualified, you should do it. I'll even help you find one. It won't hurt my feelings. I just want an opportunity to work with you."

"It sounds too good to be true."

"I suppose so. Think of it this way. It's about being on the right spot of the wave at the right time. Take your time to think about it."

Shia shrugged. "We might as well try it. What's the first step?"

"Well, I already called a couple of places, and both of them said they'd talk to us. One is Seaside Café, and the other is Sierra Vista. I know they aren't the sexiest. We'll aim for Quick Silver and Roxy once we get a few professional shots of you on some waves."

Shia shook her head and sat on the steps next to Mikayla. "This is so weird."

Mikayla was excited. She and Shia talked for a few more minutes and made plans to meet up for a swim the next day. She wished she could say the conversation got her mind off how much she missed Gem, but she would have been lying. She wasn't going to sit around the house pining away, either.

CHAPTER TWENTY-NINE

Gem couldn't stop thinking about Mikayla. Specifically, the way she'd looked the last time they'd seen each other. Unbelievable hurt had turned to a stonelike mask. Both expressions haunted her, but the hurt was the one that she couldn't bear. She'd cut Mikayla to the bone, and she'd do anything to take it back.

She'd reminded herself of her father when he'd yelled at her for two days straight after she'd suggested they hire a property manager. It hadn't felt good, but she knew at the time it was anger masking his fear of losing something he cared so much about. Hours after Mikayla had left, when Gem was curled up in a ball in bed, she'd realized her bad behavior had come from the same kind of fear. Only she didn't have the justification of having a medical condition. She was just an asshole.

She had no idea what to do about it.

She'd turned her misplaced anger on the person who meant the most to her. It took her breaking down while on a call to Margo to help her figure out what had gone wrong:

She dialed the phone and before Margo could say hello, she jumped right in. "I know I've been all over the place about this, but is the position still available?"

Margo made a couple of clicking sounds with her tongue, which meant she was trying to make a decision. Gem hoped it didn't mean she'd lost her opportunity. She could get a job somewhere else, but she wanted to work with Margo. "It depends."

Gem's gut clenched. Had she ruined her chance? "On what?"

"On whether you really want it."

"What do you mean?

"It seems you have quite a bit going on, and I don't want to add to it. I realize I've been nagging you for weeks, and I probably wasn't being very intuitive about why you weren't jumping at it. I don't want you to take the job just to make me happy. I want you to want to be here. Previously, when we chatted, you seemed overwhelmed. Do you want to talk about it?"

"About the job or being overwhelmed?" Gem stalled, feeling vulnerable.

"What's overwhelming you?"

"Are you offering me a counseling session?" The question reminded Gem of the conversation with Mikayla several weeks ago, and it made her sad.

"I'm offering you a friendly shoulder. Let's pretend this is a Friday palaver."

Nostalgia filled Gem at the reminder of the impromptu coffee dates Margo used to have on Friday afternoons when someone on the team had finished a rough week. She believed good therapists couldn't help but be affected by their clients' troubles, and they sometimes needed a safe place to talk it out. "I miss the palavers."

"Me, too. Tell me about your week."

"Let's see," she said, shrinking into her chair. "I told you about my dad's stroke last week."

Margo hummed. "And the doctors think previous strokes are the cause of his decline in cognitive function. Is he still improving?"

"Apparently, he's surpassing expectations. He's feeling so much better that he's decided to take back the operations of Oceana."

"Are you worried he's taking on too much?"

"Yes. Especially since he fired me and handed me an eviction notice."

Margo hummed again before responding. "On the surface, it sounds like an opportunity to get your previous life back. But…" She paused, clearly in therapist mode. It annoyed Gem, but at the same time, she knew she needed it. "After the push-pull of recent months, I can guess you're grappling with a lot of mixed emotions. It's hard facing our parents' mortality. You've been dealing with that, plus you've been his caretaker, and you've chosen to sacrifice your own life to a certain extent. Just when you became resigned to it and maybe believed you were even good with it, the entire thing gets rearranged. Am I on the right track?"

"You couldn't be more on track." She wasn't surprised. Margo was good.

"And I'll bet you don't trust it not to change again."

"You scare me sometimes." It was only a partial joke. One of the reasons Gem wanted to go back to social work, and specifically with Margo, was because she knew she'd learn so much more from her. "I've been seeing someone, and she's the one who told my father I wasn't happy, so I think he's doing all of this in a misguided attempt to make me happy again."

"Why do you think this?"

"I know my dad. His identity is embedded in his ability to help people."

"Sounds like some social workers I know."

Gem accepted the soft dig, but it could describe most social workers she knew. Social work was a calling more than a job. She also recognized how much it applied to her father and Oceana, too. "He isn't used to accepting help."

"I know the story of how Oceana came to be, and it started with him accepting help from the previous owner."

"True. He believes help goes both ways. I think it's more about his role as father. As in, it's his duty to be the protector and fixer. He hasn't been either one of those things in a long while. I think he may be trying to reclaim them now that he's on the mend." This idea had just dawned on her. It was as if a light bulb had turned on in her mind.

"So he's worried about you. Are you upset he talked to the person you're seeing about it?"

"I don't think it was her place." Had Mikayla understood her father's actions better than she did? Was that the real reason why she was so upset?

"Did she bring it up?"

"She told me he asked her about it." Saying it out loud made it seem as if maybe she'd twisted the situation in her mind from one in which her father and Mikayla were motivated out of concern for her rather than betraying her trust. Shame burnt a hole in her stomach.

"I see. You don't think your father would have decided to go back to work on his own?"

"I don't think it would have happened like this."

"How do you think it would have gone?"

"I didn't expect this." Her answers were almost automatic as she wondered if she'd misconstrued everything. Could she ever fix it? Did she want to?

"Let me ask you this: *were* you unhappy?"

The question made her pay more attention to the conversation. "About being able to help my father? Not at all. It's what family does. Oceana is his dream, and there is no way I would have turned my back on it."

"Of course not. You're not that kind of person. But is running Oceana *your* dream?"

What was she after? "I love Oceana. I grew up there. It's a huge part of my life."

"You didn't answer the question. Is running Oceana what you've always wanted to do? What about your sisters?"

"My sisters have their families. My passion is social work. That's what I always imagined I'd be doing, what I *want* to be doing. But—"

"Hold on. You've reminded your dad that you want to go back to social work, right? Your sisters, too?"

Gem felt like she was being pushed into a corner, but she also trusted that Margo was trying to get her to see something.

"It's complicated. When he hurt his back…I took temporary leave to take care of him and the property. He resisted, so I led him to believe I was burnt out with the job and needed the break. For his pride."

Margo hummed yet again. "When things started to drag, and you ended up resigning, you did it out of obligation?"

Gem had never been more aware of Margo's humming. She'd always thought it was just a habit she fell to when she was thinking or making a decision. But maybe it meant something else. "His memory and confusion issues came on so suddenly…and now we know why."

"So you took care of your dad who was in a sort of limbo with issues that were concerning but not bad enough to make serious decisions about advanced care. It's a stressful position. And you were doing it for how long?"

Irritation flared inside her for losing so much time doing something she didn't want to be doing. "Four years." Margo hummed. *Again with the humming.*

"It's a long time. Makes it hard to get back to a normal life."

"Exactly."

"Do you think your father was aware of your unhappiness before he talked to the person you're seeing?"

"I did my best to not let it show." He knew. She knew he knew, but she pretended not to know. She'd figured if she tried to hide it, he'd know she was unhappy to have left her life on hold but happy that it was to help him.

"You live together. How could he not see it?"

"Well, he had his own problems with memory and confusion." But he wasn't completely lost to it yet. She'd blocked his view of her essence, but it wasn't completely blocked to that, either.

Margo's hum proceeded her next words. "I'll bet you were both trying to be kind. I mean, you and he are cut from the same cloth. You're a kind and caring person. I'll bet you get a lot of it from your dad."

The hum seemed to indicate something big, as if Margo was marking the comment or question as having some sort of significance. "Both my parents are kind. The kindest people you've ever met." Gem wanted to cry. She missed her mom, but it hit her for the first time in a long time, as if the feeling was brand new. And until recently, she'd been in start-and-stop mourning for her father, too. He was back now. A surge of joy struck her, along with all the other emotions she'd been holding on to, both good and bad. They all crashed over her, and she started to cry, overwhelmed. She knew Margo had to hear the catch in her breath, but her throat remained too tight to speak.

"You poor thing. You've been doing all of this on your own, not letting anyone help you, taking responsibility for everything."

Gem wiped her nose on her sleeve and struggled for composure. She wanted to deny it. None of this had ever been about her. She wasn't a poor anything. People needed her. Her father needed her. Of course, she did it alone, but no one needed to feel sorry for her. "Yeah, I guess." She sighed. "My dad needed help. Everyone did what they could. I managed okay."

Margo hummed again, and Gem knew what came next was what all the humming had been leading up to.

"I think we all need the reminder—myself included—that just because we know why we feel the way we feel, it doesn't make it go away, and it doesn't mean it's our job to deal with it all by ourselves. You were making decisions for everyone. Now, your dad is making decisions for you. All in an effort to protect one another. I'll bet if you talk to your dad honestly and tell him what you want, you'll manage things better together because you won't be trying to read each other's minds."

The realization felt like a cold blanket being laid over her. Gem had always relied on her gift to know what people around her needed, including her father. But some of her access had been lost when he was sick. In a similar way, her father had lost access to her, too, some of it by her own doing in an effort to not make him worry about her. When he started feeling better, they both continued to try to help each other, but they were lacking critical information.

"Mikayla got caught up in the crossfire on all of this."

"Mikayla?"

"The woman I've been seeing. I was horrible to her."

"You can fix it. I believe in you."

When Gem had hung up, she'd felt better for having shared her worries. She'd been operating alone for so long. For a short time, Mikayla had been there for her, and the relief had been so sweet.

And that was the thing. Mikayla cared. How could she not think Mikayla would want to help her? She needed to figure out how to fix things. If it wasn't too late.

Gem waited in her father's room for him to get back from physical therapy. He was always tired afterward, but his mind was clear, and they had things to talk about. The trouble was, she wasn't even sure *what* she wanted to say. She just needed to release the stranglehold around her heart.

A noise at the door took her out of her contemplation. Annabel, the nurse her dad had a crush on, rolled a cart into the room. "Your father will be here in a few minutes for his lunch." She winked as she moved plates around. "I brought you a little something, too. He ordered the burger and selected the margarita pizza for you. Hope you like it. It's one of our chef's best meals, in my opinion."

She could see why her father liked her. "Thank you. I appreciate it. Um…can I ask you something?"

"Sure."

"Has my dad…uh…been out of line at all? I know it's a weird question." Gem pushed her hair behind her ear.

Annabel clasped her hands together. "He's been a perfect gentleman. Your father is very sweet. He did ask if I would consider going on a date with him when he leaves the facility, and I had to reluctantly decline. It wouldn't be appropriate. I think he might have been relieved. Either way, we laughed about it, and he's been a delight."

"I'm so glad to hear it," Gem said, finding comfort in her father being fine enough to laugh about it.

Speaking of her father seemed to have manifested him because his voice and laughter rang through the empty doorway, and he soon followed, walking into the room using a cane but standing tall.

"Look at you. What happened to the walker?"

"I traded it in for the sports model," he said, giving her a kiss on the cheek before sitting on the edge of his bed and leaning the cane on his bedside table. He pulled the tray over, removing the plate covers. "What do we have here?"

"I'll leave you to your lunch," Annabel said. "Give me a shout if you need anything."

Gem waved good-bye and removed the plate cover in front of her. The pizza looked delicious.

"They won't give me fries the way I like them. I have to settle for mixed fruit," he said, picking up a raspberry and popping it into his mouth. "I'm starving. Therapy kicks my caboose."

She marveled at the difference a few days had made in him. "I can't believe how much progress you've made."

"I'm working hard. Hopefully, I get to go home at the end of the week. So far, so good."

Tears stung her eyes. Hope had been so far away not so long ago. "That's wonderful."

"At the risk of sounding boastful, I think so, too. I'm thankful for regaining my health, such as it is. I will never again take it for granted."

"I second the sentiment." She lifted her water glass in a sort of toast, and he raised his juice. Less than a week ago, she would never have predicted this dramatic show of improved health for him.

"In the same vein," he said, "I may have been hasty in making my plans."

"What do you mean?" she asked, looking up from the pizza.

He finished chewing and took a sip of juice. "Well, for one thing, I should have talked some of it over with the people involved. Namely, you and a certain nurse."

"How did you come to this realization?" This topic wasn't a surprise to her after the call with Margo, but she wondered how he'd come to the same conclusion.

"The dear woman I attempted to woo very nicely let me know she is not available, and it got me to thinking that I was jumping into the water without looking for rocks first."

"I'm sorry, Dad."

He waved. "It was a relief, actually. I don't want to date. It was all your mother's idea. She thinks I'm lonely. I'm not." He narrowed his eyes, and she realized she'd rocked her body back when he'd mentioned her mother. Classic body language for someone not believing what they hear. "Don't shrug it off on me being nuts. I realize how crazy it sounds, but your mother has been with us since she passed. I never said anything because I knew people would think I was crazy. Now they already do, so what do I have to lose?"

"I'm sorry, Dad." She thought he had a lot to lose, but there was no use saying it. So many conflicting emotions always rose in her when he mentioned her mother being with them, and it had been going on since his mental issues had started. Some had to do with the fear she always had when he demonstrated his decline because it reminded her of his mortality. She wasn't ready to lose her father and every day, every reminder, was one step closer, one more small good-bye to the only parent she had left.

Almost as painful was wondering why her mother came to him but not her. Were her sisters getting visits and not telling anyone because they were worried about what people would say? All of this was on top of her general agnostic view about whether ghosts even existed. Thinking about it now, she almost laughed about the diametric opposition of her contradicting views. She believed one-hundred-percent in a mystical energy that enveloped Oceana. She believed in her and her father's ability to divine a person's essence by looking at or sensing the energy they manifested. Why would she be skeptical about a spirit visiting the people she loved? The tumult within her made her want to cry. "Is she here now?"

"No. She usually comes when I'm alone. I get too distracted."

"I see," she lied. She didn't see, but part of her very much wanted to even though it kept going through her mind that if her mother had ever been there, she would have felt her.

He watched her for a moment. "You don't have to pretend to believe or understand if you don't."

Her chest tightened with emotion. "I don't know what to believe, Dad. Someone once said something to me about how nice it must be to communicate with a dead loved one regardless of whether it's real or not. If you find happiness with Mom being with you, I don't think it matters if I believe it or not." Except for wondering why she didn't get to see her, too.

He tipped his head again. "Sometimes, I wish I had your wisdom when I was your age."

Gem snorted. "Wise? I'm not sure about that."

He gazed tenderly at her. "You've opened your heart. There's nothing wiser than following your heart."

Gem almost made a crack about him sounding like a yogi but didn't. She was jealous that he believed. Just because she didn't understand didn't mean it wasn't real…even if it was only real to him.

"Yep. Your heart is open, and you accept the pain that comes with understanding…and loving." He took another bite of his burger. "Another thing is you, me, and Oceana. You love Oceana. But it's not your passion. When I said I was going to start managing it again, it was because I could see you didn't want to, and I wanted to release you. I did it ungracefully. It's not my decision to make. I don't know how we'll resolve this, but I won't be stepping back in, and I'll work with you to find the right solution."

"Are you sure?" She'd never imagined having this conversation with him. She believed they'd lost the chance when his mind began to slip. A glimmer of hope bloomed within her.

"As sure as I can be for now." He shrugged as if it would take care of itself, and for some reason, she believed it would, too. "And this brings me to a final thing."

There was more? She was emotionally drained. "Final thing?"

"Thank you."

Not what she expected, let alone thought she deserved. "For what?" She was so spun around. After having to manage things on her own for so long, all of this was disorienting but not in a bad way. Just strange…and exhausting.

"For watching over me. For not only keeping me safe but for letting me continue to live as normal a life as could be, in light of the challenges we were going through. I don't know how we managed or how you summoned the grace to accept what was going on and made decisions because my mind is"—he wiggled his fingers next to his ear—"still a little Swiss-cheesy, but I have this gratitude in me. It's coming from trust and love. It's unwavering, and it's because of you. I never doubted you. We've built a community and nurtured it, and you've continued to nurture and protect it. I can't tell you how much it means to me. Thank you, my Angel. Thank you."

His eyes glistened more and more as he spoke, and for the first time in several years, she felt hopeful and free. The fear that had been slowly crushing her without her even knowing it had evaporated. The paralyzing dread of having no options and the suffocating sense that it was solely up to her to manage her father's dream and legacy was gone. In place of it all was the knowledge that she wasn't alone.

There was still one thing she needed to work out. She just hoped Mikayla hadn't given up on them.

CHAPTER THIRTY

From inside the toolshed, Gem watched Shia and Mikayla walk past in their shorty wet suits with the tops unzipped and hanging around their waists, their bikinis showing off their fit torsos. Shia carried her surfboard and wore a bright yellow wet suit, and Mikayla wore a black suit with pink stripes down the sides. They were having a focused conversation. It was the first time Gem had seen Mikayla since the night of their argument, except for furtive peeks across the road at windows that were dark or covered most of the time.

A lump filled her throat when she realized she couldn't shout a greeting like she wanted to. She didn't know how to fix it. She simply watched as they turned the corner toward the main gate. She hated things being like this between them, but if she wanted things to change, it would have to be her who made the effort. How could Mikayla fix it? Even Gem hadn't been sure what she'd been mad about.

With Margo's help, she now knew her anger had actually been her own fear, and she'd taken it out on Mikayla because she couldn't be mad at her sick father. Mikayla hadn't done anything wrong. She'd simply told the truth, something Gem knew she, herself, should have been doing all along. As for the actual argument, her own poor response had been because she'd been hurt and overwhelmed, and she'd simply reacted. Poor Mikayla didn't have all of the information to deal with it. No wonder she'd gotten angry.

It was a crappy situation all around, and life wasn't always tidy and easy. When it was the situation that was screwed up and emotions were connected to it, it was hard to figure out where to direct her anger. Poor Mikayla had been caught in the middle. Gem had pushed away the best thing that ever happened to her.

Without thinking about it too hard because she didn't want to talk herself out of it, she followed Mikayla and Shia to the beach. She remained a good distance behind, but they were absorbed in their discussion. While their path turned north, probably to go to the harbor side of the jetty, she turned south and walked down the strand toward the pier.

Still a little early for tourists, the pier wasn't crowded, with a handful of couples at the end, no doubt waiting for the sun to go down. Rather than be treated to a beautiful sunset with no one to share it, she stopped about halfway out. Leaning against the weathered wooden rail, she stared out over the calm water. It made for a beautiful evening but was a bust for the surfers. Nevertheless, a handful of die-hards straddled their boards, waiting for ridable waves that were few and far between.

Charlie the pelican, the unofficial pier mascot, stood in his preferred place close to a small section jutting out for fishing. No one was fishing at the moment, so Charlie had it to himself. If his feathers hadn't ruffled in the soft breeze, he'd have looked like a carving. Gem stood silently and enjoyed his stoic company.

The water beyond the breakers was calm, slow rockers and no chop, making for nice swimming conditions. Mikayla enjoyed an easy swim. Now on her fourth day with Shia and near the end of their southbound lap from the jetty to the pier, she trailed by only a few yards, which gave her a sense of accomplishment. She'd always been a strong swimmer, but Shia swam almost every day.

Mikayla wanted to keep up with her, aiming to be there in another two weeks. There was something very soothing about swimming in the ocean.

While the exercise provided her with endorphins and a sense of well-being, it also gave her time to think, which came with positives and negatives. On the positive side, it forced her to work through her hurt about Gem, releasing some of the negative emotions she tended to beat herself up with. On the negative side, she had so much time to miss Gem, and it made her sad and angry. The anger helped her swim, but the sadness was hard on her heart.

During the day, she focused on becoming Shia's agent, which she enjoyed more than she imagined she would. They'd already locked in small cash sponsorships from Seaside Café and Sierra Vista and had meetings scheduled with a half dozen more businesses, including a new start-up making handcrafted surfboards. They were also putting together an event schedule, optimizing Shia's opportunities for point accumulation in an attempt to qualify for the US Open of Surfing taking place in Huntington Beach later in the summer.

For the first time since Craig had surprised her with his request for a divorce, Mikayla felt like she was doing something meaningful. The work she'd put in to support his career had been how she'd measured her value back when she didn't know the difference between a vocation and a relationship. It had been easy to get those mixed up when they were both focused on one person, and she'd nearly made the same mistake with Gem.

She had to be thankful that she'd avoided making the same mistake. Gem had been right. Mikayla's boundaries were messed up. Now, they were clear. So clear, in fact, that she'd called Craig and had told him she was blocking his number, and he was not allowed to drop by her house or call her family. She needed time to establish herself, and this was just the beginning. Her heart might have been broken in order to figure it out, and the experience had helped her see she was a valuable person in her own right, and her happiness came through supporting and helping others but not at the expense of losing herself. Realizing that distinction was the important part, and a surge of strength passed through her. Now that she saw it, she could be careful about not losing herself along the way.

She just had to fix her heart so she could enjoy the discovery.

Somewhere in all of the newness, Mikayla had fallen in love with Gem. She couldn't deny it. The hurt pervaded every atom in her, and after four days, it had only gotten worse. She couldn't keep busy enough to make it better. Not even the excitement of making plans and working with Shia minimized the ache in her heart over how things had fallen apart with Gem. She missed her in a way she couldn't find a way to fix. No amount of distraction or helping others made her heart feel better. Not even the epiphany about her own self-worth and the feeling of being needed touched the pain she felt when she envisioned a future without Gem, the one person she needed to feel needed by. Everything inside her was certain of it.

Approaching the pier, Mikayla's arms ached from doing the front crawl, so she rolled over to backstroke. The late afternoon sun hung low on the horizon, and it was almost relaxing to stare into the sky as she swam, even if she did it through goggles, and her thoughts were focused on such difficult things.

She didn't expect the physical pang of sadness and pain sweeping through her when a memory of Gem covered in seahorse tank water and kissing her senseless filled her mind. It must have been brought on by the seawater. She'd always been prone to olfactory memories. This one was so vivid, she could almost feel Gem's arms around her, holding her. Gem's soothing voice speaking next to her ear. God. She wished for it to be real with everything inside her. She wanted so much to have Gem close, to have her lips on her skin, to be protected and loved. She ached for it.

❖

A flash of color thirty feet below and several yards into the water caught Gem's eye. Two swimmers made their way toward the pier. She recognized Shia in her yellow wet suit, which meant it was Mikayla trailing her by a few yards. Gem had expected them to swim between the two jetties closer to the harbor. A glance at shore, where several flags indicated riptides, told Gem why they'd chosen to swim between the jetty and the pier, where currents were less chaotic.

Gem watched Shia's smooth strokes bring her close to the mussel-encrusted pilings of the pier, where she did a lazy turn and began to swim back toward the far jetty. Gem got tired just watching her and shook her head at how nonchalantly Shia navigated the open water, seemingly unconcerned with the creatures lurking beneath her. Aware that her fear of sharks and other marine life was blown out of proportion, she reminded herself the chances of an animal harming a human measured far less than those of a human harming an animal. But the chance wasn't zero, so she played it safe instead of facing the terrifying prospect of becoming some ocean creature's lunch.

Shia passed Mikayla and started to swim back. A sharp arrow of longing hit Gem as Mikayla effortlessly rolled onto her back and started an easy backstroke toward the pier. Impressed with how natural Mikayla appeared in the water, Gem watched as she closed on the pilings and waited for her to turn, but Mikayla didn't. Gem sucked in a harsh breath as Mikayla swam directly into one of the giant wooden posts. It happened so smoothly and unexpectedly, Gem didn't have time to shout, she could only watch in shock as Mikayla's limbs jerked with the impact, and then she floundered in the water, touching her head, probably checking for blood as the posts at the waterline were covered in mussels and barnacles. Blood. In the water, it would draw sharks. Gem could only hear her own blood rushing in her ears. She had to do something.

Leaning over the rail to see better, she called out, but there was no response. Mikayla didn't even look up. Gem looked around to see if anyone else had seen or if there was someone official she could call on for help. But all she saw were tourists and fishermen, and none of them appeared to have seen what happened.

And now Mikayla had disappeared from view. God. Hopefully not underwater. Frantic, worried, Gem ran to the fishing spot to get a better view underneath the pier. Thankfully, she could see Mikayla holding on to the piling. But she didn't look well. She floated with her head barely out of the water, not even trying to control how the current washed over her, pushing her against the post. Gem imagined how scared she must be and that she might be holding on with fading strength.

With her heart racing, Gem shouted to the nearest people to call 9-1-1 and didn't think twice before climbing over the railing and jumping. She barely noticed the fall or when the water closed over her, so focused on getting to Mikayla. She emerged about fifteen feet away and swam directly toward her. As she neared, she saw blood streaming down Mikayla's forehead from her hair. She looked dazed, her eyes barely open, fluttering, barely conscious.

"I'm coming, Mikayla. Don't let go," she shouted, trying not to choke on the water. As soon as she reached her, Mikayla's eyes rolled back, and she went limp. She'd managed to tuck one hand underneath a waterlogged buoy rope, the only thing keeping her from slipping underwater.

"Mikayla!" Gem lifted her head, trying to wake her. Mikayla didn't react.

Treading water and jostled by the current, Gem's heart pounded. She needed to get Mikayla to shore. She grabbed the rope and slipped behind, using her body to push Mikayla so she floated on her back. Gem floated beneath her, supporting her head and shoulders and using her own body as a cushion between Mikayla and the piling, grateful she still wore her boots to brace her feet against the wood as she fought the swells.

"I'm here, Mikayla. I've got you. I'm not going to leave you." Gem hoped she could hear. The water was cold, and she didn't know how long they could hang out like this. She glanced over her shoulder and wondered if she could kick-float them from piling to piling until they reached the breakwater, and she could use the surf to push them ashore. She wasn't jazzed about trying to bodysurf while keeping Mikayla's head above water, but it was better than nothing, better than Mikayla drowning, better than bleeding to—

No! Not that. They would be fine. She'd figure out a way.

She told Mikayla the plan as she gently pulled her hand from under the rope. She'd been brilliant to grab the rope like this. Gem wasn't surprised. Mikayla was one of the most capable women she'd ever known. She loved that about her. Not only for that. She loved her for a lot of reasons. "God, I just love you," she said into Mikayla's ear, water filling her mouth, but she had to say it. She spit the water out. "I do. We're going to figure this out. I'll never leave you." Gem kissed the back of Mikayla's hand that was scratched from rubbing against the piling. She kissed her temple, spit out more water. "We're going to be okay."

Gem mustered up the courage to start for the next piling when the sound of a motor rose above the noise of the water. She looked franticly around, trying to see over swells of water as they churned around the post. Relief rushed through her when a lifeguard on a red and white Jet Ski slid to a stop a foot or so away.

"Are either of you injured?" he shouted. He scanned the water. "Are there others?"

"Just us." She spit out water. "She's unconscious."

"Is she breathing?"

"Yes. She hit her head. It's a l...lot of blood."

He throttled closer and grabbed the neck of Mikayla's wet suit. "I've got her. Can you climb onto the rescue board behind me?"

Gem pulled herself onto the board, and the lifeguard dragged Mikayla behind him. Gem helped him roll her onto the board, too.

"Can you hold her while I get us to the beach? If not, I'll lash her to the board."

"I've got it," Gem said, lying over Mikayla and grabbing the handles on either side. There was no time to waste.

She barely noticed the ride to the beach. It seemed to take forever as she struggled to maintain her grip on the handrails as the Jet Ski maneuvered through the surf and slid directly onto the wet sand. First responders rushed toward them. Gem tried to get out of the way, her leaden arms barely able to push herself up, her legs barely working. Someone might have pulled her up from behind, but she found herself struggling to stand on the fringe of the group of responders, trying to see Mikayla, who looked so small lying among the people gathered around her. "She hit her head on the piling and she passed out," Gem said, but they all had their backs to her.

"She's breathing, and her lungs sound clear," one of the paramedics said. "Pulse is strong."

Gem found strength and hope hearing those words.

"She has some superficial lacerations on her scalp," said the other, placing a gauze pad on her head.

"I think it's safe to move her to the gurney." One looked at Gem. "How do you know her?"

Gem swallowed around the tightness in her throat. "She's my girlfriend."

"You can ride with her to the hospital if you want."

"What happened?" Shia was running up the beach, her face displaying a terrified expression. "Oh my God. Is she okay?"

Someone near the gurney said, "Stable for now. The emergency room docs will give you more information."

Shia grabbed Gem's arm. "What happened?"

"She swam into one of the pilings. I jumped in and found her holding on to a rope, but she lost consciousness as soon as I got to her."

"That's a long fall," the lifeguard said, sounding impressed.

"I don't even remember doing it," she said, and then turned to Shia, resting a hand on her arm to keep from falling over but mostly because she needed to touch someone she knew and cared about. It comforted her, but it made her want to cry, too. "I'm going with her. I'll tell you what the doctors say," she said through a tight throat and jogged to catch up to the ambulance.

It wasn't until they loaded Mikayla that Gem thought to call her family, but her phone had been in her pocket when she'd jumped. Expecting it to be fried, to her amazement, it still worked, but her fingers were shaking too hard to enter the password.

"Looks like you're crashing from the adrenaline rush," the paramedic said as he draped a blanket over her shoulders. "Hop in." He helped her up because her legs had lost all strength.

Mom, she thought as she sat in the tiny jump seat, staring at Mikayla, willing her to be okay, *if you're hanging out here somewhere, can you please stick close to her so she isn't afraid?*

She sucked in a deep breath that hitched in her chest and didn't bother to hold back her tears. Right now, being able to identify her feelings evaded her because they all seemed to be pummeling her at once. But for a second, a warm wave washed over her entire body, and she had hope. She grabbed Mikayla's hand and squeezed.

CHAPTER THIRTY-ONE

Mikayla got out of the car while Gem apologized to the Lyft driver for the soggy extra five she gave above the tip she'd already given via the app. Mikayla stood next to the car and held a plastic bag with her wet suit against her chest. She tilted her head back with her eyes closed and breathed deeply of the magnolia-scented cool night air, a contented grin curving her lips. The car drove away, and she became aware of Gem drawing near without having to open her eyes.

"You don't look like a woman who nearly drowned," Gem said.

"I don't feel like one." Mikayla opened her eyes. Gem's bag of wet clothes swung beside her in the strong ocean breeze. "Do you see the moon?"

Gem turned, and Mikayla noticed her shoulders relax for the first time all night. Mikayla placed the bag on the ground next to her and rested her hands on Gem's shoulders, standing close to her back, not quite letting their bodies touch. "Isn't it beautiful?"

"Yes." Gem's response was a whisper, and Mikayla leaned against her briefly before stepping away and picking up the bag. The motion reminded her of the mild concussion she'd sustained, but only because it made her a little dizzy. The meds kept the pain at bay. She couldn't remember much of what had happened from the time she'd entered the water and the moment she opened her eyes in the ambulance on the way to the hospital, where the first thing she saw was Gem's worried face. And it was probably the pain meds that kept her from feeling anything but a general sense of well-being, even after Gem told her what had happened.

Although she felt bad for Gem for the emotional hangover she described during their time in the emergency room, her own prevalent emotion at the moment was gratitude for being okay and for being with Gem.

She made her way up her porch steps and paused at the top when she realized Gem wasn't following. "It's almost midnight, but can you come in for a few minutes?" When Gem hesitated, she walked to the front door. "I have some scones from Seaside, and I'm going to fix a cup of tea."

By the time Mikayla switched on the living room light, Gem was next to her, but when she started walking toward the kitchen, Gem stepped in front of her and relieved her of her bag. "Let me do it. Why don't you go sit?"

Mikayla sat on the couch, pulling her legs up. She smoothed the soft blue material covering them. "I need to thank your sister for giving us these scrubs. I couldn't get warm enough in my damp wet suit, and I can't imagine how uncomfortable you were in all those wet clothes."

Gem glanced over her shoulder with a tired smile as she took cups from a cupboard. "I needed a new pair. It's been a while since Gabriela swiped some from the hospital for me. They make great pajamas."

Mikayla tipped her head to the side. "I love it when you smile."

Gem faced her after lighting the stove under the kettle. "You've seen me do it a million times."

"Not tonight. Not in several days."

Gem dropped her gaze. "I guess there have been other things on my mind for a while."

"Things we should talk about." While Mikayla felt a general sense of well-being at the moment, she hadn't forgotten how painful the last several days had been. But somehow, waking to find Gem at her side and sensing nothing but love coming from her, she couldn't imagine that they couldn't get past the fight that had led to them being apart. Of course they had to talk about it, but she was confident that they'd be okay. Better than okay.

Gem looked up. "You just got released from the hospital with a concussion. Maybe now isn't the right time."

"Is there ever a good time?" Mikayla patted the couch. "Come here while the water heats." She shifted on the couch so her back was against the arm as Gem took a seat, looking stiff and uncomfortable. She wanted to look at her while they talked, but Gem stared at her own hands. She slipped her toes under Gem's thigh. She craved the contact, and it elicited a smile from Gem, which sent bubbles floating in her stomach. "You jumped into what could have been shark-infested waters to save me."

Gem's smile faded, and Mikayla's heart ached at the tears in her eyes. "You could have died."

"But I didn't because you did something terrifying to help me."

"The only thing on my mind was getting to you."

Tears welled in Mikayla's eyes for the fear mixed with determination she saw in Gem's expression. "You kept me safe."

"You were unconscious." Gem seemed to be reliving the whole ordeal.

Mikayla wanted to save her from the pain. "I watched you swim to me, and I felt you holding me and heard you talking. I knew you were there." A warm glow filled her chest.

"But you weren't moving."

"My senses were working, and they told me you would make everything okay."

"I was so scared." Gem's voice cracked on the last word, and she started to cry.

Mikayla took her hand and pulled her close, and Gem curled against her and cried. Mikayla smoothed her hair and brushed it from her face. The waves of emotion emanating from Gem weren't all about the accident. Mikayla understood. They needed to address the fight. She knew they would get through it but only after talking about it. When the pot started to whistle, Gem got up to turn it off.

She fixed the tea and brought their cups and a couple of scones on small plates. As she sat, she put everything on the coffee table and took a deep breath. "I've been miserable the last few days. You don't know how many times I wanted to come see you, talk to you, touch you, but I was paralyzed with shame. I'm so sorry for acting the way I did. A dam of everything I've been trying to hold together over the last four years burst, and I took it out on you. You didn't deserve it. Not the unfair accusation about your boundaries, which are just fine, by the way. Not about talking to my dad. Not any of it."

Mikayla slid her toes under Gem again, who rested a hand on her knee. Mikayla rested her hand on Gem's and rubbed little circles along her fingers. The touch seemed to validate their connection and she felt Gem relax, which made her relax. "Thank you. I've been kicking myself for walking away. I never walk away. I always stay until it's all talked out. I didn't, and I think it made things worse." Mikayla felt a pang of regret at this admission and wondered if the meds were already wearing off.

Gem squeezed her hand. "Never and always are dangerous words. Sometimes, it's better to trust your gut, which is what you did. Besides, I have no idea how it would have gone if you'd stayed. I was in a bad state of mind. It took you walking away to snap me out of it."

"I don't want to be the kind of person who walks away." Mikayla knew this about herself and was proud of it. In fact, she had been willing to stay with Craig and had even begged him to stay when he asked for a divorce. A little resentment rose in her. Maybe she needed to find a middle ground. She stored this revelation away for future consideration.

"You don't have to be. I've never acted the way I did with you. Never." Gem hung her head.

"I believe you." Mikayla knew Gem had acted out of character. If she could go back, she'd have tried to focus on getting Gem to talk about her stress. Maybe Gem would have—

She stopped that train of thought. This was something she could help Gem with, but it was Gem's responsibility to communicate better. She set her cup on the table and took Gem's hands. "You've been under constant pressure for years without an outlet or an end in sight. Your kind heart and dedication to your family have been keeping you going, and you did it willingly while watching your father's health decline. Everyone has a breaking point, Gem. Even therapists." She tilted her head. "That's a lot to manage. And then your father upset this house of cards you've put up, and he used the information I gave him to do it. I'd be mad at me, too."

Gem took in a deep breath and let it out. "I'm not mad at you. I'm one-hundred-percent convinced your conversation with my father would have ended up exactly as it did either way. By the time I got to him, he'd already changed his mind. He said he overestimated his capabilities when he started feeling better, and it caused him to make unrealistic plans."

Mikayla was relieved that Gem seemed to have already worked through some of it. "I'll bet it's been a wild few days for him."

"He seems fine. Better than fine, actually. He said my mom's been telling him what to do."

Gem looked at her through her lashes as if gauging her reaction. Mikayla wondered what that was about. "He still thinks your mom is talking to him? How long will it take for him to recover from the brain trauma?"

"They won't make a guess. The time frame and damage estimates are different for everyone. But he insists my mom is truly with him and has been since she died, and she's not part of the stroke damage. The strokes just made him talk about it openly." She shrugged.

Mikayla sensed this was a significant topic. "What do you think?"

Gem leaned her head against the back of the couch. "I don't know what I think about it."

They sat quietly in an almost comfortable silence. Mikayla didn't feel the need to fill the pause. She had a feeling Gem would talk when she was ready.

When Gem looked up, she had an expression of wonder. "I went to see him a couple of days ago. He thanked me. He said that he knew people were trying to help him all along, and it overwhelmed him with a sense of gratitude that he wasn't able to express, and when he tried, it came out all wrong, and so all anyone could see was his frustration and fear. But all along, he felt love from people and for people."

Mikayla couldn't help but imagine how Gem felt. Certainly relieved and probably some sort of grateful to have her father back for whatever time the future gave them. Having taken care of her dad for so long, getting a glimpse of what might come, thinking it was an inevitable decline, knowing him to be a different man; all of it had probably taken a toll on her. More than that, Mikayla wondered if Gem was aware of what she glimpsed of herself: her own fears, her abilities and inabilities to let others help her, her difficulties in communicating her fears. She tried to think of a way to bring it up when Gem started speaking again.

"I never knew he was aware of how hard people tried to maintain normalcy and give him autonomy. Even with my gift, I didn't know when people were doing that for me. If I had, I would have responded with his kind of gratitude instead of anger when I believed you and he were making decisions for me. I'm not sure I'm making much sense, and I know they were two very different situations, but the heart of it is, people cared, and I knew it. I would have responded much differently if I had focused on being grateful for the help instead of my fear. I'm ashamed, and I want to…I *need* to fix it."

Mikayla felt those words settle inside her and was impressed that Gem had figured it out on her own. It would make it easier for them in the future if Gem could accept help without a struggle because Mikayla knew she was at her best when she felt needed. In a way, things seemed to be resolving themselves. "That's...wow. I'm glad you and your dad are in a good place now. What you have is special, and it would have killed me if I'd damaged it. So your job and home are safe?"

Gem tipped her head from side to side. "In flux. I accepted the job with Margo. Part-time but I expect to eventually go to full. I'm going to start training Rose as you suggested. She's perfect."

Mikayla clapped. "Was she excited?"

"Very."

"Things have a way of working out the way they need to. I've been told Oceana has a way of helping with it." Mikayla winked while trying to hide a yawn. The excitement of the day had set in, and fatigue had her in its grasp.

"You have to be exhausted," Gem said, getting up to put their cups in the sink.

Mikayla sensed that Gem was planning to leave and was wide-awake again. She met her in the kitchen. "I was fading for a moment, but I don't want you to leave."

"I planned to get you settled in bed and camp out on the couch. You know, what with the concussion."

A balm of contentment warmed Mikayla for the care Gem was giving her. She felt...cherished to know that Gem planned to watch over her through the night, and the knowledge led to a sort of revelation brought on by a dawning memory. "It's only a slight concussion, but if it convinces you to stay, I'll play it up. I might even be forced to remind you of a promise you made."

Gem smiled, responding to her teasing. "What promise is that?"

"Your promise to never leave me. You said it while you were saving me in shark-infested waters."

Gem's smile remained but a seriousness claimed her eyes as she closed the distance between them and cradled Mikayla's face in her hands. "You don't have to convince me to stay, Mikayla. You said something when you woke up in the ambulance. 'I belong, and I matter.' If I made you feel otherwise, I'm sorry. You definitely do belong, and you absolutely matter to me. I won't leave. I can't leave."

Something settled inside Mikayla, a calm she'd never experienced before. "Did you mean the other things you said?" Her heartbeat thumped in her chest. She took a deep breath and bit her lip, waiting for the answer. Gem's voice echoed in her mind. She hoped the words that had helped her swim up from the depths of unconsciousness were real and not wishful thinking.

Gem's eyes held her suspended. "I meant it all. Especially the part where I said I love you. I will love you through high tides, low tides, or riptides. I love you. I mean it more than anything I've ever said."

Mikayla placed her hands over Gem's, knowing why she had such overwhelming confidence that everything would be okay. It wasn't the drugs. It was three simple words. "I love you, too."

CHAPTER THIRTY-TWO

A half dozen tiny red-throated hummingbirds zipped around the feeder hanging outside Mikayla's kitchen window as Gem finished washing the last of the breakfast dishes. Despite being up late, both she and Mikayla had woken at sunrise, the effects of the day before heavy on their bodies but seemingly light in their hearts, and they'd both risen from bed starving. She'd whipped up a spinach and cheese scramble that they'd eaten in bed, after which they'd made love. Now, Mikayla was sleeping again, and Gem was wide-awake, but she didn't want to leave.

Drying her hands, she approached the fish tank. She'd already restocked the feeders and watched the seahorses eat. Clyde had played elusive, not having moved from his place deep inside the seagrass, and since he hadn't been interested in eating earlier, she decided to give him a snack with the turkey baster. As soon as she did, the other seahorses swam over for their own treats, and Clyde came out from the seagrass appearing healthy as ever.

"Hi, gorgeous," Mikayla said from behind her, dropping a kiss on her shoulder before coming to stand beside her. Gem's mouth went dry when she saw her wrapped in one of the sheets from the bed and nothing else. With her hair tousled, she looked like a character in a sexy movie, and Gem wanted to take her back to bed. She almost missed it when Mikayla's eyes widened. "Hey, is that what I think it is on Clyde's belly?" She bent to look more closely, and Gem did the same.

"I think it is. He's pregnant?" Gem said.

"I had no idea until now."

Gem examined him as best she could through the tank glass. "His tummy isn't as round as Othello's gets. It would explain why he didn't want to eat. We should probably move him over, right?"

"I'll get the bowl," Mikayla said. "Oh, I should video call Brandi. She'll want to know."

Gem transferred Clyde over without much trouble or getting soaked like last time, but she did smile, remembering first kisses.

"Hi, Brandi. You'll never guess what," Mikayla said.

"You forgot to do laundry and are forced to wear bed linen?"

Mikayla had her phone on video, and Gem turned in time to watch Mikayla turn bright red. She clutched the sheet higher on her chest. "Um…well no. I'll be right back."

Gem couldn't help laughing as Mikayla handed her the phone. Brandi's laughter bubbled from the speaker. "Hey, Brandi. How's London life?"

Brandi wiped her eyes and caught her breath. "It's good. Not nearly as rainy as I expected. I guess they're having an unseasonably dry spring."

"I don't want a weather report. I wanna know if you're having fun or at least enjoying the job."

"Yes, to both of those." She pointed into the camera. "But what's with Mikayla being wrapped in a sheet and both of you with bedhead?"

Mikayla came back and leaned into the frame. "Sorry. I just woke up. Did Gem tell you she saved my life?"

"*What*?" Brandi almost screeched.

Gem laughed and gave a quick explanation of the events from the day before. All of the terror from the event rolled over her as she recounted the details. She hoped it would fade over time. In the meantime, it took everything in her not to wrap Mikayla in her arms in front of Brandi. They hadn't discussed telling her about them, yet.

"And that's why my hair is a mess," Mikayla said. "I have a zillion tiny cuts all over my scalp that no doubt were attracting sharks, by the way." She glanced at Gem, who was still having flashbacks about the day, but her heart raced, and her stomach clenched at the thought of the sharks who could have been circling them without them even knowing it. Mikayla just winked, and she wondered how she was not absolutely horrified about the shark attack that had possibly nearly happened. "Guess I'll be wearing hats until I can properly brush it again. Wait. But first, you have to check this out." Mikayla turned the camera toward Clyde.

"Is that Bonnie or Clyde?" Brandi asked.

"It's Clyde. Notice he's in the nursery part of the tank?"

"Why...holy shitballs! Did Clyde have his first brood?" Brandi asked.

"Not yet, but any time now," Gem said, finally regaining her voice. As soon as she said it, Clyde sort of straightened out and then jerked. Nothing else happened, but he'd started having contractions. "Did you see what just happened?" Gem asked, excitement surging inside her, the memory of fear disappearing. She picked up her phone to start recording Clyde's big day.

Both Mikayla and Brandi squealed.

"He's definitely ready," Gem said.

"You two are amazing. Thank you for calling me and letting me watch this."

As she spoke, Clyde did the straightening and jerking thing again, and a little cloud of tiny seahorses spurted from his pouch. He did it three more times, and the water around him teemed with fry.

"Not as many as Othello. I'd say there's about a hundred of them," Gem said. She zoomed in on the little specks swimming around their dad, who totally ignored them.

"I can't believe Rick didn't pick up on this," Brandi said. "He's going to freak out."

Mikayla draped an arm around Gem's waist. "I guess I understand why people have babies. This is exciting. But I'm glad it's the seahorses and not me," she said.

"Amen," Gem and Brandi said in unison.

Booming footsteps pounded up the stairs, and the screen door burst open. "Did I miss it? Did Clyde have the babies?" Shia sounded like a kid who believed they might catch Santa Claus.

"It just happened. Check it out," Gem said, stepping aside to give Shia room to view the babies. Clyde wrapped his tail around a strand of seagrass near the bottom of the tank while most of the babies swam near the top.

"They're cute, but I'm bummed I missed it."

"Gem's recording it," Mikayla said. "Including your dramatic entrance. How'd you know it was happening?"

"Brandi texted me. Can you send me the video?"

"Yes. And speaking of the devil, we're on a video call with her."

Shia stretched her neck to be seen in the video. "Hey, Brandi. Congratulations on being a grandmother for the four-thousandth time."

"Girl, when I see you, I'm gonna hafta inflict great harm upon you for calling me a grandmother. You've been warned. Actually, Gem? Give that sassy girl a pinch for me."

Gem made a move for Shia with no real intention of pinching her, but Shia squealed and hid behind Mikayla. "You don't have to stoop to her level, Gem. The consequences are not worth it."

Gem paused. "What consequences are those?"

"Eternal damnation."

"Did I hear eternal damnation? Who has done what to earn such a terrible fate?" Alice stood outside of the screen door, her earnest face concerned.

Gem pushed the door open. "Brandi told me to pinch Shia for calling her a grandmother, and Shia told me if I did the pinching, I would suffer eternal damnation."

Alice waved a hand dismissively. "Pinching is a venial sin, if that. I assure you, no one will be greeting the man downstairs for a good-natured pinch. I heard from Shia that one of the seahorses is giving birth."

Gem gestured toward the nursery side of the tank. "Say hello to Clyde and his one-hundred offspring."

Alice squinted at the tank. "Those little specks are baby seahorses? They look like miniature copies of the big ones. Amazing." She stared for a minute and then turned to leave. "I paused my power walk to stop in. I have to get back at it. Good to see you all."

Alice squeezed through the little crowd by the tank, and on her way, her hand darted out, and Shia squawked. "Alice! No fair. She pinched me."

Alice threw a mischievous grin over her shoulder and sashayed out of the house. "Being bad feels so good."

"I'm not safe here," Shia said with a laugh. "Sorry I barged in. I was just excited. Send me the video when you get a chance, okay? I'll call you later, Brandi!" And with that, she left, and the house fell quiet again.

"So when did you two become a thing?" The tip of Brandi's finger moved back and forth in the foreground of her video, and Gem followed it. "Don't you play coy, either. Mikayla wore that same T-shirt when we talked last week."

Gem peered at the shirt she'd borrowed from Mikayla with the Julian Apple Festival logo on the breast pocket, then laughed at the look on Mikayla's face reflected in the small square. She'd hoped they'd dodged the thing about Mikayla wrapped in the sheet. The explanation had sounded innocuous enough. She glanced at Mikayla, who shrugged. "A few weeks ago?" Gem said, peering at Mikayla, who nodded.

"Damn. I would have figured it out by the googly way you look at each other. You two move fast. And why am I just now hearing about this? I talk to Mikayla at least once a week."

"It never came up," Mikayla said.

"Well, I can guess who's going *down*," Brandi said wiggling her eyebrows.

Mikayla's eyes grew wide, and Gem couldn't help but chuckle. "Don't let Brandi fool you. She's got a dirty mind."

"Asexual doesn't mean no sense of humor," Brandi said. "And I'll leave you to your own devices, folks. Love you like a sister. Give a kiss to each of the babies." And her face disappeared off the screen.

The quiet pressed in on the sudden departure of everyone.

Mikayla turned to her with a sexy gaze. "I'm glad I moved here."

Gem took a small step, placing her hands on Mikayla's hips. "Me, too."

Their kiss was familiar and soft and promised time for them to learn a lot more about one another. Gem melted into it, vowing to keep their love at high tide as much as she could, accepting there might be a few low tides. Either way, she was looking forward to every minute of it.

About the Author

Kimberly Cooper Griffin is a software engineer by day and a romance novelist by night. Born in San Diego, California, Kimberly joined the Air Force, traveled the world, and eventually settled down in Denver, Colorado, where she lives with her wife, the youngest of her three daughters, and a menagerie of dogs and cats. When Kimberly isn't working or writing, she enjoys a variety of interests, but at the core of it all she has an insatiable desire to connect with people and experience life to its fullest. Every moment is collected and archived into memory, a candidate for being woven into the fabric of the tales she tells. Her novels explore the complexities of building relationships and finding balance when life has a tendency of getting in the way.

Books Available from Bold Strokes Books

Before She Was Mine by Emma L McGeown. When Dani and Lucy are thrust together to sort out their children's playground squabble, sparks fly leaving both of them willing to risk it all for each other. 978-1-63679-315-3)

Chasing Cypress by Ana Hartnett Reichardt. Maggie Hyde wants to find a partner to settle down with and help her run the family farm, but instead she ends up chasing Cypress. Olivia Cypress. 978-1-63679-323-8)

Dark Truths by Sandra Barret. When Jade's ex-girlfriend and vampire maker barges back into her life, can Jade satisfy her ex's demands, keep Beth safe, and keep everyone's secrets…secret? 978-1-63679-369-6)

Desires Unleashed by Renee Roman. Kell Murphy and Taylor Simpson didn't go looking for love, but as they explore their desires unleashed, their hearts lead them on an unexpected journey. 978-1-63679-327-6)

Maybe, Probably by Amanda Radley. Set against the backdrop of a viral pandemic, Gina and Eleanor are about to discover that loving another person is complicated when you're desperately searching for yourself. 978-1-63679-284-2)

The One by C.A. Popovich. Jody Acosta doesn't know what makes her more furious, that the wealthy Bergeron family refuses to be held accountable for her father's wrongful death, or that she can't ignore her knee-weakening attraction to Nicole Bergeron. 978-1-63679-318-4)

The Speed of Slow Changes by Sander Santiago. As Al and Lucas navigate the ups and downs of their polyamorous relationship, only one thing is certain: romance has never been so crowded. 978-1-63679-329-0)

Tides of Love by Kimberly Cooper Griffin. Falling in love is the last thing on either of their minds, but when Mikayla and Gem meet, sparks of possibility begin to shine, revealing a future neither expected. 978-1-63679-319-1)

Catch by Kris Bryant. Convincing the wife of the star quarterback to walk away from her family was never in offensive coordinator Sutton McCoy's game plan. But standing on the sidelines when a second chance at true love comes her way proves all but impossible. (978-1-63679-276-7)

Hearts in the Wind by MJ Williamz. Beth and Evelyn seem destined to remain mortal enemies but are about to discover that in matters of the heart, sometimes you must cast your fortunes to the wind. (978-1-63679-288-0)

Hero Complex by Jesse J. Thoma. Bronte, Athena, and their unlikely friends, must work together to defeat Bronte's arch nemesis. The fate of love, humanity, and the world might depend on it. No pressure. (978-1-63679-280-4)

Hotel Fantasy by Piper Jordan. Molly Taylor has a fantasy in mind that only Lexi can fulfill. However, convincing her to participate could prove challenging. (978-1-63679-207-1)

Last New Beginning by Krystina Rivers. Can commercial broker Skye Kohl and contractor Bailey Kaczmarek overcome their pride and work together while the tension between them boils over into a love that could soothe both of their hearts? (978-1-63679-261-3)

Love and Lattes by Karis Walsh. Cat café owner Bonnie and wedding planner Taryn join forces to get rescue cats into forever homes—discovering their own forever along the way. (978-1-63679-290-3)

Repatriate by Jaime Maddox. Ally Hamilton's new job as a home health aide takes an unexpected twist when she discovers a fortune in stolen artwork and must repatriate the masterpieces and avoid the wrath of the violent man who stole them. (978-1-63679-303-0)

The Hues of Me and You by Morgan Lee Miller. Arlette Adair and Brooke Dawson almost fell in love in college. Years later, they unexpectedly run into each other and come face-to-face with their unresolved past. (978-1-63679-229-3)

A Haven for the Wanderer by Jenny Frame. When Griffin Harris comes to Rosebrook village, the love she finds with Bronte de Lacey creates safe haven and she finally finds her place in the world. But will she run again when their love is tested? (978-1-63679-291-0)

A Spark in the Air by Dena Blake. Internet executive Crystal Tucker is sure Wi-Fi could really help small-town residents, even if it means putting an internet café out of business, but her instant attraction to the owner's daughter, Janie Elliott, makes moving ahead with her plans complicated. (978-1-63679-293-4)

Between Takes by CJ Birch. Simone Lavoie is convinced her new job as an intimacy coordinator will give her a fresh perspective. Instead, problems on set and her growing attraction to actress Evelyn Harper only add to her worries. (978-1-63679-309-2)

Camp Lost and Found by Georgia Beers. Nobody knows better than Cassidy and Frankie that life doesn't always give you what you want. But sometimes, if you're lucky, life gives you exactly what you need. (978-1-63679-263-7)

Felix Navidad by 'Nathan Burgoine. After the wedding of a good friend, instead of Felix's Hawaii Christmas treat to himself, ice rain strands him in Ontario with fellow wedding-guest—and handsome ex of said friend—Kevin in a small cabin for the holiday Felix definitely didn't plan on. (978-1-63679-411-2)

Fire, Water, and Rock by Alaina Erdell. As Jess and Clare reveal more about themselves, and their hot summer fling tips over into true love, they must confront their pasts before they can contemplate a future together. (978-1-63679-274-3)

Lines of Love by Brey Willows. When even the Muse of Love doesn't believe in forever, we're all in trouble. (978-1-63555-458-8)

Manny Porter and The Yuletide Murder by D.C. Robeline. Manny only has the holiday season to discover who killed prominent research scientist Phillip Nikolaidis before the judicial system condemns an innocent man to lethal injection. (978-1-63679-313-9)

Only This Summer by Radclyffe. A fling with Lily promises to be exactly what Chase is looking for—short-term, hot as a forest fire, and one Chase can extinguish whenever she wants. After all, it's only one summer. (978-1-63679-390-0)

Picture-Perfect Christmas by Charlotte Greene. Two former rivals compete to capture the essence of their small mountain town at Christmas, all the while fighting old and new feelings. (978-1-63679-311-5)

Playing Love's Refrain by Lesley Davis. Drew Dawes had shied away from the world of music until Wren Banderas gave her a reason to play their love's refrain. (978-1-63679-286-6)

Profile by Jackie D. The scales of justice are weighted against FBI agents Cassidy Wolf and Alex Derby. Loyalty and love may be the only advantage they have. (978-1-63679-282-8)

Almost Perfect by Tagan Shepard. A shared love of queer TV brings Olivia and Riley together, but can they keep their real-life love as picture perfect as their on-screen counterparts? (978-1-63679-322-1)

Corpus Calvin by David Swatling. Cloverkist Inn may be haunted, but a ghost materializes from Jason Dekker's past and Calvin's canine instinct kicks in to protect a young boy from mortal danger. (978-1-62639-428-5)

Craving Cassie by Skye Rowan. Siobhan Carney and Cassie Townsend share an instant attraction, but are they brave enough to give up everything they have ever known to be together? (978-1-63679-062-6)

Drifting by Lyn Hemphill. When Tess jumps into the ocean after Jet, she thinks she's saving her life. Of course, she can't possibly know Jet is actually a mermaid desperate to fix her mistake before she causes her clan's demise. (978-1-63679-242-2)

Enigma by Suzie Clarke. Polly has taken an oath to protect and serve her country, but when the spy she's tasked with hunting becomes the love of her life, will she be the one to betray her country? (978-1-63555-999-6)

Finding Fault by Annie McDonald. Can environmental activist Dr. Evie O'Halloran and government investigator Merritt Shepherd set aside their conflicting ideas about saving the planet and risk their hearts enough to save their love? (978-1-63679-257-6)

Hot Keys by R.E. Ward. In 1920s New York City, Betty May Dewitt and her best friend, Jack Norval, are determined to make their Tin Pan Alley dreams come true and discover they will have to fight—not only for their hearts and dreams, but for their lives. (978-1-63679-259-0)

Securing Ava by Anne Shade. Private investigator Paige Richards takes a case to locate and bring back runaway heiress Ava Prescott. But ignoring her attraction may prove impossible when their hearts and lives are at stake. (978-1-63679-297-2)

The Amaranthine Law by Gun Brooke. Tristan Kelly is being hunted for who she is and her incomprehensible past, and despite her overwhelming feelings for Olivia Bryce, she has to reject her to keep her safe. (978-1-63679-235-4)

The Forever Factor by Melissa Brayden. When Bethany and Reid confront their past, they give new meaning to letting go, forgiveness, and a future worth fighting for. (978-1-63679-357-3)

The Frenemy Zone by Yolanda Wallace. Ollie Smith-Nakamura thinks relocating from San Francisco to her dad's rural hometown is the worst idea in the world, but after she meets her new classmate Ariel Hall, she might have a change of heart. (978-1-63679-249-1)

A Cutting Deceit by Cathy Dunnell. Undercover cop Athena takes a job at Valeria's hair salon to gather evidence to prove her husband's connections to organized crime. What starts as a tentative friendship quickly turns into a dangerous affair. (978-1-63679-208-8)

As Seen on TV! by CF Frizzell. Despite their objections, TV hosts Ronnie Sharp, a laid-back chef; and paranormal investigator Peyton Stanford, have to work together. The public is watching. But joining forces is risky, contemptuous, unnerving, provocative—and ridiculously perfect. (978-1-63679-272-9)

Blood Memory by Sandra Barret. Can vampire Jade Murphy protect her friend from a human stalker and keep her dates with the gorgeous Beth Jenssen without revealing her secrets? (978-1-63679-307-8)

Foolproof by Leigh Hays. For Martine Roberts and Elliot Tillman, friends with benefits isn't a foolproof way to hide from the truth at the heart of an affair. (978-1-63679-184-5)

Glass and Stone by Renee Roman. Jordan must accept that she can't control everything that happens in life, and that includes her wayward heart. (978-1-63679-162-3)

Hard Pressed by Aurora Rey. When rivals Mira Lavigne and Dylan Miller are tapped to co-chair Finger Lakes Cider Week, competition gives way to compromise. But will their sexual chemistry lead to love? (978-1-63679-210-1)

The Laws of Magic by M. Ullrich. Nothing is ever what it seems, especially not in the small town of Bender, Massachusetts, where a witch lives to save lives and avoid love. (978-1-63679-222-4)

The Lonely Hearts Rescue by Morgan Lee Miller, Nell Stark, Missouri Vaun. In this novella collection, a hurricane hits the Gulf Coast, and the animals at the Lonely Hearts Rescue Shelter need love, and so do the humans who adopt them. (978-1-63679-231-6)

The Mage and the Monster by Barbara Ann Wright. Two powerful mages, one committed to magic and one controlled by it, strive to free each other and be together while the countries they serve descend into war. (978-1-63679-190-6)

Truly Wanted by J.J. Hale. Sam must decide if she's willing to risk losing her found family to find her happily ever after. (978-1-63679-333-7)